A TALENT for TROUBLE

Books by Jen Turano

A Change of Fortune
A Most Peculiar Circumstance
A Talent for Trouble

A TALENT *for* TROUBLE

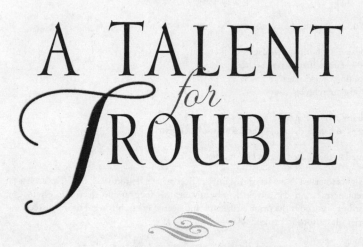

JEN TURANO

BETHANYHOUSE
a division of Baker Publishing Group
Minneapolis, Minnesota

© 2013 by Jennifer L. Turano

Published by Bethany House Publishers
11400 Hampshire Avenue South
Bloomington, Minnesota 55438
www.bethanyhouse.com

Bethany House Publishers is a division of
Baker Publishing Group, Grand Rapids, Michigan

Printed in the United States of America

Library of Congress Cataloging-in-Publication Data
Turano, Jen.
    A Talent for Trouble / Jen Turano.
        pages cm
    Summary: "After getting into one scrape after another in 1880s New York City, are Grayson and Felicia destined to spend the rest of their lives keeping each other out of trouble?"— Provided by publisher.
        ISBN 978-0-7642-1126-3 (pbk.)
        1. Life change events—Fiction. 2. Man-woman relationships—Fiction. I. Title.
    PS3620.U7455 T35 2013
    813'.6—dc23   2013023299

Cover design by John Hamilton Design

Author represented by The Seymour Agency

13 14 15 16 17 18 19   7 6 5 4 3 2 1

For Al . . . just because.

All my love,
Jen

1

New York City, 1881

Miss Felicia Murdock was wallowing.

She did not normally have the propensity to wallow, but given the trying circumstances of the day, she felt she was entitled, at least for an hour or two.

Leaning her forehead against the cool pane of glass, she stared out her bedroom window, watching the traffic that paraded past the Fifth Avenue mansion she called home. Carriages sporting liveried servants jostled for space amongst delivery wagons, while well-dressed ladies and gentlemen strolled down the sidewalk arm in arm, all of them apparently enjoying the lovely spring day.

Her nose wrinkled at the sight of so many cheerful people, and when one of the couples stopped in the middle of the sidewalk and shared a quick embrace, Felicia jerked her head from the glass and trudged across the oriental carpet, coming to a halt in front of her bed.

Normally the sight of her whimsical bed, with its frothy bit of blue silk scooping gracefully from the canopy and comfortable quilted ivory coverlet, brought a smile to her lips, but on this particular day, smiles were difficult to produce.

Feeling the need for a dramatic gesture in order to continue with her wallowing, Felicia turned, held out her arms, and fell backward, anticipating the moment her bed would cushion her in a soft cocoon of luxury and allow her to descend into a much-needed bout of self-pity.

As she landed, a sharp stabbing of her behind sent all thoughts of self-pity disappearing in a split second. She bolted upright, beat down the voluminous skirt of the putrid pink gown tangled around her legs, struggled to her feet, and permitted herself the indulgence of releasing a good grunt.

Acts of a dramatic nature were clearly not advisable when one still had the required fashion accessory of the day, the dastardly bustle, attached to one's backside. Disgruntlement now flowing freely through her veins, she reached around and twisted the dreaded contraption back into place.

Kicking off her shoes, she eyed the bed once again and, unwilling to abandon her dramatic gesture, took a few steps back, hitched up her skirt, and lunged forward. She flung herself into the air and landed on top of the coverlet with a resounding bounce.

Air was difficult to come by, as her tightly laced corset protested such strenuous activity, but determination to continue with her wallowing had her breathing in shorter breaths as she cushioned her head with folded arms. She was hardly comfortable, but at least she was in an appropriate position to sink into misery. She closed her eyes and forced herself to recall the horrors of the day.

Reverend Michael Fraser, the gentleman she'd held dear to her heart for over four years, was now married.

Unfortunately, *she* had not been his bride of choice.

That honor had gone to Miss Julia Hampton, a young lady Felicia might have actually liked if the lady hadn't absconded with the man Felicia adored—the man she'd for so long believed God had selected for *her* to marry.

It appeared she and God had experienced a slight misunderstanding of late. Quite frankly, she couldn't help but be distinctly put out with Him.

She'd been so certain He would intervene today—with a bolt of lightning or something equally impressive—right in the middle of the wedding, which would have proven once and for all that she was meant for Reverend Fraser, not Miss Hampton. But even though she'd kept a sharp eye on the ceiling throughout the ceremony, no such divine intervention had occurred.

A trickle of unease caused her eyes to flash open.

Good heavens, if God would have intervened, Miss Hampton, or rather Mrs. Fraser now, would have been devastated. All of Julia's hopes and dreams would not have come to pass, and . . . The sheer selfishness of what Felicia had hoped for hardly spoke well of her character.

It was little wonder God hadn't answered her many and varied prayers regarding Reverend Fraser. She was a sad excuse for a self-proclaimed woman of faith.

How in the world could she have convinced herself she was destined to become the wife of a minister?

It was ludicrous—that's what it was. And now, since she'd spent so many years pursuing Reverend Fraser, she'd reached the ripe old age of twenty-four and couldn't help but think she'd landed herself in a bit of a pickle.

None of society's eligible gentlemen would want to court a lady so long in the tooth, which meant she was destined to remain a spinster forever.

An image of herself ten years in the future sprang to mind, and it did absolutely nothing to calm her nerves—especially since the image she'd conjured had her wearing a ratty old shawl with dozens of cats slinking around her feet.

She didn't care for cats. They made her sneeze. They also seemed to spring out at her when she least expected it.

Groping out with one hand, Felicia yanked a velvet pillow of periwinkle blue toward her and pressed it against her face, trying to force her thoughts away from anything to do with cats. To her dismay, trying to push cats out of her mind only caused more cats to prance through her thoughts. Pushing the pillow aside, she began to whistle a jaunty tune she'd picked up from one of the grooms, and thankfully, images of cats disappeared, replaced with sailors walking on bowed legs down at the dock.

It wasn't much of an improvement, given that she wasn't terribly familiar with sailors, but at least it was better than cats.

"What in the world are you whistling?"

Pressing her lips tightly together, Felicia glanced out of the corner of her eye and, much to her dismay, saw her mother striding determinedly across the room. She squeezed her eyes shut and summoned up what she hoped was a credible snore.

"I know you're awake."

"I'm not."

A chuckle was Ruth Murdock's only reply before Felicia felt the mattress shift and then shift again as her mother went about the business of getting comfortable, apparently intent on a bit of a chat.

"It was a beautiful wedding, wasn't it?"

The last thing she wanted to discuss was the wedding. The disappointment of it was still too fresh, but her mother had no way of knowing her daughter had suffered a blow today. Felicia had never admitted to anyone the troubling fact that she held Reverend Fraser in high regard.

"I thought Miss Hampton looked lovely."

Felicia forced open her eyes, pushed herself up and then off the bed, shook out the folds of her gown, and summoned up what she hoped would pass for a smile. "She did."

"You looked lovely as well." Ruth's eyes began to gleam. "I noticed the marked attention Mr. Zayne Beckett was sending your way."

Felicia looked past her mother and caught sight of her reflection in the full-length mirror that stood next to the entrance of her dressing room.

Lovely was hardly the term she would have chosen to describe her appearance.

White-blond hair was pulled ruthlessly away from her face, the tightness of the chignon causing her deep blue and heavily lashed eyes to tilt up at the corners. Her cheekbones were high and her nose slim, but her face looked strained and pale, and she resembled a lady of forty instead of twenty-four. Her eyes skimmed over plump lips that were entirely too full and settled on her gown, the sheer volume of it hiding curves she knew perfectly well were considered voluptuous. She winced when the sun took that moment to stream through the window, the beams of light causing the pink tulle she was wearing to glow.

"Are you planning on seeing Zayne again soon?" Ruth asked, causing Felicia to pull her gaze from her appalling reflection and settle it on her mother.

"Mother, honestly, the only reason Zayne was paying me 'marked attention' was because I knocked him over that pew after you shoved me a little too enthusiastically in his direction. Zayne, being a most considerate gentleman, was concerned for any embarrassment his rapid plunge to the ground might have caused *me*."

She blew out a breath. "Besides, you're forgetting the pesky little fact that he's firmly off the marriage market, given that he's practically engaged to Miss Helena Collins."

Ruth's eyes turned shrewd. "Reverend Fraser was firmly off the market as well, but that didn't seem to stop you from continuing to hold the man in affection. Really, Felicia, the manner in which you were staring at the ceiling throughout the ceremony today was somewhat disturbing. Why, I was convinced you expected a bolt of lightning to disrupt the service."

Sometimes her mother knew her just a touch too well, but . . . Her eyes widened. "You knew?"

Ruth scooted back on the bed and took a moment to plump up some pillows behind her. "Of course I knew, darling." She folded her hands over her stomach. "It is my fondest hope that, now that he's well and truly married, you'll finally be able to put the gentleman behind you once and for all. I also wouldn't mind if you'd set aside the rather demure attitude you've assumed over the past four years."

"You've taken issue with my 'demure attitude'?"

Ruth bit her lip. "Oh dear, that might not have come out exactly right." She tilted her head. "I certainly expect you to be ladylike at all times, my dear, but ever since you made the acquaintance of Reverend Fraser, you've ruthlessly pushed aside your exuberance for life. That is what I long for you to embrace again. I also wouldn't be opposed to seeing a dramatic change in the fashions you choose to wear. Your rather outlandish sense of style, while always a topic of conversation at every society event, has bothered me for years."

"You're the one who bought me my first 'outlandish' gown."

"I truly do love you, darling, but I'm not going to take responsibility for the manner in which you've been dressing. Did I, years ago, purchase you a somewhat hideous gown bedecked in ribbons? Yes, I did, but I only did so because the designer assured me it would make you appear years younger. If you will recall, at that time you'd almost reached the ripe old age of twenty and did not have a suitor to call your own."

"Only because my coming out was delayed due to Grandmother's death and Grandfather's ill health."

Ruth's lips curled into a smile. "It was truly commendable, your diligence to your grandfather, but . . . that has nothing to do with the horrible dress I bought you." She gave a delicate shudder. "The moment you stepped out of your room garbed in that ridiculous creation, I knew I'd made a horrible mistake. Unfortunately, we were running late. There was nothing to do but tell you how charming you looked and pray you'd someday forgive me."

"You never told me you thought I looked ridiculous."

"I had every intention of doing so, dear—after the ball, of course—but you made the acquaintance of Reverend Fraser that very night. He rather foolishly, yet out of kindness, I'm sure, proclaimed you looked delightful . . . and charming."

"He sounded sincere."

"I'm certain he was, since he's a lovely man. But he is woefully deficient in the matter of fashions. I cannot tell you how appalled I was when the very next day you asked me to go shopping, ordered an entirely new wardrobe comprised of questionable styles, and discarded your old wardrobe. You haven't worn anything remotely fashionable since."

Something that felt remarkably like regret swept through her. "I was trying to impress Reverend Fraser, and I thought I was on the right track because he did compliment my appearance quite often."

"Again, he's a kind man and probably came to the conclusion you needed extra compliments because you always looked so peculiar." Ruth released a sigh. "I've never understood why you decided he was the right gentleman for you."

"I thought God had sent him to me."

"Because . . . ?"

Felicia walked over to a settee, sinking down on it as her

skirts billowed up around her. "I knew perfectly well after I returned from Grandfather's house that I was rapidly approaching spinsterhood, so right before the Patriarch Ball, I had a talk with God. I told Him that I wanted to find a suitable gentleman that very evening, and then, much to my delight, Reverend Fraser turned up."

"Did it never cross your mind that you might have been mistaken? Surely you must have considered, given your slightly mischievous nature, that you were hardly suited to a life as a minister's wife."

Felicia leaned forward, earning herself a faceful of pink tulle in the process. She brushed it aside. "I would make a fine minister's wife."

"You've done an exceptional job helping the needy and attending church, but tell me, have you done those things because you desire to do them, or was it simply a means to spend time in Reverend Fraser's company?"

The answers to those questions weren't something Felicia cared to delve into at the moment. She'd already come to the conclusion she was a horrible person for wanting a bolt of lightning to end Miss Hampton's dreams. The last thing she wanted to contemplate was whether or not actions she'd told herself were selfless had actually been done in an attempt to further her appeal to Reverend Fraser.

A knock on the door provided a welcome reason to avoid answering her mother. She rose from the settee, walked across the room, pulled open the door, and found one of the housemaids, Gladys, on the other side.

Gladys bobbed a curtsy. "There's a gentleman here to see you, Miss Murdock."

"A gentleman?"

"Yes. Mr. Sumner has come to call."

Apprehension was immediate. "Are you certain about that?"

Gladys nodded and pressed a calling card into Felicia's hand. She glanced at it, and sure enough, it did appear as if Mr. Grayson Sumner had come to call. She jumped when her mother suddenly peered over her shoulder.

"Ah, how lovely. The card does read *Mr. Sumner*. My, I wonder what he's doing here."

Felicia turned and quickly recognized that her mother was batting innocent-looking eyes back at her—something she did quite often when she was in the midst of a plot. "I can't help but wonder the same, Mother."

Ruth ignored her and beamed at Gladys. "Please tell Mr. Sumner that Felicia will be right down."

"I don't think so. Gladys, please tell him I'm indisposed."

"She'll be right down," Ruth repeated.

"I'm indisposed."

Ruth seemed to grow a little larger even as her face turned red. "You're not indisposed; you're sulking—which is quite unattractive, by the way." She nodded to Gladys. "Again, you may inform Mr. Sumner that Felicia will be down momentarily."

Not giving Felicia an opportunity to argue further, Gladys barely bobbed a curtsy before she spun around and beat a hasty retreat.

"Why is Grayson Sumner here, Mother?"

"Because he enjoys your company?"

"Mr. Sumner and I have rarely spent time in each other's company."

Ruth smiled. "Why, that's it. He saw you today at the wedding, realized he wishes to become better acquainted with you, and here he is, in our house, waiting for you to go greet him."

"I'm afraid I don't think that's the reason a member of British aristocracy is currently waiting for me to go greet him."

"I disagree."

"Out with it, Mother. What have you done now?"

"You're always so suspicious."

Felicia arched a brow.

Ruth arched one right back at her before she seemed to deflate on the spot. "Oh, very well. If you must know, Mr. Sumner is here to escort you to his sister's house. Eliza's decided to host a late-afternoon tea, and she specifically sought me out in order to extend an invitation to you." Ruth let out a breath. "She was quite concerned when no one could locate you after the wedding. You'll be relieved to learn that I explained your mad dash from the ceremony with as few words as possible, stating something to the effect that the fabric of your gown had brought on an unfortunate rash."

"You told everyone I have a rash?"

"Well, not everyone—just Eliza, Grayson, and oh, that delightful Agatha Watson." Ruth frowned. "The thought did spring to mind, right after the word *rash* escaped my lips, that it probably wasn't the best explanation I could have come up with, considering rashes are hardly desirable. However, ladies have been known to suffer from wearing an excess of tulle, which you *were* wearing today, so it certainly was a believable comment."

Ruth's frown turned into a smile. "At least now your friends will be considerate of your tender condition instead of recognizing the real reason you fled the wedding was due to your unfortunate infatuation with Reverend Fraser."

There were no words at Felicia's disposal to respond to that bit of nonsense, and oddly enough, since her mother had mentioned a rash, her skin had begun to itch somewhat dreadfully underneath the swaths of fabric she wore. Scratching her arm, she took a moment to consider her mother. "Tell me, why can't I simply ride over to Eliza's house with you?"

"Ah, well . . . I wasn't invited."

Her mother was getting more incorrigible with each passing

day. "Eliza would never neglect to extend you an invitation, Mother."

"I think it's a tea for young people."

They were getting nowhere fast.

"How did it happen that Mr. Sumner was coerced to come fetch me?"

"I wouldn't say he was *coerced*. It seemed to me he was quite eager to make the offer." Ruth's eyes began to sparkle. "You should feel extremely honored that a gentleman of Grayson's caliber has come to call. Why, with that delicious accent of his and his all too handsome face, he's a gentleman any lady can appreciate."

Here it was—clear proof that her mother was indeed plotting.

"Are you sure your name isn't Ruthless instead of Ruth?"

"Pardon me?"

"You're scheming, Mother, and not very subtly. You've set your sights on Grayson Sumner as a prospect for me."

"My goodness, Felicia, I never realized you have such an overactive imagination. All I did was point out that he's a fine candidate, er, suitable escort for you today."

"Grayson Sumner is out of my reach. He's an aristocrat, as in a real-life earl."

Ruth began inspecting the sleeve of her gown. "You'd make a lovely countess, and just think how adorable any children you might have would be. When you're not downplaying your looks, you're beautiful, and Grayson . . . Well, need I say more?" Ruth looked up. "Would they be little lords and ladies, your children, or do children of earls not get honorary titles?"

"Mr. Sumner abandoned his title."

"He can always resume the use of it with a bit of prodding."

The conversation was quickly going downhill. "I've never aspired to become a member of the aristocracy."

"That's not entirely true. When you were ten, you declared to me you wished to become a princess."

"All little girls wish to become princesses."

"Now you can contemplate becoming a countess. They're almost the same thing."

Felicia sucked in a deep breath of air, the action causing her corset to brush against skin that, strangely enough, was still itching. "You're going to have to tell him I'm not feeling well. In fact, I do feel as if I might be coming down with a rash."

"You're not, and I'll do no such thing."

"Then tell him I have nothing suitable to wear."

"Your wardrobe is stuffed to the gills with clothing."

"That's exactly what my gowns resemble, gills."

"You're determined to be difficult, aren't you."

"Yes."

Ruth reached out and patted Felicia's cheek. "Darling, I understand that you suffered a great disappointment today, but the last thing you should do is hide away in your room. You need to reclaim your life and pursue a future that will allow you to embrace who you truly are, not who you've been pretending to be of late."

"May I assume you believe I should do all of those things while in the company of Grayson Sumner?"

"He's a charming gentleman, Felicia, and the times I've seen the two of you together, both of you have always been smiling."

"I'm quite certain the only reason I smile while in his company is to mask the fact he makes me incredibly nervous."

"Hmm . . ." Ruth's eyes began to sparkle once again.

Chaos normally followed that particular sparkle, which meant Felicia was going to have to nip this subject in the bud before her mother got any truly crazy ideas.

"Grayson Sumner clearly has a mysterious past, and I think that past has caused him to be a rather dangerous man."

"I've always found dangerous gentlemen to be very intriguing."

There was going to be no reasoning with her mother. Felicia's hope of extended wallowing was rapidly slipping away. "Fine, I'll find something to wear."

"That's the spirit, dear." Ruth patted Felicia's cheek once again as her eagle eyes skimmed over Felicia's hair. "You might want to do something different with your hair, darling. I'm afraid it looks quite disastrous." With that, Ruth hurried through the door and disappeared from view.

Felicia's shoulders sagged ever so slightly, knowing there was no option but to change and then travel to Eliza's tea. She stiffened her spine and headed for her dressing room, striding through it before she yanked the door to her wardrobe open. She refused to allow herself the luxury of a good sigh when the sight of pinks, yellows, pale greens, and far too many bows, ribbons, and, more alarmingly yet, feathers met her gaze.

Temper took her by surprise. She moved into the wardrobe and began rummaging through the garments, anxiety quickly replacing the temper as realization finally began to sink in over what she'd actually done over the past four years.

She'd changed who she was in the hope of attracting the attention of a gentleman.

She'd spent hour upon hour at the church, volunteering for everything from feeding the needy to distributing used clothing, and, occasionally, even scrubbing down the pews.

She'd prided herself on never missing a church service, when in actuality she'd gone to every single one only to gaze at Reverend Fraser.

She was a fraud, and it was past time she did something to rectify that.

Her hands stilled when a flash of dark met her gaze. She reached into the farthest recesses of her wardrobe and snatched at it, pulling out the black gown she'd worn to her grandfather's funeral.

She tore the pink tulle from her body, not bothering to ring for a maid, and slipped into the black dress, buttoning up the front before she strode back to the mirror. She eyed her reflection and then began to pull pins as rapidly as she could from her hair. Her fingers flew faster and faster as something that felt very much like panic settled over her.

She'd wasted years of her life.

She'd become someone she didn't know and really didn't care for in the least.

Her mother was right. It was time for her to reclaim her life, but she had no idea how to go about that.

An image of Grayson Sumner sprang to mind.

Her mother was not mistaken—he was a handsome gentleman, wealthy too, and he did possess a title, as well as a compelling British accent—but . . . he really was dangerous. She'd realized that the first time she'd made his acquaintance.

She pulled out another pin, tilted her head, and then nodded. Perhaps a tiny slice of danger was exactly what was needed to get her life back on track.

2

*G*rayson Sumner picked up the china teacup the house-maid had so thoughtfully provided for him, taking a sip of the pleasant brew before he glanced around the tastefully decorated drawing room. He'd never been in this part of the Murdock residence before, and quite frankly, he was surprised to find his surroundings so understated, without a single bold color in sight.

He'd been expecting fussy, given the eccentric manner Miss Felicia Murdock chose to dress, and was slightly disappointed to discover everything so normal.

Amusement replaced disappointment when the thought came to him that Felicia could never be mistaken for normal, no matter the conventional state of her home. She garbed herself in highly unusual fashions, her gowns always dripping with bows and ribbons, but he'd realized shortly after making her acquaintance that underneath the yards and yards of fabric draping her form, there resided a lady who possessed the spirit of a hoyden.

How he'd come to that realization, he really couldn't say. It wasn't as if he'd ever seen her behave in an untoward manner. Felicia presented herself to the world as a demure young lady, but there was just something about the way her eyes twinkled with mischief every so often that lent credence to his impression regarding her true nature.

For the life of him, he hadn't been able to understand why she'd assumed such a retiring manner—well, retiring except for her peculiar taste in clothing—until just a few hours ago. He'd watched her as she'd perched on the very edge of the pew throughout the wedding ceremony, looking for all intents and purposes as if she were about to take flight. When he'd remarked on Felicia's odd behavior to his sister, Eliza, she'd leaned closer to him and whispered that she'd come to believe Felicia held Reverend Fraser in affection, affection of the romantic kind.

That had explained much, at least in regard to her demure attitude. He wasn't certain anything could explain her taste in fashion. What had taken him aback though, once he'd had a moment to think about it, was that a clear feeling of disgruntlement had settled over him right after Eliza whispered her thoughts into his ear.

What had caused the disgruntlement, he really couldn't say, but he'd been downright grumpy for the rest of the ceremony, which had been rather odd, since weddings normally left him in a pleasant frame of mind.

Grayson took another sip of tea, set the cup aside on a table next to the chair, and pulled out his pocket watch, wondering when, or even if, Felicia would appear.

Perhaps her rash had gotten worse.

If she did appear, was he expected to inquire about the rash, or should he simply pretend Mrs. Murdock hadn't divulged that rather personal information?

Deciding pretending ignorance would be for the best in this situation, he leaned back and stretched out his legs, rising to his feet a mere moment later when Mrs. Murdock charged into the room, her face wreathed in its customary smile. He stepped forward and took the hand she offered him, bringing it to his lips, which caused her smile to widen and her cheeks to turn pink.

"I do beg your pardon for keeping you waiting so long," Ruth Murdock exclaimed when he let go of her hand. "Felicia will be down in a moment."

"I hope she's been able to address to satisfaction that, er, little problem you mentioned."

Ruth winced but then smiled. "Indeed she has, but it might be for the best if you don't bring that up around her. Ladies are extremely sensitive about such matters." She waltzed over to a settee done up in watered silk and motioned him forward. "We might as well get comfortable while we wait." She sat down and gestured to the space beside her.

Grayson smiled and took a seat, his smile widening when she reached over and patted his knee in a motherly gesture.

"I must thank you again for coming to fetch Felicia this afternoon. I know she would have been quite bereft if she'd missed having tea with her friends."

"I was more than happy to offer my services."

Leaning closer to him, Ruth lowered her voice. "Come now, Mr. Sumner. I know full well that you only offered so quickly because Eliza was treading on your foot."

"You saw that?"

"I'm a mother. I see everything." She patted his knee again. "Don't fret about it though. You are a gentleman, and gentlemen don't always see the opportunities that present themselves as well as we ladies do."

"Opportunities?"

"Exactly. Which is why it's so fortunate your sister is such an observant sort. It's clear she only has your best interests at heart, so do be certain to thank her when you see her next for stepping on your foot."

He no longer possessed any idea regarding what the conversation was about, or where it was leading.

Ruth charged ahead. "You're very indulgent with Eliza, aren't you?"

He opened his mouth to respond, but she continued on as if she hadn't just asked a question. "Tell me, dear, do you think that indulgence was brought on because you abandoned her for far too many years?"

There was no denying that.

He had abandoned his sister for years, and the guilt he suffered over that abandonment was the motivation behind his granting Eliza her every whim.

He'd left her and his father without a single word, without thought for that matter, turning his back on his responsibilities as he'd set out on an adventure of a lifetime after he graduated from Oxford. He'd never considered the possibility that his father might die, their man of affairs would steal all of the family money, and Eliza would be left to fend for herself.

She'd believed him dead.

His sister had mourned him while he'd been off in China securing a fortune for himself through reprehensible means. For that reason alone, Grayson would forever be plagued with remorse.

Regret was his constant companion, because what had eventually happened in China had been entirely his fault. His actions had caused his wife and the rest of her family to suffer the most brutal of deaths.

Only he and Ming, the child he was raising as his daughter, had managed to escape that horrifying end.

Ruth suddenly let out a cough, causing him to remember he was supposed to be in the midst of a conversation with the lady. "I do beg your pardon, Mrs. Murdock. What were you saying?"

"I was inquiring about that adorable daughter of yours. I missed seeing her at the wedding."

Mrs. Murdock's ability to change the subject at the drop of a hat was truly amazing.

"Ming's fine—thank you for asking—but since she has just turned three, I felt it unwise for her to attend today. She's at that age where you can never tell what she may do."

"I well remember those years. Felicia was a terror."

Silence settled over the room, most likely because Mrs. Murdock had snapped her lips together and was perusing the carpet as if something had captured her interest.

Resisting the urge to laugh, Grayson placed his hand on her arm. "I'm certain Miss Murdock was completely precious in her youth."

Ruth's head snapped up, and she began nodding, vigorously. "But of course she was. Why, whenever she found herself in the midst of a bit of trouble—not that she got into trouble often, mind you—she'd turn those big eyes on me and I was helpless to resist her." She smiled. "I'm sure Eliza must have used the same tactics with you in her younger years."

Eliza *had* been precious in her youth, with her flyaway red hair and large blue eyes. She'd adored him, had followed him everywhere, which made it all the more disturbing that he'd so carelessly turned from her.

"You need a mother for little Ming."

This was what happened when one let down one's guard while in the presence of a matchmaking mother. They were relentless in their determination to see their daughters well married and pounced when a man least expected it.

He considered Mrs. Murdock for a moment, unable to attribute the gleam in her eyes to anything other than speculation.

He'd come to truly enjoy Mrs. Murdock and her manipulating ways, even though that manipulation was currently directed toward him. She was obviously a lady who loved her family, especially her daughter. He appreciated that about her, even though he had no intention of going along with whatever diabolical plan she currently had prowling around her mind.

He was going to have to be honest with her, firm as well, and make her understand that he was not the gentleman for Felicia, or for any other lady for that matter. He'd vowed to never marry again, and he intended to keep that vow. He was too damaged, too filthy, if the truth were known. He would never be good enough to become someone's husband, let alone a husband to a lady like Felicia, who was entirely too captivating for her own good.

He felt a bead of sweat pop out on his forehead and begin to dribble down his face as trepidation rolled through him. It was a bit concerning even thinking the word *captivating* and Felicia in the same breath. Granted, it lent a bit of an explanation as to why he'd been grumpy at the wedding, but . . . he needed to make a hasty retreat before other words such as *alluring*, *enchanting*, and *compelling* started swirling around his mind, but . . . apparently, they already were.

Searching for an excuse that would allow him to take an immediate leave, he casually pulled up the sleeve of his jacket, wondering if he could hope Felicia's rash had been a contagious thing and was even now rapidly spreading through the wedding guests. He leaned closer and peered at his skin, unable to detect a single blemish. He scratched it just to be sure.

"Good gracious, Mr. Sumner, are you itching?"

Itching to get out of there, but he couldn't very well make that proclamation without giving Mrs. Murdock a perfect reason to speculate, and that wasn't something he was willing to do, not given her devious mind.

The sound of an uneven stomping gait right outside the drawing room broke through his panicked thoughts. He turned toward the door and felt the breath leave him in one single whoosh when Felicia stormed into the room, the sight of her causing his mouth to drop open even as he belatedly remembered to get to his feet.

"Oh . . . dear," Ruth whispered as she got up from the settee as well.

Mrs. Murdock's exclamation summed it up nicely. The lady standing in front of him in no way resembled the Felicia he'd come to know. Instead, he was faced with a lady gowned all in black, the cut of the garment emphasizing curves he'd never noticed and certainly never imagined. Her hair was unbound and tumbled to a waist that was incredibly small and accented her . . . charms.

His mouth ran dry as another bead of sweat formed on his forehead and trickled down his face.

Who would have ever thought such an enticing figure was lurking under the vast amount of fabric Felicia normally wore?

Realizing he was gawking, and with a mother bent on match-making standing only feet away from him, he pulled his gaze from Felicia's surprising attributes and decided a safe part of her to concentrate on would be her hair. Unfortunately, random pins sticking haphazardly out of her tresses captured his attention, causing his mouth to curve up in a grin, something he quickly strove to control when Felicia's eyes began to shoot sparks in his direction.

Ruth took that moment to clear her throat, loudly. "Felicia, what could you be thinking wearing that particular gown, and where are your manners? You've neglected to greet Mr. Sumner."

"Mr. Sumner," Felicia all but purred in a husky voice, the huskiness causing his mouth to feel as if it were suddenly full of sand.

"Miss Murdock," he managed to say, wincing when he realized his voice sounded unnaturally high. He swallowed, drew in a deep breath, and tried again, pitching his tone a few octaves lower. "Don't you look . . . delightful."

Felicia frowned, narrowed her eyes, and folded her arms over her chest.

Oddly enough, it seemed as if she took offense at the term *delightful*. He tried again. "Charming?"

Her eyes narrowed to mere slits.

"Different?"

Felicia's frown disappeared as her lips curved into an enchanting smile, causing all rational thought to flee from his mind.

She was stunning when she smiled.

"Thank you, Mr. Sumner."

"Really, Felicia, I'm not certain he was extending you a compliment," Ruth muttered before she waved a hand at Felicia's dress. "Would you care to explain why you've garbed yourself all in black? It's not as if anyone has died recently."

Felicia lifted her chin. "I had nothing else to wear. And there has been a death recently, very recently—the death of the old me. I've decided to assume a new identity, at least for today. Today . . . I'm going to be Clara."

Grayson exchanged a glance with Ruth, who was looking decidedly worried, before he returned his attention to Felicia. Curiosity stole over him. "Why Clara?"

Felicia swept a strand of hair out of her face, the action causing some of the hairpins to tumble to the floor, which she ignored. "If you must know, Clara was a character I ran across in a moldy old book years ago. Given that she possessed a remarkable zest for life, I've long admired her." She smiled. "She was a complete nuisance and came to an exceedingly bad end, but she was an incredibly compelling character—so compelling, in fact, that I've decided to emulate her."

"You long to come to a bad end?" was all Grayson could think to ask.

"If it's an interesting end, certainly."

What could he possibly say to that bit of nonsense?

He opened his mouth but was spared a response when Ruth suddenly made a *tsk*ing noise under her breath, grabbed him rather roughly by the arm, and began tugging him toward the door.

"Thank you so much for coming by today, Mr. Sumner, but I fear my *dear* daughter's rash must be far worse than I first imagined and is causing her to be out of sorts. You'd best get on your way quickly before you contract whatever vile disorder Felicia's evidently picked up."

"Forgive me, Mrs. Murdock, but I don't believe a rash is causing her behavior—more like insanity, and I don't think insanity is contagious."

Ruth tightened her grip on his arm. "We mustn't take any chances."

They made it to the hall and were moving at a brisk pace down it before the sound of footsteps echoed behind him. Even though Ruth kept trying to prod him along, he slowed to a stop, turned, and found Felicia limping after them. He looked to her feet and couldn't help but grin. She was wearing two completely different shoes, one with a high heel and one with a low heel, which went far in explaining her lopsided gait.

"You should have kept moving," Ruth mumbled, right before Felicia teetered to a stop in front of them and plopped her hands on her hips. Ruth released a dramatic sigh. "Are you aware, dear, that you're wearing two different shoes?"

Felicia lifted her black skirt, looked down for a moment, dropped the skirt back into place, and shrugged. "So I am. How odd."

"Yes, it is odd, much like your demeanor, which is why you're going to bid Mr. Sumner a good day and return to your room. I suggest you spend the rest of the afternoon taking a good, long nap."

"I'm not tired."

"Be that as it may," Ruth returned between now clenched teeth, "it's past time Grayson took his leave."

"I'm going with him."

Ruth shook her head. "That wouldn't be wise."

"I can't ignore Eliza's invitation, and it would be beyond rude to Mr. Sumner if he came all this way to fetch me but then was forced to leave me behind." She turned to him. "I'll be right back. I just need to change my shoes." With that, she began to limp down the hall.

"If you're determined to continue on with this madness," Ruth called after her, "you might want to fetch a hat as well."

Felicia looked over her shoulder. "Clara never wore a hat."

Ruth closed her eyes for just a moment, opened them, and shook her head. "It is beyond me at times like this why people feel inclined to have children."

"To bring you joy and comfort in your old age, of course," Felicia said briskly before she turned her head and hurried off down the hallway.

"She's in an unusual mood," Grayson said to fill the silence Felicia's departure had caused.

"I'm afraid I can't argue with you about that." Ruth sighed. "I should not have agreed to the plan of having you come after her, especially knowing the disappointment she suffered today. I think the only prudent thing to do now is to summon my carriage and accompany Felicia over to your sister's house myself. Eliza did, in fact, issue me an invitation, but . . ." Ruth suddenly looked a little shifty. "It might be for the best if you didn't mention that to Felicia."

"Should I even bother to ask why you've allowed your daughter to believe you weren't invited?"

Ruth began to fan her face with her hand. "Probably not, and it hardly matters now. What does matter is rescuing you from my somewhat deranged daughter." Ruth stopped fanning her face. "Do forgive me, for you have no idea what I'm speaking about, but I'm afraid I'm not at liberty to disclose the particulars."

"Eliza told me about Reverend Fraser and Felicia's affection for him."

"I was under the impression Felicia had kept that affection a well-guarded secret."

"I'm sure she did, but Eliza's always been intuitive, and she's great friends with Agatha, one of New York City's rising journalists. It probably didn't take much pondering for them to figure out Felicia's secret. I must admit, learning about Felicia's interest in Reverend Fraser explained quite a few things about her, especially why she's never shown an interest in any of the gentlemen I've watched you parade before her."

Ruth's eyes turned cunning. "I think she's shown a little interest in you."

Once again he'd forgotten he was in the presence of a determined mother. "She hasn't, as you very well know, and I must be up-front with you, Mrs. Murdock. I'm not looking for a wife."

"You need a mother for your daughter."

"I employ several nannies who are more than capable of seeing to her needs."

"I'm certain they do an admirable job, but there's nothing quite like a mother's touch, is there?"

Grayson laughed. "You are tenacious, aren't you?"

"I'll take that as a compliment."

"It was intended as such, but I don't want to give you false hope. Your daughter obviously hopes to settle down with a respectable and faith-filled man, given her affection for Reverend Fraser. I readily admit I'm far from respectable and even further from faith-filled."

"I'm sure that's not true."

"Do you think it will ever be possible, Mother, for you to *not* try and pawn me off on some poor, unsuspecting gentleman every time I leave a room?"

Grayson looked up and found Felicia marching toward them, her hair, surprisingly enough, stuffed underneath a revolting hat of lime green, pieces of it sticking out here and there, and one of her hands was clutched around a parasol of brightest orange. Determined to avoid the subject of wardrobe choices, he stepped forward and smiled. "Your mother wasn't really trying to pawn you off on me."

Felicia's eyes turned stormy. "Oh fine, take her side." She lifted her chin. "Perhaps I should simply drive myself over to Eliza's."

"I'm afraid that's not an option, because I promised Eliza and Agatha I'd do my very best to entertain you out of your doldrums while . . ."

Pain had a way of making a gentleman forget what he'd been saying.

"Did you just poke me with your parasol?"

"Why would Eliza and Agatha have you make any promises?"

"Ah, well . . ." He looked to Ruth for assistance, but she didn't appear to be giving him the slightest bit of attention and was instead staring at the ceiling as if she'd never before noticed the cheerful cherubs frolicking above their heads.

"What else did you promise Eliza and Agatha?" Felicia demanded.

He summoned what he hoped was a pleasant smile. "I promised them I'd be charming."

Felicia drew in a sharp breath and rounded on her mother. "I thought you only told everyone I had a rash."

Ruth stopped looking at the ceiling and fixed her gaze on him. "Isn't that exactly what I told you?"

"Is it permissible for me to admit I have been privy to that type of personal information?"

Felicia began to tap the parasol in a slightly menacing manner against the floor. "I don't have a rash. Well, I have a small one, but I think it was brought on by the mere suggestion of . . . Oh, never mind." She narrowed her eyes on Ruth. "Why would Eliza and Agatha send Grayson to charm me if they didn't know, and if you didn't tell them, how did they find out?"

Grayson resisted the urge to bolt when Felicia stopped tapping the parasol against the floor and shook it in his direction. When it appeared Ruth was at a loss for words, he cleared his throat. "I expect Eliza and Agatha, being the nosy ladies I'm sure you realize them to be, simply figured it out."

Felicia's eyes widened. "I thought I hid my feelings quite well." Her shoulders slumped for a moment, but then she straightened her spine and nodded. "Well, there's nothing I can do about it now. What's done is done, and I'm just going to have to face everyone's pity head on."

"I'm more than certain everyone is going to pity Grayson far more than you, my dear, especially if you let it be known you've decided to be Clara for the day," Ruth muttered.

Felicia looked at her mother, lifted her chin even higher, stepped closer to him, and grabbed his arm. "We should probably be on our way. I would hate to be late for tea." With that, she prodded him toward the front door, barely waiting for the butler to open it before she pulled him through it.

Their progress came to an abrupt halt when three gentlemen, all of them bearing a marked resemblance to Felicia, ambled up the steps and blocked their way. He heard what sounded like a sigh escape her lips.

"On my word, Felicia, you're looking a bit frightful," Jeffrey Murdock, the oldest of the clan, exclaimed. "Are you aware that you're dressed in black?"

Felicia's grip on Grayson's arm tightened. "Don't be ridiculous. Of course I'm aware of what I'm wearing, Jeffrey. And I'll thank you to not call me Felicia."

Confusion immediately clouded Jeffrey's eyes. "What, pray tell, would you have me call you, then?"

"Clara."

Jeffrey simply stared at her for a moment with his mouth somewhat slack before he turned to Grayson. "Am I allowed to call you Grayson, or have you assumed a new identity as well?"

"He's Frank," Felicia supplied before Grayson could get a word out of his mouth.

"Forgive me, Felicia, but I don't recall agreeing to change my name to Frank, even for just today," Grayson said.

"Did you or did you not promise your sister you were going to charm me?"

"Well, yes, but that agreement had nothing to do with assuming a new identity."

Her eyes began to sparkle in a slightly mischievous way, causing him to completely lose his train of thought.

"Don't you want to do everything in your power to charm me?"

He suddenly found he wanted to do much more than charm her, which caused him to immediately turn from her, and move toward her brother Robert, his action causing her hand to fall away from his arm.

"It's nice to see you again, Robert."

"And you as well, Grayson, but tell me, have you really agreed to charm my little sister?" Robert was regarding him somewhat warily.

"It was Eliza's and Agatha's idea."

Felicia's third brother, Daniel, stepped forward, a huge grin on his face. "Well, that certainly fits, considering the antics of those two." He held out his hand and Grayson shook it. "They must have figured out Felicia's affection for Reverend Fraser and wanted to do whatever they could to cheer her up." Daniel shuddered as he glanced at his sister and then back to Grayson.

"I can't say I envy you at the moment. Charming Felicia might be a bit of a daunting task today."

Grayson couldn't say he'd argue that point, especially when all the mischief disappeared from Felicia's eyes to be replaced with distinct irritation.

"You knew about Reverend Fraser?" she asked, moving close enough to Daniel to give him a sharp poke with her parasol.

Daniel looked at her for a moment, reached out, and much to Grayson's relief, snatched the parasol from her hand before he smiled. "Don't ever do that again, and yes, we've known about Reverend Fraser forever." He looked over her shoulder, and his smile widened. "Oh look, here comes Mother, and is that roast I smell coming out the door? I'm starving."

"Me too," Robert exclaimed, and without another word, the two brothers turned, greeted Ruth with a somewhat hurried hello, and fled into the house.

"Cowards," Felicia called after them.

"Felicia, really, it's not well done of you to throw insults at your own brothers," Ruth said as she marched up to join them. "Ah, Jeffrey, this is a fortunate surprise. You can accompany Felicia and Grayson over to Eliza's house. They're going there for tea."

Grayson thought that was a wonderful suggestion. He nodded in full agreement but stopped mid-nod when Felicia shook her head.

"Jeffrey wasn't invited, nor were you, if you'll recall."

Ruth waved the comment away. "Eliza adores Jeffrey, and he can assume the role of chaperone, or rather, guardian."

"I'm twenty-four, Mother. I haven't needed a chaperone for years."

"Not for you—for Grayson. The poor man is going to need all the guarding he can get, considering your state of mind."

Grayson grinned, extended his arm once again to Felicia,

who'd begun to sputter, and sent Ruth a nod. "We'll be fine, Mrs. Murdock, but I do appreciate your concern." He looked down at Felicia. "Ready?"

"Of course I'm ready, Frank. Lead the way."

With Ruth's voice echoing in his ear, saying something that sounded remarkably like "Your sister has lost her mind and there's nothing any of us can do to help her get it back," Grayson helped Felicia down the short flight of steps and then heard the front door shut behind them.

"I like your mother," he said, patting the gloved hand Felicia had placed over his arm. "She's very managing."

"You should try living with her."

"I said I liked her, but I don't think I'd be up for living with her."

Felicia laughed, sounding much more like the Felicia he knew, and then she took over the task of steering them toward his phaeton, reminding him of one of the few times he'd danced with her and she'd taken to leading him around the dance floor.

Felicia brought them to a stop right beside his horses and surprised him when she let out what sounded remarkably like a whistle. "Nice phaeton. Is it fast?"

Trepidation was immediate. "It has been known to move rather quickly."

She moved up to it and trailed a gloved hand along the polished surface. "Will you allow me to drive it?"

"Hmm . . ."

She turned her head and smiled a smile that was just a bit too cunning. "Did you, or did you not, make certain promises today?"

"Well, yes, but those had nothing to do with allowing you to drive my phaeton."

"Driving such a remarkable conveyance would go far in lifting my flagging spirits."

Not only was she captivating at times, it appeared she was also rather diabolical.

"Do you know how to drive?" he heard himself ask before he could stop the words from escaping his mouth.

"My mother tells everyone how proficient I am with the reins."

Five minutes later, as Grayson hung to the seat for dear life, he came to the realization that Mrs. Murdock was not above exaggeration when it came to her daughter's abilities.

3

The next morning, Felicia was somewhat surprised to find herself in a delightful frame of mind. Even though she'd slept little—having spent far too many hours contemplating her future *and* the disturbing events of the wedding *and* what had occurred afterward with Grayson—she felt better than she had in weeks, perhaps even months.

Unfortunately, feeling in tip-top shape was causing her a slight bit of distress, given that she was currently being fitted for a new wardrobe. She was supposed to remain perfectly still while pins were being thrust her way, but her high spirits kept urging her to fidget.

She needed to think of something distracting, something that would allow her to relax and not get poked with any pins, something that might amuse her.

The perfect distraction immediately sprang to mind.

Grayson was worthy of more contemplation, especially since he'd finally proven to her without a shadow of a doubt that gentlemen really were dramatic creatures.

She'd never dreamed Grayson Sumner would overreact simply because she might have—oh, very well, she definitely had—lost a smidgen of control while she'd been attempting to drive his obviously high-strung pair of horses.

There certainly hadn't been any reason for him to throw himself out of the seat once they'd arrived at Eliza's and kiss the ground numerous times. After he'd finished that alarming business, he'd jumped to his feet and proceeded to give her a blistering lecture regarding something to the effect that lying about one's abilities with the reins simply wasn't done. He'd then proclaimed, in a very loud voice, that she'd taken leave of her senses.

Why everyone believed him to be an amiable and pleasant sort was beyond her comprehension.

After he'd apparently run out of words, he resorted to grumpiness and spent the remainder of their time at Eliza's keeping his distance from her. He even went so far as to let it be known to one and all that he'd rather someone else see her home. That had earned him the old cold shoulder from Eliza and Agatha, but she hadn't been bothered in the least.

The last thing she'd wanted to deal with was his continued surliness, so when Agatha offered her a ride, she'd jumped at the chance. She hadn't even bothered to wish Grayson a good night, though it was unlikely he'd noticed, given his continued attempts to avoid her.

He really did possess the ability to be extremely annoying when he set his mind to it.

She shifted on her feet and let out a yelp when a sharp pain pierced her side.

"I do beg your pardon, Miss Murdock," Mrs. Brown, an alteration lady at B. Altman's department store, said as she pulled a pin out of the waistband of Felicia's new gown. "I wasn't expecting you to move yet again, considering you promised me not five minutes ago you were going to stay still."

"I did promise that, didn't I."

"You did, several times."

Felicia squared her shoulders. "This time I mean it."

Mrs. Brown smiled and returned to the task of sticking additional pins into the material but paused when a knock sounded on the door and Agatha stuck her head in.

"Ah, there you are, Felicia. I was hoping I'd find you here."

It was rapidly becoming apparent that everyone was under the misimpression she was heading for a nervous breakdown. While she appreciated having family and friends who cared about her, it was becoming downright annoying.

She was not some delicate miss who needed to be coddled or, for that matter, pitied.

"I thought you were going to be working on a story today," she said as Agatha moseyed into the room.

"I got the first draft written for the *New-York Tribune* earlier than expected and decided to take the rest of the afternoon off."

"Of course you did," Felicia muttered. "How did you know where I was?"

Agatha strolled over to a gilded mahogany chair upholstered in red velvet and sat down, taking a rather long time to rearrange her skirt before she looked up. "Your mother told me. She showed up at my house an hour or two ago and thought it would be entertaining for me if I joined you."

"It's hardly entertaining to watch a lady get fitted for a new wardrobe, so please don't feel I'll take offense if you decide to seek out true amusements."

"Ah, tea, how lovely," Agatha said as she rose from the chair, glided across the room to the tea cart, poured herself a cup, and took a sip. "Delicious." She raised the cup in Felicia's direction, moved back to the chair, resumed her seat, and sent Felicia a cheeky grin.

It was apparent Agatha was not going anywhere anytime soon.

"That's a lovely color of green," Agatha remarked with a nod toward the dress Felicia was currently wearing. "Although I do believe your mother is a touch upset you turned down her offer of a trip to Paris to secure new fashions."

Now they were beginning to get somewhere.

"Is that why she sent you, to convince me to take a trip across the ocean to visit the House of Worth?"

Agatha took another sip of tea, swallowed, and shook her head. "No, especially after I told her I balked at the same idea, even though my mother believes I would look divine in gowns created by Charles Worth. Lucky for me, my position at the *New-York Tribune* gives me a ready excuse to avoid taking a leisurely jaunt across the sea."

"Perhaps I should look into securing a career. Maybe then my mother would cease her relentless worrying and discontinue sending my friends to check up on me." She caught Agatha's eye. "I'm fine, by the way, even though I'm sure Mother told you differently."

"That remains to be seen." Agatha set her teacup aside. "But returning to the idea of a career, how is your writing?"

"Mediocre at best."

"Then I'm afraid you probably wouldn't make it as a journalist." She tapped her finger on her chin. "Are you any good at snooping?"

"Snooping?"

"You know, ferreting out information. Arabella Wilder has taken to helping Theodore with his private investigation business, and I'm sure they'd be more than happy to bring you on if you're any good at that sort of thing."

"I used to be proficient at running down my brothers when they tried to avoid me, but that was years ago." Felicia wrinkled her nose. "Besides, Arabella and Theodore, even though they've been married for a few months now, still seem overly enthralled with each other. While that's a lovely state for them to be in . . . considering I've recently suffered a direct blow to the heart, I hardly think it would be wise for me to be in constant contact with a couple so in love."

"Aha, so you really aren't fine."

It truly was unfortunate Agatha was such an intelligent sort, but since Felicia had no intention of discussing her recent heartache, especially since she was in a lovely frame of mind at the moment, she settled for waving Agatha's comment away with one deliberate flick of her wrist. "Yes, well, getting back to a career choice for me, I'm afraid I have no real skills, and isn't that a sad state of affairs for a lady of twenty-four to recognize?"

"You're very good at helping the needy. Perhaps you should continue on with that."

It wasn't as if she hadn't thought about continuing on with her charitable efforts, even though she knew full well it was hardly likely she'd ever help out as much in Reverend Fraser's church. That would be somewhat awkward, especially since it appeared far too many people had discovered her feelings about the gentleman. It would only be a matter of time until he found out about them, or worse yet, his wife.

The new Mrs. Fraser was truly a compassionate soul, but her compassion might not extend quite so far as to embrace a lady who'd longed to be with her husband.

The pesky little problem of what to do with her life now that reality had smacked her in the face had plagued her endlessly throughout the night. She'd taken to having a rather long chat with God, not that He'd sent her any clear solution to her problems as of yet, but in the midst of that chat, she'd come to a few uncomfortable truths.

She'd changed her identity in order to secure the affections of a gentleman.

She'd thrown herself into charitable endeavors to please that gentleman, and . . . although she'd gone to more church services than she could count, she'd barely listened to any of the sermons.

She'd been completely ridiculous.

She needed to make amends, and in order to do that, she needed to honestly and quietly help the less fortunate—not in a manner that would draw attention to her actions and have everyone exclaiming how wonderful and selfless she was.

That made what Agatha was suggesting a bit of a problem. "Felicia?"

Felicia blinked. "Good heavens, I do beg your pardon, Agatha. I fear I was lost in thought. What were we talking about?"

"A career for you, but maybe we should change the subject, considering the very suggestion sent you into a trance."

Worry was clearly evident on Agatha's face.

Maybe it was time to change the subject. She looked down and then back to Agatha. "What do you think about the color of this gown?"

For a moment, Agatha said nothing as she considered Felicia, but then she shook her head ever so slightly and smiled. "Fine, we'll talk fashion, although I already mentioned I thought the color was lovely." She tilted her head. "Moss green does wonders for bringing out the blue of your eyes, and I find the richness of the shade much preferable to the pastels you normally favor." She bit her lip. "Oh dear, that was hardly amusing for me to say."

Felicia laughed. "It was honest, and honesty is something of which I've heard relatively little the past few years." She grinned. "You'll be happy to learn that I haven't purchased a single pastel gown today, nor have I requested any frills or ribbons."

Agatha's eyes grew round. "You're worse off than anyone imagined."

"I'm fine."

"You keep saying that, but you just admitted you ordered gowns without frills. You're far from fine."

"Agatha, you and I both know a lady of my advanced years should never wear frills in the first place. Instead of being concerned with my selections, you should be relieved. At least now no one will have to avoid eye contact with me when I arrive at a society event dressed in revolting styles." She glanced down when Mrs. Brown paused in her work. "No offense, Mrs. Brown. It wasn't your fault I demanded you attach bows and ribbons to all my purchases." She blew out a breath.

"Truth be told, I dressed that way because I believed—wrongly, of course—that a gentleman who shall remain nameless thought I looked delightful drowned in ribbons and bows."

"That explains a lot," Mrs. Brown said before she stuck one last pin in the hem and straightened. "There, all done. I'll have this altered within the week, and then I'll send it to your house along with the other garments you've chosen."

Felicia smiled her thanks and stepped off the raised platform, turning to allow Mrs. Brown access to the buttons running down her back. When Mrs. Brown finished, Felicia held the bodice of the gown in place with one hand as she moved over to a rack of clothing that held many of the garments she'd purchased. Pulling out a darling navy-and-white-striped walking dress that had already been altered for her while she shopped, she folded it over her arm and stepped behind the privacy screen. It took her only a moment to shrug out of the pin-ridden gown and slip into the new dress. Mrs. Brown joined her behind the screen, making short shrift of fastening her up. She moved out into the main room and winced when she heard Agatha release what sounded like a snort.

"You don't like it?"

Agatha rose from the chair, walked up to Felicia, looked her up and down, and then wrinkled her brow. "It's lovely to be sure, but you look . . . different."

Different was rapidly becoming one of Felicia's favorite words.

"Wonderful. That's exactly what I wanted to hear." She smiled at Agatha, who was once again watching her in concern, and then strode across the room, plucking the hideous confection of palest orange she'd worn to the department store from a chair. She held it up to Mrs. Brown. "Now then, let us move on to discussing my old clothing."

Alarm flickered across Mrs. Brown's face. "I don't believe my talents are such that I can turn that into anything resembling the latest styles."

And didn't that speak volumes about how she'd been parading around the city for the past four years?

She absolutely refused to sigh—even though if there'd ever been a time to sigh, this was certainly it. "I wasn't suggesting you alter the gown, Mrs. Brown. Skilled as you obviously are in the art of alteration, even you have your limits. Do you know of anyone who could benefit from my old wardrobe?"

Mrs. Brown eyed the massive amount of fabric in Felicia's hand. "I do have a cousin who works in the theater district. He's constantly lamenting the dismal state of their budget. I imagine he would be thrilled to receive your old garments, and I would be happy to furnish you with his address."

She'd apparently been garbed in outfits best suited for the theater.

She managed to nod, which sent Mrs. Brown hurrying over to a desk, rummaging through it for a moment until she finally located a piece of paper. She took a moment to scribble something down, walked back to Felicia, and handed her the paper, taking the orange gown from her in return. "I'll send this along with your order so you won't have to lug it around, but before you go, would you care to show Miss Watson the gown you've chosen for the ball?"

Agatha frowned. "What ball?"

"The ball Mrs. Beckett is holding for Zayne," Felicia reminded her.

"Oh, that ball." Agatha's expression turned somewhat glum, but then she drew in a breath and practically stomped across the room, coming to a stop in front of the rack that held Felicia's new clothing. She began to sort through the garments, exclaiming every now and then over the cut of a gown, or the color, but then her hand stilled right before she plucked out a gown of brilliant red and shook it in Felicia's direction.

"I'm going to assume this gown has been hung here by mistake."

Felicia frowned. "That's what I'm wearing to the ball."

"Have you lost your mind?"

Felicia eyed the wispy bit of silk Agatha was still shaking at her and smiled. "Not at all. I've come to the conclusion red is a wonderful color for me. Mrs. Brown believes it makes my eyes sparkle."

"It does," Mrs. Brown added with a nod. "And it fits her form to perfection."

"I don't think you're helping me," Felicia muttered as she glanced at Agatha, who was now staring back at her as if she'd suddenly acquired two heads.

"Too right you are," Mrs. Brown exclaimed before she consulted a watch pinned to her sleeve. "My, would you look at the time. I've almost missed lunch." She hurried across the room, set Felicia's old gown on a table, and plucked up a hat. "I must thank you once again, Miss Murdock, for your order today, and . . . best of luck to you at the ball, and . . ." She shot a look to Agatha, snapped her mouth shut, strode to the door, and disappeared a second later.

"You cannot wear this gown."

Felicia moved to Agatha's side, took the gown from her, and hung it back on the rack. "There's nothing wrong with it."

"I disagree. For one, it's red, and for two, well, it seems to be missing a bodice."

"It's not missing a bodice. It's simply a little low-cut. I'm quite certain there will be other ladies at the ball, younger and more appealing ladies at that, who will be wearing similar styles. I'm an old spinster. No one will even notice me." She smiled. "Besides, it's the off-season. Most members of society are languishing at their summer homes, enjoying the sun and sea, so they won't even be in attendance."

"Oh, please, this is a Beckett ball. Everyone will come back to enjoy it." Agatha planted her hands on her hips. "All the sticklers for propriety will be there, and I can guarantee you that the talk of the evening won't center on the fact that Zayne is finally going off to join his soon-to-be fiancée, Miss Helena Collins. No, talk will center on you, no matter your proclamation in regard to your spinster status. Honestly, Felicia, spinsters don't wear bright red gowns, and they certainly don't possess a remarkable figure such as yours—a figure, I must add, that no one is even aware you possess."

"The gown I wore yesterday afternoon showed off my figure" was all Felicia could think to respond.

Agatha arched a brow. "Did it?"

"You didn't notice?"

"Forgive me, but I was more concerned regarding your mood, and over the fact that Grayson was so obviously put out with you. I didn't happen to notice the curves you've been hiding for years."

"Grayson might have noticed."

Agatha's mouth went slack. "He did?"

"He was rendered somewhat mute when he first saw me at my

house, and then, when he did speak, his voice was remarkably high." She bit her lip. "Although, he might simply have been surprised I was wearing two different shoes, my hair looked like a rat's nest, and I told him and my mother I was going to be Clara for the rest of the day."

"Ah, hmm" was all Agatha seemed capable of saying for a moment. She crossed her arms over her chest. "I can't fathom why you'd declare yourself a Clara for a day, but an explanation regarding that troubling matter will have to wait." She tilted her head. "Tell me, was your decision to purchase a red gown influenced at all by what Grayson might think?"

Needing a moment to craft a response to that rather uncomfortable question, Felicia headed toward a mirror hanging on the wall and took a moment to secure her new hat on her head. For a second she admired its navy base paired with a single white ribbon wrapped around the body and not one bow in sight, but then she heard the sound of Agatha's toe tapping all too impatiently on the floor and forced herself to turn, having no idea how to reply.

Had the thought of Grayson and how he might react to seeing her in the red gown come to mind the moment she'd spotted the gown hanging on a dress form?

Yes, it had, but she didn't understand why, nor had she taken the time to ponder the matter, which meant she wasn't prepared to discuss it with Agatha.

She loved the lady dearly, had enjoyed getting to know her better the past year, but Agatha was a meddler—everyone knew that. If Agatha discovered she was even remotely attracted to Grayson—not that she was admitting she was—well, that would simply never do.

"I think Grayson's interested in you."

Felicia blinked rapidly out of her thoughts. "Come again?"

"He allowed you to drive his prized horses."

"What does that have to do with anything?"

"Eliza told me he's never trusted a woman with the reins."

"Nor will he ever do so again, judging by his reaction to my driving."

Agatha's eyes turned cunning. "It was quite chivalrous of him to escort you yesterday over to Eliza's—very telling, don't you think?"

"There was nothing *telling* about it," Felicia argued. "You and Eliza badgered him into it, and don't even think about arguing that point."

"There was only a small amount of badgering involved, and perhaps a bit of toe stomping." She smiled but then sobered. "You need to reconsider your gown choice for the ball."

"It's a very fashionable piece, Agatha. I know you'll find this hard to believe, but before I turned delusional and thought my life was meant to be spent as a minister's wife, I used to be highly particular about fashion. I need to make changes in my life, and one of those changes—not one of the largest changes, I know—is that I'm going to dress to please myself.

"That dress pleases me. It's bold, but not in a forward way, and the color makes me feel feminine. If it causes a few tongues to wag, so be it."

"Please tell me you're not planning to continue on as Clara in order to get the tongues wagging." A frisson of awareness swept over her, the masculine voice causing her to stiffen.

She did not have to turn to know who was standing behind her, because there was only one person she knew in New York who possessed such a distinctive, and slightly intriguing, British accent.

What in the world was Grayson doing at B. Altman's?

He was supposed to be extremely put out with her, but for some unknown reason, his tone seemed more amused than annoyed.

She drew in a steadying breath and turned. The sight of Grayson lounging oh so casually against the doorframe, looking every inch the aristocrat, caused the unusual reaction of her breath catching in her throat.

Her reaction to the man was ridiculous. Granted, he was extremely attractive, especially when he grinned—the grin bringing into sharp attention the two dimples her mother made mention of rather often. Her gaze drifted to his jacket, and she found no fault with the impeccable cut of gray, or with the waistcoat underneath, or even with the subtle dark tie that was tied to perfection around his neck. Her gaze lowered, taking in the pinstriped trousers and stopping at his shoes, unable to help but notice their glossy shine.

He'd obviously secured the services of a well-trained valet since he'd come to America, which explained his immaculate appearance, but it didn't explain why he was grinning. She lifted her head and, sure enough, he was still at it.

What was wrong with him?

They'd parted on less than amicable terms. She knew full well—even if no one else appeared to realize it—that he wasn't the type of person to blithely set aside a grudge, especially considering he seemed to believe she'd almost caused him a horrible death due to her driving abilities.

She finally realized he was waiting for a response, given that he was staring back at her with a trace of expectation in his eyes. "I've decided Clara is only to be brought out in extenuating circumstances, and since there's nothing extenuating about shopping, she's not around today."

"Well, we can thank the good Lord for that."

Funny, but it almost seemed as if there was now a touch of surliness edging his tone. Oddly enough, that thought had her feeling slightly better. A surly Grayson she could handle. "What are you doing here?"

Grayson pushed away from the doorframe and stopped right in front of her. His nearness caused her pulse to once again go galloping off through her veins.

It was a peculiar feeling, and one she didn't happen to care for in the least.

"A Mrs. Brown found me wandering aimlessly amongst the dresses and took pity on me, telling me I would find you in here." Grayson took a step back and looked her up and down.

A sliver of disappointment slid over her when he didn't bother to remark about her new gown or hat but simply nodded, just once, and continued on with what he'd been saying.

"She assured me it was acceptable for me to enter what can only be described as a feminine domain because, in addition to telling me both of you were respectably gowned, she felt there might be a need for a distraction, and apparently I fit that bill." He grinned yet again. "So, why do the two of you need a distraction, and more importantly, why are tongues going to wag?"

Felicia blew out a breath. "Hasn't anyone ever told you it's rude to eavesdrop?"

"Hasn't anyone ever told you that if you plan on saying something you don't want overheard, you should make sure the door's shut?"

Her pulse slowed immediately. He might be an attractive gentleman who dressed to perfection, but he was also irritating, arrogant, and far too sure of himself.

Knowing full well it would hardly be productive to continue bantering with him, she decided her best option was to keep him a little defensive. "You never said what you're doing here, and I must confess I'm a little surprised you'd seek me out. I was under the impression you were annoyed with me because of what happened with your carriage yesterday."

"Just to be clear, it is not a carriage; it is a phaeton, which you had no business even attempting to drive, limited as your abilities obviously are. As for what I'm doing here, Eliza sent me."

It seemed to her that although his lips were still curved in somewhat of a grin, his voice was now sounding distinctively surly, proving once and for all that underneath his pleasant and affable appearance, there really did lie the soul of a grumpy gentleman.

His grumpiness begged the question of why he'd agreed to Eliza's request in the first place.

"That was sweet of Eliza to be concerned about me, but I assure you, I'm fine."

"How lovely, but she didn't send me after you." He turned to Agatha. "I've been all over the city trying to track *you* down. I finally stopped at Felicia's house as a last resort, and that's when I learned you were here."

Agatha frowned. "Has something happened?"

Grayson returned the frown. "You're supposed to be distressed."

"Eliza told you I was distressed?"

"Yes, and she also gave me strict instructions that I was to"— he held up his hand and began to tick items off his fingers— "improve your spirits"—one finger went up—"charm you out of your bad mood"—another finger went up—"and put myself entirely at your disposal."

"Eliza sent *you* to complete those arduous tasks?"

"Really, Agatha, you wound me. Do you not think I'm up for coaxing you out of your gloomy mood?"

"I'm not in a gloomy mood."

"Since I've traveled all over the city in order to cheer you up, you're going to have to humor me and get in a gloomy mood."

"But I don't feel gloomy."

Grayson quirked a brow. "You're not upset that Zayne is moving out west to join his Miss Collins?"

Agatha rolled her eyes. "Really, everyone believing I'm distraught over Zayne Beckett is getting a bit ridiculous. We're simply friends. He's the brother of my dear friend Arabella. Did I at one time suffer a small infatuation for him? Yes, I did—as I've admitted time and time again. I've also insisted, on numerous occasions, that I have come to my senses. Zayne's intentions toward Miss Collins were formed years ago, and since he's determined to carry through with those intentions, I've firmly pushed aside any romantic affection I once felt for the gentleman. I'm happy for him and wish him nothing but the best for his future."

Felicia sucked in a sharp breath as yet another one of her flaws came into glaring evidence. She'd been so consumed with her own problems in life that she'd not even realized Agatha might be in need of a bit of cheering up.

Though her friend had claimed time and time again she'd abandoned all hope in regard to Zayne and his affections, everyone knew she wasn't exactly telling the truth.

The very idea that she'd neglected to even consider the plight of her friend spoke volumes about her selfish character.

She was a sorry excuse for a friend.

"Is something the matter, Felicia?"

Felicia pulled herself out of her thoughts and found Grayson watching her closely. "No."

"You're looking a little pale."

"To think Eliza truly does seem to be under the misimpression that you're capable of charm." Felicia shook her head. "Telling a lady she looks anything other than delightful is not charming in the least, and I suggest you remember that."

"I thought you took exception to the term *delightful*?"

All the breath left her in a split second. He'd remembered their exchange. No one ever bothered to pay marked attention to anything she said.

Chills swept down her spine, followed quickly by alarm. What in the world was the matter with her? Grayson Sumner was not the sort of gentleman who should be causing her chills.

He was too worldly, too jaded, and—as she'd mentioned to her mother—too dangerous.

Why then did she suddenly find him rather fascinating, even though she knew perfectly well he was less than fond of her at the moment? Could it be possible she was instinctively drawn to gentlemen who were completely unacceptable for her?

Pushing that disturbing idea aside, she forced a smile. "I readily admit the word *delightful* does annoy me upon occasion, especially since I've come to believe it was used to humor me instead of compliment me."

Grayson crossed his arms over his chest, and time seemed to stop moving as he looked her up and down again.

Heat flooded her face, but then he stepped closer to her and smiled a smile that actually appeared to be genuine. "Today you, my dear Felicia, look incredibly delightful, and I assure you, I'm not trying to humor you in the least."

His words swirled around her mind, and much to her surprise, her vision suddenly went a little misty as unexpected tears stung her eyes.

It was a sincere compliment, something she hadn't received in quite some time, if ever, from a gentleman. She blinked rapidly to hold the tears at bay, even as she spun on her heel and walked as quickly as she could to the small table where she'd left her reticule. She opened it, pulled out a handkerchief, dabbed at her eyes, and when she felt sufficiently composed, turned to find Grayson and Agatha watching her closely.

"Good heavens, Felicia, are you all right?" Agatha asked.

Felicia waved the handkerchief in the air. "Don't mind me. I seem to get overwrought at the strangest things these days—not that I get overwrought on a regular basis—but . . . I'm fine now."

Grayson frowned. "You don't appear fine."

"There you go again, being charming," she muttered. "I just want everyone to stop pitying me."

Grayson's lips twitched ever so slightly. "Dissolving into tears when someone tells you that you look delightful is a *wonderful* way to go about seeing that happen."

"He does make a good point," Agatha added as she stepped up to Felicia's side and took her arm. "I've just had a marvelous idea, one that will forever stop people from pitying you."

Apprehension was swift, replaced with outright alarm when Agatha began towing her toward the door. "What's your idea?"

"I'll tell you when we get to the restaurant."

"We're going to a restaurant?" Grayson asked.

Agatha nodded. "Of course we are. I'm starving, and I won't be able to explain my idea properly until I get something to eat."

Felicia dug in her heels, causing Agatha to lurch to a halt. "I'm not going anywhere until you explain at least a little of this plan of yours."

Agatha tightened her grip and tried to pull Felicia forward, but when Felicia wouldn't budge, blew out a breath.

"Fine, but I'm telling both of you right now that I expect full cooperation from each of you."

Grayson blinked. "I'm involved in this plan?"

"Indeed."

He narrowed his eyes. "The last plan I agreed to that involved me being in Felicia's vicinity almost got me killed."

"That's a little overly dramatic," Felicia muttered.

"Did you, or did you not, lose control of the horses and drive them along the sidewalk instead of the road, causing too many people to count to throw themselves out of your way?"

"There were only three people who had to dive out of our way."

Agatha held up her hand. "Children, behave."

Felicia closed her mouth, as did Grayson.

"My plan is not a complicated one, and shouldn't involve anything of a dangerous nature." Agatha's smile widened. "We're simply going to have Grayson escort you to the Beckett ball, and since he's currently considered one of the most eligible gentlemen in New York City, no one will think to pity you again."

4

*D*isgruntlement, mixed with apprehension, was immediate.

Grayson couldn't help but notice that there seemed to be a disturbing trend occurring—a trend that had thrust him directly into the position of knight in shining armor on an all too frequent basis.

Granted, he'd willingly gone along with Eliza's demands, fetching Felicia the day before and agreeing to seek Agatha out today, but his participation with his sister's demands was only due to guilt, not because he was inherently chivalrous.

Couldn't anyone see that his armor, what little he actually possessed, was remarkably tarnished—and because of his past was hardly likely to ever shine again?

The last thing he wanted to do was escort Felicia to a ball. It would require he spend hours in her company alone, hours that he was fairly certain would be vastly uncomfortable, given that he was rapidly becoming fascinated with the lady.

He'd distanced himself from her at Eliza's house not because he was annoyed about her driving abilities—or lack thereof, as the case seemed to be—but because he'd been helplessly drawn to her as she'd driven his horses haphazardly down the street—and an occasional sidewalk—her shrieks of laughter doing odd things to his heart.

His heart had once again begun acting rather peculiarly when she'd gone all misty-eyed simply because he'd proclaimed her appearance delightful.

He hadn't actually been truthful in that moment, because . . . she was more than delightful today, wearing a new gown that molded to her charming curves and sent his temperature rising.

He was becoming obsessed with the lady.

He should have remembered a pressing engagement when he visited the Murdock home seeking Agatha's whereabouts and Mrs. Murdock had informed him she was at B. Altman's with Felicia—especially since it had been abundantly clear that Mrs. Murdock was still cherishing hopes of him becoming better acquainted with her daughter. She'd not been bothered in the least when he'd reiterated time and time again that he needed to find Agatha, not Felicia, but had simply patted him on the cheek, told him to say hello to her daughter for her, and practically pushed him out the door.

What could he have been thinking, traipsing off to B. Altman's, knowing full well it was madness to spend additional time in Felicia's company? Eliza would have understood if he'd been unable to track Agatha down, but here he was, standing only a few feet away from the lady who'd begun to occupy his almost every thought.

An elbow placed none too gently in his side brought him rapidly back to the situation at hand. He glanced at Agatha, who looked as if she longed to do more to him than stick her bony elbow in his ribs, and then at Felicia, who was a delicate shade of pink but who was glaring back at him, her amazing eyes blazing with heat.

He'd apparently been lost in thought longer than he'd realized, but what to do now?

Should he give in to Agatha's request and agree to escort Felicia to the ball, even though doing so was against his better judgment? What would happen if she formed an attachment to him, which would cause him to disappoint her, and then . . .

"I'll pick you up at eight." He heard the words come out of his mouth before he could stop them.

To his immediate annoyance, instead of smiling and accepting his less-than-gracious offer, Felicia stuck her nose in the air. "I think not," she announced before she spun on her heel, stalked to the fitting-room door, and disappeared from view.

"Well, hmm . . ." was all he seemed capable of responding, which caused Agatha to let out a snort right before she stomped out of the room as well, leaving him standing there by himself.

At this rate, it wouldn't be long at all until everyone realized he was no knight in shining armor. Then he'd be left in peace, not expected to run at the drop of a hat after ladies who seemed to have the propensity for running amok.

That idea, surprisingly enough, hardly sent relief flowing through him.

He made for the door and increased his stride, edging around shoppers and racks of clothing until he finally caught up with Felicia and Agatha, who were standing in front of the steam elevator.

Neither of the ladies bothered to speak a single word to him as they waited for the elevator to arrive, but to his further annoyance, they became downright chatty with the elevator operator once the door opened and that gentleman ushered them inside.

Before their descent began, Felicia asked if she could operate the lever that controlled the elevator, and the operator was only too happy to agree. Grayson couldn't say he blamed the man. When Felicia was smiling, much like she was doing at that moment, her smile seemed to bring out the best in people. The operator, appearing absolutely thrilled that a beautiful lady was giving him her undivided attention, briefly explained how the lever worked and with a besotted smile handed it over to Felicia—and she handled that lever in much the same way she'd driven his horses.

By the time they finished their jerky ride to ground level, he was afraid he was about to lose his breakfast. The moment the operator opened the gilded doors, Grayson stumbled out of the dreaded contraption, so determined to get out of what he'd come to think of as a death device that he completely forgot to allow the ladies to go first. Felicia didn't even appear to notice his blunder, though, as she bid the elevator operator a good day and brushed past Grayson with nothing but a very loud sniff.

"What in the world is the matter with you?" Agatha snapped, drawing his attention as she stepped up beside him. "You've hurt Felicia's feelings."

"I told her I'd pick her up at eight."

"In a remarkably unpleasant tone of voice." Agatha grabbed his arm and prodded him forward. "Felicia's in a precarious state of mind at the moment, and you're hardly helping that situation. Go apologize, and then tell her you'll be completely disheartened if she doesn't agree to accompany you to the ball."

"That might be stretching the truth just a touch, and she needs to apologize to me for scaring a good ten years off my life just now. Did it escape your notice that she had a heavy hand with that lever? Quite frankly, I'm not certain elevators are supposed to stop and start that abruptly. We're lucky the silly thing didn't break altogether and plummet to the ground, killing us in the process."

Agatha ignored his little speech and pointed a finger toward Felicia's back. "Go."

"Has anyone ever told you you're annoyingly bossy?" he mumbled before he set after Felicia, having no idea what he was going to say to her when he caught up with her, but realizing he couldn't simply let her leave without some words being spoken between them.

Perhaps he should just be candid and explain that he wouldn't care to hurt her in the future, but . . . no, that would hardly do.

Knowing Felicia, she'd take that as a clear indication of his arrogance, and now that he thought about it, it was beyond arrogant to assume she'd develop feelings for him.

She'd never given him any reason to believe she held him in affection, so perhaps assuming she would develop feelings for him in the future was strictly wishful thinking on his part—and thinking he shouldn't even be contemplating in the first place.

He saw the back of her skirt swish through the main doors of the store and increased his stride, nodding his thanks to the doorman before he raised his hand to block the sun that hit him squarely in the eyes. He looked around and felt a moment of panic when he couldn't locate Felicia.

"Young lady, have you lost your mind? Let go of my packages."

Grayson's mouth dropped open when his attention settled on an elderly lady engaged in what could only be described as a fierce tug-of-war with none other than Felicia. He forced his mouth shut and moved forward, coming to a stop right beside the struggling ladies.

"Mrs. Shaffer, I'm not trying to steal your purchases. I'm simply trying to help you. You were about to lose one of the bags."

The lady, apparently one Mrs. Shaffer, abruptly released her hold on all the packages, causing Felicia to stumble backward. He caught her and held her close to him for just a second, but when he began to enjoy the feel of her softness, he quickly set her back on her feet even as he took the bags away from her.

"Good heavens, Miss Murdock, you must forgive me," Mrs.

Shaffer exclaimed, stepping closer to them and squinting at Felicia. "I didn't recognize you at first. I thought you were one of those thieves who dress up in pretty clothing and try to prey on elderly shoppers."

She reached for her reticule, pulled out a pair of spectacles, shoved them over her nose, and proceeded to look Felicia up and down. "May I say you look positively delightful today? I always knew there was an incredibly lovely lady lurking under those voluminous fashions you so oddly embrace. Dare I hope you've given those up?"

Protective instincts he hadn't realized he possessed caused him to step forward, intent on interceding on Felicia's behalf, but to his amazement, instead of hurt lurking in her eyes, there was clear amusement.

"I must thank you for your kind words, Mrs. Shaffer, and yes, I have firmly abandoned my wardrobe of old, which is why I was at B. Altman's today. But enough about me. Whatever possessed you to try and manage all of these packages on your own? I thought you were about to collapse under the weight of them—which is why I rushed over to help you. Although I must apologize if I startled you. That certainly wasn't my intent. Did you not bring an attendant with you?"

It took everything Grayson had to not drop the packages he was holding for Mrs. Shaffer and charge immediately in the opposite direction. If there was any question remaining regarding Felicia's kind heart, that question had just been answered and lent further proof to the idea she was too good to be sullied by his company.

Few young ladies he knew would rush to the aid of an elderly woman burdened with too many packages. In fact, few ladies would have noticed that assistance was needed in the first place.

She truly was a compassionate soul, and that meant he was

going to have to maintain his distance from her. It would be a true tragedy if his blackened soul damaged the goodness of hers.

". . . and I have my driver with me, but he remained with my carriage," Mrs. Shaffer was saying. "I had no intention of purchasing so many items, and didn't realize how many bags I'd procured until I got out here."

Grayson cleared his throat. "I'll be happy to deliver these to your carriage if you'll tell me where it's parked."

Mrs. Shaffer's eyes widened right before they turned speculative. "You're Mr. Sumner."

He inclined his head. "Indeed."

"This is Mrs. Shaffer," Felicia supplied. "I know her from church."

Grayson smiled. "It's a pleasure to make your acquaintance, Mrs. Shaffer."

"And yours as well, Mr. Sumner." She slipped the spectacles down her nose and surprised him with a wink. "Dare I hope that you and Miss Murdock are enjoying this fine day together?"

"Ah, well . . ."

She continued before he had an opportunity to come up with a response. "I do hope you realize how fortunate you are to be in Miss Murdock's company, my good man. Why, I don't believe there's another lady in the entire city who possesses such a compassionate spirit." She winked again. "Any gentleman would be lucky to secure her affections."

And that exactly explained the root of his problem. Felicia might have abandoned her repulsive fashions, but she couldn't abandon her innate goodness, and that goodness would compel her to try and save him in the end, even though he didn't deserve saving.

"Miss Murdock's compassion does, indeed, put the rest of us to shame," Agatha said, stepping up beside them and saving him from having to pull out some type of benign response. "It's lovely to see you, Mrs. Shaffer."

Pleasantries were exchanged, and then Grayson followed Mrs. Shaffer to her carriage, handing an embarrassed-looking driver all the packages, and helped Mrs. Shaffer up and into the carriage. But he wasn't fast enough to escape her before she opened her mouth.

"Treat her well, Mr. Sumner, or you'll have to answer to me."

He summoned up a smile, kissed the elderly lady's hand, placed it back on her lap, and decided silence was the only answer he was comfortable giving her. He had the sneaky suspicion there were many in society who felt protective of Felicia—no matter that she thought everyone found her ridiculous—and because of that protectiveness, he was definitely going to have to maintain a good deal of space between them.

He shut the carriage door and turned, suppressing the urge to sigh when he noticed Felicia and Agatha waiting for him—both with their arms crossed over their chests, and both watching him rather disgruntledly.

"Ladies, while it's been lovely seeing the two of you today, I do think it's time I bid you goodbye."

"You agreed to have lunch with us," Agatha said, barely batting a lash when Felicia let out a grunt.

"I did not."

Agatha narrowed her eyes. "Well, you did tell Eliza you would do whatever I wanted today, and I want lunch and for you to join us. I'm thinking French cuisine might be in order."

"I'm just going to go home," Felicia mumbled.

Agatha's expression turned stubborn. "No you're not. I promised your mother I would spend the day with you, and I'm not one to take my promises lightly. We're having lunch, all three of us, together, and you two will be happy about it and entertain me with amusing stories as we dine."

Grayson narrowed his eyes. "I never promised to be amusing."

"You promised to charm me out of my bad mood," Agatha countered. "Since you're responsible for ruining the perfectly fine mood I was in with your less than pleasant response to my stellar idea regarding the ball, it's now up to you to rectify that situation." She smiled a rather grim smile. "Or I could just run back to Eliza and tell her how carelessly you discarded her request."

He'd always known Agatha was annoying, but he hadn't realized how manipulative she was, almost as manipulative as Felicia's mother. He blew out a breath. "I adore French cuisine." He caught Felicia's eye and lifted a brow.

For a second, he thought she was going to refuse, but then her eyes began to gleam, causing him to blink. "I know a perfectly adorable French restaurant, but it's quite a few blocks up the way. Did you bring your phaeton?"

These ladies were going to be the death of him.

He forced a smile. "My phaeton is at home, having a nice long rest after the horror it suffered yesterday. I brought my carriage today, and it possesses a driver, so your services are not required."

The gleam in her eye was quickly replaced with disappointment. "But it's such a lovely day, and carriages are enclosed." She turned to Agatha. "Did you bring an open vehicle today?"

"No, I brought a carriage as well."

Felicia bit her lip but then brightened. "I'll drive us, then. It might be a tight squeeze, but we'll manage."

Before Grayson could get a single protest past his lips, Felicia sailed forward, turning her head a second later. "Well, are you coming?"

"I'm not feeling famished at all anymore," Agatha called after Felicia's retreating back, but either Felicia didn't hear her or was simply ignoring that telling remark, because she didn't pause but continued marching along.

"Just think," Grayson said as he took Agatha's arm and drew her forward, "we won't have to concern ourselves much longer with your gloomy mood, considering we're both going to be dead soon."

"Yes, that certainly improves my mood," Agatha muttered before she lifted her head and suddenly grinned. "Would you look at that?"

Grayson turned his attention to where Agatha was staring and couldn't help but return her grin. Felicia was standing beside what looked to be a pony cart painted bright red with an ancient-looking pony attached to the hitching post, its head lowered and emitting noises that sounded remarkably like snores.

He pulled Agatha to a stop right beside the beast and noticed the troubling fact that Felicia was cooing to the animal and placing kisses on its intricately braided mane.

He had a feeling the braids were Felicia's handiwork.

"As I said before, it'll be a tight squeeze, but you can sit on the seat with me, Agatha, and you, Grayson, can hop in the back."

Grayson eyed the space Felicia was indicating but was spared the need to respond when Agatha let out a laugh.

"Forgive me, Felicia, but I don't believe your pony is up for the arduous task of pulling all three of us."

"He's stronger than he appears."

Grayson frowned. "I think he might be sleeping."

"Of course he's sleeping. He sleeps all the time, but it'll just take me a second to rouse him, and then we can get on our way." She patted the pony's head. "Time to wake up now, Thor."

"His name is Thor?" Grayson couldn't resist asking.

Felicia sent him a scowl. "It is, but don't talk in such a disbelieving tone. You'll hurt his feelings."

"He's still sleeping."

"He'll wake up soon." Felicia patted Thor a little harder than before. But if anything, the pony began to snore louder.

"The poor dear appears to be exhausted." She bent over and whispered something in Thor's ear, but he didn't open his eyes. Felicia straightened and shrugged. "I might need a little more time, and maybe . . . some oats." She moved to the cart, pulled out a feed sack, moved to stand in front of Thor, and swung the bag of oats several times in front of his nose. Unfortunately, the pony continued sleeping.

"We could always walk," Agatha suggested.

Felicia looked as if she wanted to argue, but then threw the oats back into the cart and took Agatha's arm. "Cherie's is just down the street if you really have French cuisine on your mind."

"Why didn't you suggest that when Agatha first remarked she wanted French?" Grayson asked.

Felicia looked at him for a second and then turned her attention back to Agatha without bothering to give him the courtesy of a response.

How was it that she could be so irritating and yet so fascinating?

He watched as Felicia drew Agatha's arm into her own, steered her back onto the sidewalk, and took off without even checking if he was trailing along after them.

He caught up with them and took Agatha's other arm, feeling the need to put at least a body between him and Felicia as they continued to stroll down the street.

"See, isn't this pleasant?" Agatha asked, fluttering her lashes at him even as Felicia muttered something he probably didn't care to hear under her breath.

"Very pleasant," he agreed, smiling ever so slightly when Felicia raised her head and scowled back at him.

"Now, none of that," Agatha admonished. "We're going to enjoy a lovely lunch. In order to do that, the two of you are going to agree to play nicely with each other."

"He started it."

Grayson was about to argue but then thought better of it. "You're right. I did start this, and for that, I do apologize."

"Wonderful," Agatha exclaimed. "I'm so glad that's settled."

"Nothing's settled," Felicia said slowly.

"Of course it is. Grayson will pick you up at eight the night of the ball, everyone will discontinue pitying you, and all will be right with the world. But . . . enough about that dreary subject. I'd rather discuss poor old Thor. Why in the world are you using such an ancient creature? I've seen your brothers out and about, and they ride prime horseflesh."

Felicia gave a rather sad shake of her head. "If you must know, I've been pestering my father for quite some time for my own means of transportation, but he seems remarkably reluctant to provide me with a real horse—hence the arrival of Thor and his cart a month or so ago."

Grayson smiled. "A concern for the safety of all the good citizens of New York is probably responsible for his decision."

Her eyes turned stormy, and she increased her pace, causing Grayson and Agatha to do the same since they were all linked together.

"I have yet to actually run anyone over, although I did take out a hitching post a few weeks back, but in my defense, it was not really my fault. Thor has the propensity to stop when one least expects it, and on that particular occasion, I was not paying close enough attention. When he came to an abrupt halt in the middle of the street, I might have given the very smallest of shrieks, which unfortunately prodded him into motion. He barreled directly into a hitching post, which turned out to be quite the disaster. I was forced to endure a scathing lecture from the owner of said hitching post, and it cost me five dollars before I was able to get away from the man."

Grayson quirked a brow. "That seems a bit steep for a hitching post."

"Well, there was the slight matter of the hitching post crashing through the man's front window, but luckily, Thor wasn't injured in the mishap. Since then I've been careful to keep my shrieking to a minimum whenever I take Thor out and about."

"I know I'll probably regret asking this, but why did you name him Thor?" Grayson asked.

"He's such a decrepit-looking creature that I felt he deserved a noble name."

Grayson stopped walking, effectively causing the ladies to do the same. "Surely you could have talked your father into providing a less decrepit beast."

"I couldn't just send him away. If I didn't accept him, I feared he was headed for a bad end."

Something that felt very much like panic caused Grayson's throat to constrict, and he found it difficult to breathe.

She was an incredible lady—one he, if truth be told, wanted to get to know . . . desperately.

But . . . that would never do. He'd made vows in regard to ladies and relationships, and he needed to remember those vows, no matter the disappointment that was going to cause him.

He prodded the ladies back into motion without speaking a word, diligently ignoring the confused looks both of them were sending his way.

5

Felicia was having a difficult time keeping up with Grayson's many moods as well as with the rather rapid pace he was currently setting.

Honestly, it wasn't as if the restaurant was going to disappear if they didn't reach it in the next few minutes, but since they were practically racing down the sidewalk, it seemed as if he feared he would not get lunch.

What had caused him to react so oddly?

One minute she was talking about Thor, and the next, Grayson's eyes had gone rather tender—that tenderness directed toward her—but then, in a mere blink of an eye, he'd gotten grumpy again. And it seemed his grumpiness had resulted from their discussion about her pony.

Thor was pathetic, to be sure, but there was no reason he would cause anyone to sink into a state of depression or, in Grayson's case, a fit of the sulks.

It was rapidly becoming clear the gentleman possessed a complicated, and confusing, nature.

"Grayson, slow down," Agatha suddenly complained. "You rushed right past Cherie's."

Grayson came to an abrupt stop, forcing Felicia and Agatha to do the same. "Why didn't you say so? It's not as if I know where we're going. I'm the foreigner, remember?"

"You've been here for months, and I would have said something sooner if I'd realized we were almost at our destination, but I was concentrating more on pulling in breaths of air as you rushed Felicia and me forward." Agatha rubbed at what was evidently a stitch in her side. "I must inform you that you are sadly deficient in your attempt at charming me out of a gloomy mood. I'm definitely going to be taking my complaints directly to your sister."

"You said you were famished," Grayson countered. "I was simply getting you to your food in a timely fashion."

"No you weren't, but I'm not up for arguing with you on an empty stomach—and while I'm still trying to suck air into my poor depleted lungs."

Felicia grinned as Grayson turned them around and marched them back to the entrance of Cherie's, where a gentleman dressed in formal attire held the door open for them and ushered them into the dimly lit restaurant.

"This is a charming place," Grayson said as he looked around, earning a smile from the gentleman who'd opened the door for them. "Tell me, sir, how does the food here compare to what they serve in Paris?"

"I think you'll find it compares very well indeed," the gentleman replied. "You've been to Paris?"

"I spent a bit of time there after I finished my studies at Oxford."

"You're English," the gentleman said with a nod. "I thought I detected a British accent." He tilted his head. "Tell me, have you ever met the queen?"

"I have met the queen. She's a lovely lady, although a bit intimidating, if you must know."

He'd met the queen.

Every now and again, especially when Grayson wasn't speaking, she forgot he was a member of the aristocracy, probably because she'd never expected a gentleman of noble birth to be quite so moody, which might—

Her thoughts were interrupted when a large gentleman with a burly build, formal black attire, and a ruddy complexion hurried forward to greet them.

"*Bonjour*," he said, sweeping into an elaborate bow. "Welcome to Cherie's. I am Mr. Bonchamp, the owner of this fine establishment."

Felicia stepped forward. "Mr. Bonchamp, we've met before. Remember? I'm Miss Murdock. My mother and I come here on a frequent basis."

Mr. Bonchamp's mouth dropped open for a brief second before he snapped it shut. "Mademoiselle Murdock, I would never have recognized you. Your face is normally buried beneath one of those . . . *chapeaux*, but today . . . Ah, I can see you for once." He took her hand and brought it to his lips. "You are *très charmante*."

Felicia bit back a grin as Mr. Bonchamp proceeded to lavish compliments on her, all of them spoken in a horrendous French accent and delivered in a booming voice.

"I shall have Andre show you to our best table," Mr. Bonchamp proclaimed as he let go of Felicia's hand and snapped his fingers, which had a waiter appearing immediately. "Andre, please seat Miss Murdock and her companions in front of the window."

A loud clearing of a throat set her teeth on edge, and she turned to find Grayson scowling once again.

"What is the matter now?"

Grayson didn't bother to respond but directed his words at Andre, who was looking decidedly nervous—probably because he was faced with an obviously annoyed gentleman.

"I'd prefer a seat in a less conspicuous location, if you please, Andre."

Felicia leaned closer to him and lowered her voice. "Are you hiding from someone?"

"Of course not. I'm trying to protect you."

Felicia blinked. "From what?"

"Those gentlemen over there."

Felicia glanced to where Grayson was currently glaring and felt her mouth drop open.

Four gentlemen sitting at a nearby table all seemed to be craning their necks her way. She glanced behind her, found no one there—not even Agatha, who was already moving across the floor with Andre—and then realized the gentlemen were gawking at her.

She'd never had gentlemen gawk at her before, but what was she expected to do now?

Did she acknowledge the gentlemen, wave to them, or perhaps nod her head?

Maybe a curtsy was in order, but no, that didn't seem right.

She settled for sending them a smile, but the smile quickly slid off her face when Grayson took a firm hold of her arm and began to rapidly escort her across the room. "That'll be quite enough of that," he growled as he towed her rather forcefully over to a table where Andre was seating Agatha.

The amiable gentleman everyone believed Grayson to be seemed to be missing once again.

"There is absolutely no reason for you to haul me to my seat," Felicia said as she shook her arm out of his hold and smiled at Andre when he held out a chair for her.

Andre beamed back at her, pushed her chair in, and then

extended an elegant bow before he walked away, promising to return shortly to take their orders.

Grayson tugged out a chair, slouched down into it, and sent her a surly look.

"Good heavens," Agatha exclaimed, "what is the matter now?"

"Felicia has, for some strange reason, taken to flirting."

"How delightful," Agatha proclaimed with a nod in Felicia's direction. "I didn't know you were proficient in the art of flirting."

Grayson rolled his eyes. "It's not something you should encourage her to do, Agatha. Ladies can come to rather nasty ends by flirting, especially when that flirting entails come-hither looks."

Felicia drew herself up. "I have never sent a come-hither look to anyone in my life."

A loud cough pulled Felicia's attention away from Grayson, and to her horror, it settled on one of the gentlemen who'd been staring at her, a gentleman who was now standing right beside their table and who seemed to be looking directly at her bodice instead of her face.

"Good day," the gentleman exclaimed with a bob of his head, even though his focus didn't waver from her bodice. "My friends and I were wondering if you would care to join us at our table."

"Oh . . . my," Agatha whispered.

The table suddenly shook, and the next thing Felicia knew, Grayson was on his feet, a vein throbbing rather prominently on his forehead. "She's with me."

It would seem he possessed traits much like a chameleon. One minute he was charming, the next surly, and now . . . hmm . . . *dangerous* was the only word that came to mind.

"I say," the gentleman blustered, "who do you think you are, sir?"

"I'm the Earl of Sefton, and you would be wise to rethink your intentions."

The gentleman eyed Grayson for a brief moment, swallowed, and then turned on his heel and strode quickly out of the café, his friends following him a split second later.

Grayson waited until the last gentleman exited before he resumed his seat, his brilliant, yet incredibly cold, blue eyes focused on Felicia. "And that, my dear girl, is what happens when one decides to gallop down the road best left untraveled."

She must have misheard him, because surely he wouldn't have called her "dear girl."

She stuck her nose in the air, reached for the linen napkin lying on the table in front of her, snapped it open, and placed it over her lap. When she felt she'd gotten her temper somewhat under control, she opened her mouth. "If memory serves me correctly, you've been known to do more than your fair share of flirting, and you haven't come to a bad end yet."

"It's different for gentlemen."

She arched a brow. "That's ridiculous, unless you're admitting that the ladies you've flirted with came to bad ends."

"Of course they didn't."

"Then I'm quite certain I've just won this argument, even though, again, I wasn't flirting. It's hardly my fault those gentlemen took a simple smile as an invitation."

Agatha leaned forward. "Need I remind both of you that we're supposed to be enjoying a nice lunch?" She nodded to Grayson. "It was impressive, the way you handled that boorish gentleman, but tell me, do you think it was your title that scared him away, or could it have possibly been the rage that was pouring out of your eyes?"

Grayson flipped his napkin open and shoved it over his lap. "I was not enraged."

"I thought you abandoned your title," Felicia said slowly.

"I bring it out upon occasion, if the situation warrants it."

"Miss Murdock," Mr. Bonchamp said, bustling up to their table as quickly as his large frame would allow. "I must extend to you my most sincere apologies. Andre informed me some lout was attempting to proposition you right in the middle of my café."

Felicia smiled. "There's no need to apologize, Mr. Bonchamp. I'm not distressed in the least, but I do fear those gentlemen left in somewhat of a hurry. I've just now realized that they most likely didn't settle their bill."

"Don't concern yourself, *ma chère*," Mr. Bonchamp said with a wave of his hand. "I've already sent one of my men after them. He will track them down and divest them of their money. May I extend to you a complimentary bottle of wine to distract you from your recent unpleasantness?"

Grayson's eyes turned downright menacing. "Miss Murdock doesn't drink wine."

Mr. Bonchamp took one look at him, glanced to Felicia, and then, without a word, bolted as fast as he could away from the table.

Felicia drew in a steadying breath and, when she was somewhat certain she wasn't in danger of throwing the silver at Grayson, turned in his direction. "You don't know me well enough, *Mr. Sumner*, to make a decision regarding whether or not I enjoy wine with my meals."

"From all accounts, *Miss Murdock*, you are considered a woman above reproach. It hardly seems much of a stretch to come to the conclusion regarding your alcohol consumption, or lack thereof, as the case may be."

A woman above reproach.

That was what her efforts to land Reverend Fraser had gotten her—a reputation of a pious and evidently moral lady who would shock everyone if she so much as thought about consuming a glass of wine at lunch.

Felicia squared her shoulders. "I've had wine on numerous occasions. The church serves it on a regular basis."

"Yes, but that would be during communion, a slightly different circumstance than guzzling it with a meal."

"I don't recall proclaiming the urge to guzzle anything."

"I wonder if they're serving salmon today," Agatha interrupted, her voice unusually loud. "I always adore a well-prepared dish of salmon. If done properly, it practically melts in one's mouth."

Felicia pulled her attention away from Grayson and settled it on Agatha. "Do you find it difficult to believe I would enjoy a glass of wine with my meal?"

"Hmm . . ."

Felicia's mouth dropped open. "You would find it difficult to believe."

"Ah . . . well . . . Oh look, it's Mr. Bonchamp."

Felicia looked up, and sure enough, Mr. Bonchamp had returned and was standing right next to the table, looking a touch wary. "Have you come to a decision regarding the wine?"

She opened her mouth, intent on asking him to bring the bottle, but then blew out a breath as she shook her head. "I thank you for the offer, Mr. Bonchamp, but I don't actually care for wine, so I think I'll settle for lemonade."

Her temper flared when Grayson had the audacity to grin a little too smugly.

"On second thought . . ."

"I'll have iced tea," Agatha said, cutting Felicia off midsentence. "What will you have, Grayson?"

"The same."

Mr. Bonchamp nodded and took his leave, promising to send Andre back with their drinks as everyone picked up their menus and disappeared behind them.

A moment later, Felicia set hers down. "Am I really considered a woman above reproach?"

Grayson peered at her from over the top of his menu. "I don't know why you've taken issue with that notion. You should feel honored you've managed to obtain such a lofty position in life. People respect you because of your strong and abiding faith."

"I'm not a nun," Felicia returned. "Nor do I understand why everyone believes I should act like one. Take Agatha, for example."

"Oh, I don't think there's any reason to pull me into the conversation," Agatha said as she buried her entire face behind her menu.

Felicia pretended she hadn't heard her friend's remark. "Agatha is a lady possessed of a deep faith, and yet no one expects her to be perfect. She's landed in jail . . . twice."

Agatha peeked over the menu, lowered it just a touch, and then smiled at Grayson. "Tell us about China."

Grayson returned her smile. "I'd much rather discuss you and jail."

Agatha's menu lowered another inch. "I'm sure you would, but alas, I don't feel up to obliging you. Let's return to China. I must say I've been dying to ask you how you managed to learn that language. From what little I've heard spoken here in the city, it seems to be a complicated tongue, one I'm quite certain I wouldn't be able to master."

"I don't speak Chinese."

Agatha's brow wrinkled. "Eliza told me you lived in China for over five years. Are you saying you never picked up the language?"

"As you mentioned before, it's a difficult language to learn."

Agatha's wrinkles increased. "You were married to a Chinese woman. Surely you picked up a smattering of words?"

"No, not a one," Grayson said cheerfully, although Felicia thought there was another of those pesky edges to his tone. "I'm just not very clever, and since it would be incredibly rude of you to question me further on the subject when I've freely admitted my intellectual deficiencies, perhaps we should move on to something more exciting—like the weather."

It hit Felicia then, out of nowhere. China was the reason behind the darkness Felicia knew resided in his very soul.

She wanted to ask about his wife but found herself hesitating, not really knowing if she truly wanted to know about the woman who'd apparently captured his heart years ago.

The feeling of annoyance that had immediately run over her at the mere mention of his deceased wife was disturbing. Not wanting to contemplate the matter further, Felicia looked up and let out a small sigh of relief when Andre suddenly appeared out of nowhere and everyone settled into the task of placing their orders.

Andre had barely left the table before Agatha shifted in her seat right as her eyes went wide. "Oh no, here comes Mrs. Amherst."

Felicia felt the distinct urge to duck under the table.

Mrs. Amherst was one of the biggest gossips in the city. She never had a pleasant word to say about anyone, and she was one of the few people who'd openly questioned Felicia's wardrobe choices, usually in a loud voice.

"Good afternoon," Mrs. Amherst exclaimed as she came to a stop in front of their table. Grayson set aside his napkin and rose to his feet. "Lord Sefton, this is a pleasure. Please, sit down, although I do appreciate your stellar manners."

She smiled as Grayson resumed his seat and directed her attention to Agatha. "Miss Watson, lovely to find you doing something normal, such as eating, instead of running wild about the city snooping for stories, and . . ." Her gaze settled on Felicia. "Good heavens, would you look at you, Miss Murdock. Done a bit of shopping lately, have you?"

Before Felicia could even think of a suitable reply to that bit of snippiness, Mrs. Amherst had pulled a pair of wire-rimmed spectacles out of her bag—much like Mrs. Shaffer had done a short time before—shoved them onto her nose, and leaned forward. Her gaze traveled down and lingered on Felicia's gown for a long moment before she straightened, whipped the spectacles off, stuffed them back into her reticule, and then nodded, just once.

"Much better, Miss Murdock. You don't look hideous in the least today." She shook her head and sent Felicia a rather pitying look. "I do hope this new you was done for the right reason and not because you're trying to change yourself because of that unfortunate business with Reverend Fraser."

It was rapidly becoming clear her little secret about being infatuated with Reverend Fraser hadn't been much of a secret, but . . . Since when had she decided she'd only been infatuated with the gentleman and not head over heels in love?

"Rest assured, Mrs. Amherst, Miss Murdock has not changed her style because of Reverend Fraser."

Felicia drew in a sharp breath at the same moment Agatha did. She exchanged a glance with her friend, realizing in that moment that Grayson's casual statement made it sound as if she'd changed her style because of him.

What could he be thinking?

Word would sweep like wildfire through society the moment Mrs. Amherst left their side.

Everyone would come under the misimpression she and Grayson were romantically attached.

Felicia blinked. For some reason, that idea didn't bother her nearly as much as it should have, but no, she wasn't thinking clearly.

"On my word, I had no idea you and Miss Murdock had an understanding," Mrs. Amherst exclaimed. "May I presume an announcement will be forthcoming soon—perhaps at the Beckett ball?"

Grayson settled back in his seat, smiling somewhat pleasantly, but his eyes had turned hard. "I wouldn't presume anything if I were you, Mrs. Amherst."

"Hmm" was the only response Mrs. Amherst gave to that, although her eyes did narrow right before she directed her attention to Agatha.

"Are you going to the Beckett ball, dear?"

Wariness immediately crossed Agatha's face. "But of course. I've been looking forward to it."

"I would have thought you'd be dreading it, seeing as how it's a going-away ball for Mr. Zayne Beckett."

Agatha began to sputter, but Mrs. Amherst ignored her as she shifted her gaze back to Grayson. "I saw your daughter the other day with your sister, Mrs. Hamilton Beckett. What is your daughter's name again?"

The vein on Grayson's forehead began to throb. "Ming."

"Ah yes, I knew it was something foreign. She's Chinese, isn't she?"

"Her mother was Chinese."

"I see," Mrs. Amherst replied with a nod before she inclined her head. "Well, I don't want to take up any more of your time. Enjoy your lunch." She turned on her heel and strode away without speaking another word.

It was somewhat odd.

"You shouldn't let her bother you, Grayson," Agatha said softly. "She only attacked because you didn't give her any details regarding what she assumed was an alliance between you and Felicia. It's just ignorance on her part."

Felicia pulled her attention away from Mrs. Amherst's retreating back and settled it on Grayson. A shiver ran over her when she spotted the rage lurking in the depths of his eyes.

"It is ignorance this entire country seems to share."

She'd obviously missed something of an important nature.

"I'm sorry, but what ignorance are we talking about at the moment?"

For just a second, she thought he wasn't going to answer her, but then Grayson sat forward. "I thought this country would accept my daughter. Unfortunately, the United States is not as progressive as I wished."

Agatha nodded. "There does seem to be a strong anti-Chinese sentiment. I've heard whispers at the paper concerning a Chinese Exclusion Act, which will curtail any new Chinese laborers from entering the country."

"I've heard the same whispers," Grayson said. "Only I've heard that not only will the act make it impossible for new Chinese laborers to enter the country, it will also exclude the family members of those laborers already in the country from being allowed access to the United States. Wives and children will be stuck in China while the men will be stuck here, forced to stay because there are limited opportunities in their home country."

Felicia frowned. "I thought you amassed a fortune over there."

"Only because I possessed connections to the white world, connections that were . . ." His voice trailed off, his brow furrowed for a brief moment, and then he smiled. "Ah, look, here's our lunch."

Felicia smiled her thanks as Andre set her meal in front of her and settled into it as Agatha and Grayson did the same. The fact that no one spoke as they ate was telling, but even though it was clear Grayson had been relieved when lunch arrived and the talk of China interrupted, Felicia still had numerous questions she wanted to ask. All she had to do was gather up enough nerve to ask them. She set down her fork.

"Has Ming suffered from the sentiment against the Chinese?"

Grayson took a sip of tea and shrugged. "Not overly much as of yet. I've been trying to keep her out of the public eye as much as possible. In fact, I've recently been considering changing her name. I think Mary has a nice ring to it."

Agatha dabbed her lips with her napkin and shook her head. "You can't change who she is simply by changing her name, Grayson. Ming looks nothing like a Mary, and besides, don't you think it would have concerned Ming's mother if she would have known her daughter would not grow up being proud of her ancestry?"

"As her mother is quite dead, along with the rest of her family, that's a moot point."

Felicia's eyes grew wide. "What happened to them?"

"I'm not comfortable speaking of it," Grayson muttered before he smiled. "Why don't we talk about something pleasant, like your decrepit pony or perhaps the weather?"

"Have you considered going back to England?" Agatha asked, ignoring Grayson's request.

Grayson sent Agatha a glare. "I have."

"Again, I thought you abandoned your title," Felicia said slowly, the thought of him putting an ocean between them causing something strange to happen to her heart.

"I recently discovered you can't actually abandon a title," Grayson said. "I received a letter from my cousin, who assumed the role of earl after my father died and I was believed dead. Turns out, Eliza's old fiancé, Lord Wrathshire, has spread it about London that I'm alive and well."

Agatha paused with her glass of tea midway to her lips. "What does that mean?"

"It means that Spencer, my cousin, is no longer accepted as Lord Sefton."

"He's been stripped of the title?" Agatha pressed.

Grayson shook his head. "Not really, since the title didn't actually belong to him in the first place. He's agreed to continuing managing all of the estates—for a substantial salary, I might add—but I got the impression he'd really like to return to his own home and put the whole business behind him. I don't think London society has been very kind to him after it was discovered I'm alive. English aristocrats are sticklers for the proprieties, after all."

"But . . . are you willing to accept the responsibilities that come with resuming your title and . . ." Felicia stuttered to a halt as Grayson suddenly stiffened in his seat and his expression became downright frightening.

"Are you insinuating I'm incapable of handling responsibilities?"

How in the world had he gotten that from what she'd asked?

"Of course not."

Before she could formulate a better response, Grayson got to his feet and pulled out his billfold. He tossed some bills on the table and sent her a nod. "I've just recalled an urgent matter that demands my attention." He bowed in her direction, turned and did the same to Agatha. "You'll make certain Felicia gets home all right in your carriage?"

"She drove herself today, remember, in her pony cart?"

"Ah, exactly right, I almost forgot, and you did bring your own carriage, didn't you?"

Agatha nodded. "I did, but . . ."

"Then since the two of you have a means of transportation to see you home, I'll bid both of you good day." With that, Grayson, not bothering to even look in Felicia's direction again, stalked rapidly from the restaurant.

6

Three long days after storming out of the restaurant, Grayson was coming to the uncomfortable realization he was a coward. Quite frankly, after trailing behind Felicia for several hours in the slums of New York, never allowing his horse to catch up with her so that he could actually apologize to her, there was no other explanation. Cowardice was exactly why he was currently lurking behind a parked delivery wagon, watching Felicia from a distance as she chatted with a group of ladies who were clearly ladies of the night.

That she seemed remarkably comfortable around such women was beyond disturbing. She had no business even being in this part of town, let alone unescorted.

Where were her brothers? Did they even know their sister apparently spent a great deal of her time in the slums? Her comfort in the midst of squalor and her ability to mingle comfortably with ladies society deemed unacceptable was concerning.

He edged his horse forward but then brought it to a stop when one of the ladies let out a peal of laughter, pulled out a gown from a bag in Felicia's cart, and shook out a garment of red and green that Grayson distinctly remembered Felicia wearing at the ball her mother had given that past Christmas.

It was suddenly evident that, not only was she delivering baskets of food to the needy today, she was also distributing her old wardrobe, something that caused an odd pang to settle in the region of his heart.

He liked her old clothes. They were unusual to be sure, but they effectively hid her figure from view. And that would have come in handy today, seeing as how as she'd traversed through the streets of the city, she'd commanded far too much attention from every gentleman who happened to catch sight of her.

There'd been numerous times he'd reached for his pistol in order to come to her aid, but instead of displaying any menacing attitudes toward her, the gentlemen—and he used that term loosely—all showed her a distinct measure of respect. That was probably a direct result of the fact that Felicia's goodness practically oozed out of her every pore, but it had also reminded him that she was far too good to spend any of her time with the likes of him.

"Have a good day."

Grayson blinked and then frowned when he realized Felicia was already back on the road, waving goodbye to the ladies of the night as she set Thor into motion, steering him into the crowded street.

He kneed his horse and directed him into traffic, keeping a close eye on Felicia as she and Thor plodded along, apparently unaware that they were causing carriages and wagons to pile up in a line behind them.

The slowness of Thor's gait made it incredibly easy to watch her, however, while giving him plenty of time to think.

It seemed ages ago since he'd fled the restaurant and subsequently buried himself inside his house with only Ming and his army of nannies and servants to keep him company. During the first two days, he'd descended into what could only be described as a fit of the sulks, staring morosely out the window as life passed him by and refusing all company, including his sister.

Eliza hadn't seemed exactly thrilled when she'd stomped out of his house after he'd had his butler tell her he was indisposed. In fact, as he'd peered through a crack in the curtain, she'd lifted her head, shook a finger directly in his direction, as if she'd known he'd been spying on her, and then marched back to her carriage. She'd flung herself inside and sent him one last shaking of her finger through the window.

He'd spent the majority of his time after Eliza had taken her leave feeling very put upon and annoyed with the world, or more specifically, Felicia, but then something had gradually begun to change. Embarrassment replaced the annoyance, which had led him to some less-than-comfortable conclusions.

For one, he was an idiot.

He'd completely overreacted to Felicia's question regarding whether or not he'd want to resume his title and all the responsibilities that went with that, because, quite frankly, he'd always been irresponsible when it came to his inheritance, blatantly turning his back on his many estates and the work those estates demanded.

For two, he'd allowed himself to use Felicia as a handy target for his disgruntlement, which was completely ridiculous now that he'd had time to ponder the matter. Felicia didn't have a mean bone in her body and certainly hadn't been trying to point out his deficiencies by asking a simple question regarding his desire to return to England and take up his title again.

His deficiencies were, and had always been, a sore spot with him, and it had been all too convenient to turn his resentment toward Felicia instead of simply owning up to the truth that he'd led a despicable life. It was past time he stopped blaming others for circumstances he'd brought about all on his own.

He needed to make amends with Felicia, but he had yet to figure out what he should say. He was not, after all, a gentleman who apologized on a regular, if ever, basis—hence his conclusion regarding his cowardly nature.

If only he would have made himself known to her as she'd pulled away from her house, he wouldn't be skulking behind her in the midst of the slums. He'd been so close, but his courage had mysteriously disappeared, and he'd been trailing after her ever since.

During the hours he'd been following her, she'd first stopped at a disreputable-looking boardinghouse, leaving poor Thor unattended and snoozing on his feet while she sauntered up to the door. She'd pounded on it in a most enthusiastic manner, and when the door had opened, revealing a rather careworn-looking lady, she'd thrust what appeared to be a freshly baked pie into the lady's hand and disappeared into the house.

It had taken everything Grayson had to not follow her into that dismal excuse for a home, but he'd bided his time, and she'd eventually reappeared, looking cheerful and happy as she kissed four dirty and ragged children goodbye and called back to the woman in the doorway that she'd return in a few days so they could finish their conversation.

Grayson was fairly certain Felicia intended to return in order to make sure the children and woman were fed, but when that notion began to make him feel all fuzzy inside, he'd quickly abandoned the thought and settled for concentrating on keeping her in his sights as she traveled to her next destination—an even more deplorable house in one of the worst tenement slums Grayson had ever seen, but a slum that didn't appear to phase Felicia in the least.

She'd traveled into numerous ramshackle neighborhoods after

that, depositing pies and bags of what appeared to be food to one downtrodden family after another. Dirty children seemed to delight her, and the more Grayson watched, the more he came to realize exactly how special Felicia was.

There was a glow about her as she interacted with the people in the slums, a glow he'd come to realize was a direct result of the pleasure she took in her work. She truly was a child of God, called by Him to help the needy, which was why, after he finally apologized for his dismal behavior, he needed to leave her alone.

She needed a gentleman of faith by her side to help her along in life, and he was fairly certain, considering the sins of his past, that God had given up on him.

Felicia took that moment to suddenly steer Thor to the opposite side of the street, cutting off a large delivery cart in the process. A sigh of relief escaped his lips when a disaster didn't occur, but the relief was quickly replaced with trepidation when she brought Thor to a stop in the middle of the sidewalk right in front of what appeared to be a theater. His eyes narrowed on the sign nailed over the door.

Rogue's Theater.

He watched in dumbstruck amazement as she jumped off the cart, looped Thor's reins around the hitching post, kissed her pony on the head, and then hitched up her skirts and hurried to the door, completely oblivious to the crowd of seedy-looking men directing their attention her way. She pounded on the door, and a moment later, it flew open and four exuberant men bounded through it, greeting Felicia as if they were long-lost friends.

He couldn't hear what was being said, but Felicia kept pointing to her pony cart as the men nodded eagerly. They walked over to the cart, and Felicia extracted a dress from one of the remaining bags. The men's eyes widened, and they began to ooh and aah over every dress she pulled out.

His patience waning, Grayson decided to put an end to the

nonsense once and for all. He swung off his horse but paused yet again when Felicia gave the men a cheery goodbye, got back into her pony cart, flicked the reins, and . . . simply sat there when Thor didn't budge.

He couldn't help but grin when she flounced out of the cart and gave the pony a stern talking to. She grabbed hold of the reins and tried to pull Thor back into the street, but the pony wouldn't move—not even when Felicia leaned down and kissed it soundly on the nose.

It was rather odd to feel jealous of a pony.

Deciding there was nothing to do but step in or otherwise remain stuck in the slums forever, Grayson began to stride forward but froze on the spot when two men stepped in front of him, speaking rapidly in Chinese. The rhythm of their speech sent a wave of revulsion through him as they pushed past. Sweat immediately beaded his forehead as he followed them and moments later watched them disappear into a building seeping smoke with a familiar scent. Grayson's gaze lifted and settled on the sign swinging slightly above the building's door.

Posey's.

The sweat rolled off his forehead and down his face, stinging his eyes, but he found he couldn't blink, couldn't move, as he continued staring at what could only be an opium den.

Why had he never considered there would be opium dens in this less than reputable part of the city?

The demand for opium had been increasing in the United States, no matter that the government had passed a law banning the importation of the substance. That ban had not decreased in the least what the Wu family had garnered from providing America with an abundance of the substance. Granted, they'd had to pay quite a few bribes to get the opium through the docks and into the proprietors' hands, but money easily opened doors. One of Grayson's main responsibilities had been to organize the massive ships to transport the drug to these shores. He'd become richer by the minute while countless men and women became addicted to the vile substance.

He watched a group of well-dressed men enter the establishment, and then it hit him—Felicia was on a street that sported an opium den.

He swung his attention back to her . . . and felt an icy hand of terror clench his heart. She was gone, but Thor still remained exactly where Grayson had last seen him.

Pulling his horse through the crowded street, he threw the reins over the hitching post next to Thor's and set his sights on an older gentleman sitting on a stoop.

"Begging your pardon, my good man, but did you happen to see a woman standing next to that pony just a moment ago?"

The man nodded and then grinned. "She couldn't get that there pony to move, so she shook her finger at the beast and began walking down that way." He pointed to his right. "Maybe she decided to travel home on foot."

Felicia would never abandon her pony.

"Thank you," Grayson called over his shoulder as he strode down the sidewalk, peering into dirty window after dirty window as he went. His panic grew until he stopped in front of a place called the Wild Rose and heard a familiar tinkling laugh drift out the open door.

What was wrong with the woman?

He stalked through the door, coming to a complete stop when he spotted her.

His terror turned to disbelief.

Felicia was sitting at a dirty table, surrounded by men, with a glass of what appeared to be whiskey in front of her.

She'd obviously lost her mind.

He squared his shoulders and strode over to her table. He came to a stop and simply waited for her to see him.

It turned into a rather long wait.

Felicia was completely engrossed in a conversation with a man who was missing most of his teeth, not that Felicia seemed to mind. She was giving the man her full attention, and suddenly, Grayson's anger simply melted away.

She truly was a wonderful woman, no matter that she seemed to have abandoned all of her principles by waltzing into a pub of all places.

Felicia lifted her gaze and her eyes widened.

"Frank," she exclaimed, rising to her feet. "What are you doing here?"

Grayson swallowed a laugh at the guilty expression on her face. "Clara . . . you're right, it's Frank, and might I ask you the same question?"

"You know Clara?" the man sporting no teeth asked. "Who are you—her gentleman friend?"

It was a bit disturbing to learn he'd been right about what name she would assume, the name of the character who'd come to a bad end in one of her favorite novels. "I do know Clara, and I *am* her gentleman friend."

Felicia's eyes narrowed. "Frank *is* a gentleman friend of mine, but he's not *that* type of gentleman friend."

"Come now, Clara," Grayson said. "Didn't we enjoy a lovely drive just the other evening? If memory serves me correctly, it was quite remarkable."

"You're right, Frank," Felicia said, "but I distinctly remember you making a rather abrupt departure while we dined a few days ago. That led me to believe we were no longer in accord."

"That's the reason I've sought you out, Fel . . . er . . . Clara. I wanted to speak with you about the incident."

"Pull up a chair, then, Frank," the toothless man said. "I'm Jessie, and I love a good tale. Care for a whiskey?"

"No, thank you," Grayson said as he sent a look to a man

on Felicia's right, which had the man bolting out of his chair and scooting away. Felicia rolled her eyes before resuming her seat. Taking that as a sign it would be safe to join her without any physical repercussions, such as a slap across the face or a whiskey poured over his head, he settled into the chair. "Care to explain what you're doing here?"

"I thought we were going to discuss you, not me."

"Seems as if I might need another drink," Jessie muttered. "Now, don't say a word until I get back."

"You can have Clara's drink," Grayson said. "She doesn't care for whiskey."

He knew it was the wrong thing to say the moment the words left his mouth.

Felicia's face turned red, and she glared at him for a brief second before she grabbed her glass, sent him a rather mocking salute, and bolted down the contents as if she were an old hand at imbibing in hard spirits—an old hand until the glass dropped to the table with a thud and she turned her head and spit the contents of her mouth onto the floor. She wiped her mouth with the back of her hand and, without a single glance to him, lurched to her feet and dashed through the throng of people crowding the pub.

Grayson pushed back his chair but didn't have an opportunity to rise because Jessie stopped him with a hand to his arm.

"She won't appreciate your help," Jessie said. "Women like to be alone with their embarrassing moments."

"But . . . she's probably off to toss up her accounts."

"Yep, she probably is, which is why you should stay here. She'll be back. I promised the little lady she could accompany me when I play the piano."

Grayson tilted his head. "When you say 'accompany' you, what exactly do you mean?"

A man sitting on the other side of Grayson leaned forward

before Jessie had an opportunity to respond. "The lady told us she loves to sing, and she agreed to entertain us."

The day just kept getting better and better. What could have possessed the woman to agree to sing in this derelict pub where the majority of patrons were men? Didn't she realize the danger? Didn't she realize that most of the men were three sheets to the wind, a certain recipe for disaster? He got to his feet. "I really must go fetch Clara."

"She's fine," Jessie said with a jerk of his head. "See, she's over there with Dot."

Grayson peered through the crowded pub and breathed a silent sigh of relief when he located Felicia chatting with a woman who looked vaguely familiar. He frowned and leaned forward.

"You said that woman's name is Dot?" he asked.

Jessie nodded. "Yep."

Here was yet further proof that Felicia spent a great deal of her time mingling in places she didn't belong, with people she probably shouldn't even know. Dot was an acquaintance of Theodore Wilder, and Grayson knew perfectly well she spent quite a bit of her time working the streets.

"That's it," he muttered, ignoring the men who hissed advice behind him as he stalked across the room and stopped in front of Felicia. He blinked when he noticed she didn't look the worse for wear. She certainly didn't look as if she'd recently gotten sick.

"Are you all right?" he asked, more annoyed than he cared to admit that she looked to be in the best of health.

"Frank, you're still here," Felicia said with a smile that was entirely too charming. "I thought you'd leave."

"As if I'd even consider that option," Grayson muttered. "Again, are you all right?"

"I'm fine, although I willingly admit the taste of that whiskey was simply dreadful. Thank goodness I ran into this lovely lady.

She fixed me up a special concoction to get the taste out of my mouth, and now I feel back to my old self."

"You drank something a complete stranger gave you?"

"Dot's hardly a stranger, Frank, seeing as how she's acquainted with Agatha. Granted, I've never actually made her acquaintance until just a few moments ago, but I knew who she was and was more than appreciative when she handed me that tonic as I made my way past the bar. Drinking her remedy was certainly preferable to a trip to the back alley. And just so we're clear, I'm not a complete idiot. Do you really believe I'm so naïve that I'd accept a drink from a stranger?"

Grayson arched a brow. "Did that whiskey just appear on its own, Clara?"

"Jessie procured it for me, and I'll have you know, he's a nice man."

"He's barely coherent."

"Nonsense. He seems perfectly sober, or mostly so." Felicia lifted her chin. "If you must know, I made his acquaintance when I was strolling down the sidewalk and saw him stumble to the ground when his cane got stuck in a hole. He was appreciative when I came to his assistance, and . . ." She lowered her voice. "I know full well this is hardly the place I should be patronizing, but I didn't have the heart to refuse his offer of a drink, and it's not so bad in here. I mean, it has its own charm in a strange sort of way."

Grayson glanced around and suppressed the urge to strangle her.

It was a rough and derelict place, and she had absolutely no business being there, no matter that it seemed as if she'd been invited in because of yet another good deed she'd been doing.

Sometimes he expected to find a halo circling her bright locks.

"We're going to leave . . . now, and I don't expect you to give me any trouble," he finally said.

"I'm not going anywhere with you, Frank. In fact, now that I think about it, what are you even doing here? It seems a little convenient that you'd just happen to stumble into me in a place like this."

"Why, this is delicious," Dot said as she stepped forward, sent Grayson a subtle wink, and saved him from an immediate response to Felicia's question. "I never took you for the type of gentleman who would assume a secret identity, Lord Sefton."

Felicia's eyes suddenly began to gleam in the dim light. "You know Frank?"

"Of course I do," Dot purred, which caused Felicia's mouth to drop open and Grayson to grin.

"Not intimately, and you need to behave, Dot."

For some odd reason, his response caused Felicia to smack him upside the head.

"That was a rude thing to say to Dot, Frank. You need to apologize to her."

Grayson felt the strangest desire to laugh. Here they were, in the midst of a disreputable pub, and she was demanding he apologize to a woman of the night whom he was fairly certain he hadn't actually insulted.

The day was becoming stranger by the second.

He assumed what he hoped was an adequately somber expression and nodded as he turned to Dot. "Forgive me, Dot, if I offended you, because that was not my intention." He took a deep breath. "Now, since that is firmly behind us, I really must insist we take our leave."

"I can't leave yet," Felicia announced. "I promised Mr. Jessie I would sing. I would hate to disappoint the darling man. He and his friends were enthusiastic when I agreed to entertain them."

Grayson reminded himself it would hardly be considered appropriate if he flung Felicia over his back and carted her out of the pub. "This is not the type of establishment where you

100

should promise to entertain anyone, Felicia. They might have misunderstood your intentions."

Dot nodded. "He's right, Clara, or Felicia, or whatever your name is. You probably should reconsider your offer."

Felicia's expression turned mulish as she crossed her arms over her chest and began tapping her foot against the dirty floor.

He blew out a breath. "If you insist on being so unreasonable, may I at least inquire whether or not you have the ability to sing?"

"My mother claims I'm very proficient."

"Oh . . . no . . . not again."

"And," Felicia continued as if she hadn't heard him, "everyone at our church believes I have a *delightful* voice, and I sing in the choir whenever my services are required."

"Do you stand in the front?" Grayson asked hopefully.

"Surprisingly enough, I don't."

"This should be entertaining," Dot said, taking Felicia by the arm and escorting her rapidly across the floor before Grayson had the presence of mind to stop them. Apprehension settled over him when Dot brought Felicia to a stop beside a rickety old piano right as Jessie ambled over to join them. His apprehension increased when Jessie handed Felicia a piece of sheet music. She looked it over briefly and then leaned over and whispered something into the man's ear.

Surely she wasn't requesting a hymn, was she?

Felicia straightened, clasped her hands demurely in front of her, and sent Grayson a smug smile.

Knowing he had no choice but to see the fiasco through to fruition, he moved to an empty space along the wall and slouched against it, trying to prepare himself for what was about to occur.

Nothing could have prepared him for the sounds that came out of Felicia's mouth.

They were a cross between the cry of a wounded animal and the shrieking of an unknown creature, but the sight of Felicia belting out a tune he'd never heard before, and was fairly certain *she'd* never heard before, did strange things to his heart.

Not wanting to dwell on that disturbing notion, he shifted against the wall and tried not to wince as Felicia tried to hit a particularly high note, something, it turned out, she wasn't remotely capable of reaching.

7

*I*t was incredibly liberating, abandoning one's normally reserved demeanor and bellowing out a song in the midst of the seediest establishment Felicia had ever frequented. She knew she was making a complete mess of the words to the little ditty Jessie was banging out on the piano, but she really wasn't that concerned about it. She probably should have taken a closer gander at the notes on the page he'd handed her, but she wasn't exactly competent when it came to reading music, much to her mother's despair. Oh, she'd tried her best throughout the years, but for some reason, notes on a page just seemed like a bunch of random dots and lines to her. She could only hope her enthusiasm made up for the liberties she was currently taking with the tune.

The words to the song were a bit of a puzzle to her too. It seemed as if the theme of the story was something regarding a dock, a sailor, and some woman who didn't return said sailor's affections. She heard her voice wobble just a touch when the realization came to her that the lyrics might be referring to an illicit liaison. It was probably best not to contemplate the matter too closely. She shook the thought away, increased her volume, and stifled a laugh when she noticed a man standing close to her take a few steps back.

She was perfectly aware she couldn't carry a tune.

Taking a deep breath, she hit the last high note of the song and held it for as long as she was able. She finally ran out of air and closed her mouth, feeling a stab of disappointment run through her when Jessie abruptly stopped playing and jumped to his feet.

She smiled at him. "Shall we do another?"

A slightly pained expression slid over Jessie's face before he sent her a toothless grin. "My fingers ain't what they used to be, Clara. It might be best if we call it a day."

Bless his heart. Lurking underneath that shabby exterior lived the soul of a true gentleman.

Felicia smiled, stood on tiptoe, and kissed his cheek, causing Jessie to turn a deep shade of red even as his grin widened. She took the arm he offered her but ended up helping him back to the table when he began to wobble. Pulling out a chair, she held on to him as he lowered his lanky frame, then released his arm and turned, feeling a sudden need to find Grayson and learn what he'd thought of her performance.

She still had no idea what he was doing here, not that she'd had much time to contemplate the matter. Logic told her he had to have been following her, but why he would have been doing that, well, she couldn't really say.

Taking a deep breath, she set her attention to where Grayson was lounging against the wall on the opposite side of the pub. She'd known his position the entire time she'd been singing but had deliberately avoided his gaze. Sometimes he was simply too aristocratic, too proper, and since she'd hardly been behaving in a manner that anyone could have called proper, she'd kept her attention front and center, directed at the gentlemen who'd lined up to hear her sing.

In hindsight, that might not have been the best decision she'd ever made, especially since, when those gentlemen weren't grimacing in obvious pain over a sour note she'd hit, they'd been staring back at her with expressions that were somewhat frightening.

Taking another deep breath, she began to weave through the crowd, a grin edging her lips when she realized everyone seemed to be giving her a bit of a wide berth.

Perhaps they were afraid if they so much as smiled at her she'd jump back over to the piano and belt out another tune.

She slipped around a dirty table filled with empty glasses and looked up, her steps faltering ever so slightly when she caught Grayson's gaze. All the air squeezed out of her chest when she noticed something warm and more than a little disturbing in his eyes.

"Well?" she asked when she stopped in front of him. "What did you think?"

Grayson pushed away from the wall and smiled, causing what almost felt like disappointment to flow over her. He was going to tell her she'd been wonderful, just like all the other well-meaning people in her life. She felt tears well in her eyes and blinked rapidly to hold them at bay.

"You're a horrible singer."

Her blinking stopped. "I beg your pardon?"

"As you should, since my ears will never be the same."

Right then and there, Felicia's heart began to beat a rapid tattoo, even as her knees went a little weak.

He'd actually proclaimed, out loud, the fact that she was horrible.

Blood rushed through her veins, and she felt a little light-headed. She planted her hands on her hips and attempted a scowl, even though she was completely delighted with him.

"I've been told I have the voice of an angel."

"A demon more like."

"I'm not *that* bad."

Grayson released a bark of laughter. "You are, and I think you're perfectly aware of that. The question I must ask now is why you would even consider singing in front of people. You possess absolutely no ability to carry a tune."

Her delight with the gentleman immediately increased. She took the arm he offered, shivered when the heat from his skin scorched its way through the sleeve of her gown, and allowed him to escort her through the crowd. Surprise stole over her when, instead of immediately hustling her out of the pub, he steered her to a table for two, held out a chair for her, helped her into it, and once she was settled, took a seat.

"So?" he prompted as he reached over the small table and placed his hand over hers, causing a small shiver to travel up her arm. "How long have you been aware you're a horrible singer?"

"You don't really need to continue using the word *horrible*, Grayson. I got your point the first time you used it."

Grayson smiled. "But if I bring it up often, perhaps it will compel you to refrain from singing, and that will save people from experiencing such pain in the future."

"I wouldn't go so far as to claim I cause people pain."

Grayson rubbed his ear. "That's debatable, but again, how long have you known you can't sing?"

"Forever."

Grayson arched a brow, causing Felicia to laugh. "Maybe not forever, but at least since I was fourteen or fifteen." She shrugged. "When you're young, everyone is more tolerant and finds you adorable, no matter your abilities." Drumming her fingers against the sticky table, she released a breath. "I only started singing again in the choir at church about four years ago.

I knew, as did everyone else in the choir, that I didn't possess what anyone could call dulcet tones, but . . ."

"Ministers' wives are expected to sing in the choir," Grayson finished for her.

It was unsettling, the way he seemed to understand her.

"Tell me, were you truly in love with Reverend Fraser, or were you in love with the thought of becoming a minister's wife?"

She pulled back the hand that had been resting under his. "That's somewhat insulting."

"It might be insulting, but I notice you're not exactly denying it."

Felicia blinked. He was right. She wasn't denying it, probably because that particular thought had crossed her mind on an annoyingly frequent basis of late.

"Did he compliment you on your singing abilities?"

The man was too astute for his own good.

"Reverend Fraser never complimented my voice, but he never tried to dissuade me from singing in the choir."

"He seems like a kind man."

"I'd prefer not to talk about Reverend Fraser, if it's all the same to you."

"That's fine by me. What would you care to talk about?"

Tilting her head, she thought for a moment, then smiled. "Didn't you mention something earlier about your having something to say to me about the café incident?"

"I might have."

"And?"

Grayson shifted in his chair, regarded the ceiling for a long moment, switched his attention back to her, stared unblinkingly at her for a good long time, and finally opened his mouth. "I behaved like an idiot at the café, and for that I truly must beg your pardon."

Good heavens, he was apologizing. She hadn't expected that.

She reached across the table and patted his hand. "Thank you for that, but since we're clearing the air, I must admit to you that, after a thorough consideration of what I said that day, I believe I owe *you* an apology. I fear my words came across in an accusatory manner, but I certainly didn't mean them as such."

Grayson smiled. "I'm perfectly aware that you didn't mean to insult me. If you must know, your words struck a nerve, hence my abysmal behavior." He paused for a moment, glanced to the right, and then a scowl crept over his face. "We're going to have to continue this conversation elsewhere."

"What do you mean?"

"Evidently, I've been an idiot once again by not escorting you directly out of here after you finished your song. You've picked up some admirers, and unfortunately, they're heading this way."

Felicia swiveled her head and found a group of slovenly dressed and staggering men making their way toward their table.

It hit her then—the danger she'd allowed herself to so ridiculously stumble into. Granted, she'd only entered this deplorable pub to assist poor Jessie, but she should have seen him into a seat and taken her immediate leave. Her curiosity regarding the seedy establishment, and a longing to embrace a life she'd hidden from for far too long, had obviously made her lose all good sense. She looked back to Grayson. "You have no idea how thankful I am you somehow managed to find me here."

"Save your thanks for later," he muttered. "I need to get you away from here—now."

Before Felicia could even push back her chair, Grayson was right next to her, offering her his hand. She looked up and blinked, finding that somehow, in the span of a few seconds, the charming and agreeable man who'd been sitting across from her had been replaced once again with the dangerous man from the café. Her heart began to beat a little faster.

"I say there . . . Frank, wasn't it?" one of the men asked, coming to a stop in front of the table. "Where are you going with fair Clara?"

"That's really none of your concern."

The man cracked his knuckles. "I'm making it my concern."

One minute Felicia was sitting in her seat, and the next she was standing against the wall, Grayson blocking her from the men, who were now looking remarkably ugly as they crowded closer to them. She found herself admiring the width of his shoulders and then shook herself. It was a completely inappropriate moment to ogle the man. Their lives appeared to be at risk, or at least Grayson's did. The men didn't seem to have a problem with her, which, now that she thought about it, might not be a good thing.

"Gentlemen, I suggest you maintain your distance," Grayson drawled, sounding for all intents and purposes the aristocrat he actually was.

"Oh . . . fancy," one of the men hooted. "I have a feeling you're no ordinary Frank."

Felicia watched in stunned disbelief as Grayson shrugged out of his jacket and calmly handed it to her.

"Watch this for me, love."

Even though the word *love* in regard to her was entirely too appealing, Felicia didn't have a moment to savor the appeal. It seemed as if Grayson was actually considering engaging in a brawl with these men. She clasped his jacket to her chest, stepped forward, and tugged on his arm.

"Grayson," she whispered.

He turned his head ever so slightly. "Yes?"

"This is madness. There's at least six of them and only one of you."

"True, hardly fair odds," Grayson said with the strangest smile on his face. "Perhaps I should give them one last chance to back down."

Clearly the man was a lunatic. Before she could voice that opinion, Grayson spread his hands out. "I don't want to hurt any of you, so if you'd be so kind as to move, we'll just be on our way."

"You're one of them fancy toffs from across the sea," a big, brawny man with wild eyes said. "I don't much like foreigners." With that, he hurled himself at Grayson.

A small squeak was all Felicia could manage as bodies began to fly through the air. Grayson was moving fluidly across the floor, almost like a dancer—although no dancer Felicia had ever seen radiated the sheer raw power and destruction Grayson was emitting. He suddenly turned, caught her eye . . . and grinned.

Felicia lost the ability to breathe.

He was not the gentleman everyone assumed him to be. He was dangerous, exciting, and seemingly insane, but there was something incredibly compelling about him that—

Her breath came back in a split second when she realized one of the men had noticed Grayson's distraction and was stealthily advancing on him, rage evident in his eyes. She tried to yell a warning, but her voice wasn't up for the task of traveling through all the grunts and moans. She waved her hands to capture Grayson's attention, but he'd already turned to deal with another one of the rowdy patrons. Not knowing what else to do, and fearing the advancing man was going to do Grayson a good deal of harm, she snatched up a large tankard filled with ale from a nearby table, rushed up behind the man, and swung with all her might.

Ale splashed everywhere, soaking her from head to toe, but the resounding thud of the tankard meeting its mark and the subsequent act of the man dropping to the ground caused a glimmer of satisfaction to run through her.

"Clara, honestly, get back against the wall," Grayson yelled as another body sailed through the air and landed by her feet.

Even though Grayson was sounding distinctly surly once again, Felicia couldn't help herself—she grinned. Grayson scowled in her direction, gestured to the wall with one deliberate point of a finger, and then threw himself back into the fray, taking care of the last man standing with relatively little fuss.

"What an extraordinary man," Dot purred, causing Felicia to jump even as a trace of annoyance spread over her at the all too admiring look Dot was sending in Grayson's direction. "Why, there's just something downright delicious about a gentleman who can handle himself well in a dangerous situation."

Felicia took a moment to consider Grayson. Blood marked his shirt here and there, his waistcoat was sporting several rips, as were his trousers, and his hair was standing on end, but all in all, he did look somewhat . . . delicious.

She pulled her attention away from him and glanced around the floor, taking in the vast amount of carnage Grayson had caused. Men were lying everywhere, some holding their heads, others holding their stomachs, and one barely moving at all.

Apprehension was swift.

How was he even capable of delivering such destruction, and without a weapon—well, except for his hands?

He was an aristocrat and had been born to wealth and privilege, but he fought like a man who'd grown up on the streets, although not streets Felicia had ever seen.

"Is there anyone else who has an issue with me taking Clara out of here?" Grayson suddenly demanded as he looked to the left and then to the right, a surprising touch of disappointment flashing over his face when no one else stepped forward.

Good heavens, it appeared he'd enjoyed the brawl. What did that say about his true character?

Grayson took that moment to stride over to Felicia, stopping right in front of her, the heat from his body, causing goose bumps to erupt under the thin and wet material of her gown.

She would have taken a step away from him, but her back was already against the wall, so she suppressed the urge to shiver and forced herself to meet his gaze. What she discovered there had her mouth running dry.

He was furious, and it seemed as if that fury was directed at her.

"You're soaking wet."

She blinked. "True."

"You'll catch your death of cold."

She blinked again. "It's hardly cold out today, Grayson, and if I hadn't hit that man over the head with the tankard of ale, he might have harmed you."

Grayson let out a snort. "I doubt that, but either way you shouldn't have intervened. You could have been harmed."

"I wasn't."

"That's beside the point, but tell me, how are you going to explain to your mother why you're covered in ale?"

"I forgot all about my mother."

"Apparently, as you're currently in a pub, a place I'm certain your mother would hardly approve of," Grayson said before he turned to Dot, who'd picked his jacket off the floor where Felicia had dropped it and handed it to him. He smiled his thanks and opened his mouth, but then his entire body stiffened and his eyes went hard. He reached forward with one hand, grabbed onto Felicia's arm, and yanked her behind him, shielding her once again with his body.

Interestingly enough, although he'd barely broken a sweat while he'd been engaged in the brawl, he was now perspiring, and profusely at that.

Felicia leaned to the right and peered around him, searching for whatever new threat awaited. All she saw were two slightly built Chinese men, standing across the room, their attention decidedly locked on Grayson.

"Is there a back door?" Grayson muttered out of the side of his mouth.

Dot nodded.

"Take Felicia outside and stay with her. I'll join you momentarily."

Before Felicia could protest, Dot had her firmly by the arm and halfway across the bar. Felicia tried to dig in her heels, but Dot was remarkably strong for a lady of her size and tugged Felicia along, sending her a glare when Felicia tried to shake off her hold. "Stop that. We have to get out of here."

Felicia stopped resisting but didn't allow Dot to increase their pace, dragging her feet once again, which slowed them down to a mere crawl. "Who are those men, and how can you believe it's remotely acceptable to leave Grayson to face them alone?"

"Honey, I have no idea who those men are, but I do know this. Something dangerous is afoot, and we need to let Grayson deal with it. After what I just saw, he's more than capable of setting matters to rights."

The next moment, Felicia found herself outside the pub, standing in a rubbish-strewn alley. Her nose wrinkled at the pungent smell that smacked her in the face. She lifted a hand and covered her nose, looking around their derelict surroundings. "I think it was safer inside." She spun on her heel, but before she could take a single step, the door flew open and Grayson stomped through it. He stopped and narrowed his eyes.

"You weren't thinking about coming after me just now, were you?"

Felicia pretended she hadn't heard him. "Who were those men?"

For a moment, Felicia didn't think Grayson was going to answer her. His eyes turned to hard shards of ice-blue glass, and she felt the unusual urge once again to step away from him, but stubbornness caused her to hold her ground. She planted her hands on her hips and simply waited.

"You're not going to let this go, are you," he said.

She shook her head.

He sent her another glare and then released a grunt. "Fine, if you must know, my past just caught up with me."

Without another word, he sent Dot a nod, took Felicia's hand, and pulled her down the alley.

8

Rage flowed freely as Grayson hustled Felicia over the rough cobblestones, trying not to dwell on what might be following them.

It was glaringly clear that he had yet to put his irresponsible ways behind him. Throwing himself wholeheartedly into a brawl in some obscure seedy establishment had been beyond idiotic and had most likely put Felicia in great peril.

He should have ignored the miscreants and tried to get Felicia out of the pub without incident. Unfortunately, the undisguised hunger directed at Felicia he'd observed pouring out of each and every one of their beady eyes had caused him to throw caution to the wind.

If the logical part of his brain had been functioning as he was contemplating the brawl, he might have considered the troubling little fact that he was only doors away from an opium den. Using fighting skills he'd learned in China while so close to that den had been foolish in the extreme. Of course word had quickly spread about a man systematically destroying numerous men, and the Chinese had come to investigate. One of those men, a man with a ragged scar marking his face, had looked familiar.

Grayson stumbled to a stop when Felicia suddenly stopped moving. He tugged on her hand, his gaze roaming around the alley, searching for danger, but for some reason, the stubborn lady refused to budge.

"Felicia, this is no time to dawdle."

"I'm not dawdling. A rat just ran over my foot."

He switched his attention to her and was surprised to feel a trace of amusement flow over him. Felicia was standing in the midst of the filthy alley, hitching up her skirt as she peered at her feet. Ale was dripping from her hair, she was missing her hat, and she had a look of clear horror on her face.

"You just took on a man three times your size with nothing more than a tankard of ale, and yet you're concerned about a rat?"

She dropped her skirt, shuddered, and lifted her chin. "I loathe rats. They carry diseases, and those diseases can be entirely more deadly than one inebriated man."

"If it makes you feel any better, I don't see any rats, so we really must get on our way."

Her expression turned stubborn. "They're just waiting to ambush me, the rats, and it's not as if I can blame them. I probably smell horrible, and you must realize that rats are attracted to odors."

"We really don't have time for this."

"Why not?"

"I'll tell you once I get you to safety."

"But what about the rats?"

Grayson narrowed his eyes. "Could you, for once, try to refrain from being difficult?"

"They scare me."

Three little words were all it took to completely vanquish the rage that lingered in his veins. Felicia was looking back at him, her eyes huge and her lips trembling slightly, and he wasn't up for the task of resisting her. He moved closer, scooped her up into his arms, ignoring her sharp intake of breath, and began striding down the alley.

"This is hardly proper," she muttered.

"I don't think anyone will see us, and just to refresh your memory, it was hardly proper for you to enter that pub in the first place."

A soft sigh was her only response before she put an arm around his neck and seemed to snuggle closer to him, her movement causing him to get a distinct sniff of ale mixed with something that was all Felicia.

The something that was all Felicia began to distract him, but knowing they were still in danger, he forced the distraction aside and increased his pace.

"Who were those Chinese men back in the pub?"

"I'll tell you once we get to Theodore's office."

Felicia's hand tightened around his neck. "We need to involve Theodore in this?"

"I'm afraid so."

"Good heavens, Grayson, you really do have a past."

"Don't we all?"

Felicia relaxed her grip. "I suppose we do. Although, I have to say, your past seems to be far more interesting than mine."

"Don't envy me my past, Felicia. It was more reprehensible than interesting."

"And those Chinese men in the pub have something to do with your reprehensible past?"

"I'm afraid so."

Felicia lapsed into silence, but it only lasted a moment. "Do you think they came over to the pub from that opium den?"

"Please tell me you didn't considering going into Posey's."

He felt Felicia's breath against his throat when she let out a huff of annoyance. "Of course not, although I have to admit, I was curious. If you must know, at first I thought it might be a flower shop, until that large cloud of smoke poured out the door when someone opened it. That's when I figured out it was an opium den."

Grayson came to a stop and looked down at her. "You thought it was a flower shop?"

"Because of the name . . . Posey's. You know—flowers, bouquets . . . There's no need to look at me that way, Grayson. It was a mistake anyone could make, but after I figured out what the place really was, I didn't consider allowing my curiosity to get the better of me. An opium den is hardly a respectable haunt for a lady."

"The entirety of Mott Street is hardly a respectable haunt for a lady, yet that didn't stop you from traveling up and down it—speaking to ladies of the night and then traveling to that theater and . . . "

The moment the words were out of his mouth, he wanted to call them back. Felicia's eyes were gleaming with something indescribable, and her cheeks were flushed.

"So you were following me?"

"Maybe." He began walking again, trying to ignore the satisfied smile on Felicia's face.

"I thought perhaps you might have been. I mean, really, how else could you have found me in that pub?"

"How else indeed, but, tell me, what possessed you to travel to this part of the city without a proper escort?"

"I travel around parts like this all the time on my own. I've been doing it for years. No one ever pays me any mind."

"They were paying you mind today."

He looked down and saw that, instead of looking concerned, she looked rather delighted. "It must be my new wardrobe."

It was certainly true that wearing gowns that accentuated her figure was one of the reasons she was drawing attention, but there was something else about her now that drew even more interest. It seemed to him that with the abandonment of her old fashions, she'd gained confidence and a desire to embrace the world head-on.

Unfortunately, no matter that she appeared to believe otherwise, she was an innocent at heart and far too trusting of people, and that disturbing situation was bound to land her in trouble. Which meant . . . he was not going to be able to keep his distance from her quite yet.

She brought out protective instincts in him that he'd barely remembered he possessed, and those instincts were causing him a bit of discomfort, especially with her pressed so thoroughly against him. Slowing to a stop once again, he carefully set her down and nodded to a small walkway just ahead of them between two buildings.

"We should be right by the theater if I've judged the distance right. I'll walk with you to the end of this building, and then I want you to get in your pony cart and travel as quickly as you can to Theodore's office."

"You're not coming with me?"

"We can't afford to allow anyone to see you with me. I'll follow you as soon as the coast is clear."

For just a second, what looked like fear clouded her eyes, but then she squared her shoulders and nodded. He sent her a smile, took her hand, and helped her through the narrow space between the buildings, stopping at the end to peer into the street for a second before he turned back to her. "Thor's just ahead. Simply walk as nonchalantly as you can to him, and then get on your way. I'll watch from here, and if I think anyone is following you, I'll step in."

"Won't that defeat the purpose of not allowing people to know we're together?"

"If anyone's following you, they'll have already figured that out."

Felicia's eyes went round, but then she drew in a breath and nodded.

"Remember," he cautioned before she stepped out onto the sidewalk, "try to appear nonchalant, but do everything you can to get Thor moving faster than a plod."

Felicia looked down at her sopping gown, then looked up and grinned. "That might be a tall order. Thor has never moved faster than an amble—well, except for the time he plowed into that hitching post."

She lifted her chin and stepped forward, causing Grayson to smile when she began to stroll toward her pony as if it were an everyday occurrence to mosey down the sidewalk while wearing a gown soaked with ale.

She made it to Thor with no mishaps, moving to release her pony's reins from the hitching post before she leaned closer and began to whisper something in his ear. Seemingly satisfied that Thor was going to listen to whatever she'd told him, she walked to the cart and climbed in.

Relief swept through him when she flicked the reins and Thor began to move, but it changed to frustration when the door to the Rogue's Theater burst open and two men rushed out, both of them waving madly to Felicia and both of them wearing what appeared to be her old gowns.

"Miss Murdock, hold up a moment," one of the men shouted as he raced toward her.

"Don't do it," Grayson muttered through gritted teeth, even though he knew full well she couldn't hear him.

"We wanted to show you how we look," the other man yelled as he skirted around some people on the sidewalk and stopped right by the pony cart that Felicia had, annoyingly enough, pulled to a stop.

Felicia's laughter soon drifted back to Grayson as she exclaimed over the men, but when one of them gestured to her gown, she sobered immediately and said something Grayson couldn't hear. Then, to his amazement, one of the men jumped on the seat right next to her while the other climbed into the cart. Before Grayson had the presence of mind to step forward, Felicia flicked the reins and Thor—an animal that rarely cooperated—jolted into motion and headed down the street at what appeared to be almost a trot.

The day just kept getting more unusual by the minute, but perhaps the sight of a drenched and disheveled lady riding in a pony cart with two men dressed in outlandish gowns would be enough of a distraction to allow Felicia to get safely on her way.

He watched the cart until it disappeared from view and then took one step onto the sidewalk, considering how he was going to get across the space to his horse without being detected. A street urchin caught his attention. Grayson smiled in satisfaction and motioned the urchin to join him as he stepped back between the buildings.

The dirt-encrusted boy regarded him warily across the space that separated them for a moment before he darted across the sidewalk and hesitated at the entrance of the walkway.

"Did you need something, sir?"

Grayson nodded. "I could use your assistance, if you're willing to help me."

"Help you with what?"

Grayson nodded to his horse. "See that horse over there? I'll pay you a dollar if you'll fetch it for me."

"You a horse thief?"

"No, it's my horse."

"What's its name?"

"Spot."

The boy's brow wrinkled. "That's a dog's name."

"True, but you see, my daughter wanted a dog, and I came home with a horse—hence the name."

The boy tilted his head and then nodded as if that made perfect sense. "How come you just don't go and get Spot yourself? A dollar's a lot of money."

"It *is* a lot of money, which means if you want me to give it to you, you're not entitled to questions."

"Can I see the dollar?"

Grayson shoved his hand into his pocket and pulled out some bills. "I'll give you all of this if you stop talking and fetch my horse."

Before Grayson could utter another word, the boy darted away and was soon by Spot's side. Grayson watched as the child, whistling in a nonchalant manner, unhooked the reins, pulled Spot away from the hitching post, and began traveling in the wrong direction.

When the boy disappeared around a corner, Grayson feared he had been conned by a horse thief. He stood there for a moment, wondering if he should go after the boy, when the sound of galloping hooves sounded behind him. He turned and found the boy on top of Spot at the other end of the walkway. He strode to join them.

"How'd you get back here so fast?" he asked as the boy jumped to the ground and handed him the reins.

"I live on the streets. I know all the shortcuts."

A pang of pity spread through Grayson as he looked the boy over. He couldn't be more than twelve years old, but his eyes were far too old for his years.

"What's your name?"

"Sam."

Grayson handed Sam the bills and then reached back into his pocket. The thin hand Sam had extended to him was almost frail, and Grayson couldn't imagine how difficult it must be to live on the streets. "Wait," he called when Sam turned and began walking away.

"You want some of your money back?" Sam asked, holding up the bills.

"No, and put that away before anyone sees it. It'll do you little good if it gets stolen."

"Nobody steals from me."

The boy's spunk caused Grayson's lips to curl. He pulled his hand from his pocket, stepped forward, and pressed more money into Sam's outstretched hand. "Use that wisely, and if you ever need assistance, I'm renting a house on Fifth Avenue. Just ask for the English lord and someone will direct you to me."

"Why?"

"Pardon?"

"Why would you help someone like me?"

That was a difficult question to answer. But the truth suddenly smacked him in the face. He needed to seek redemption. Perhaps, just perhaps, if he tried to help even one unfortunate soul, he'd find a small measure of peace.

"Mister, are you all right?"

Grayson forced a smile. "I'm fine, Sam. Now, hide that money, and remember, if you need help—"

"Fifth Avenue, English lord," Sam finished for him.

"Good boy," Grayson said, swinging up on top of Spot. He looked down. "You didn't happen to notice any Chinese men on the streets out there, did you?"

"They're all over the place."

"Wonderful," Grayson muttered.

"Where do you need to go?"

"Broadway."

"I could show you a shortcut where you wouldn't run into any of those men."

Grayson smiled, held out his hand, and pulled Sam up behind

him. They were soon traveling through one back alley after another, Sam regularly calling instructions.

By the time they reached Broadway, Grayson's anxiety level had reached an all-time high, and he could only pray Felicia had made it out of the slums safely.

He'd hated to let her out of his sight, but he'd had little choice in the matter, since he didn't want anyone to know of their association. If he'd stayed with her, he would have only drawn more attention to her.

"You can set me down here, sir," Sam said, breaking into Grayson's thoughts.

Grayson brought Spot to a halt and felt Sam slide off the horse. He looked down. "How will you get back?"

"Not to worry," Sam said. "I'll just jump on an omnibus, seeing as how I have some spare money."

Grayson reached into his pocket and pulled out a handful of coins, surprised when Sam shook his head.

"You already paid me plenty."

"That was for fetching my horse. Besides, you'll draw less notice if you pay your fare with coins. No one expects a street boy to be carrying around a bunch of bills."

Sam hesitated for a moment and then, almost reluctantly, held out his hand. Grayson dropped the coins into it and smiled, but his smile faded when he found himself wondering how often Sam found something to smile about.

"Thank you, sir. My sisters will appreciate having a decent meal, and the money you gave me will last us awhile."

Grayson closed his eyes for a moment and then slowly opened them. "You have sisters?"

"I do, sir, two. Both younger than me." He puffed out his thin chest. "I've been taking care of them ever since my parents got killed down at the mill."

"Do you have a home?"

"We used to rent a room, but the landlady threw us out when my parents died."

"Did no one think to send you to an orphanage?"

"We're better off on the streets."

Pain sliced through Grayson at the injustice life offered some. He took a deep breath. "Not all orphanages are bad, Sam. My sister and her husband just opened one on the outskirts of the city. I have a feeling you might like it there."

Sam's eyes grew round. "Is your sister Lady Eliza?"

"You've heard of her?"

Sam ignored the question. "That's why you said to ask for an English lord. You really are one."

"Yes, I am, whether I want to be or not."

"You don't like being a fancy gentleman?"

"Not particularly."

"But . . . haven't you got a house and plenty of money?"

Grayson actually had five houses—or maybe it was six—not that he was going to admit that to the poverty-stricken boy gazing up at him. "I do have a house and money."

"Then you should be happy," Sam said. "Someday I'm going to have me a house, or at least a room of my own, and rooms for my sisters. I'm going to get a job at the mill once I get taller."

Shame burrowed into Grayson's soul. He'd thought he'd matured greatly during his years in China, but in reality, the boy standing by him, who was little more than a child, shouldered more responsibilities than Grayson had ever managed.

It was humbling, being faced with the reality of his true character.

He'd allowed himself to be pulled into a brawl with little consideration of the consequences. He was apparently still capable of whining about having been born an aristocrat.

It was past time he grew up.

"Is something the matter, sir?"

Grayson shook himself out of his thoughts. "Nothing of any great importance. Now then, I have nothing with which to write this down, so you'll need to listen carefully to what I'm about to say."

"I don't read real well, sir, so I'd have to listen anyways."

Another bout of shame descended. He'd always taken his education for granted.

"Right, you can't read well," he muttered. "We'll have to do something about that."

"Sir?"

Grayson leaned forward on Spot. "I want you to seek out my sister, but I can't recall her actual address, so you'll need to go to that big church down the way, the one with the lovely stained-glass windows."

"Reverend Fraser's church?"

"That's the one, but he won't be there."

"I know. He just got married."

"You are aware of everything that goes on, aren't you?"

Sam grinned. "Sometimes it comes in handy."

"I imagine it does," Grayson replied, unable to help grinning back at the boy. "Anyways, go there and tell them Grayson Sumner sent you. That will get you access to my sister, and she'll get you and your sisters off the street and settled."

"I heard there's no room right now at that orphanage."

"My sister will make room for you and your sisters," Grayson said. "I'll tell her to expect you."

"That's kind of you, Mr. Sumner."

Grayson's heart ached as he looked at the boy watching him now so earnestly. The boy's life was beyond difficult, and yet he still minded his manners. It was clear he was an intelligent lad, and Grayson swore then and there he'd do whatever was in his power to help him. But first, he needed to get to Felicia.

"I don't remember the last time anyone called me kind," he

finally muttered before he leaned farther over his horse and held out his hand. Sam looked completely delighted as he shook it. "I have your word you'll seek out my sister?"

"I'll do my best to find her."

It wasn't a promise, but it would have to do.

"See that you try your hardest," Grayson said, "and now, I have to be on my way. I need to ascertain that a good friend hasn't landed herself in more trouble."

"Miss Felicia?"

"You know her?"

"She roams the streets, looking for the needy and for stray orphans."

Grayson frowned. "If you know that, why didn't you let her find you?"

Sam shifted on his feet. "She just started looking for orphans a few months back, but everyone knows she's one of those religious ladies. I don't like when they try to lecture me."

"Felicia tried to lecture you? That doesn't sound like her."

"Not Miss Felicia—some of the other ladies. But that's why I never approached her."

"May I assume one of those ladies said something distasteful to you?"

"Just one, she called me the spawn of . . . Well, it doesn't really matter. But I didn't like that at all, and then . . . she tried to dump water over my head. She said it would cure me of any evil lurking inside me."

"I hate to tell you this, Sam, but you're going to encounter nutty people throughout your life," Grayson said. "That one lady doesn't represent all people of faith. Felicia's a wonderful lady and remarkably good."

"Why was she singing in that pub if she's so good?"

"You heard her?"

"The whole street heard her. It was horrible."

"If you ever run into her, you might want to keep that information to yourself."

"My pa always taught me to treat girls with respect," Sam said. "I would never tell her she can't sing."

"You're a better man than I."

"You told her she couldn't sing?"

"Well, yes, but strangely enough, it seemed she liked hearing it from me."

"She's a bit of an odd duck."

Grayson laughed. "Speaking of Felicia, though, I do need to find her."

"She'll be fine," Sam said. "I saw the men from the theater get into her cart. They're good men, and they won't let her come to any harm."

"How do you know that?"

Sam shrugged. "The men at the theater have been real kind to me and my sisters. They even let us sleep in the theater when it gets cold outside, and they offered to let us sleep there all the time, but I'm not keen on having my sisters live in such a . . . different place."

"We'll have to work on finding you a normal place to live, Sam," Grayson said before he tightened his grip on the reins. "Make certain you look up my sister. She'll be expecting you."

Sam grinned, nodded, and then spun around, disappearing a moment later down an alley. Grayson stared after him for a long moment, hoping the boy was good for his word. Otherwise, he would be forced to intervene, whether Sam wanted his assistance or not.

That thought took Grayson aback. He'd never been one to involve himself in the lives of others. For one, because he was an aristocrat, people usually gave him a wide berth, and for two, well, he didn't really know how to go about assisting people.

He had the sneaky suspicion his new attitude was a direct result of being in close contact with Felicia.

He nudged Spot out into the street, anxious now to locate the exasperating woman.

It didn't take him long to find her.

She was sitting on the seat of her pony cart in front of Theodore Wilder's private investigation office, poor Thor already asleep in his tracks, his bedraggled mane blowing in the breeze. The gentlemen from the theater were seemingly doing their best to entertain her, because Felicia was laughing quite enthusiastically as one of the men gestured wildly with his hands.

Grayson urged Spot forward and pulled to a halt right in front of Felicia, who looked up and sent him a smile that caused his mind to go numb.

"There you are, Grayson," she exclaimed. "I was beginning to worry."

The very idea that Felicia was worrying about his welfare had a chunk of the ice surrounding his heart melting ever so slightly. Before he could so much as think of a response, though, the door to Theodore Wilder's office opened, and Theodore and his wife, Arabella, rushed out, both of them brandishing pistols pointed at the now somber men in the cart.

"Get away from Miss Murdock," Arabella Wilder snarled, "or I swear I'll see you dead."

9

*F*elicia strolled down the hallway of Theodore Wilder's investigation office, pausing for a moment to allow Arabella Wilder time to catch up with her. "Do you think it might have been a slight overreaction, threatening to shoot those poor gentlemen from the theater?"

Arabella stopped by her side, grinned, and flicked back a strand of golden hair that had evidently escaped her pins while she'd been racing around trying to shoot people. "How was I to know those gentlemen hadn't abducted you and stolen your gowns?"

"I doubt gentlemen bent on abduction would direct their victim to park in front of a private investigator's office."

"A valid point," Theodore Wilder said, striding up to join them. He moved next to his wife, placed a kiss on her forehead, and then smiled. "Although, I must admit, the fact that they were wearing your clothing was somewhat suspicious, Felicia."

"I found that suspicious as well."

Felicia glanced past Theodore and found Grayson walking

through the door, his expression once again a bit disgruntled. He really was a moody sort of gentleman.

"You'll be happy to learn I was finally able to flag down a carriage for hire," he said as he joined them, "even though I was forced to pay the driver an exorbitant sum in order to convince him to cart men dressed as women back to the theater. He wasn't convinced by my explanation for their appearance." Grayson shook his head. "I'm not even sure I was convinced. And it didn't help when one of the men kept crying."

Felicia waved that comment aside with a flick of her hand. "The reason they were wearing my old gowns was because they're about ready to begin rehearsals for a new production, a bit of a farce. They were waiting for me to return to the theater so they could express their appreciation over my donation to their cause, and they also wanted me to see how well my dresses fit them." She blew out a breath. "As for why the one man was crying, I would think that would be obvious. Everyone knows theatrical people are a somewhat dramatic lot, and considering they'd just faced down two crazy people shoving guns their way, I'm not surprised in the least one of them dissolved into tears. I would have done exactly the same thing."

Grayson suddenly stepped closer to her, reached into his trouser pocket, pulled out a handkerchief, and scrubbed at a smear of grime staining her sleeve. He released a grunt as he continued scrubbing. "You didn't cry a single tear back in the pub, and believe me, you were in more danger there than those men were from Theodore and Arabella."

"You two have gotten yourself embroiled in something concerning, haven't you?" Theodore asked.

"You could say that," Grayson muttered before he stopped scrubbing at Felicia's sleeve. "I'm only making it worse. I'm afraid this new frock of yours is damaged beyond repair."

Felicia glanced down. "It's a pity, to be sure, but I think I knew it was headed for the ragbag the moment all that ale spilled over me."

"Perhaps our first order of business is finding you something dry to wear," Arabella said. "Unfortunately, I don't believe I have a spare gown here at the office."

Theodore smiled. "You know, I think we might just have a spare gown lying around here." He walked down the hallway and opened a door that appeared to lead to a broom closet.

"Really, darling, I don't think Felicia will be too keen to wear what you're searching for in there," Arabella said, pitching her voice a little louder when Theodore disappeared into the closet.

"Why won't I be keen to wear it?"

"Because it's an opera gown, one I wore when Agatha solicited my assistance in tracking down a story."

"And a gown you should never wear again, seeing that it managed to land you in jail," Theodore said, backing out of the closet with an overabundance of fabric clutched in his hand. He walked back to Felicia and handed it to her. "There's a powder room at the end of the hall and to the right. We'll be in the room right across from it when you've finished changing."

Felicia shook out the gown. "It's . . . lovely?"

"Almost reminds me of some of those gowns you gave to the theater," Grayson muttered.

"Honestly, Grayson, my gowns weren't this bad." She lifted her chin. "Now, if everyone will excuse me, I'll be right back." She headed down the hallway, the stiffness of the skirt of her gown, now having dried just a bit, making it somewhat difficult to walk. She reached the powder room and shut the door behind her, jumping in fright at the sight that met her gaze in the mirror, until she realized it was her reflection. She peered closer and grinned.

She looked deranged.

Her hair was matted to her head, bits of dirt were clinging

to her face, held there by remnants of ale, and her gown was filthy and splattered with what appeared to be specks of blood.

It was no wonder the men from the theater had insisted on accompanying her off Mott Street. She looked as if she'd suffered a traumatic experience.

It took her several minutes to wash her hands and face in the sink and then get out of her ruined garments. It took even longer to get into the monstrosity that was the opera gown. It might have helped if she had a maid, or Arabella, for that matter, to assist her, but she knew Arabella would be hard-pressed to keep a straight face in the midst of such a disaster, so she struggled to reach the buttons in the back and moved to the mirror, giving her appearance a critical look.

If anything, she now looked more frightful than when she'd first entered the room.

The opera dress billowed around her, which was perfectly fine since she'd been wearing billowing styles for years, but the bodice . . . It did not leave much to the imagination. She took a deep breath and blanched when a part of her body that was meant to be kept strictly out of sight almost spilled out of the gown.

She grabbed a pretty green hand towel by the sink and stuffed it over her exposed skin.

There, one problem managed.

She tilted her head and settled her attention on her hair. Pins were sticking out at odd angles, and when she reached up to shove them back into place, she discovered that her hair was incredibly unpleasant to the touch. She picked up a brush lying on a nearby table, thought better of using it, and set it back down. She didn't want to ruin Arabella's brush, and besides, she doubted even the sturdiest of brushes would be up for the task of taming the disaster on her head.

There was no help for it—she would just have to leave well

enough alone, and it wasn't as if Grayson hadn't already seen her deplorable condition.

That notion had her eyes growing wide before she backed away from the mirror and busied herself with bundling her ruined gown into a ball. She could not allow herself to dwell on thoughts of Grayson, or to wonder what the gentleman might think of her appearance. After what she'd witnessed today, it was clear she'd been right all along—he was a dangerous man.

He wasn't simply dangerous—he was lethal—and it was clear there was much more to him than she'd imagined.

It would serve her well to remember that, and it was past time she got some answers as to exactly who he was and exactly what he might have gotten her involved in.

She straightened her spine, opened the door, and trudged across the hallway to the room Theodore had indicated, the dragging skirts of her gown impeding her progress. She edged through the door but came to an abrupt halt when she saw Grayson, Theodore, and Arabella sitting on the far side of the room, all looking her way and all looking remarkably guilty.

She resisted the urge to roll her eyes. "Were you talking about me?"

"My, don't you look delightful." Arabella nodded to Theodore and Grayson. "Doesn't she look delightful?"

Theodore sent her a rather weak smile, while Grayson just looked at her with his mouth hanging open as if he had no words at his disposal to describe her appearance.

Felicia hitched up her skirt just a touch and made for the nearest chair, sinking into it and then taking a moment to pummel the fabric of the skirt that had puffed up around her the moment her behind hit the seat of the chair. Finally managing to beat the skirt into submission, she folded her hands in her lap and turned her attention to Arabella.

"So, what were the three of you talking about before I entered the room?"

"The weather?"

That didn't even deserve a quirk of one of her still-sticky brows. "Did Grayson tell you I went to a pub?"

Arabella winced. "He might have mentioned it."

"Did he explain that I only went in there because I was helping a poor elderly gentleman who'd lost his balance due to a hole in the sidewalk?"

"He wasn't exactly clear about that."

Felicia narrowed her eyes at Grayson before she turned back to Arabella. "Did he tell you about the whiskey?"

"Well, ah, yes."

Felicia lifted her chin. "I know it wasn't exactly responsible for me to try the whiskey, but there were extenuating circumstances that prodded me to act a little rashly."

Grayson shook his head. "I think she believes I was behind those 'extenuating circumstances,' but I didn't think she'd actually take a large gulp of the stuff after I insisted she doesn't drink whiskey."

"I did spit it out."

"True, all over the floor," Grayson muttered. "I must say, that did take me by surprise."

Arabella looked at Felicia, then at Grayson, then shook her head even as she smiled. "I must admit I might have felt compelled to do the exact same thing, Felicia, especially if Grayson was sounding somewhat high-handed when he made his declaration."

Grayson frowned. "She doesn't need to be encouraged, Arabella. If you're forgetting, she entered a pub, unescorted except for some elderly gentleman she'd never seen in her life, and instead of getting him settled and taking her leave, she sat down with him at a table filled with men." He glared at Felicia. "You're lucky I was following you, or else you might not have gotten out of there unscathed."

"But she didn't get out of there unscathed," Arabella pointed out. "Look at her. She's a mess—as are you, in case you've neglected to realize it."

Felicia felt Grayson's gaze on her once again, but when she turned her head to meet it, she didn't find him looking at her face. He seemed to be staring at the towel she'd shoved into her bodice.

"Do you know there's a towel stuffed right . . . er . . . well . . . there?" he asked as he waved a hand toward her bodice.

Felicia felt her cheeks heat but was spared a response when Theodore suddenly scooted his chair closer to Arabella, let out what sounded remarkably like a laugh disguised as a cough behind his hand, and then cleared his throat. "While stuffed towels are certainly a riveting topic of conversation, may I suggest we finally get around to an explanation of why the two of you are really here?"

"I'm afraid Grayson will have to answer that," Felicia admitted. "I'm somewhat confused as to what actually happened back on Mott Street, except I believe it has something to do with two Chinese men and Grayson's past."

Right before her eyes, Theodore became all business as he leaned forward and settled his attention on Grayson. "You'll need to start at the beginning."

Grayson took the next few minutes to fill Theodore and Arabella in on what had occurred, glossing over Felicia's singing abilities, or lack thereof, which had her feeling slightly warm and fuzzy all over. He could have easily used the singing incident to add a bit of humor to his story, but he was keeping the particulars to himself, which seemed to her to be his way of protecting her yet again, if only from an embarrassing situation.

He was a complicated gentleman, one she didn't understand

in the least, but he'd stepped up and defended her honor in the pub, carried her out of a rat-infested alley, and before that, told her the truth about her singing. All of those things combined were enough to turn any girl's head, but . . . she wasn't a girl anymore. She was a woman grown, and she needed to keep her attention on the conversation at hand, and remember she'd only recently gotten over a painful disappointment. She had no business even considering forming feelings for another gentleman, no matter that her heart sometimes ignored her head.

"If I'm going to help you," Theodore said, dragging Felicia rapidly out of her disturbing thoughts and back to reality, "you're going to have to explain to me—in exceeding detail, mind you—what happened in China."

Grayson slid a glance to Felicia, then to Arabella, and finally back to Theodore. "Perhaps we should repair to your private office and leave the ladies to chat about more pleasant matters."

Felicia pushed herself out of her chair and plopped her hands on her voluminous skirts. "You can't leave me in the dark now, not after what happened back at the pub."

"I can if I believe leaving you and Arabella in the dark will help keep you safe."

"You do realize that my husband and I are now working together on cases, don't you?" Arabella asked, rising from her chair and moving to stand beside Felicia, continuing before Grayson could reply. "If you don't agree to allow Felicia and I to stay, I'll just have Theodore tell me everything that was said after you leave."

"Not if I pay him for his services and request complete confidentiality."

Arabella's eyes turned stormy. "Fine, be that way. Felicia, would you care for a cup of tea? I have a lovely little parlor that I call my own. We can repair there while the gentlemen discuss their *manly* business."

Grayson nodded. "That might be for the best."

"Her parlor is actually a broom closet that provides the opportunity to pick up conversations throughout the office," Theodore said with an exasperated glance to Arabella before he turned back to Grayson. "Unless you've got something to tell me that really isn't fit for delicate ears—not that I'm remotely suggesting your ears are delicate, darling," he added with a smile to Arabella—"it might be easier to simply allow the ladies to stay so that we can get on with things."

It almost seemed as if Grayson was going to balk, but then he shrugged and blew out a breath. "I suppose I could skim over some of the nastier aspects."

That was hardly what Felicia had wanted to hear, but at least—given that he was gesturing toward the chairs she and Arabella had abandoned—it appeared they'd be allowed to stay, for the moment.

She resumed her seat, as did Arabella, and then Grayson settled back in his chair, took a moment where it appeared he was gathering his thoughts, and finally began to speak.

"While growing up, I was a wild and impetuous young man— your typical spoiled aristocrat, if you will. I spent my time, when I wasn't at the university, carousing through the city and causing all sorts of mayhem. My father finally had enough of my irresponsible ways and demanded I return to our main estate after I finished my studies. I, of course, balked. All of my friends were taking their Grand Tour, and I wanted to travel with them."

Theodore frowned. "A Grand Tour is far different from moving to China."

"True, but my father, having no idea how to handle me, opted to limit my funds so I wasn't financially able to take my Grand Tour. I was furious with him, and harsh words were spoken before I gathered up what little money I could scrape together and went off without another word."

He got up from his chair, moved to the window, looked out it for a moment, and then turned, his gaze settling on Arabella. "You and Eliza have gotten remarkably close since you've returned to town, but I doubt she's ever disclosed to anyone, except perhaps Hamilton, how poorly I treated her. I abandoned my own sister without a second thought and barely considered her at all the entire time I spent away." He released a bitter laugh. "I was busy securing myself a fortune of my own, you see."

"I'm fairly certain Eliza doesn't hold that against you," Arabella said softly.

"She should. Because of my immaturity, she was forced to deal with the death of my father, the abandonment of her fiancé, and the loss of a good portion of our fortune on her own."

Arabella lifted her chin. "Sometimes, Grayson, events happen for a reason. If you hadn't gone to China, Eliza would never have been forced to come to this country. She'd never have met, nor married, my brother. She's been given a wonderful life and has gained not only Hamilton, but Piper and Ben as well.

"You must realize how much she loves those children. I do hope I won't make you uncomfortable with what I'm about to say, given that you and I have never discussed matters of faith before, but I believe Eliza's life has turned out exactly how God meant it to be." She smiled. "I honestly don't believe Eliza holds your past against you, so perhaps it's time for you to let it go."

Grayson's eyes turned hard. "Unfortunately, that's not possible. My past has defined who I am, and I'm afraid there's no changing that." He moved from the window only to begin pacing around the room, seemingly unable, or unwilling, to meet anyone's eye.

"After I left England, I traveled for a good six months, and when I landed in Spain—almost out of money, I might add—my luck changed. At the time, I thought it had changed for the better, but in hindsight, it was the worst thing that could have happened to me."

He stopped pacing and stared at the floor. "I made the acquaintance of a young gentleman in Spain, a Mr. Francisco Coronado. He was from a prominent family and he, like me, possessed a taste for freedom. He had ample funds at his disposal and was more than willing to share, seeing as how he enjoyed my company and didn't want to travel alone. We both agreed we were far too young to be hampered with family responsibilities. I allowed him to convince me that China was the place to make our fortune, so away we went."

"How in the world did you get to China?" Felicia asked. "Isn't it a long journey from Spain?"

Grayson lifted his head and nodded, although he didn't meet her gaze. "It is a long journey, but again, we were young and thought we were on the greatest adventure of our life. We took our time getting there, sometimes traveling by coach, sometimes by horseback and occasionally by boat, but it was while we were traveling by coach that we met another gentleman who made us an offer we couldn't refuse, an opportunity of a lifetime, so to speak."

Arabella shifted in her chair. "Should we assume it was an opportunity of a rather shady nature?"

"It was a lucrative opportunity," Grayson countered, "an opportunity that turned out to be more dangerous than shady." He moved back to his seat and sat down, his shoulders drooping ever so slightly. "I accepted the gentleman's offer and became indebted to the Wu family, a powerful and ruthless Chinese family who were involved in an intricate exporting business."

Theodore narrowed his eyes. "Where did you fit in with this exporting business?"

"Well, that's a little complicated, but to put it as simply as possible, Francisco and I were chosen because Wu Wah Hing,

the head of the Wu family, needed the services of socially prominent gentlemen who could assist him with brokering deals with
shipping lines. It turned out that many captains flatly refused
to negotiate with Chinese businessmen, having a difficult time
understanding them and also believing the Chinese to be less
than trustworthy."

"And this Wu Wah Hing placed two men someone from his
company just happened to meet on a coach in incredibly important positions with little background information? What made
him trust you?" Theodore pressed.

"Well, Francisco and I had to agree to a . . . side deal." Grayson moved back to his seat, sat down, and began to take an
extreme interest in the crease marking his trousers. He finally
lifted his head. "I had to agree to marry Wu Wah Hing's eldest
daughter."

10

*G*rayson braced himself when Felicia jumped out of her chair, tripped over her gown, wobbled for a moment, and then advanced directly toward him.

His first instinct was to leap to his feet and dash out the door, but for some odd reason, her gaze had him pinned to his chair. He found he couldn't give in to his instinct to flee. In fact, he was having a remarkably difficult time even sucking in a single breath of air.

Even though he'd vowed to distance himself from her, he couldn't help but admit she was incredibly magnificent when she was in a foul frame of mind, what with her blue eyes shooting sparks and her cheeks flushed a becoming shade of pink. Those thoughts disappeared in a flash when she took one last step, got her foot tangled yet again in her skirt, and tumbled . . . straight into his lap.

The smell of state ale wafted from her hair, causing him to feel the strangest desire to laugh.

Knowing full well Felicia would be unable to appreciate his

amusement, he grabbed hold of her shoulders and tried to pull her out of his lap, his desire to get her a safe distance away from him increasing when he suddenly realized the warmth from her body was beginning to play havoc with his senses. To his relief, Theodore came to his rescue, lifting Felicia up easily by the waist and plopping her down on her feet a second later.

Felicia, to give her credit, appeared perfectly composed after her less than graceful plunge. She patted her hair, sent Theodore a lovely smile, and looked down her nose at him. "Did I understand you correctly? Your marriage was nothing more than a business opportunity?"

Most women who blushed got rather splotchy, but not Felicia. Her temper had resulted in a lovely pink glow over her entire face, drawing attention once again to her startling eyes.

"Well?" Felicia prompted.

Grayson cleared his throat. "Well, yes. Soon after our introduction to the Wu family, Wu Wah Hing presented me with a surprising proposition—marriage into the family. I know it sounds mercenary, but if it makes you feel any better, I was doing Lin a favor by agreeing to marry her." He swallowed. "She wasn't considered very attractive, you see."

Felicia's only response was a sharp intake of breath.

He cleared his throat yet again and continued, knowing he had no choice but to get everything out in the open, or at least the more pertinent parts. "China is a completely different world from what we're used to. Women are not well thought of to begin with, and when one is not pleasing to the eye, she's often neglected.

"Unfortunately for Lin, she was the eldest daughter, and as such, she was expected to marry before any of her younger sisters could take husbands. Because she was unattractive, she'd had no suitors, so Wu Wah Hing proposed that if I married Lin, he would turn over a large amount of gold to me *and* the responsibility of securing new shipping routes for the family business. It was an opportunity that benefited everyone."

Arabella frowned. "Why wasn't that Francisco fellow asked to marry Lin?"

"He wanted to marry Mei, the other daughter Wu Wah Hing wanted to get off his hands. Mei was far more attractive than Lin, and since Francisco had been the one to fund our expedition to China, he insisted it was only fair that he be allowed to marry the attractive sister and leave Lin to me."

"Lovely taste in traveling companions you had there, Grayson," Felicia said, sarcasm dripping from her every word. "Did you ever consider how humiliating it must have been for Lin to marry a man who was only doing so for personal gain?"

"I never got the impression she was humiliated by our marriage, Felicia, only that she appreciated having been given a means to escape her father's constant belittlement. I must admit I'm not entirely certain about that though. As I mentioned before, I knew nothing of the Chinese language. But she was never abused after entering into marriage to me—not from her relatives, and certainly not from me." He cleared his throat. "It was a marriage in name only."

Complete silence settled over the room, causing Grayson to wince. He wasn't certain he should have let that little tidbit escape, but now that it had, he was—

"Explain Ming," Felicia demanded. "Is she illegitimate?"

"No, she's not."

Felicia blinked, and then her eyes widened. "You had more than one wife?"

Her incredulous tone saddened him, as did her apparent assumption he would be capable of assembling a harem.

"I freely admit my behavior in China is not something I'm proud of, but I never stooped so low as to marry more than one woman."

Felicia considered him for a long moment, plopped back down in her chair, folded her arms across her chest, and simply stared at him, apparently waiting for him to continue.

He was somewhat hesitant to do so, knowing that what he still had to say was far more troubling than his marriage to Lin and his relationship to Ming.

"Ming is Francisco's child. Francisco and Mei were killed along with Lin, and I took responsibility for their daughter," he finally admitted. "When I left China, I decided it would be easier all the way around if I simply let people believe she was mine."

"Why didn't Mei's father take responsibility for the child?" Theodore asked. "Ming is his granddaughter, after all."

Grayson forced himself to continue, knowing that to do so was going to cause him quite a bit of discomfort and might, perhaps, lose him the friendship of the people currently sitting in the room. "The night Francisco, Mei, and Lin were killed, they weren't the only ones who lost their lives. Everyone connected to the Wu family was murdered—except for me and Ming, that is."

He drew in a breath, slowly released it, and looked up at the ceiling, unwilling to see the horror in everyone's eyes as he continued his tale. "The Wu family wielded incredible power in China, and yet they were the object of envy amongst their competitors, especially the Zang family. I believe this family took exception to one of our acquisitions, and so . . . they attacked the estate and slaughtered every person there, setting the buildings on fire after they finished, which burned all the bodies beyond recognition."

"But . . . how did you manage to escape?" Felicia's question was barely a whisper.

Grayson forced himself to meet her gaze. "I was not there at the time of the attack. I was dealing with a captain who wanted to renegotiate his terms, and the meeting went much longer than I'd expected." He tilted his head. "I was beyond annoyed with the captain at the time, but now I'm remarkably grateful he was so difficult. If it hadn't been for him, I'd have been killed as well."

Arabella sat forward. "How did you end up with Ming?"

"After I finished with the captain, I headed home, but it wasn't long before I spotted the flames. Licks of fire were traveling high into the sky directly over the Wu family's grand estate.

"The compound was empty when I arrived, the fire consuming everything in sight. As I stood amidst the flames, I realized the destruction had to have been caused by one of our rivals—and my life was in danger because someone had gone to great lengths to wipe out the entire Wu family. Even though I was only a son-in-law, I was considered part of that family. I returned to where I'd left my horse, already having made the decision to leave China as quickly as possible."

He looked up at the shocked faces surrounding him. "That's when I found Ming. She was just standing there, in the midst of all that chaos, her little face streaked with soot, jabbering in the way two-year-olds do. She was the only true Wu left alive, which meant her life was in great peril too. I scooped her up, headed for the docks, and paid a small fortune to get us safely out of China."

Theodore began to drum his fingers against the arm of the chair. "She's the heir to the Wu fortune, isn't she? That's why her life would have been in such peril."

"She might be, although the thought has crossed my mind that I might actually be an heir as well since I was Wu Wah Hing's son-in-law."

Theodore's gaze sharpened. "Would these rivals of the Wu family bother to track you down all the way to America?"

"I don't know why they would, especially since I've given no indication I'd ever try to claim any part of the Wu fortune—for

Ming or myself. However, the Chinese do seem to hold revenge close to their hearts, and they might try to eliminate me and Ming simply to complete their vendetta against the Wu family."

"That could explain the interest you drew from those Chinese men in the pub," Theodore said.

Grayson shifted in his seat. "There is one other possibility. I left China with a rather large fortune in gems from Wu Wah Hing's office down at the docks. I figured Ming deserved some type of inheritance, and those gems are rightfully hers, given to the Wu family generations ago by an emperor who'd been pleased with services rendered." He released a breath. "Upon further reflection though, considering the attention I garnered today, I have to wonder if perhaps I should have left Ming's inheritance behind, because someone probably knows those gems went missing, and those gems are worth the time and expense to cross an ocean after them."

Felicia sucked in a sharp breath. "We should go fetch Ming immediately."

"I've already seen to Ming's protection," Grayson said. "I hired guards to watch out for her the moment we reached England. They traveled with us here, and believe me, they're the very best. I'm more worried that someone might have realized you were with . . ." His voice trailed off when rapid footsteps suddenly sounded in the hallway.

"Hello? Is anyone here?"

Grayson immediately rose to his feet when Ruth Murdock sailed into the room, followed by Jeffrey. She stopped and smiled at everyone before she set her sights on her daughter. "Jeffrey and I were delivering some of the pies you couldn't fit in your cart today when we just happened to see your pony cart parked outside and . . ." She stopped talking and frowned. "What, pray tell, are you doing once again dressed in your old style, and what have you done with your hair?"

Felicia smoothed down the skirt of the opera gown and narrowed her eyes at her mother. "I have never, ever, worn a gown like this. Well . . . not before today."

Ruth ignored the statement as she leaned forward. "Is that ale I smell?"

"It might be a little ale," Felicia admitted slowly before she brightened. "Did you know that ale is the latest remedy for controlling curl in a person's hair?"

Ruth ignored the statement. "What have you gotten yourself into now, Felicia?"

"It wasn't intentional, and I certainly didn't plan on becoming involved in a brawl in the midst of that pub."

Ruth's mouth formed the word *pub* before she spun around, looked at Arabella, then Theodore, and then settled her sights on Grayson. "Since you have what appears to be blood on your shirt and your clothing is shredded, Mr. Sumner, may I assume you've shared the company of my daughter today?"

He refused to wince. "I must admit that I have, Mrs. Murdock."

"And did you encourage my child to go into a pub?"

"He didn't encourage me, Mother," Felicia said, rising to her feet. "I went in there all by myself. Grayson just happened to be trailing me at the time and followed me into the pub, apparently because he felt it wasn't a suitable place for me to go, especially unescorted."

She smiled and nodded to him. "It was a fortuitous circumstance indeed that he followed me there, especially since I attracted a wee bit of attention, which might have caused the brawl in the first place."

Ruth tapped her finger on her chin, and her eyes turned speculative. "Tell me, Mr. Sumner, why *were* you following my daughter?"

"Ah, well, you see . . ."

"He wanted to apologize to me for his behavior a few days ago," Felicia explained before he could finish.

The speculation turned to outrage. "You didn't tell me you'd seen Grayson a few days ago."

"Her sneaky ways have apparently come back to her," Jeffrey proclaimed, speaking for the first time. "I always knew they would, once she abandoned her desire to become a minister's wife and returned to her normal self."

Felicia lifted her chin. "I've never had sneaky ways, Jeffrey. Mischievous, perhaps, but never sneaky."

"Was it your mischievous ways that caused you to forget to mention your rendezvous with Grayson?" Ruth demanded.

"I did not have a 'rendezvous' with Grayson, Mother. He simply joined Agatha and me for lunch. It was completely innocent."

"If it was so innocent, why did he feel the need to follow you today in order to apologize?"

"Mother, you're reading entirely too much into this."

"You're covered in ale and wearing a dress you weren't wearing when you left the house today. I don't think I've even begun to start reading enough into this."

Grayson couldn't help but feel a stab of sympathy for Felicia. Granted, she had gone willingly into the pub on her own, but what had happened in there, and the danger she might even now be facing, was not her fault. It was his, pure and simple. He moved to Ruth's side and touched her arm. "I take full responsibility for your daughter's condition, Mrs. Murdock. It's my fault she's covered in ale."

Jeffrey let out a sound that seemed almost a growl. "You dumped ale on my sister?"

Grayson glanced to Jeffrey's now-fisted hands and couldn't really say he blamed the gentleman for his anger. Felicia was not looking her best, nor had they apparently explained the situation well. He opened his mouth to add more details, but before he could get a single word out, Felicia stepped forward and shook her finger at her brother.

"Of course Grayson didn't dump ale on my head. I dumped the ale on myself when I hit that man over the head with a full tankard of the substance."

Grayson knew even before Ruth turned red in the face and began yelling that Felicia's statement had been exactly the wrong thing to say.

11

*M*inutes later, Felicia shifted on the seat of the pony cart and swiveled her head, a distinct flash of disgruntlement settling over her when she saw the rather ferocious gentleman Theodore had sent to guard her trailing her cart from a discreet distance. Why she even needed a guard was still a little confusing because the discussion they'd been having regarding Grayson's past had come to an abrupt end the moment Ruth had begun yelling.

It hadn't escaped her notice that Grayson had been relieved by the abrupt change in conversation. He'd used Ruth's dismay over her daughter's participation in a brawl as a means to get Felicia, accompanied by Jeffrey, quickly out of Theodore's office and on her way with barely another word said. She had heard Grayson tell Theodore something about "ruthless Chinese practices" and that "anyone who shared an association with him might be in danger," but since her mother had been delivering a blistering lecture to Felicia regarding the impropriety of a lady being in a pub, she hadn't been able to hear anything else.

No, she'd been sent on her way, none the wiser as to what was actually transpiring. She was decidedly put out with Grayson. He'd evidently made the decision she didn't need to be well informed but was simply supposed to go along with being saddled with a guard and not be given answers to her questions. Such as . . . why would anyone still believe him to be alive if the whole Wu family had been slaughtered and . . . what dastardly business had the Wu family, and Grayson, been involved with in the first place?

The guard took that moment to yell something in her and Jeffrey's direction, which caused her to turn front and center, not wanting to even acknowledge the man. But when she did so, she realized he'd been yelling out a warning, because poor Thor was drifting toward the wrong side of the street, directly into the path of a large delivery wagon. She uttered a small shriek, snapped her mouth shut when she remembered Thor didn't appreciate those, tugged on the reins, and breathed a sigh of relief when she missed the delivery wagon with inches to spare. The disgruntlement that had been plaguing her for quite some time turned to downright grumpiness when Jeffrey let out a laugh by her side, even as he gripped the edge of his seat all too dramatically before making an elaborate production of wiping nonexistent sweat from his brow.

"You could have told me Thor was veering into traffic."

Jeffrey grinned. "True, if I'd actually been paying attention. I don't think you noticed, but there was a delightful-looking young lady walking down the sidewalk. Since I foolishly forgot for a brief moment that you possess abysmal driving abilities, I was giving her my full attention instead of diligently looking after our lives."

That didn't deserve a response.

"You've landed yourself in what appears to be a fine mess," Jeffrey said cheerfully, causing her state of grumpiness to increase. "Why, I can't recall a time when Mother's been so distinctly put out with you. Makes for a nice change of pace, don't you think? She normally reserves her ire for me."

"She's never annoyed with you."

"Except for when she's nagging me to find a wife and lamenting the fact that I've apparently allowed so many fine catches to slip through my fingers."

Felicia wrinkled her brow. "Who did you allow to slip through your fingers?"

"Well, first there was Eliza, whom, if you must know, I found completely delightful, until Hamilton stole her right from under my nose; and then there was Arabella." Jeffrey released an exaggerated sigh. "She's entirely too beautiful and intelligent for her own good, which was why I was somewhat hesitant to approach her, but then Theodore swooped in and swept her off her feet, and now, well, I'm left with slim pickings. Not that Mother seems to understand that, as she nags me on an almost daily basis to choose a wife."

"She just wants to see you happy."

"I think she wants grandbabies to dangle on her knee. Since you haven't been kind enough to oblige her on that account, she's turned her full attention to me."

"I would have been perfectly content to settle down as a wife and mother by now, but . . . apparently I was completely misguided as to whom I should set my sights on. Now I'm quite certain the only mothering I'll ever get to experience will be to the dozen cats I keep seeing slinking around my feet in my future."

"My, my, you are feeling sorry for yourself today, aren't you? And just to remind you, you loathe cats, so I don't think that picture you keep seeing of yourself in the future will actually ever come to pass."

Felicia felt her lips curl ever so slightly. "Yes, well, I'm in no mood to contemplate my murky future at the moment, so let us return to your dilemma of securing yourself a wife so Mother will stop nagging you. What about Agatha Watson? She's charming, and I would adore having her as a sister-in-law."

"Agatha is indeed charming, but there is that pesky little problem of her being in love with Zayne Beckett. I'm not keen on pursuing a lady who has firmly placed her affection on another gentleman."

"I wasn't aware so many people knew about Agatha's affection for Zayne."

Jeffrey smiled. "I'm not certain many people are, but I took note of Agatha's interest in Zayne at Mother's Christmas ball."

A thread of discomfort sliced through her. She'd had no idea Jeffrey had been interested in Eliza, Arabella, or even Agatha, for that matter. In fact, she couldn't really remember a time she and Jeffrey had exchanged anything other than simple pleasantries over the past four years. Glancing at him out of the corner of her eye, she was shocked to discover he had distinct traces of white mixed in with his golden hair. She turned toward him, reached out her hand, and yanked one of the hairs out, bringing it closer to get a better view.

Jeffrey rubbed his head. "Honestly, Felicia, what's gotten into you? That hurt."

"I thought I saw some white in your hair."

"Of course you did. It's been turning white for years, but even though some take issue with white hair—you apparently included with that bunch—I prefer leaving it on my head, if it's all the same to you." He crossed his arms over his chest. "I've come to believe the white lends me an appearance of distinction."

She was shocked to realize she no longer knew Jeffrey, or truth be told, any of her brothers. How could she have possibly allowed that to happen? Granted, none of her brothers lived in the family mansion anymore, but they were frequent visitors, and they went to the same society events she attended.

Was it possible that she'd allowed her pursuit of Reverend Fraser and her charitable endeavors to stand in the way of establishing true relationships with everyone, including her own family?

For someone who'd made the staunch claim numerous times that she was a devoted woman of God, her actions did not lend much credence to that particular claim. God could hardly be pleased with her at the moment, considering her quest to obtain her own selfish desires had resulted in the dreadful neglect of her family and friends.

It was past time she corrected that situation and past time she began living a life that would actually allow her to become the faith-filled woman she'd been portraying herself as for years.

She closed her eyes for just a moment to send God a prayer, asking Him for forgiveness and assistance as she vowed to rectify her life and strive to do better in the future.

She opened her eyes and felt them widen in horror when she saw a man step directly in Thor's path. Before she could even think, Jeffrey wrenched the reins out of her hands and yanked them to the right, which resulted in Thor giving a single toss of his head right before he came to an immediate stop.

Felicia winced. "Oh dear, that was not well done of you. You've insulted poor Thor most grievously, and I doubt we'll be able to prod him into motion anytime in the foreseeable future."

"I wouldn't have had to do anything if you'd been paying attention. Really, Felicia, what could you have been thinking, closing your eyes while in the midst of driving? It wasn't the appropriate time to take a little snooze. And as for insulting Thor, I did no such thing."

"I wasn't sleeping, I was praying, and you insulted Thor by taking the reins. He only lets me drive him."

Jeffrey let out a grunt. "While I am not opposed to prayers, you might want to reconsider praying in the middle of a street while you're trying to drive. I'm not sure God will look too kindly on you running people over willy-nilly, even if you've done so because you were deep in prayer."

"Hmm, you might have just a wee bit of a point." Felicia reached over and took back the reins, gave them a wiggle, and then sighed when the wiggle did absolutely nothing to coerce Thor back into motion. "He's definitely annoyed."

Thor tossed his head as if he were in full agreement and then pawed an ancient hoof against the street.

"You'll have to apologize to him if you ever want to get him moving again."

"I most certainly will not. I did absolutely nothing worthy of an apology."

"Then prepare yourself for a long wait."

Jeffrey considered her for a moment, then turned his attention to Thor. "Sorry."

Thor tossed his head again but remained stubbornly still.

"You'll have to do better than that. Maybe you should get out and croon to him a bit, or you could try whistling in his ear. He loves that."

"I should have ridden home with Mother," Jeffrey muttered before he jumped off the seat, moved to Thor's head, and began crooning a bit of nonsense into the pony's ear.

"What is he doing?"

Felicia jumped in her seat, lifted a hand to her chest, and then raised her head to meet the gaze of the ferocious-looking guard Theodore had insisted accompany her home. "Good heavens, sir, you scared me half to death."

The guard didn't so much as blink or acknowledge that she'd even spoken. "You need to get out of the middle of the street. You're beginning to attract attention."

"That's a lovely suggestion, to be sure, but Thor has other ideas." Felicia summoned up a smile. "Perhaps you have an idea as to how to get my pony moving, Mr. . . . . er . . . ?"

"Blackheart."

"Is that really your name or is it one you've assumed to lend credence to your frightening demeanor?"

"Do you really think now is the appropriate time for idle chit-chat, especially since it appears Mr. Blackheart is in no mood to appreciate your odd sense of humor?" Jeffrey asked as he moved from Thor's head and climbed back into the cart.

"I must beg your pardon, Mr. Blackheart. I realize you've been given the daunting task of watching out for my sister—not that I claim to even understand why that's necessary—but I'm afraid we have no control over this animal at the moment, or ever, for that matter. Because of that, I'm afraid we're going to draw unwanted attention for some time to come, unless we can figure out a way to get the decrepit beast moving."

Mr. Blackheart, not speaking a single word, edged his horse up beside Thor. He leaned over, slapped Thor soundly on the behind, and ignoring Felicia's sputters of outrage, eased his horse to the side. Thor let out a snort and jerked forward, his short little legs moving at a remarkably fast clip.

"Just wait until I get ahold of Theodore," Felicia said as she tightened her grip on the reins. "What could he have been thinking, assigning me such an unpleasant chap? Poor Thor will require weeks of rest and special oats to get over this trauma."

"Thor will be fine, as you very well know, but since he is almost moving at what some might call a gallop, I do believe we'll reach our destination sooner than I anticipated. Perhaps it would be prudent, before we meet up with Mother again, if you could explain to me a few things, such as why you've been given your own personal guard."

"I don't really know."

"Should I assume it has something to do with that brawl in the pub? Are Theodore and Grayson afraid you attracted someone's interest there and are simply being cautious regarding your welfare?"

"Well, I definitely attracted interest from quite a few gentlemen in that pub, but considering Grayson dispatched all of them, except for the one I hit over the head, I hardly think it's likely any of them were physically capable of following me off Mott Street." She blew out a breath. "I think I've been assigned the guard because of the Chinese men who came into the pub after Grayson had finished the fight."

"You've lost me. What do Chinese men and Grayson Sumner have in common?"

"Far too much from what little I've been able to understand."

Jeffrey shifted on the seat. "I'd forgotten he's recently returned from China. It almost sounds as if . . ."

"His past was somewhat disturbing?" Felicia finished for him.

"Exactly. I doubt we'll be able to sufficiently puzzle the mess out though, considering the limited facts we've been given. I'll try to track Theodore down later on today or tomorrow and see if he'll be able to explain matters to satisfaction, but until then, let me return to you."

"I don't believe that's necessary."

Jeffrey continued as if she hadn't spoken. "What in the world were you thinking, going into a pub on your own? I mean, it's evident you've decided to make some changes in your life ever since Reverend Fraser got married, but I don't think spending time in a pub—especially one on Mott Street—is exactly the way you should go about it."

"I didn't plan on going into a pub when I started out today." Felicia took a moment to steer Thor back to their side of the street before she shot a glance at Jeffrey, who was watching her with one brow raised. "If you must know, I only went to

Mott Street to drop off some of my old clothing at the Rogue Theater."

"And the members of that theater convinced you to go have a drink with them?"

Felicia rolled her eyes. "Of course not. Those gentlemen were too busy trying on my clothing when I left them to even think about extending me a drink."

Jeffrey grinned. "I'm not even going to ask why that occurred."

"It does sound odd, but they're soon to be performing a farce, which I think is why they were so pleased with my clothing, but I digress. When I got back to Thor, he turned obstinate and refused to move, and in the past, if I walked away from him and allowed him to believe I was going to abandon him, he was much more apt to cooperate when I finally returned to his side."

"So you went strolling down Mott Street in order to get Thor to turn from obstinate to accommodating? Have you lost your mind?"

Felicia lifted her chin. "I've been traveling around the city, and the seedier parts of the city at that, for years. I've never run into a problem. In fact, most of the time it appeared to me that people, especially gentlemen, went out of their way to extend me a wide berth."

Jeffrey simply stared at her for a moment, the intensity of his gaze causing her to return her attention to the road—not that she really needed to do so, considering Thor was seemingly running out of energy and was now barely moving.

"Felicia, I do adore you, and I hope you'll remember that when I tell you that the reason gentlemen gave you such a wide berth was because, well, given your peculiar fashions over the past four years, I'm afraid you've caused people to believe you're a little insane."

Her lips began to curl. "I didn't look that bad."

"I'm afraid you did. But now, since you've abandoned those atrocious fashions, and you're wearing hats—well, when you haven't misplaced them—that allow a person to see your face, you've once again become the beautiful lady you were always meant to be. That means no more traveling around to the seedy parts of the city unescorted."

Tears caused her vision to go a little misty. "I do think that's quite the nicest thing you've ever said to me."

Jeffrey placed his hand over hers. "I'm sure you're mistaken, but that's neither here nor there. Getting back to the pub, what possessed you to go in there?"

"It was all very innocent."

"I somehow doubt that, but continue."

All traces of tears disappeared in a flash. "While I was waiting for Thor to come to the belief I'd abandoned him, I saw an elderly gentleman get his cane stuck in a hole, and then he stumbled and fell to one knee. I couldn't leave him like that, could I?"

"If you were on Mott Street, certainly."

"Anyway," Felicia continued, "I went to his assistance, and then he insisted on purchasing me a drink after I helped him into the pub. It would have been rude to disappoint him, and he was looking at me ever so hopefully that I just couldn't refuse him, and . . . that's where Grayson found me."

"He just happened to be in the same derelict pub that you found yourself in?"

"No, as I told you and Mother—although it seems you might not have been paying attention to me—Grayson had been following me."

Right then and there, Jeffrey turned into the consummate older brother. "It appears I'm going to have to have a little chat with Grayson and find out exactly why he would be following you around." His eyes narrowed. "Don't think I haven't noticed that he watches you as if you're a tasty treat he wants to snap up."

She would not allow herself to consider why that notion caused pleasure to course over her. "He most certainly does not."

Jeffrey's eyes narrowed another fraction. "You watch him the same way."

Felicia opened her mouth, intent on arguing that ridiculous point, but then snapped it shut. Did she look at Grayson as if he were a tasty treat? Granted, he was incredibly handsome, and his good looks did cause a person to look at him every now and again, but Theodore Wilder was incredibly handsome as well, yet she knew for certain she'd never looked at him as a tasty treat.

What was it about Grayson that caused her to watch him so consistently? It had to be something other than his looks.

Maybe it was simply because he'd come to her rescue more than once, which, if she were honest with herself, made him incredibly appealing, almost as appealing as . . . cake. She adored cake, especially chocolate—loved the taste of it, and it definitely was a treat—but did she look at Grayson the same way?

"If I wasn't certain he'd just put your life in danger, and certain it's hardly appropriate for any gentleman to follow you about the city, I'd almost encourage you to further your association with him."

Felicia blinked. "I beg your pardon?"

"He suits you, strange as that may seem, suits you in a manner Reverend Fraser never did."

All lingering thoughts of cake evaporated in a split second. "I thought Reverend Fraser would suit me well because he possesses such a strong faith."

"You don't need to set your sights on a minister to ensure you end up with a gentleman of faith, Felicia. Why, if that were the case, there'd be very few Christian ladies actually married."

"I don't think Grayson possesses any faith."

There. She'd said it, out loud. She hadn't even realized that had been bothering her, but evidently it had been lurking in the back of her mind all along, mixed in with her somewhat concerning attraction for the man.

"You might be right, but have you even asked him what he believes?"

"Well, no."

"Then I wouldn't simply make the assumption he has no faith. Many people, myself included, aren't comfortable discussing matters of faith on a regular basis. Perhaps he's the type who just keeps his thoughts about God to himself."

"But . . . he's no Reverend Fraser."

"It would be difficult for any gentleman to live up to the esteemed Reverend Fraser, but the man is no longer available, and forgive me for being direct—he was never meant for you. You would have driven the poor man batty within weeks of spending any great amount of time alone together.

"Miss Hampton, or rather, Mrs. Fraser, is a demure young lady, whereas you . . . you've played a rather convincing role of it over the past few years, but you're not demure, Felicia. Even though you've disguised it well, within you lurks the soul of an adventurous lady, and you'll never be happy until you embrace that."

While her brother had gained white hair with age, he'd evidently lost part of his mind in the process.

"Is that why you think I'd do well to cultivate an alliance with Grayson? Do you find him an adventurous gentleman?"

"I never suggested you form an alliance with the gentleman—especially since, again, he seems to be responsible for placing you in danger. However, I do think he's an adventurous sort, or perhaps a better term would be *worldly*, and I have the impression that at heart he's a good man."

Thor took that moment to turn on his own accord into a dirt

alley, effectively ending the conversation when Felicia realized they'd somehow reached home.

A groom ran out to greet them, and much to Felicia's amusement, after she climbed down from the cart with Jeffrey's assistance, Thor, rather than balking at the groom taking the reins, allowed the man to lead him away, his ears drooping and his demeanor forlorn.

She smiled and took the arm Jeffrey offered her, walking with him up the pebbled path toward the house. "I bet Mother beat us home," she said, pausing before the front door.

"I'm sure she did, and I'm sure she's used the time alone to craft a suitable lecture to give you once we step inside." He grinned. "Perhaps I should bid you a good day now and avoid all the drama that's sure to erupt."

"Don't be a coward," she said, gripping his arm tighter and prodding him forward, pausing again when the front door opened and, surprisingly, Agatha stepped out.

"It's about time. Your mother got home ages ago, and I must say, she's in an unusual frame of mind."

Felicia dropped her hold on Jeffrey and stepped forward, giving Agatha a quick hug and then releasing her as a grin stole over her face. "Thor was being difficult."

"Of course he was," Agatha said with a returning grin before she turned to Jeffrey. "It's good to see you, Mr. Murdock."

"It's lovely to see you as well, Miss Watson."

It really was unfortunate Agatha's affections were firmly centered on Zayne. She would have made a more than excellent sister-in-law.

"To what do I owe this unexpected pleasure?" Felicia asked as she took Agatha's arm and Jeffrey took her other, and together they stepped through the door and into the house, stopping for a moment in the entranceway.

For a second, Agatha's eyes went stormy, but then she blinked and the storminess disappeared. "Gloria Beckett came to pay my mother a visit, and the two of them immediately turned their attention to talk of the upcoming ball. I soon found I needed an escape to, ah, more peaceful surroundings, so I thought I'd come over here and see if you were home."

Here was further proof that Agatha had not completely abandoned her feelings for Zayne and was, indeed, bothered by his impending departure.

"However," Agatha continued with a cheerful grin, "when I arrived, I found your mother in an agitated state, but since she wouldn't divulge to me the reason for her mutters, of which there have been many, I'm afraid I have no idea what has sent her into such a tizzy." She frowned. "What is that smell?"

Jeffrey laughed. "I'm afraid it's my sister." He shook his head. "I was thankful we were in an open pony cart. Otherwise, well, I'm afraid her scent might have upset my tender stomach."

Felicia glared at him. "And here I was just thinking how delightful you'd become with age, when in reality, you're still the annoying little boy who used to torment me endlessly."

She switched her attention back to Agatha, who was staring at her with what could only be described as pure horror on her beautiful face. "It's only a bit of ale, Agatha—nothing to warrant any concern."

"I'm not concerned about the ale, although I'm sure that's a riveting story. Why have you abandoned your lovely new wardrobe and gone to back to your former style?"

Honestly, her wardrobe hadn't been *that* revolting.

"This isn't my gown, Agatha. Arabella lent it to me because my gown was soaked with ale and other nasty things—mostly blood." When Agatha's eyes grew huge, she hurried to say, "But it wasn't mine."

"Thank goodness for that, and thank goodness that isn't one of your old gowns. I was worried we were going to have to start from scratch." Agatha considered Felicia for a moment. "Why does that gown look so familiar?"

"It's the one Arabella wore the night the two of you got carted off to jail."

Jeffrey blinked at Agatha. "I never heard about you and Arabella getting carted off to jail."

"I'm not surprised," Agatha said. "My parents, along with Arabella's, have done their best to keep the matter hushed up, but I assure you, it was all a huge misunderstanding—as was the first time I landed in jail."

Felicia released a dramatic sigh. "I've never even had the pleasure of landing in jail once, let alone twice."

"Don't let Mother hear you say that," Jeffrey muttered. "And speaking of Mother, I suppose, being the wonderful older brother I am, I should go pave the way for you—especially since, from what Agatha said, she's still fit to be tied. Where is she? In the drawing room?"

"She's in the ballroom," Agatha said. "I think she needed a large space that would allow her plenty of room to pace back and forth as she mutters things like 'I'm a horrible mother' and 'Where did I go wrong?'"

Jeffrey grinned. "Well, this should be a cheerful experience." With that, he strode to the curving staircase and bounded up it, leaving Felicia standing in the entranceway with Agatha.

"I don't envy him breaking the ice with Mother."

"I can't say I do either," Agatha replied. "I don't believe I've ever seen your mother quite like this. Do you know that while I was waiting for you, she consumed three cups of tea and four pieces of cake?" Her eyes began to sparkle. "When I set down the plate of cake she thrust at me—before I'd taken one bite, I might add—she absconded with it."

"She's always been a nervous eater, but perhaps I can hope the cake has put her in a better frame of mind, or maybe caused her to forget some of the more distressing things she learned today."

"She muttered something about a pub, Chinese men, and Theodore setting a guard to watch you."

"Good heavens, I forgot all about Mr. Blackheart." Felicia walked back to the door and opened it. Sure enough, there was Mr. Blackheart, sitting on his horse and staring, unblinking it seemed, at the house. She sent him a nod and closed the door. "He's right outside."

Agatha arched one delicate brow. "Are you going to explain to me what happened? I fear I must tell you that when we heard you'd returned, your mother discontinued muttering just long enough to instruct me to get all the pesky details out of you."

"Felicia."

Felicia turned her attention to the stairs and found Ruth at the top of them, glaring down at her.

"Why are you dawdling down there with Agatha while I've been forced to wait forever to speak with you? You must realize I still have numerous things I long to say and numerous questions that have yet to be answered."

"I thought Jeffrey was going to start explaining."

"He knows just about as much as I do—which isn't much."

Felicia refused to sigh. "I'll be right up. Although I must warn you, Jeffrey's made numerous comments regarding my smell. I'm afraid my less than pleasant odor might linger awhile in the ballroom. I wouldn't be surprised if it lingered all the way to the next ball you host."

"Perhaps it would be for the best if you were to bathe first. Take Agatha with you."

"I don't believe Agatha needs to take a bath. She looks remarkably well groomed and smells pleasantly of lemons."

"Do not try to humor me, my dear. You're in enough trouble as it is." Ruth directed her attention to Agatha. "Remember what I asked of you, and don't—I repeat, don't—disappoint me." With that, she turned on her heel and disappeared.

"And I thought *my* mother was scary," Agatha mumbled as she followed Felicia through the hallway, up one set of stairs and then another, until they finally reached Felicia's room. Agatha strode through the door, plopped down on a settee upholstered in deep blue, and smiled. "This is not what I imagined I'd find."

"Were you expecting something more dramatic?"

"I must admit I was."

Felicia smiled and moved toward her bathroom, turning around when she reached the door. "I won't be long."

"Don't hurry on my account," Agatha said as she lifted up her skirt, yanked a notebook from what appeared to be a string tied around her leg, dropped her skirt back into place, and leaned back against the settee. "I need to come up with some new story ideas, so I'll use the time it takes you to make yourself present-able to see if anything comes to me. I've been considering doing a feature on the less than effective sewage disposal systems in the tenement slums, but I'm not certain how much interest that story will garner from my editor, or my readers, for that matter."

An intriguing thought immediately sprang to mind. Felicia took a few steps toward Agatha and stopped. "Perhaps you could do a feature on the Chinese immigrants who've settled in the city, or the ones who've settled down to do business on Mott Street."

Agatha's eyes began to gleam. "Ah, the opium dens. Now, that might make a compelling story, but . . ." Her eyes lost their gleam as they narrowed on Felicia. "Why would you think to bring up opium dens?"

"I didn't bring up opium dens. I brought up the Chinese who live or work on Mott Street."

Agatha waved a hand in the air. "They're one and the same, Felicia. Everyone knows that."

Of course they were. How could she have neglected to consider that? Here she'd been confused about Grayson being somewhat evasive concerning the business he'd done for the Wu family, but it had been in front of her face the entire time—starting with Grayson's warning her about Posey's. He'd been, in some capacity, involved with the opium trade.

She bit her lip. "What do you know of Grayson's past?"

"Truthfully, not much, except for the fact that he lived in China and evidently was able to make a rather large fortune there."

"And how do you think he made that fortune?"

Agatha's eyes widened. "Good heavens, I never really considered it before, but surely you're not suggesting he was involved in the opium trade, are you?"

"I wouldn't go as far as to say I'm suggesting it, but it is possible . . . isn't it?" She walked over to a chair and sat down. "What do you know about those opium dens on Mott Street?"

"Well, they're opium dens and . . . a lot of people seem to like to visit them—even society people."

"Aren't they illegal?"

"I'm hardly an expert on the subject of opium, Felicia, but from what I understand . . . Hmm, no, I don't actually know the answer to that. I do know that the police occasionally make raids on them, probably when funds are running low, but for the most part, those dens are left undisturbed."

"So . . . chances would be slim, if you *were* to ever investigate one, that it would be raided. Right?"

"That's not just a rhetorical question, is it."

"Not really."

Agatha got up from the settee. "And if I were to investigate an opium den, could I expect you'd want to go with me?"

"Is that a rhetorical question?"

"Not in the least."

Felicia smiled. "Then yes, I would want to go with you. I have this peculiar feeling that answers to Grayson's past just might lie in the midst of those dens, or at least the den that's close to the Wild Rose."

"Visiting an opium den won't be pleasant—what with all the smoke I'm certain will be hanging in the air. Nor will it be pleasant if Grayson finds out. He won't thank either one of us for meddling."

"I'm willing to take my chances."

Agatha looked at her for a long moment. "All right, I'll look into it, but I'm warning you now, I have to get approval from my editor, and I'll need time to come up with a viable plan. We can't simply go wandering into an opium den without giving it some thought."

Excitement, mixed with trepidation, surged through Felicia's veins as she sent Agatha a grin. "I bet we're going to uncover a wonderful story for you."

Agatha sighed. "While that's normally my intent when searching out a story, this time I'm almost hoping I don't discover anything of interest."

As Felicia turned to finally retreat to her bathroom, she found there was a small part of her, the part slightly intrigued with Grayson, that was hoping exactly the same thing.

12

Contrary to what Agatha had said the day before, it hadn't taken her long to come up with a plan—especially after she'd traveled to the *New-York Tribune* and gotten an enthusiastic go-ahead from her editor. That enthusiasm was the reason Felicia was currently standing behind a privacy screen as the afternoon sun flooded Agatha's room, trying to squeeze into a pair of trousers that didn't seem to want to go over her curves. She gave them a sharp tug, got them over her hips, and was contemplating how she was going to get them to fasten when Mrs. Watson's voice suddenly sounded from the other side of the screen.

"Agatha, I picked up the most adorable . . . Good heavens, you're dressed like a man . . . again. I suppose the question I must ask now, considering I am your mother, is why are you dressed like a man?"

Felicia sucked in her stomach and managed to fasten the trousers before she stepped out from behind the screen. Cora Watson stood in the middle of the room, holding some type of garment in her hand as she stared at her daughter with what seemed like resignation in her eyes.

"No need to fret," Agatha said as she shrugged into a jacket and took a moment to button it up. "We're working on a story my editor has asked me to submit to him in the next few days, and that story requires a little snooping and disguises."

"We?" Cora pressed.

Felicia cleared her throat and stepped away from the privacy screen.

Cora swung around. "I do beg your pardon. I thought Agatha was alone. I'm Cora Watson, Agatha's mother."

Felicia flicked the spectacles she was wearing down her nose, wincing when the hair from the long mustache she'd attached to her lip got tangled in the wire, causing the tender skin of her upper lip to feel as if it were in danger of pulling off. She gingerly picked the hair out of the wire and felt the mustache droop over her lip. Evidently, she wasn't proficient with the special glue Agatha had given her. She looked up, realized Mrs. Watson was regarding her somewhat oddly, and summoned a smile. "Mrs. Watson, it's me—Felicia Murdock."

Cora's face paled. "Good gracious, child, what are *you* doing involved in one of my daughter's schemes?"

It was becoming only too clear that over the last four years she'd done a rather good job of convincing *everyone* she lacked an adventurous spirit.

"Felicia's agreed to be my assistant today," Agatha said, sparing Felicia a response. "I've given her the task of recording details in my notebook because I discovered she has lovely penmanship."

Cora crossed her arms over her chest. "An unlikely story if I've ever heard one, but—heed me well, Agatha—do not, under any circumstances, allow anything to happen which will result in the two of you being carted off to jail. I highly doubt

Ruth Murdock would appreciate being summoned to post bail for Felicia. She's always been rather proud of the fact that her daughter is a stickler for the proprieties."

An unusual desire to be taken away in shackles and thrown into a dingy cell was immediate. Perhaps if she was carted off to jail, everyone would discontinue the absurd notion that she was so perfect.

It wasn't as if she wanted to be thought of as scandalous, but she was tired of being perfect, or at least pretending to be. The assumptions everyone had about her were getting rather bothersome.

"Mother, as I said before, there's absolutely no reason for you to fret. We're only going out to gather information for a story. It's not as if we're going to be dabbling in anything illegal. Besides, it's the middle of the day. How much trouble could we possibly find?"

Cora rolled her eyes. "I do believe I've heard all this before, young lady. You're the only person I know who has the propensity for getting arrested even when you're *not* breaking the law. The fact that it's the middle of the afternoon certainly won't ensure that the two of you won't end up in trouble."

"Hmm, interesting point, but to relieve your anxiety," Agatha continued rather loudly when Cora began to sputter, "Zayne's agreed to go with us."

Cora's sputters ceased immediately as she brightened, all signs of anxiety disappearing from her face. "Ah, well, that's lovely. I suppose I have no need to continue protesting so vehemently then. Zayne will keep the two of you in line."

"That might be giving the gentleman too much credit," Agatha muttered before she lifted her chin. "Tell me, are my whiskers on straight?"

"I truly never thought I'd be having that question asked by my daughter, but yes, they're straight." Cora smiled. "Now, tell me, dear, where are you, Felicia, and Zayne heading off to this afternoon?"

Felicia blinked. She'd come to the conclusion that Cora was a remarkably progressive mother, seemingly willing to allow her daughter to waltz off dressed like a man, but the tone of her voice, even though she was smiling, indicated she wasn't blasé about the matter at all. It seemed Cora had sprung the question out of the blue, most likely in an attempt to catch her daughter off guard.

It was rapidly apparent Agatha was quite used to her mother springing questions in just such a way, because she barely batted an eye as she dismissed the question with a breezy wave of her hand. "It would probably be for the best if I didn't allow you too many details, Mother. That way, if Mrs. Murdock just happens to show up on your doorstep, searching for Felicia, you truthfully won't be able to tell her our whereabouts. It certainly wouldn't help me ferret out all the facts I need for my story if Felicia's mother showed up on the scene."

Cora closed her eyes for a brief moment before opening them and settling her attention on Felicia. "Your mother isn't aware of what you intend to do?"

"My mother isn't actually speaking to me right now, so I didn't have an opportunity to explain to her my plans."

"I've never known your mother not to speak to someone. She's constantly speaking."

"I think she believes, if she gives me the cold shoulder, I'll reform my recent trying ways."

Agatha moved over to her side and patted her arm. "Speaking of your trying ways, Zayne believes his purpose in accompanying us today is to cheer you up. I told him you were somewhat distraught."

"Why would you tell him that?"

"I couldn't very well tell him exactly what we planned to do. He'd never have agreed to come along." She shot an innocent look to her mother. "Not that we're going to be in danger or anything."

"But I'm not distraught in the least," Felicia pointed out, even as Cora began sputtering once again.

"You're going to have to pretend you are, because I told Zayne you're a touch dismayed that Grayson isn't escorting you to the ball."

Felicia's mouth dropped open for a brief moment. "If you'll recall, Grayson and I never had set plans for him to escort me. You're the one who brought it up, and then he balked, only agreeing after you badgered him about it, but I never consented to go with him. I'm hardly dismayed about it. Besides, I have three brothers, all of whom are perfectly capable of escorting me to the ball."

"Yes, but they're your *brothers*."

Cora cleared her throat, quite loudly, and walked over to stand directly in front of Felicia, edging Agatha out of the way. "Am I to understand you and Grayson Sumner have formed an attachment?"

"Not at all."

"But he wanted to escort you to the ball?"

"No, your daughter tried to meddle and told him to escort me, but I refused." Felicia smiled. "Even if we'd planned on going together, I'm afraid that would no longer be possible since my mother is decidedly put out with the gentleman at the moment."

Cora frowned. "I thought she was put out with you."

"Oh, she is, but I do think she might be just a tad more annoyed with Grayson. He is the reason my life could be in danger, and he is the reason there's a very disturbing guard by the name of Mr. Blackheart dogging my every step."

Agatha took that moment to smack herself in the head, the action causing the wig she'd put over her hair to wobble. "I forgot all about Mr. Blackheart. He's certain to complicate matters."

Felicia shook her head. "No, he won't, because he didn't see me leave home. I climbed out a back window and snuck off down a side street."

"Why didn't you just walk out a back door?"

"I thought it was entirely more cloak-and-dagger to use the window. It helped me get into the right frame of mind for what we're about to do."

Agatha wrinkled her nose. "You're somewhat odd. You know that, don't you?"

"I'll take that as a compliment."

"It wasn't meant as such, but I have to tell you, Mr. Blackheart is not going to be happy in the least when he discovers you've given him the slip."

"I don't think Mr. Blackheart is ever happy."

Agatha grinned. "True, but he's incredibly loyal to Theodore and takes his job seriously. I've had him escort me to the tenement slums on numerous occasions, and while he is a dreary sort, he's very capable."

Cora began to tap her toe against the floor. "If he's so capable, I must ask why neither of you seemed to consider asking him to go with you today?"

"Oh, I don't think that would have been wise, Mrs. Watson," Felicia began when she realized Agatha didn't seem to have an answer available to her and had taken to staring at her reflection in the mirror, incredibly focused on making certain her whiskers were securely patted into place. "Mr. Blackheart seems to be the sort who believes in following a strict rulebook, and . . ." Felicia stuttered to a stop when Cora seemed to swell on the spot.

"Do not even tell me the two of you are going to be investigating brothels today." Cora rounded on Agatha. "Is that why you mentioned you didn't tell Zayne where you're going, knowing full well he'd balk?"

"We're not investigating brothels, Mother. I do plan on traveling back to some of those in the future, but not today."

"Where are you going, then?" Cora pressed.

"Mother, we've been over this, numerous times in fact. My position as a journalist for the *New-York Tribune* requires me to travel to all parts of the city, and some of those parts, if you knew exactly where I was going, are bound to distress you. Since I'm not willing to give up my position with the paper, and you and Father did finally agree that I should be allowed to pursue my dream, you're simply going to have to trust me and accept that I'm a responsible lady."

Cora narrowed her eyes. "Felicia's mother has not been given the courtesy of knowing what her daughter is getting into today."

Felicia stepped closer to Cora and laid a hand on her arm. "Mrs. Watson, forgive me, but I'm twenty-four years old. I'm quite old enough to make my own decisions without seeking out my mother's permission."

"You're twenty-four?"

"I reluctantly must admit to it."

"Then I suppose I really am going to have to hold my tongue and allow the two of you to get on with things. But I do expect both of you to promise me to be careful and to try your hardest to avoid arrest."

Felicia smiled. "We'll do our best."

Cora opened her mouth, but before she could give what was certain to be another piece of motherly advice, Agatha suddenly grinned and waved toward the door.

"Ah, Grace, I was wondering when you were going to stop lurking outside the door and join us."

Felicia watched as Agatha's younger sister sidled into the room, her appearance so similar to Agatha's that Felicia couldn't help but grin. By her shifty expression, much like the one Agatha frequently wore, it was clear that Grace had been lurking for quite some time.

Grace came to stop in front of Agatha and gave Agatha's beard a tug. "That's an interesting disguise. You do realize that your wig doesn't match your beard though, don't you?"

"I had to work with what was available, and no one will actually see much of my wig once I get my hat into place." Agatha gestured to Felicia. "What do you think of Felicia's costume?"

"Very nice, except those trousers are a bit tight." She smiled. "I'm Grace by the way, Grace Watson. I've seen you before, Miss Murdock, but I don't think we've ever been formally introduced." She lifted her chin. "I'm not old enough to come out into society quite yet."

Felicia smiled, unable to help herself from immediately adoring the young girl. She was completely charming, and Felicia knew that when she did reach the age where she could come out, New York would never be the same.

"It's a pleasure to meet you, Grace. Please, call me Felicia, and tell me, are my trousers really too tight?"

Agatha strode across the room and picked up what looked to be a gentleman's jacket, in a rather unusual shade of lime green. She tossed it to Felicia. "That should take care of the problem, but Grace is right, they are a touch snug. I hope they don't burst a seam."

"I didn't think about that," Felicia said, swiveling her head to try and gauge exactly how tight the fabric was stretched across her bottom. She shook out the coat, eyed it for a moment, and then tossed it on. "I don't believe I've ever seen a gentleman wear this particular color."

"At least you won't attract any attention from the ladies," Grace said with a laugh. She eyed Felicia for a moment, and then her face turned pink. "I saw your brother the other day on his horse, your brother Daniel."

Felicia felt her lips begin to curl, but she quickly stifled the urge to grin when she realized immediately why Grace had been lurking for such a long time outside the door. She'd probably been contemplating exactly how to bring Daniel—oh so casually—into the conversation, because it was obvious that, although Grace couldn't be more than eleven or twelve, she'd developed a wee bit of an infatuation for Felicia's younger brother.

Remembering all too well her first infatuation, with a boy by the name of Rupert, no less, Felicia paused to consider how she should reply.

While she'd been in the midst of her infatuation with Rupert, she'd trailed him around rather obviously, and that trailing had been noticed by Rupert's older sister—either that or he'd complained to her about Felicia's unwanted attention. His sister had been less than careful with her choice of words, ruthlessly telling Felicia that Rupert was far too old for her and only liked ladies who were possessed of grace and charm. She'd then warned that if Felicia didn't leave her brother alone, she'd be sorry indeed.

The embarrassment of that encounter lingered still, which was why Felicia needed to be very careful with Grace's tender young feelings.

She caught Grace's gaze and found the girl staring back at her rather intently. She summoned up a smile. "Daniel's just recently returned from Harvard, but I do believe he intends to head up to our summer home in Newport soon. After that, he's planning on traveling to Pittsburgh with our father in order to learn a bit about the family steel business."

Grace's slim shoulders sagged. "We don't have a summer home in Newport. Our house is on the Hudson." She brightened and looked to her mother. "We should buy a house in Newport. Why, I bet it would be a wonderful investment, and you know how Father dearly loves investing."

To give Cora credit, she barely batted an eye. "That's a wonderful idea, Grace, and I'll bring it up to your father at my earliest convenience."

Grace frowned. "How early is your earliest?"

"The next few years or so, but certainly before you turn eighteen."

Felicia swallowed a laugh, knowing full well that if Grace still had the same feelings for Daniel when she turned eighteen, Cora, being one of the most diligent matchmaking mothers in society, would not only speak to her husband, she'd make certain a house was bought in Newport as well. She'd probably go about trying to purchase the home right next to Felicia's family, even if that meant disposing of the family who currently owned the place.

"But, that's forever away," Grace said slowly.

Agatha nodded. "Indeed it is, but for now, how about if you help Felicia get that mustache back on properly?"

As a distracting factor, including Grace in their preparations worked wonders. Her shoulders straightened, her lips curved into a smile, and a moment later, she was holding a jar of glue as she considered Felicia's mustache. "How much do you think I should use?"

"I have no idea, but try to put on enough so I don't lose my mustache in the middle of our investigation," Felicia said. "That would be a sight, wouldn't it, if I were to lose my mustache in the midst of speaking with someone?"

Grace leaned closer, dabbed some glue on Felicia's upper lip and lowered her voice. "I know where the two of you are going."

Felicia turned to find Cora was engaged in adjusting Agatha's costume, but even so, she spoke softly. "How do you know that?"

"Agatha talks to herself when she's plotting, and I just happened to be standing right outside her door."

Felicia knew without a doubt she'd just discovered a kindred spirit. She leaned closer to Grace and lowered her voice even further. "While I can hardly lecture you for eavesdropping, seeing as how I used to do quite a bit of that myself in my younger years, it might be best if you didn't disclose that information to your mother. It'll only make her worry. Although . . . if your sister and I don't happen to return in the next day or so, feel free to tell everyone our destination."

Grace grinned. "You know, I heard Agatha say you're rather odd, but I don't find that to be the case at all." She pressed Felicia's mustache firmly into place and held it for a second. "I think it'll stay, but I'm afraid it might sting when you try to remove it. Hopefully it won't leave too much of a mark, although, with your fair complexion, you might be rather red for a while."

She really should have considered that before she'd encouraged Grace to plaster her mustache back on her face. Although her dress for the Beckett ball was red, she really didn't care to have a matching face. It would hardly allow her to impress . . .

She pushed that disturbing thought right out of her mind. Honestly, she had a dangerous assignment ahead of her, and the last thing she needed was Grayson and how he'd react to seeing her at the ball stomping around her mind.

"Are you all right?" Grace asked. "You've turned pink."

It was time to redirect the conversation. "Don't you have a younger sister? Where is she?"

Grace looked as if she wanted to continue discussing Felicia's pink face, but then she shrugged. "Lily's over at Mr. Hamilton Beckett's house. Eliza used to be our governess, before everyone learned she was an aristocrat and before she met up with Hamilton. Now that she's turned all respectable, Mother allows us to visit her."

Cora let out a sniff. "I never forbade you access to Eliza."

"You threw her out of our house," Agatha reminded her.

"Your father threw her out of the house," Cora corrected, "and you know full well it was a simple misunderstanding. I adore Eliza."

"You made her wear Aunt Mildred's hideous gown and attend one of your dinner parties," Grace added.

"And since that turned out incredibly well for her, seeing as that is where she met Hamilton, I don't understand why everyone still brings that up."

Agatha smiled. "We bring it up because it's amusing to watch your reaction." She turned to Felicia. "Grace and Lily have taken to helping Eliza entertain the children, especially since Ming's been spending a lot of time over there."

Grace nodded. "Ming has been driving everyone batty lately. Eliza keeps telling everyone it's just a stage."

"Why didn't you stay with Eliza and help if Ming's being so difficult?" Cora asked.

The shifty expression returned, causing Felicia to swallow a laugh.

Grace rolled her eyes. "Lily's much better at it than I am. Besides, I'm twelve. Lily's only ten, and she has nothing better to do with her time. I came home because . . . I need to find something to wear tomorrow night." The last part of the sentence came out very fast and somewhat mumbled.

Cora drew herself up. "And where, pray tell, do you think you'll be tomorrow night?"

"Eliza told me I could help their nanny watch the children during the ball."

Cora frowned. "You need to worry about what you're going to wear to Eliza's house?"

"I won't actually be at Eliza's house, Mother. Piper didn't want to miss out on the festivities, and since Zayne Beckett is her uncle and the ball's being held in his honor, Eliza felt it was acceptable to indulge her just this once."

"Hmm," Cora began. "Well, I'll allow you to go, but I better not find you shirking your duties and slipping into the ball."

"Piper's tricky, and you know she won't be content to peer over the banister. I might have to go after her, which means I'll have to be dressed appropriately."

"As long as it's not at your suggestion she makes a dash for it," Cora said dryly.

Grace opened her mouth, obviously to proclaim innocence in regard to that idea, but whatever she was about to say was interrupted when a housemaid stuck her head into the room.

To Felicia's surprise, the maid's eyes widened only a bit as she looked at Agatha, even though her lips were quivering ever so slightly, as if she were trying not to laugh.

"Begging your pardon, Miss Watson, but Mr. Zayne Beckett has arrived."

Grace stepped forward. "How does he look?"

The maid frowned. "What do you mean?"

"What's his disguise?"

"Oh, he's not wearing a disguise. He looks perfectly normal in a jacket, trousers, and appropriate hat."

Cora headed for the door. "I should go speak with him while you two finish up."

Agatha rushed to the door and blocked Cora's way. "I don't think there's any need for you to speak to him."

"He'll find it rude if he's made to wait without anyone keeping him company."

Agatha nodded to the maid. "Rosie, you should go keep Mr. Beckett company."

Rosie looked downright alarmed at that idea. "I don't think . . ."

"Ignore Agatha, Rosie. You may go back to whatever you were doing before you came up here," Cora said, which had Rosie spinning on her heel and disappearing a second later. "Honestly, Agatha, sometimes you make the most outlandish demands, asking poor Rosie to entertain Mr. Beckett, one of the most socially prominent gentlemen in New York."

"I'd rather she speak with him than you. You know you'll end up badgering him about going out west to join Miss Collins."

"I wouldn't dream of it," Cora said before she sailed out of the room without another word.

Agatha's brow wrinkled. "We'd better hurry. I can't allow Mother to spend too much time alone with Zayne. The good Lord alone knows what she'll say, and I can guarantee you, whatever she says will be certain to cause me no small amount of embarrassment." She hurried over to a chair and plucked up an opera gown that greatly resembled the one Arabella had previously lent Felicia.

"What are you going to do with that?" Felicia asked.

"It's Zayne's costume."

Felicia exchanged a glance with Grace, who was grinning. She turned back to Agatha. "Is there really a need to have Zayne dress up as a lady, or dress up at all, for that matter?"

"Of course there is. I've thought it out thoroughly, and since he's a rather large gentleman, and we're rather small ladies who are trying to pass ourselves off as men, well, it will only bring more attention to us if we're in the company of a normally dressed man. If he goes as a lady, his height alone will garner attention, and then no one will even notice us, and we'll be able to proceed with our investigation with relatively little fuss."

Felicia rolled her eyes. "That was a pretty speech indeed, but are you sure you're not trying to force Zayne to wear a gown as a subtle attempt at revenge over his leaving New York to join Miss Collins?"

Agatha's eyes hardened for just a second, but then she waved a hand in the air. "That idea never entered my mind." She grabbed a hat from a table, plopped it on top of the dress, and marched out of the room.

"I wonder how Zayne will react when he gets a gander at that gown," Grace said as she took Felicia's arm and they began to follow after Agatha.

They didn't have long to wonder.

13

A haze of smoke burned Grayson's eyes, and a persistent itch plagued his scalp. He pushed a finger under the edge of the wig he was wearing and rubbed it back and forth, his movement stilling when he noticed a patron of Posey's watching him through bleary eyes. Realizing his scratching was causing his red locks to wiggle, he lowered his hand and sent the patron a smile.

He really couldn't say he blamed the man when he blinked and rubbed his eyes. It wasn't every day one saw a lady well over six feet tall slouching against a wall.

Thankfully, the man was soon distracted by the appearance of an opium pipe, which allowed Grayson to direct his attention back to the crowd. It came as no surprise that there was little space unoccupied. Customers lounged on the floor, reclining on questionable-looking pillows, drawing smoke into their mouths from long, thin pipes with balls on the ends of them. The stench from the opium was overpowering, and Grayson felt slightly light-headed due to the fumes that hovered in the air.

He'd never been tempted to try opium, even though he'd been around it daily when he lived in China. There was just something off-putting about it—from the smell, to the smoke, to the idea that it caused men, and quite a few ladies, to descend into a permanent state of oblivion, their only goal in life being that of enjoying their next pipe.

A thread of regret stole through him as his gaze traveled over his surroundings. It had been his job to secure transportation for the opium the Wu family produced, and he'd been very good at his job, securing new trade routes to faraway countries, one of those countries being America.

How many lives had he been responsible for ruining while he'd been in the midst of securing himself a fortune?

Pushing aside that unanswerable question, he shoved away from the wall, knowing he would never complete his mission if he continued observing people instead of mingling with them. He stepped forward, hoping none of the men in Posey's would take his mingling as a sign he would welcome their attentions. Quite frankly, he had no idea how he'd react if someone extended him a proposition.

It wasn't that he thought he made a lovely lady, but opium was known to cause hallucinations in some people, and it would be just his luck if some poor soul decided he was attractive.

He stepped over a gentleman lying on the floor and edged around another who was rocking back and forth, his eyes vacant and an odd humming noise coming out of his mouth. He was forced to a stop when a group of men blocked his way, none of them seeming to realize Grayson wanted to pass, their attention solely fixed on a pipe they were passing around between them.

If he hadn't been dressed like a woman, he would have simply jostled his way through them, but he didn't want to draw more attention to himself than was strictly necessary. He turned on his heel and headed back in the direction he'd just come, reaching an empty spot against the wall a moment later. He leaned against it and twitched the skirt of his garish red gown back into place, effectively hiding his less-than-feminine boots.

He hadn't intended to dress as a lady, even though he'd known he would have to disguise his appearance somewhat in order to snoop around Posey's in an attempt to ferret out a bit of information to give to Theodore. He'd been thinking more on the lines of obtaining a beard and perhaps a mustache, but then he'd had the brilliant idea to request assistance from the gentlemen he'd met from the Rogue's Theater. He'd sent them a note bright and early that morning inquiring whether or not they'd be interested in helping him, adding in that note that he'd be more than happy to pay them for their time and counsel. To his amazement, instead of sending him a return reply, the two men who'd escorted Felicia back to Theodore's had simply shown up on his doorstep a few hours later, lugging a huge trunk between them, smiles of obvious delight on their faces.

Evidently money was always short when one worked in theater, and they'd been only too happy to relieve him of his funds as they went about disguising him.

Before he'd even had the presence of mind to balk, they'd stuffed him into the red gown—stating too gleefully that it was the only one they had on hand that would fit him—smothered his face in rouge after they'd made him shave it, attached some gooey substance to his eyelashes that he thought made him look as if he had caterpillars hanging over his eyes, and proclaimed him perfect.

A second later, one of the men eyed him closely, declared that Grayson wasn't quite perfect, and made the outlandish suggestion that he would need to shave his chest.

Grayson had balked then, even though he realized that ladies weren't normally possessed of hair on their chest. After conferring with the men, a compromise was struck. They pulled a shawl out of the trunk and wrapped it securely around his shoulders and chest, and fastened it with a lovely cameo brooch. The only thing that hadn't been in the trunk were shoes that would fit him. So, much to the theater men's dismay, Grayson had been forced to wear his own boots. It had taken him a good five minutes to convince his helpers that no one would see the boots, as they were well hidden beneath the flaring skirt of the gown.

As he twirled a bit to show how well the boots were hidden, Ming had toddled into the room. She'd taken one look at him, let out a wail, and turned and fled from the room, screaming at the top of her lungs for one of her nannies. It seemed his identity had been safely concealed.

No amount of coaxing on his part had convinced the child that he was actually her father, so with a quick apology to the nannies, who were going to have to deal with a distraught child for the rest of the day, Grayson had taken his leave.

An opium pipe was suddenly thrust into his hand, distracting him from his thoughts.

"Go ahead. Smoke it. I don't mind sharing."

"No. Thank you, but . . ." Grayson paused when he realized the gentleman who'd passed him the pipe was looking back at him, his expression decidedly bemused.

He had to remember to use a higher voice. He cleared his throat and pitched his tone appropriately. "You're too kind, but no."

He handed the pipe back to the man, took a step forward, and stumbled over the hem of his gown. He regained his balance, hitched the skirt up just a tad, and shouldered his way through the crowd, coming to an abrupt stop when he caught sight of a dark-haired man who looked vaguely familiar. Grayson squinted and tilted his head as he considered the man.

He *had* seen the man before, and if he wasn't mistaken, the man was one of the captains Grayson had dealt with.

Here was a man who would know without a doubt if anyone, or rather any Chinese, were searching for Grayson.

Grayson took off after the man but was forced to stop yet again when the man disappeared through a back doorway right as five Chinese men, obviously guards, stepped through that same doorway, blocked the entrance, and began to scan the crowd.

Ducking his head, he took off in the opposite direction, not stopping until he found a spot along the wall and quickly slouched against it.

Bright light suddenly hit him squarely in the eye. Peering toward the front door, his gaze settled on an odd sight indeed.

Three people were entering the den, two slight gentlemen and one rather large lady, all of whom paused in the entranceway, almost as if they had no idea what to do next.

The front door slammed shut and the room went dim again, casting the new arrivals into shadows before they disappeared into the crowd.

Reminding himself that he was supposed to be obtaining information and not gawking at the odd patrons who kept walking through the door, Grayson put his head down and edged around the room. He finally came to a stop almost where he'd started, but this time in a position hidden behind numerous patrons that enabled him to be near the back doorway without allowing the guards to see him. He inched closer, and satisfaction flowed over him when he caught the sound of what seemed to be a rather heated discussion.

". . . and there was some unwanted attention by the police," a voice was saying. "They were all over the dock area, and another ship from China that was right behind mine actually pulled back. I have no idea if they'll try to drop their shipment anytime soon, which means you might want to watch how you're speaking to me. You can't run an opium den if you don't have any opium."

Grayson strained to hear the muttered reply and then realized that someone was translating the words into Chinese.

It really was unfortunate he'd refused to learn the language. By the loud guffaws now drifting out the door, he had a feeling the demands of the first man—probably the captain he'd noticed earlier—were being scoffed at. Hopefully the man was a bright sort and wouldn't attempt to argue. He'd seen all too often what happened to those who stood in the way of profit.

A large body suddenly lurched into him, sufficiently distracting him from the conversation he'd been straining to hear. Reaching out, he steadied an unusually large woman, frowning when he realized the arm he was clutching seemed to be made of steel. Before he could contemplate that realization, the woman shrugged away from him, squared her shoulders as she patted her hair, and ducked her head, making it impossible for Grayson to see her face.

"I do beg your pardon," she said in a high, slightly nasal voice. "These dastardly dresses can be a bit of a menace at times." The woman lifted her head and then . . . her eyes widened. "Grayson? Is that you? And if it is, what are you doing here?" she said in a voice that greatly resembled Zayne Beckett's.

Grayson's mouth dropped open right before a snort of laughter shot out of it. "On my word, Zayne, you make a lovely lady."

Zayne eyed him for a moment and then grinned. "I wish I could return the compliment. Why do you have that . . . thing wrapped around you?" he asked, gesturing to Grayson's shawl.

Pulling the shawl closer, Grayson returned the grin. "This is to hide the low bodice of this adorable gown. I'm wearing it because I didn't believe showing an overabundance of chest hair would lend me the look I was attempting to achieve, and I didn't particularly care to shave."

Zayne glanced down at his own bodice. "Why didn't anyone think to lend me a shawl? Agatha made me shave, and I must tell you, it was not a pleasant experience."

"Agatha's the reason you're here?"

"She's working on a story."

"Hmm, that explains a lot, but tell me, why are you dressed like a lady?"

Zayne rolled his eyes. "Agatha spouted some nonsense about me not being recognized and not drawing undue attention to her disguise, but quite honestly, I think she just insisted I dress up this way in order to make me look completely ridiculous."

"And yet you went along with her."

Zayne frowned. "So I did, which begs the question of why."

"I don't think that question should be difficult for you to answer, but tell me, where is Agatha?"

"She's right over there," Zayne said with a nod toward a group of patrons standing a few feet away. "I'm not exactly comfortable leaving her side, but she insisted I would be too distracting and that would result in her being unable to gather any information. She then threatened me with pouring something of a nasty nature down my bodice if I didn't comply. Since my skin is remarkably sensitive due to the shaving business, I thought I'd keep my distance but stay close enough to help if she requires my assistance." He shook his head. "She and Felicia have turned out to be incredibly annoying ladies today."

All the breath left Grayson's body in a split second. "Felicia's here as well?"

"She is."

She was going to be the death of him. Did she not remember the danger she was in, and more importantly, that the danger she was facing was a direct result of him being seen by the Chinese?

She was an intelligent lady, so one would think she would have put two and two together and realized that the last place on earth she should be at the moment was an opium den.

She was the most exasperating woman in the entire world.

"Where did you say they were?"

Zayne gestured with his head. "I told you, right over there, and no, I don't think it would be advisable for you to go storming up to them—something the expression on your face clearly states you're about to do. They will not thank you for disrupting their investigating, so take a couple of breaths and calm down."

"Investigating? What are they investigating?"

"I'm not certain. Agatha was remarkably stingy with any details."

Grayson's temper began to simmer. "How could you agree to escort them to an opium den without learning the details regarding why you were coming here in the first place and what was to take place once you got here?"

"I agreed because I knew they would come here on their own if I refused."

He did make a most excellent point.

"What are you doing here?" Zayne asked.

Grayson glanced over to the crowd Zayne had indicated, unable to pick Felicia or Agatha out from the swarm of gentlemen gathered in a tight bunch. He began to ever so discreetly inch that way but was brought to an almost immediate halt by Zayne's hand on his arm.

"They're fine."

"Believe me, they are not," he countered. "I have more than my fair share of experience with places like this. Anything can happen, and normally does, in the blink of an eye."

Zayne frowned. "You have experience in opium dens?"

"I do, but you'll have to wait until after we get Felicia and Agatha safely away from here for an explanation."

"Do you really want them to hear your explanation?"

The truth was, no, he didn't—although, since Felicia was currently standing in an opium den, Grayson was somewhat certain she'd figured a few things out on her own, things he'd been hoping she would never discover about him.

"It'll be safer for them if I'm the one who discloses the information they're obviously searching for, which means we need to go get them."

Zayne, irritatingly enough, didn't move. "But again, what are you doing here?"

"It doesn't really matter right now, and . . ." His words trailed off as a laugh he recognized only too well met his ears. He turned and couldn't believe his eyes when he caught sight of a small man with abundant whiskers on his face and an overly large jacket dwarfing his frame—a man he knew without a doubt was actually Felicia.

She was going to be found out any moment now, especially since she seemed to have forgotten she was supposed to be a man and was laughing in an all too feminine voice.

His mouth dropped open when she slapped the gentleman standing to her right on the back, right before she puffed out her chest and spit on the floor, causing the man she'd just slapped to jump out of the way even as he sent her a disbelieving scowl.

"Do you think she knows that gentlemen don't normally spit on the floor, even in places like this?" Zayne asked slowly. "But I must say, it does seem as if she's having a great deal of fun."

"And that is exactly why we're going to escort them out of here right now. Felicia has a remarkable talent for attracting trouble, especially when she's in the midst of enjoying herself." Grayson took a step forward, tripped on what appeared to be part of his shawl that had somehow managed to start dragging on the floor, shoved it back into place, and sent a man who was gawking in his direction a smile. To his amusement, the man spun on his heel and charged away in the opposite direction.

"Smooth," Zayne declared with a laugh.

"Yes, well, smoothness aside, it's past time we fetched the ladies."

Zayne began to shake his head, but then stopped in midshake

and began to nod. "You might be right because, if I'm not mistaken, the police have just arrived. There's one standing over by the door."

"What?"

Before Zayne could answer, a shrill whistle sounded, the front door burst open, and policemen began swarming around the room, grabbing people left and right and hauling them out as chaos descended.

"We have to get Felicia and Agatha," he called, stepping over two men lying on the floor. He spotted Felicia tugging Agatha toward the back room and changed directions. Unfortunately, his skirt was tangled around his legs. He fell to the floor and felt someone walk over him, but then hands grabbed him and pulled him to his feet. He shook out his skirt and lifted his head, wincing when he saw a policeman staring back at him, a look of pure astonishment on the man's face.

"I hope you've got some spare money to pay for your bail, missy, because you'll never get released from jail on your looks alone."

14

Agatha had made the claim that opium raids were few and far between, but apparently, given that they were currently being marched in the direction of a waiting police wagon, her friend had been greatly mistaken.

At that time Felicia had oh so casually lamented that she'd never been carted off to jail, but now, faced with the prospect of soon finding herself behind bars, she wasn't feeling much excitement regarding her situation. In fact, she was rapidly coming to the conclusion that she might have bitten off entirely more than she could chew.

Her mother was going to have an absolute fit when she learned of the afternoon's outcome.

As the policeman who had hold of her arm tightened his grip, Felicia winced, knowing full well she was sure to have bruises come morning. "My good man," she finally said, "I assure you, there is no need to hold me so tightly. I'm not going to make a mad dash in a foolish attempt to escape."

The policeman turned his head and nodded at a fellow officer who was tugging Agatha along. "I hate dealing with opium eaters. Their grasp of reality is severely limited."

Felicia released a snort. "I'm not an opium eater, thank you very much, and again, I'd appreciate it if you'd loosen your grip."

The policeman came to an abrupt stop, swung her around to face him, and took a moment to consider her. His gaze traveled to her hat, then to her face, where he took a great deal of time to examine her whiskers. He turned his attention to her jacket and then leaned over to peruse her shoes. He finally straightened. "You're a girl."

"I prefer *lady*, but who am I to split hairs at this particular moment."

The policeman glanced to Agatha. "You're a girl too, aren't you?"

Agatha lifted her chin. "I'm a reporter for the *New-York Tribune,* and the lady you're holding is my assistant. If you'll allow me to get into my pocket, I have proof."

"Good thinking, Agatha. Show them the proof, and then perhaps we won't have to continue on to jail."

"I've heard some strange excuses to explain why miscreants are in places they really ought not to be, but this one takes the cake," the policeman muttered before he prodded Felicia back into motion again. "Do you think we should put them in the wagon with the other men, or should we take them to the one with the ladies?"

"Better make it the ladies," the policeman who was once again dragging Agatha by his side said. "If you ask me, these raids are much more trouble than they're worth. Sure, the city will get some cash from our efforts today, especially from the owner of that den, but quite honestly, I think our efforts would be better spent tracking down real criminals."

"Opium's illegal," the policeman holding Felicia returned. "Rules are rules."

"It is illegal to bring opium into the country," Agatha said. "I looked it up last night in a book from my father's library, but local laws vary. I couldn't find anything clearly stating that opium dens are illegal in the city of New York."

"I guess you'll have to take that up with the judge."

Felicia heard Agatha begin to mutter under her breath, but she couldn't tell what her friend was saying, and since her policeman was now prodding her forward at a more hurried clip, she wasn't able to move closer to Agatha to hear. Before she knew it, she was standing in front of a police wagon, and her nerves were beginning to make themselves known.

"Did you hear Larry found a man dressed up like a woman?" Agatha's policeman suddenly asked.

"You find all sorts of nasty business in Posey's."

Apparently Zayne had been captured as well.

"What did the man have to say for himself?"

"Not much. He seemed to be the strong, silent type." The policeman chuckled. "They put him in the wagon reserved for women though, didn't want to deal with the ruckus the other men would make if they got a good look at him. He's not what anyone could call attractive."

That was odd. She'd thought Zayne made a somewhat lovely woman, if you discounted his large frame. Before she had a chance to voice that sentiment, she was roughly hauled into the back of an enclosed wagon, Agatha following her seconds later. Strong yet gentle hands helped her take a seat. She made room for Agatha and lifted her head. "Thank you, Zayne, it . . ."

All the breath seemed to squeeze from her body in a split second. Staring back at her were eyes she'd come to know only too well, but they didn't belong to Zayne. Those eyes were currently narrowed on her face, and it was clearly evident Grayson was not exactly happy to see her as he loomed over her, having to almost double over in order to not hit his head on the low ceiling of the wagon.

"Lovely shawl," Agatha said, breaking the awkward moment.

Felicia blinked when the person sitting next to Agatha sat forward. Zayne had been apprehended too.

"The shawl is to hide Grayson's chest hair—something you, Agatha, really should have thought of before insisting I shave mine off."

Agatha gave a sniff. "I would think that shaving allowed you to get into the true spirit of the role we asked you to assume, and you could have said no."

Zayne's mouth dropped open. "I did protest."

"Obviously not adamantly enough," Grayson muttered. "But at least you can take comfort that your hair will regrow." He gestured to Felicia. "Scoot over."

Seeing no reason to refuse, she edged over, allowing him to sit right next to her, the heat from his body warming her leg through the material of her trousers.

"Do you care to explain what you were doing in that opium den?" he asked.

"It's a little tricky to explain."

"Were you trying to dig up information regarding my past?"

She should have known he'd immediately come to that conclusion. "I readily admit I was curious about a few things, especially since you neglected to include several pertinent details regarding your past—such as the whole opium business."

Zayne leaned even farther forward. "So you were involved in the opium trade?"

"Of course he was," Agatha answered for him. "It all makes perfect sense if you think about it. Everyone knows Grayson had some type of tragic past, and if you add in the fact that he lived in China for years and he made a fortune there, well, the logical conclusion—especially since he's been somewhat cagey about the whole mess—is that he was connected with the opium trade."

"If you're in with the opium gents, ma'am, can I hope you have some of the stuff on you?"

Felicia swung her attention to the lady who'd just spoken and found the woman swaying on the seat, her eyes dazed, yet her expression eager.

"I don't use opium, nor do I have any on me," Grayson said.

"Pity," the lady replied before she nodded and then, to Felicia's dismay, slid off the seat and landed on the floor of the wagon, where she promptly curled into a ball and went to sleep.

Everything Felicia had witnessed in the opium den suddenly sprang to mind. She'd seen men and women stumbling about, some of them begging others for just one more draw from a pipe when it appeared their money had run out. Speech had been slurred, eyes had been red, and for the life of her, Felicia couldn't understand the appeal of the drug. She also couldn't understand, or perhaps she could but didn't want to admit it yet, exactly why Grayson would have gotten involved with something so disturbing.

Grayson suddenly patted her knee. "You're disappointed with me."

"I'm not certain I would go that far, especially considering I have yet to fully understand what your part was with the opium trade."

For a moment, it seemed he wasn't going to reply, but then he released a breath, withdrew his hand from her knee, and settled back against the rough walls of the police wagon.

"I was in charge of distribution."

"What does that mean exactly?"

"It means I made sure the Wu family's opium was delivered to every country that wanted it."

Her stomach clenched as the truth stole into her very soul.

She'd been trying to ignore the idea that Grayson could have really done anything truly reprehensible, but there it was, from his own mouth.

He'd provided a drug that obviously ruined countless lives on a daily basis, and from what she'd been able to piece together, he'd made a fortune in the process.

Every warm and fuzzy feeling she'd felt toward the gentleman disappeared in the span of a heartbeat.

"Do you have any remorse?"

"More than I can express."

She caught his eye, saw the despair clearly visible, but refused to allow the sight to move her.

She'd known he was dangerous, known he'd possessed a mysterious past, but she'd never thought he would have been capable of such things.

She swallowed and then spoke past the lump that had formed in her throat. "Did you ever consider the many lives you were ruining?"

The despair deepened in his eyes. "Not at all, at least not until after the Wu family was slaughtered. I had abundant time to think my life through on the boat ride back to England and then to America."

He gestured to the woman still sleeping on the floor. "I realize now that the plight of that woman, and countless others just like her, is on some level my fault, but . . . there's nothing I can do to change what I caused. I can only hope that someday I'll learn to live with myself."

Agatha cleared her throat. "I'm not one to make suggestions—well, not on a frequent basis—concerning matters of faith, Grayson, but did it ever occur to you to seek forgiveness from the one source that can help ease your guilt?"

"God has no reason to grant me peace, Agatha," Grayson said softly. "And, quite frankly, I don't exactly deserve any. Greed convinced me to look the other way and ignore the destruction my actions caused. I doubt God will be willing to forgive me anytime soon."

"He will forgive you if you ask. And you could give away all the money you made in China, donate it to help the people who've become addicted to the drug you provided them," Felicia said slowly.

Disappointment stole her breath away when he sent her a small shake of his head.

"The money I made working for Wu Wah Hing was substantial, and I took that money and sent it back to England, instructing a financial man of affairs to invest it in numerous ventures. During the long trip back to England from China, I began to realize that I wouldn't be able to keep that money. Once I reached England, though, I immediately set sail for New York, convinced by Eliza's ex-fiancé that it was imperative I seek out my sister immediately.

"Since she so capably restored our family finances by tracking down the thief who'd stolen it, and those finances provide me with more funds than I'll ever be able to spend during my lifetime, I was then free to begin disbursing my ill-gotten fortune. I've spent substantial time determining charitable organizations to receive all the money my investments generated. I am no longer living off of any of that money."

He sighed and crossed his arms as he leaned back against the police wagon wall. "I expect you will not agree with my reasoning, but I took the initial amount I made from working in China and set up a special account for Ming. That money is her inheritance, and even though it was made through reprehensible means, it's hers, and I intend to keep it that way.

"We'll never be able to claim the fortune she deserves that's back in China, but at least she'll have money of her own to see her through life. And quite honestly, she's going to need it as a way to force people to accept her in a white world."

He was right. She *didn't* agree with his reasoning, but she couldn't say she didn't understand it. Ming would always be seen as different in America—or anywhere else she chose to go, unless she returned to China someday—but money would allow her to be more readily accepted.

She opened her mouth—to say what, she had no idea—but then Agatha leaned forward once again. "Correct me if I'm wrong, Grayson, but I think there was more to you accepting that position with the Wu family than simply greed. While the lure of a fortune would surely have been appealing to a young man fresh out of university, there had to have been something else."

Grayson smiled a rather sad smile. "It seems you always search for the good in everyone, Agatha, but I don't think you'll be able to find anything good about my decision. Was there something besides greed that prompted me to pursue a fortune? Certainly. In the back of my mind, I thought that if I could obtain a fortune all on my own, my father would develop a bit of respect for me and possibly come to regret the harsh manner in which he'd tried to control me. However, that reasoning seems almost silly when you take into account the lengths I went to procure money.

"In case you've forgotten, besides immersing myself in the opium trade, I also married a woman I didn't know, and a woman I never even bothered to attempt to converse with."

"If you were planning on impressing your father with your success, may I assume you were considering a return to England at some point?" Felicia asked.

"In the beginning, no, I was too consumed with work, but it wasn't long before the allure of China began to fade and I found myself missing the land of my birth."

"Why did you wait so long?" Felicia pressed. "Eliza told me you were gone for years."

"I discovered it's next to impossible to get out of China. I

206

was indebted to a man who had no intention of allowing me to leave."

"He probably didn't want you to take his daughter out of the country."

"Wu Wah Hing cared nothing for Lin. His only concern was losing a means to secure profitable routes for his opium. If he hadn't been murdered, I'd probably still be there."

Grayson's eyes turned hard. "Their deaths were my fault. I got entirely too self-assured, made reckless choices. I managed to wrest a whole fleet of ships along with their routes away from the Zang family, the biggest rivals of the Wus, and because of that, Wu Wah Hing, my wife, her sister and Francisco, a good twenty other relatives, and countless servants were slaughtered in retaliation for my arrogance."

Although he'd spoken the words in a rather casual manner, there was a world of anguish behind them.

"I've distressed you."

Felicia forced herself to meet Grayson's gaze. "You have."

"You needed to hear the full truth. At least now you understand why I initially balked when Agatha suggested I escort you to the Beckett ball. No good can come of associating with me. Even though I enjoy your company more than I can say, we need to part ways once and for all after we get out of this mess. You're too good, too innocent, and a lady like you deserves better than me."

She knew he spoke nothing less than the truth—well, not the part about her being too good and innocent—but . . . for some reason, the thought of never having him in her life again sent a sharp ache directly through her heart.

"I never intended to place you in danger," Grayson said softly. "For that, I can only extend to you my most sincere apologies and hope that I'm mistaken, that those men who came to the Wild Rose did not recognize me. And if they did, I pray they didn't realize you were with me."

Zayne blew out a breath. "I do beg everyone's pardon, but what is going on? What danger is Felicia in and why?"

Grayson took a moment to explain, and as he explained, Felicia allowed her thoughts to wander, returning to the distressing details Grayson had revealed.

He was obviously tormented about what he'd done, but his admissions had disturbed her more than she cared to admit. He'd carelessly put his own greed, his own desires, before everyone else's, even going so far as to marry a woman for nothing more than financial gain. Didn't it stand to reason, then, that he deserved just a bit of the torment that plagued him?

From out of nowhere, she felt as if someone had smacked her across the head. She glanced around, yet everyone was directing their attention to Grayson, who was still explaining.

Forgiveness.

She looked at the ceiling of the wagon, peering up at it as she strained her ears.

Nothing came to her except the idea that God was apparently trying to tell her something, something that concerned forgiveness.

She wasn't certain she had forgiveness in her at the moment, but . . . she blinked as another word entered her mind.

Judgmental.

Disgruntlement was immediate, even though she knew perfectly well that, if God was sending her messages, He was spot on with that particular assessment.

She was being judgmental, and a little bit sanctimonious, if the truth were known, but Grayson had had a direct hand in ruining hundreds, perhaps thousands, of lives. He'd admitted his actions had caused many people to be murdered. Did she feel justified in judging him? Certainly. But . . . could she forgive him? And was that what God expected her to do?

". . . so last night, the face of one of the Chinese men sprang back to mind, and I finally remembered where I'd seen him before. He has a distinctive scar on his face, and . . . he worked for the Zang family," Grayson said. "He's the reason I went to the opium den today. I wanted to find out who owned the place. If the Zang family has anything to do with opium dens in this city, I'll have to leave town immediately, because Ming won't be safe for long. If they know she survived the fire and that she has been living with me, they won't be satisfied until every last Wu is extinguished from the earth."

Good heavens, while she'd been lost in thought, she'd apparently missed quite a bit.

"You recognized one of those men?" she asked.

Grayson nodded, but before he could say anything, the wagon slowed and rumbled to a stop. The door flung open, and she squinted as light poured in from outside.

"Come on, I haven't got all day," a policeman barked, causing her to scurry to the door. She wasn't surprised when Grayson took her arm and helped her down.

It would be so much easier to dismiss the man if he'd stop being considerate.

He followed her a second later but then tripped on the hem of his gown and sprawled to the ground. The sight of his boots showing from beneath his skirt caused her lips to twitch just a touch. The amusement felt strange, given what she'd just learned, but when Zayne stepped in front of her to extend Grayson his hand, she couldn't help but grin at the sight the two men made.

"That's something you don't see every day," Agatha muttered before she took Felicia's arm and moved her out of the way as other occupants of the wagon jumped or fell to the ground.

Felicia soon found herself walking in a less than straight line as the policeman directed them toward the jail. "Is this when they'll put us in a cell?"

"I'm afraid so," Grayson said before he stumbled once again and muttered something undetectable under his breath.

"It's all in the stride," Zayne said cheerfully. "Watch me." He shook out the folds of his skirt and pranced ahead, sending Felicia and Agatha a smile. "See? It's not that difficult."

"Get back in line," the policeman ordered.

Zayne dipped into a curtsy and resumed his place beside Grayson, his eyes twinkling ever so slightly.

"Zayne? Zayne Beckett, is that you?"

Zayne looked up and grinned even as he raised a frilly sleeve and began waving madly to someone Felicia couldn't see.

"Theodore, yes, it's me, Zayne."

A moment later, Theodore came into view, striding their way, shaking his head. He came to a stop and slapped Zayne on the back.

"I must say I wasn't expecting to find you here, and my, don't you look lovely today." Theodore switched his attention to Grayson, and his eyes went wide as he looked him up and down. "I don't know how to break this to you, but red is definitely not your color."

"Do you know these people, Mr. Wilder?" one of the policemen asked, walking over to join them.

"Yes, I know these two fine-looking ladies," Theodore admitted.

"He knows us too," Agatha said, speaking up as she stepped forward, drawing Theodore's attention.

A sound that resembled nothing less than a snort escaped Theodore's lips. "Honestly, Agatha, why am I not surprised to discover you here, and dressed as a man no less?" Not giving Agatha a chance to respond, he turned to Felicia right as his mouth dropped open. He turned back to Agatha. "What could you be thinking, pulling poor Felicia into one of your madcap adventures? You have a distinct talent for trouble, but there's absolutely no reason to get Felicia involved in such a mess."

Why was it that Theodore was not surprised at all to discover her soon-to-be cellmates in trouble but was seemingly appalled to find her in the midst of this disaster?

She lifted her chin. "Today's madcap adventure was my idea, not Agatha's, so if anyone seems to have a talent for trouble today, it would be me." She lifted her chin another notch and ignored Theodore's sputters. "If you must know, blame for our situation actually should be laid squarely at your and Grayson's feet."

Theodore stopped sputtering. "How do you reason that one out?"

"You and Grayson should have sought me out and given me pertinent information that would have kept me from being forced to search for that necessary information on my own today—well, with the help of Agatha and Zayne." She drew in a deep breath, blew it out, and continued. "If I'd been given that information— such as why I might possibly be in danger and what Grayson's past really entailed—I wouldn't have even considered asking Agatha to do a story on opium dens, and then neither she nor I would be in this mess. Nor would Zayne."

She tossed a glance to Grayson. "Although Grayson would still be in this mess—he didn't travel with us to the opium den but went there on his own."

Theodore ran a hand through his hair and suddenly looked somewhat uncomfortable. "All of you were at the opium den this afternoon?"

"Until the place was raided and we got hauled here," Zayne said.

Theodore winced. "That's unfortunate."

Agatha planted her hands on her hips. "Were you responsible for that raid?"

"Well, not exactly. It was a police decision, but I might have prodded the decision along a bit, considering I met with the police chief this morning to see what he could tell me about that particular den." Theodore shot a look to Grayson. "You might have let me know you were planning to investigate on your own. I would have made certain no raids took place until you were out of there."

"But why raid it at all?" Agatha pressed. "What possible good could come of that?"

"I hoped they would pick up the men who run the place so I could talk to them and find out who owns it. That's why I'm here. Although, I have to tell you, I didn't expect they were going to cart all the patrons away."

"Funds are running a little low," the policeman muttered.

"Ah, well, good luck getting any money from the patrons," Theodore said. "From what I know about opium eaters, they tend to be considerably low on funds most of the time."

He stepped closer to the policeman. "Do you mind letting these people go with me? I assure you, they weren't participating in anything untoward."

The policeman's lips curled. "Except maybe the manner in which they're dressed."

"True, but dressing as the opposite gender is not really arrest worthy, so if I have your permission, I'll personally escort them to their respective homes."

"By all means," the policeman said. "It'll save me some paperwork." With that, he nodded, winced when he looked at Zayne and Grayson, and strode away.

"Shall we go to my carriage?" Theodore asked.

"Don't you want to stay and question the employees of the opium den?" Grayson asked.

"Normally I would say yes, but I think it's more important to get Felicia returned safely to her house."

Felicia narrowed her eyes. "Don't let my situation dissuade you, Theodore. It's not as if I'll get into any other trouble today."

If you feel the need to continue with your investigation, we can hire a carriage to take us home."

"Surely you must realize that no driver in his right mind would allow you into his carriage, and besides, we need to get you home quickly."

Her eyes narrowed to mere slits. "Why?"

Theodore cleared his throat. "I believe your mother might be under the impression you're up to no good."

"You've seen my mother?"

"She stopped by my office a few hours ago, looking for you. Apparently, she'd been to see Mrs. Watson, and because Cora was acting—your mother's words, not mine—shifty, Ruth decided you were getting yourself involved in something you shouldn't be involved in." He smiled. "I told her you and Agatha were probably shopping, but since she started muttering all sorts of dire predictions under her breath, I don't think she agreed with me."

"Maybe you should see me home."

"There'll be no need for that, Miss Murdock. You're coming with me."

Dread was immediate as Felicia slowly turned and found Mr. Blackheart standing right behind her. "What are you doing here?"

"Searching for you. Your mother and I have been to all the shops you've been known to frequent and traveled through the tenement slums calling out your name. Finally I decided to check the jail. Imagine my surprise when I spotted Theodore standing right next to the lady I'm supposed to be guarding."

"How did you recognize me?"

Mr. Blackheart quirked a brow and said absolutely nothing in response to that completely reasonable question.

Felicia swallowed and tried again. "You're not, by any chance, here with my mother, are you?"

Mr. Blackheart smiled as a carriage Felicia knew only too well clattered over the cobblestones and came to a stop directly in front of them.

Ruth stuck her head out the window, her mouth dropped open for just a second as her gaze settled on Felicia, and then she began to yell, loudly.

Felicia felt an immediate urge to seek out the policeman once again and beg him to throw her behind bars.

15

*G*rayson eased into a chair in the middle of Eliza's drawing room, enjoying the sight of Ming playing with one of her dolls. It was a relief to find her playing so calmly.

When he'd returned home last night, Ming's nannies had informed him she'd been horrible all day, but he'd explained her bad behavior away, reasoning out that it had been her way of handling the sight of her father dressed as a woman.

Unfortunately, he was fresh out of explanations as to why she'd woken up bright and early that morning and proceeded to tear the house apart, flinging her toys and not minding the nannies at all, no matter that they spoke to her in soothing tones and tried to accommodate her every wish.

He'd finally been driven to bring Ming to Eliza's house, hoping that being around her cousins, children she absolutely adored, would bring his sweet and lovable daughter back.

That hadn't happened. She'd created havoc the moment he'd set her down in the entranceway, running straight up to Ben, Eliza's son, and biting the boy's arm. Biting another child was disturbing in and of itself, but Ben was Ming's favorite person in the world, and that made the biting all that more concerning and proved there was something truly bothering her.

He had to figure out what that was.

Releasing a sigh, he settled back into the chair and considered how to proceed. He didn't have much experience with children. He'd left England before any of his friends had married, and it wasn't as if he and Lin ever considered having a child of their own. Though unspoken, they had agreed that their marriage was to be in name only.

"There you are, Grayson. Could you join me for a moment?"

Grayson looked away from Ming and found Eliza standing in the doorway. He rose to his feet, told the nanny sitting in a chair a few feet away from Ming that he'd be right back, and followed his sister into the hallway.

"Is everything all right?" he asked.

Eliza nodded. "Everything's fine. I was hoping you could help me look for a piece of jewelry. It's probably right in front of my face, but perhaps a fresh pair of eyes will be able to pick it out."

Grayson fell into step beside her, and they walked down the hallway and up a steep flight of stairs, entering her private suite of rooms a moment later. He admired the tasteful décor surrounding him. Eliza had somehow managed to turn the main room into a comfortable retreat, one that reflected both feminine and masculine tastes. It was the perfect spot for the still-somewhat newlyweds to seek out a bit of peace, because with one small boy and one very active little girl, they certainly needed a place where they could escape the hectic pace of their lives.

The house he rented a block away, even though it did bear the status of being on Fifth Avenue, lacked any vestige of charm

and definitely couldn't be considered a retreat. He'd been considering making a home purchase of his own, but he wasn't
certain New York was going to turn out to be the place he
truly belonged.

Where he and Ming belonged, he couldn't really say. Ten-
sions were ever increasing between Chinese immigrants and
the rest of the population in America. He knew it was only a
matter of time before Ming suffered from the prejudice spreading throughout the nation, no matter the extent of the wealth
he'd set aside for her.

He pulled himself from his thoughts when he realized Eliza
was motioning him forward.

"I'm looking for that sapphire necklace Mother used to
wear, the one in the shape of a lily with diamonds along the
rim. It's the one Father gave her when I was born. Do you
remember it?"

He suddenly lost the ability to breathe. He blinked and then
blinked again, trying to focus on the jewelry chest Eliza was
gesturing toward, a jewelry chest apparently filled with jewelry
once worn by his mother.

A deep sense of loss came from out of nowhere, hitting him
hard, causing a wave of pain such as he'd never felt before to
course over him.

His mother was dead, as was his father.

He'd mourned the death of his mother years before, but not
until this precise moment had he fully realized what he'd lost.
He'd never taken any time at all to mourn his father. They'd
parted on horrendous terms, and yes, he'd been dismayed to
learn of his death, but he hadn't actually sorted through or ex-
amined his grief. His heart had been too numb, the horrors of
China too fresh to add any other emotions, but now it seemed
as if his heart had unfrozen just enough to almost bring him
to his knees.

"Grayson?"

He could hear Eliza calling to him, but he didn't seem able to summon up a response.

His hand reached out right as his feet began moving, and then he was standing directly in front of the chest, picking up a delicate bracelet encrusted with rubies.

He remembered his mother wearing this bracelet, wearing it around her warm, slender wrist, a wrist that had always been dabbed with the most pleasant scent of lilacs. She'd allowed him to play with this bracelet once when he'd been a child, encouraged him to take it over to a window so that the sun could sparkle over its many gems.

Her wrist was no longer warm, nor was it scented with lilacs, considering she'd been dead for ten long years.

He hadn't made the time to visit her grave when he'd returned to London. He hadn't taken the time to pay his own mother the respect she deserved.

He'd never seen his father's grave.

Grief overwhelmed him as tears blinded him.

"Grayson."

Eliza was suddenly in front of him, her hands on his face as matching tears glistened in her eyes. She leaned closer and kissed his cheek, and he dropped the bracelet and pulled her close.

For how long they stayed that way, he couldn't say, but as his grief dissipated, he felt his soul breathe a sigh of relief. He gave Eliza one last lingering hug and took a step back.

"Eliza, I'm sorry I—"

Eliza held up her hand. "Do not apologize, Gray. I'm your sister, and it was past time you allowed yourself a moment to grieve all that you've lost. I'm just thankful I was here to grieve with you." She gave a rather watery snort. "It is lovely to have you back."

"I've been back for months."

"No, that was simply your body. Now you're finally returning to life." She smiled. "I can't help but wonder what, or perhaps who, is responsible for this improvement." Her smile widened. "If I were to hazard a guess, I would say Felicia Murdock has something to do with it."

His first instinct was to argue the point, but then he tilted his head and thought about it for a moment.

Was Felicia responsible for opening him up to the people around him, for him beginning to deal with the past?

During the time he'd spent with her, he'd come to realize she was a truly remarkable lady. She was giving and kind—even though she really did seem to have a talent for trouble. It wasn't as if she sought it out, though. Trouble just seemed to find her while she was in the midst of trying to help other people.

He'd begun to feel an odd urge to follow in her footsteps, but also an urge to further his association with her, even knowing she was far too good for the likes of him. He'd thought he'd convinced himself the best thing he could do for her was to leave her alone, but then . . . he'd revealed the worst of himself, reluctantly, of course. He'd braced himself for the rejection he'd been certain was soon to follow his revelation, but . . . it had never come.

She'd obviously been disappointed with him, and more than a little disturbed over what he'd disclosed, but she hadn't turned her back on him.

He'd thought about that throughout the night, after he'd finally gotten Ming to sleep, and as he'd thought about it, a sense of what almost felt like hope had flowed through him.

If he could ensure that she wouldn't face danger because of him, perhaps, just perhaps—

"So, any thoughts?"

Grayson blinked and smiled when he realized Eliza was watching him with clear expectation on her face.

"I'm not certain."

"Not certain about what I suggested regarding Felicia, or not certain you have any thoughts?"

"It's difficult to put into words."

"Try."

Grayson took Eliza by the arm, helped her into a chair situated next to the fireplace, and then took a seat in a chair right next to her. He folded his hands over his stomach and took a moment to gather his thoughts, even though Eliza began to fidget in her seat. She'd never really been a patient sort.

"I told Felicia about my past."

Eliza's eyes widened right before they narrowed. "How much about your past?"

"Everything."

Eliza leaned over, plucked up a book lying on the floor beside her chair, and swatted him with it.

He rubbed his arm. "And the reason for that would be?"

"You know full well you have yet to tell me everything about your past. I'm your sister. I should have been the first to know, not Felicia."

"Zayne and Agatha heard it as well, if that makes you feel any better. It wasn't as if I specifically singled Felicia out."

Eliza evidently didn't believe that deserved a response, because she stuck her nose into the air and didn't say another word. She simply began drumming her fingers against the arm of the chair, even though Grayson couldn't help but notice her other hand was still clutching the book.

He was pretty sure he'd be experiencing another hard whack any moment.

"Would you like to know what I told her?" he finally asked, still eyeing the book.

"No."

His lips twitched. He'd forgotten his sister had a distinct propensity for surliness when she felt the occasion warranted it.

He leaned back and decided to wait her out.

The ticks of the clock on the wall sounded loud in the room, and after at least one hundred of them had sounded, Eliza finally let out a grunt and waved the hand not still clutching the book in the air. "Fine, I'm listening."

"Perhaps we should order some tea first."

Eliza dropped the book to the ground, leaned forward, and patted him on the knee. "There's no reason to stall. I'm your sister, Grayson. It'll be far easier to tell me about your past than it was to tell Felicia, Agatha, and Zayne. They had the ability to reject you, while I, no matter what you say, will always love you."

Swallowing past the lump that had grown in his throat, Grayson told his sister everything, not bothering to soften what he'd done, and unable to help but notice that, although her eyes widened every now and again, they never filled with disdain.

"So I told Felicia all of this," he finally concluded, "and although I do believe she was somewhat distressed, she didn't seem as if she wanted nothing more to do with me."

"Hmm . . ."

Grayson sat forward. "What does that mean?"

"It means I'm thinking."

"Think faster."

Eliza arched a brow. "You're so impatient."

"It runs in the family."

"True." She smiled. "Very well, here's what I'm thinking. Felicia is a lady any gentleman would be proud to call his own—though not many have noticed her the past few years, given her odd sense of fashion. She's a lady possessed of an incredibly strong faith, and that faith is what probably allowed her to see beyond your many faults—current and past, I might add—and perhaps forgive you for the sins you've obviously committed." Her smile faded as she reached out once again to touch his knee. "She would make you a worthy partner."

"She's far too good for me."

"Perhaps, but I think you're selling yourself short, Gray. You're an honorable man. Yes, that honor has definitely been tarnished, but that doesn't mean your future has to continuously be affected by your past. You've admitted you've done wrong. You're accepting responsibility by that admission, and now I'm going to encourage you to finally put your past behind you and embrace a future that could be filled with love, and hopefully love with Felicia."

Grayson's throat seemed somewhat constricted. "I didn't say anything about love. I barely know Felicia, so it is entirely too soon to even consider that alarming emotion."

"Stop being such a man. Love doesn't have a time limit, Gray. Since Felicia has firmly come out of her shell—or out from her outlandish fashion sense—and she's no longer trying so hard to behave in a demure manner, other gentlemen are going to take note of her appeal. You don't want someone else to swoop in and steal her heart, do you?"

"She would be better off finding a gentleman who shares her strong faith," he heard come pouring out of his mouth, wondering when that notion had started plaguing him. "I have so much for God to forgive."

"I believe the day is quickly coming when you will finally ask Him for that forgiveness. But until then . . ." She tilted her head. "Sometimes God throws us together with people we don't believe we'd get along with, but He knows differently. That certainly can be said for me and Hamilton. I know God put us together, which makes me wonder if maybe He's doing the same for you."

"I don't believe God will ever be willing to truly forgive me,

Eliza. I've done too many horrible things—for totally selfish reasons."

Eliza straightened in her chair and looked at him for a long moment. "Hmm . . ."

"There's that 'hmm' again."

Eliza frowned. "Did you ever consider that perhaps you've accepted entirely too much responsibility for what happened to the Wu family?"

"Ah, well, no."

She tilted her head. "Was this Wu Wah Hing and his family involved with the opium trade before you landed in China?"

"The Wu family was probably involved with opium for generations."

"And they had rivals all that time?"

Grayson nodded.

"And were these rivals known to be ruthless?"

"It's the opium trade, Eliza. Everyone's ruthless."

"Exactly. So violence was expected."

"Yes, violence was expected, but what happened was not your typical retaliation. The entire family was slaughtered, and it was my fault."

"Did you lure that shipping account away through nefarious means?"

"Does it make any difference if I did?"

"It might."

Grayson released a breath. "No, I didn't do anything underhanded to win the account. I simply offered them a more lucrative profit margin, and my offer was accepted."

"To be clear, you acted in a way that businessmen around the world behave every day—except you were dealing in less than reputable goods."

"I guess you could say that, but again, I knew the risks. I knew there might be repercussions, but I still went forward."

"Are you suggesting you made this decision on your own?"

Grayson frowned. "Wu Wah Hing had the final say, but I was very persuasive."

"Even though you didn't speak Chinese and he spoke limited English?" Eliza rolled her eyes. "Honestly, Grayson, I'm surprised you haven't thought this through more thoroughly. Your deceased father-in-law wasn't the type to be easily persuaded. Quite frankly, I believe he was a horrible man. He forced his own daughters to marry you and that Francisco fellow, knowing full well it was hardly fair to expect his daughters to find happiness with men who didn't even speak their language."

"Not to interrupt your tirade, Eliza, but though we didn't communicate much, I could tell that, by marrying me, Lin was able to obtain a small amount of freedom. She also was able to escape her father's constant tormenting regarding her lack of a husband, so I don't believe she was completely miserable being married to me."

"And were you miserable being married to her?"

"I wasn't miserable, but I did have regrets. I hadn't considered the consequences when I agreed to Wu Wah Hing's deal, but it fairly quickly occurred to me that Lin and I were going to be stuck together forever."

"You could have sought an annulment."

"No, I couldn't. Lin would have been put in an incredibly difficult position if I would have abandoned our marriage."

Satisfaction seemed to ooze out of Eliza's every pore. "See, this proves it. You are an honorable man, Grayson. Don't you think it's about time you remembered that? And while you're remembering, may I suggest you finally try to forgive yourself?" She smiled. "As for the matter of God and His forgiveness, surely you must realize that all you need to do is ask. He'll take it from there."

"I'm sure you believe that, Eliza, but I can't say—" He stopped speaking in midsentence when Eliza's daughter, Piper, charged into the room, her golden curls flying about her small face and her expression decidedly put out. She set her sights on him, marched over to stand in front of his chair, plopped her hands on her slim hips, tilted her head, and considered him for a long moment.

"Have you been crying, Uncle Grayson?"

Piper was far too observant for her tender years. "I wouldn't say I was exactly crying, more like choked up."

"Are you done being choked up?"

"I believe so. Why?"

Piper wrinkled her nose. "Because I have something just awful to tell you, but if bad news is going to turn you into a watering pot, I'll come back later."

Grayson swallowed a laugh. "I have never in my life been a watering pot, so please, feel free to state your bad news."

"Ming just tore the head off my favorite doll."

Grayson frowned. "Was it an accident?"

"Ah, no, I don't think so, since she twisted it around and around until it popped off, even though I told her to stop."

"Where was her nanny?"

Piper sent him a rather pitying look. "Ming waited until the nanny left the room to fetch us a snack before she attacked my doll."

"She deliberately made certain no one was there to see her?"

Piper nodded. "Ming's very smart. How else do you think she's been able to learn English so quickly?" She shook her head, causing her curls to fly around her face. "But things with her have gotten way out of hand, so I'm afraid I'm going to have to charge you for my services tonight."

"I'm sorry?"

"I'm sorry too, because I did tell Mama I'd help keep an eye on Ming at the ball, but really, she's turning out to be work, and

Daddy always says a person should be paid for work. I think a dollar should do the trick."

Eliza got to her feet. "Piper, you're not going to charge your uncle for helping out with your cousin. She's family, and sometimes one has to put up with all sorts of nonsense when one is dealing with a small child."

"I bet no one tore the head off of your favorite doll and then made you watch over the criminal," Piper argued.

Eliza's lips curled just a touch. "Ming's not a criminal, Piper. She's just a baby."

"If I walked into a store and started ripping heads off the dolls, I'd land in jail."

Grayson turned his head to hide his grin. Piper was always relentless with her objections, which made it incredibly difficult to win a point from her. When he felt he'd gotten his grin sufficiently under control, he turned back. "Tell me, Piper, why do you think Ming is suddenly acting so differently? She used to be a shy, pleasant child, and remarkably well behaved."

Piper sent him yet another pitying look. "You don't really understand children, do you?"

Grayson chanced a glance at Eliza and found her staring in the opposite direction, much as he'd done only a moment before. Realizing there was to be no help from that corner, he set his sights back on Piper. "I'm afraid you might be right about my understanding of children, which means I'm going to have to throw myself at your feet and beg you to give me your explanation as to what's happening with Ming."

Piper grinned. "Fair enough."

"So?"

She glanced at the floor. "You're not at my feet."

Grayson laughed, pushed himself out of the chair, sat on the floor, and lifted his head. "There, I'm literally at your feet. So tell me, why is it that even though I've hired numerous highly qualified nannies to deal with my daughter, no one seems capable of controlling her unruly behavior?"

Piper looked down at him. "Uncle Grayson, that's the problem right there. Ming doesn't want a nanny—she wants a mother."

He pushed himself to his feet, but before he could even process Piper's response, Eliza swung her attention away from the wall, stepped closer to Piper, and cupped her daughter's chin with her hand. "That makes perfect sense, darling, and what a clever girl you are to realize what we've missed. Of course Ming wants a mother."

Piper moved closer to Eliza and snuggled against her as Eliza put her arm around the little girl's shoulder and pulled her to her side. "That's why I don't want to be mad at her, Mama. She's acting just like Ben used to act when he went through that biting business, but he stopped doing that soon after you and Daddy met."

Eliza kissed the top of Piper's head and met Grayson's gaze. "She's jealous, Gray. That's why she's being so horrible to Piper and Ben."

"But why would she be jealous? Ming gets to spend time with you almost every day."

Piper stepped away from Eliza, scooted over to him, gave him a quick hug, and then stepped back. "Ming sees how happy Ben and I are with a mama, and it must bother her." Her eyes suddenly went huge. "You have to get married."

Grayson blinked. "I'm afraid it's not quite that easy."

"Sure it is. You just have to find someone you think would be a good mother and then ask her to marry you." She bit her lip and then shook one of her small fingers at him. "Just don't tell whatever lady you decide to marry that you want to marry her because she'd make a good mother. Daddy tried that with Mama, and it didn't work out very well for him at first."

She drew back the finger she'd been shaking at him and tapped her chin with it, looking for all intents and purposes as if she were in deep thought, right before she nodded. "You'll need to write a love poem. Girls like stuff like that. I can help you if you don't know how."

"What could you possibly know about a love poem?" Grayson asked. "You're six."

Piper shrugged. "Mama says I have quite the imagination." She stopped talking, appeared to be lost in thought once again, and then brightened. "You can ask Miss Agatha to marry you. She's lovely, and I would adore having her for an aunt."

"I'm sure you would, seeing as how you and Agatha seem to be kindred spirits."

"Thank you," Piper said primly.

He refused to allow himself the luxury of a good snort. "I'm not certain I was complimenting you, but that's beside the point. I'm sorry to disappoint you, Piper, but I don't think Agatha and I would suit."

"She's beautiful," Piper said, a mulish expression crossing her face, reminding Grayson immediately of Felicia.

Now, there was a beautiful woman.

"You could always marry Miss Felicia."

Grayson rubbed his forehead. It almost seemed as if Piper were tiptoeing around his thoughts.

"Piper, Uncle Grayson isn't ready to marry anyone at the moment," Eliza said, finally coming to his rescue.

"But Miss Felicia would be a good choice for him when he is ready," Piper argued. "Ming adores her. She watches for her at church—I've seen her." Piper batted big eyes at Grayson. "You don't want to disappoint your daughter, do you?"

Grayson found himself shaking his head.

"Good, then it's settled," Piper said. "When you're ready, I'll help you write a love poem for Miss Felicia." She turned and skipped to the door. "I'm going to go and rescue my doll now."

"I'll come with you," Grayson said. "I need to see the damage she's done and talk to her about it. I'll replace whatever she's ruined, Piper, and I will pay you for helping with her tonight. She's obviously more difficult than I believed, and you should be compensated for your troubles."

"You don't really have to pay me, Uncle Grayson, and you don't have to buy me a new doll. I've pulled plenty of heads off dolls in the past, and I'm pretty good at sewing them back together."

Grayson grinned down at her and felt his heart warm when she took his hand in hers and pulled him down the hallway and then down the stairs. A frown replaced the grin when Ben suddenly barreled through the door of the drawing room, toy soldiers clutched in each hand as he muttered something under his breath. He stopped and looked up, and Grayson noticed his little lip was trembling. Grayson dropped Piper's hand and bent down. "Is something the matter, Ben?"

"Sorry, Uncle Gray. I don't want to play with Ming. She stomped on my men. I don't want them to be like Piper's dolls." He gave a sniff, put his head down, and rushed away.

"I'll see to him," Eliza said, hurrying after the fleeing boy.

Grayson straightened and looked down at Piper. "Did you happen to notice how Ben said dolls instead of doll?"

Piper released a sigh. "Do you want me to go in first?"

"No, I think you should stay out here. Ming and I need to have a little chat."

Piper nodded, and Grayson patted her on the head before he strode into the drawing room. Even though the house had a well-stocked nursery, it was clear to him that Eliza and Hamilton wanted their children to have the full run of the house, hence the reason there were always so many toys scattered throughout every room. Ming was standing in the midst of some of those toys, and it was immediately clear she hadn't been expecting him.

She had a doll in her hand, and right before his eyes, she began to rip the doll's head from its neck. He strode forward, and—his footsteps evidently catching her attention—she dropped the doll to the floor, stuck her hands behind her back, and began blinking remarkably innocent-looking eyes back at him.

Concern flowed through him as he reached her side and squatted down to meet her gaze. "What were you doing, Ming?"

"Playin'."

"How many of Piper's dolls did you ruin?"

Silence met his question. He picked up Ming, placed her in a chair, and began picking up headless dolls, placing each one of them at her feet. She remained silent, and almost defiant, which was more disturbing than the silence.

By the time he'd recovered eight mangled dolls, anxiety had replaced the concern. He had a real problem on his hands.

How could he have not realized she was harboring such resentment?

He pulled up a chair next to her, waved away the nanny who'd reentered the room holding a tray filled with snacks, and sat down to face his daughter. Because that's what she was—his daughter. It was time he began treating her as such instead of treating her as if she were some pampered little princess, indulged with anything she might desire, except his undivided attention.

He realized in that moment that his attention was what she needed more than anything. She was his responsibility, and because of that, he was going to have to finally act like the father he was.

"We're going to go home now, and we're not coming back here until you can promise me you're going to behave."

"I wanna go to ball."

He blew out a breath. "I'm sure you do, Ming, but I'm afraid that won't be possible now. You hurt Piper's feelings, and Ben's, and you don't deserve a treat."

Ming's bottom lip jutted out. "Don't like you."

"I'm sure you don't, at least not at the moment, but I love you, and you'll just have to learn to accept that."

Grayson rose to his feet, picked Ming up, and with her kicking and screaming through the entire house, made his way to his carriage.

16

"On my word, Felicia," Ruth said, "if you weren't so attached to the Beckett family, I swear I would seriously consider forgoing this ball tonight."

The thought flashed through Felicia's mind that she almost missed the mother who'd previously opted to give her the cold shoulder and refrain from speaking a single word to her.

That mother was nowhere to be found and hadn't been seen since Felicia had climbed into the carriage at the jail.

The fact that her mother had apparently gone along so readily with Mr. Blackheart's suggestion that they check the jail was clear testimony to the likelihood that Ruth Murdock had come to the conclusion her daughter was headed for a bad end.

"I do hope the pesky rumor mill hasn't gotten wind of your shenanigans yesterday," Ruth continued as she plopped down into the nearest chair in Felicia's bedroom and waved a hand in front of her face. "Your father and I will have to send you on an extended trip, perhaps even abroad, if word gets out you've been visiting pubs *and* opium dens."

"The only reason I was in a pub was because I was assisting an elderly gentleman, and I only went into the opium den because I was helping Agatha with a story." Felicia moved across the room and took a seat in a chair next to her mother. "I've been at loose ends lately because I no longer feel comfortable helping out as much in Reverend Fraser's church, and assisting Agatha has given me a purpose. Who knows, perhaps I'll pursue writing as a career."

Her mother's hand began waving faster. "You never enjoyed writing. Your teachers bemoaned your lack of interest in it on an alarmingly frequent basis." Ruth's hand stopped moving before she sent Felicia a glare. "I'm well aware that you were most likely the culprit behind Agatha's sudden desire to investigate opium dens. You've tried to be subtle, but you're clearly interested in Grayson Sumner. From what I've been able to gather through snippets of hushed conversations, he was somehow connected to that disreputable opium business."

Her mother gave a delicate shudder. "Quite frankly, if I'd had any idea the gentleman possessed such a . . . shady background, I wouldn't have even entertained the thought of using him as a distraction for you."

"You thought Grayson could distract me from what exactly?"

"Reverend Fraser, of course." Ruth shook her head. "How could I have possibly known Grayson would have such an abysmal influence on you and cause you to completely discard all sense of propriety? The man is an aristocrat. One would think having such a lofty pedigree would make one averse to dabbling in business that ought not to be dabbled in."

"Grayson wasn't responsible for me going into that opium den, and . . . I haven't discarded my sense of propriety."

"He's a blackguard."

"He most certainly is not."

"He's put your life in danger by exposing you to those opium people."

234

"I wandered into that pub on my own, and that started this whole fiasco. Grayson was behaving rather chivalrously by making certain I was safe. You have no idea the caliber of ruffians who were patronizing that pub, and honestly, after I finished singing, if Grayson hadn't been there to stand up for me, I probably wouldn't be here now to tell the tale."

Ruth narrowed her eyes. "You never mentioned anything about singing."

"It was a completely spontaneous occurrence."

Ruth's eyes narrowed to mere slits. "What did Grayson think of your performance?"

"He told me I was an awful singer and that only my driving abilities rivaled my proficiency in belting out a tune."

"Did he now?" Ruth muttered before she lifted her chin. "Well, there is no time left to dwell on this matter. Mrs. Sheldon will be here any minute to dress your hair. Please try not to argue with the woman, Felicia. She's the most sought-after stylist in the city, and I would regret losing her services if you insult her."

"It's not as if I argue with people on a daily basis, and I certainly don't go around insulting them."

"You've insulted me most grievously over the past few days through your less than seemly behavior, something that puts into question my abilities as a mother. As for arguing, are you really going to argue that point?" She released a dramatic sigh. "You've disagreed with almost everything I've said of late, which was why I was so relieved when you went silent for a few hours today."

"I was only silent because that mud you insisted I place over my face had dried, and I couldn't open my mouth."

Ruth eased out of the chair and moved to stand in front of her, reaching out to cup Felicia's chin with her hand. "I must say, I'm very pleased with the results of that mud. Your skin is radiant."

Given the sheer torture Felicia had been through to achieve

radiant skin, she was glad it had worked. When she'd arrived home from her almost-venture into jail, her mother had demanded she remove her whiskers immediately, as apparently the sight of them had been more than Ruth could handle. Unfortunately, the whiskers had other plans, and no amount of tugging could pry them from Felicia's face.

Her brothers, seemingly curious about the loud ruckus coming from her room, had ambled in, and that's when events took an interesting turn. Strange concoctions were produced, one viler than the next, but nothing worked. Her whiskers would not part company from her skin.

Jeffrey finally proclaimed that he'd always wanted another brother, which had earned him a glare from his mother and a trip around the house to see if anyone could come up with a solution.

Mr. Blackheart had been the one to finally suggest an effective remedy, although he hadn't actually spoken to Felicia, seeing as he was apparently still miffed that she'd given him the slip and wasn't speaking to her.

The stable master was summoned, a nasty-looking and smelly substance had been procured and placed on her face, and thirty minutes later, her whiskers were finally pried away, leaving a stark imprint on her face that resembled nothing less than the beard she'd just shed.

Certain that a restful night of sleep would set her face to rights, Felicia had escaped into her room, her mother's dire predictions ringing in her ears.

Much to her dismay, her mother's predictions had come true, because upon rising and rushing to her mirror, her appearance, if anything, had worsened. She'd let out a howl, which had caused her mother to come running. But much to Felicia's surprise, instead of the dramatics she'd expected, Ruth had let out a single sniff before quickly penning off a note to a Mrs. Brombel, requesting her immediate assistance.

Mrs. Brombel had arrived at the house in a very prompt fashion and immediately began slathering her potions onto Felicia's face, along with the rest of her body, even though it was only her face that needed attention. The lady had completely ignored Felicia's concerns regarding the odd tingling she'd begun to feel, brushing those concerns aside with an airy flick of her wrist.

Unfortunately, the tingling had been the result of an unexpected reaction. For two hours, Felicia had been forced to sit in a tub of cold water in the hopes of soothing the rather large hives that had broken out on unmentionable parts of her body.

After the bath, Mrs. Brombel had rubbed her down with a thick layer of what looked exactly like mud, and she'd been forced to lie perfectly still until the mud dried. Then it had been back into the tub. Once the mud was washed off, most of her hives had disappeared—but only most.

"Ah, there's the door. It must be Mrs. Sheldon," Ruth exclaimed, causing Felicia to shake herself out of her thoughts and away from the slight itching that what was left of her hives was causing. "Remember, dear, be pleasant and cheerful."

"I'm always pleasant and, most of the time, cheerful."

"No you're not, but that's a conversation we'll save for another day. We must have you looking your best for the ball tonight."

Her mother was still scheming. Exactly what she was scheming, Felicia really couldn't say, but because she'd been distracted of late, she'd let her guard down. She watched as Ruth sailed out of the room without another word, her steps almost jaunty.

A grin teased Felicia's lips.

Her mother wasn't nearly as put out with her as she wanted Felicia to believe, and feeling in a much improved mood over

that, because, honestly, she didn't enjoy her mother's disappointment, Felicia moved over to her vanity table and sat down,
waiting for Mrs. Sheldon to come and fix her hair.

Two hours later, she was well coiffed, gowned, wearing the
proper amount of jewelry, and ready to tell her mother she no
longer wanted to attend the ball.

What could she have been thinking, purchasing this gown?

She dropped her head, her gaze settling on the overabundance
of pale skin that apparently couldn't be covered given the skimpy
nature of the bodice she'd thought had been perfectly acceptable
when she'd tried the gown on in the store. Now, however, well,
she'd only taken one fast glance at her refection in the mirror,
and what she'd seen there had caused her to begin breathing so
rapidly she'd almost fainted.

Because she'd been forced to take deep, heaving breaths in
order not to faint, her charms had almost spilled from the low-
cut neckline of the gown, and she hadn't been brave enough to
look in the mirror again.

She'd apparently been delusional when she'd picked out this
scandalous bit of red silk. Even though the color did comple-
ment her—something she hadn't been able to ignore when she'd
taken her quick glance—she wasn't certain she was brave enough
to wear it.

It was a pity she'd given all of her old gowns away. One of
those would have come in incredibly handy at the moment.

"Maybe I could just wear one of my new day dresses," she
muttered out loud.

"There's no time for that."

She spun around and discovered Jeffrey lounging against the
doorjamb. She gave him a quick once-over. Jeffrey was impec-
cably dressed in a black cutaway tailcoat, matching trousers, a

white starched shirt paired with the required stiff collar, white silk waistcoat, and a white tie. His hair was attractively tousled, and all in all, he made a fine sight indeed. "You look *very* handsome this evening."

Jeffrey smile and pushed away from the door. "You almost sound surprised by that."

Felicia returned the smile. "Perhaps I am. I guess I've never really noticed just how handsome you are and how nicely you turn yourself out for formal events."

"You know, you're beginning to concern me with how observant you've been of late."

She blew out a breath. "I've been ridiculous the past four years, haven't I."

"Maybe a little, but that's all part of life, isn't it?" He moved closer to her and nodded. "You look lovely."

"You're just saying that because we're running late. I can't go to the ball dressed in this gown. It's too . . . scandalous."

"It's not scandalous in the least, Felicia. It's fashionable. You're just not used to dressing in gowns that suit your figure. You truly do look lovely, and if I thought you looked scandalous, as your oldest brother, it would be my job to tell you so."

"You really think I look all right?"

"More than all right—beautiful. I'll be beating the gentlemen away from you tonight."

"If you're trying to reassure me, I'm not certain that's the way to go about it."

Jeffrey laughed and extended his arm to her, guiding her out of the room. They moved down the hallway and began descending the stairs. "Is Mother still annoyed with you?"

"I've recently come to the conclusion she's plotting."

"I've come to the same conclusion."

Felicia stopped midstep. "Why didn't you tell me?"

"I would have, but I can't figure out exactly what she's

plotting." He grinned. "I think it has something to do with Grayson."

"That's what I was thinking, but why would she attempt to dissuade me from seeing him if she really wanted me to pursue him?"

"It's Mother we're talking about. Who can understand the inner workings of her mind?" Jeffrey prodded Felicia back into motion. They reached the bottom of the stairs and turned to the right, moving to join Ruth, Daniel, and Robert in the entranceway.

Felicia looked around. "Where's Father?"

"Honestly, Felicia," Ruth began, "he was called out of town on business five days ago. Didn't you think it was rather odd, given all the trouble you've caused of late, that he hasn't summoned you to have a little chat regarding matters?" She fanned her face with her hand. "I considered sending him a telegram when you almost landed in jail but then decided such distressing news really should be discussed in person."

Robert suddenly cleared his throat, loudly. "You're also going to have to discuss with Father the fact that Felicia seems to have shed all hint of modesty. Look at the gown she's wearing. It's missing huge swaths of fabric."

Daniel moved to stand in front of her and looked her up and down. "I think she looks nice."

Felicia felt her cheeks heat even as she sent Jeffrey what she hoped was a blistering glare. "I told you I should've changed."

"Robert's just being a little overprotective," Jeffrey said. "There will be plenty of ladies there with gowns similar to yours."

"But they won't be our sister," Robert argued.

"Children," Ruth said, clapping her hands together. "Enough. We're running late, and I'm in no mood for this constant bickering." She gestured to the butler, who immediately opened the door, and with one last sniff, Ruth disappeared through it.

"I don't remember the last time she called us *children*," Jeffrey said.

Robert nodded. "It's because of Felicia and her unusual behavior of late. I do believe she's almost caused poor Mother to lose her mind, something I was fairly certain you were going to do, Jeffrey."

Felicia took Jeffrey's arm and allowed him to escort her into the carriage. The bickering between her brothers continued as they rode along, but Felicia barely noticed it. Her nerves were beginning to make themselves known the closer they got to the Beckett house, and it was all she could do to resist the impulse that kept stealing over her to throw herself from the moving carriage.

What would Grayson think of her gown?

Would he be like Robert and find it somewhat scandalous, or would he be like Jeffrey and find her lovely? She looked out the window and drew in a breath, slowly releasing it, hoping that would help settle her nerves.

It didn't, but before she could try something else, the carriage slowed to a stop. Jeffrey helped her out, extended his arm to her, and then let out a grunt when she refused to move.

"I don't think I'm feeling well."

Jeffrey rolled his eyes. "I've never known you to be a coward, Felicia. Get moving."

Not being one who ever turned down a challenge, Felicia set her sights on the door and started forward, causing Jeffrey to laugh as he kept pace with her. They walked through the door a moment later and joined the receiving line, Felicia's eyes widening when she realized that it appeared as if all of society had returned from the country to bid Zayne a fond farewell.

The urge to bolt was immediate, but she wasn't given that option when Jeffrey tightened his grip on her arm and pushed her forward. Before she knew it, she was standing in front of Gloria Beckett, who looked positively delighted to see her.

"Miss Murdock, you look enchanting."

"Thank you, Mrs. Beckett, and may I return the compliment?"

Gloria beamed back at her and then shifted her attention to Ruth. "You've done wonders with her, Ruth. Why, she'll be the talk of the town by morning."

Ruth's eyes widened. "Good heavens, let us hope not."

Gloria frowned, but before she could question Ruth further, Agatha called out to them, and Felicia turned, smiling when she caught sight of her friend waving madly at her from the stairway.

"If you'll excuse me," she said to Gloria with a nod. "I should go see what Agatha wants."

"Behave yourself," she heard her mother mutter behind her.

She scooted past numerous guests who seemed to be giving her far too much attention and finally reached the stairs, stepping up a few of them until she reached Agatha's side. "You were right, Agatha. This has turned out to be a true crush," she said as she gave her friend a hug and then released her. "Good heavens, that's an unusual choice of a gown, considering it's rather warm this evening. It covers you all the way to your chin as well as covering your arms."

"I have a rash, and hives, compliments of Mrs. Brombel's special potions."

"You saw Mrs. Brombel too?"

"Your mother sent her over after she was done with you. She must have remembered that I had whiskers on yesterday as well and thought I could benefit from the lady's remedies. Turns out I had the same reaction to her potions as you did—even though she claimed right before she slathered me in the stuff that you were an odd case and hives and rashes had never occurred with any of her other clients.

"Alas, I must be odd as well, because I broke out into an immediate rash, followed by huge hives, and even though she quickly covered me in mud, the mud apparently didn't work as well on me as it did on you." She blew out a breath. "I'm sweltering in this, if you must know, but I don't think anyone would want to get near me in my rash-engulfed state. It's a bit off-putting, if you must know, and I really should have been more considerate of you when you acquired a rash after the wedding."

"I never had a rash," Felicia admitted. "That was just my mother's way of not disclosing I was a bit of a mess due to a huge case of disappointment." She smiled. "It is odd though, now that I think of it, that rashes seem to be coming into conversations quite often of late."

"Let's hope this is the end of those," Agatha said as she scratched her arm. "I was considering staying home, but this is Zayne's last stand, so to speak, so . . . here I am, sweltering hot, itching, and I think one of my hives burst just a moment ago."

"That brings a delightful image to mind," Jeffrey said as he climbed the stairs and came to stand beside them.

"Mr. Murdock," Agatha exclaimed. "And Mr. Murdock and Mr. Murdock," she said when Daniel and Robert joined them as well. "This is a surprise, seeing all three of you together like this."

Daniel let out a snort. "Mother told us to keep an eye on Felicia." He winked. "When we saw her talking to you, Miss Watson, we figured we should probably intervene. No telling what type of mischief the two of you will get into next. Now, what was that about something bursting?"

Felicia grinned. "Really, Daniel, where are your manners? Surely you must realize it's hardly appropriate to inquire about a lady's bursting propensities."

Daniel returned the grin. "You have to admit, something bursting is entirely too intriguing not to inquire about, and I'm sure I've asked you inappropriate things over the years."

"True, but I'm your sister. Agatha hasn't been blessed with any brothers, so watch yourself, if you please."

"We're supposed to be watching you."

Felicia opened her mouth to dismiss that ridiculous notion when Robert suddenly shouldered Jeffrey aside, took her by the arm, and gave her a good tug.

"What are you doing?" she asked.

"We're going to go dance. Now."

She dug in her heels. "I'm not dancing with you. You're my brother."

"You always dance with me." Robert gave her arm another tug.

Felicia shrugged out of his hold. "What is the matter with you?"

"You're being ogled, right here and now, by those gentlemen standing at the bottom of the stairs—and in a blatant manner, even though you're standing in the midst of your brothers."

Felicia shot a glance to where Robert was glaring, and sure enough, there was a whole crowd of gentlemen staring her way.

"I wouldn't go so far as to make the claim they're ogling me."

"It looks like a slight case of ogling to me," Zayne said as he slipped up behind them and smiled as he nodded to Robert. "Take it from a man who's been cursed with a beautiful sister—you might as well get used to the attention, especially as it would seem Felicia has abandoned her former appearance and turned into a lovely butterfly."

He turned to Felicia and held out his arm. "Shall we get off the stairs? I do believe we're blocking the way to the ballroom."

Felicia took his arm, waited for Agatha to take the other, and then they climbed the remaining stairs before moving across the large landing and into the ballroom, all of her brothers following her closely. She let go of Zayne's arm and turned.

"You don't need to stay with me all night."

Daniel smiled all too innocently. "Of course we do. Mother's orders. Heaven forbid you manage to land yourself in more trouble because we're not around to stop you."

There was absolutely no reason to respond to that piece of absurdity. Felicia turned back to Zayne. "It seems as if everyone has returned to town to bid you farewell. When do you leave?"

"Right after the Fourth of July. I was planning on leaving a little sooner than that, but Piper wanted me to help her with a fireworks display, and I've never been able to resist any of Piper's requests." He smiled. "I also didn't want to miss the church picnic that day. It's always so much fun to watch the bidding of the baskets." He turned toward Agatha. "Are you putting a basket up for bid this year?"

Felicia noticed Agatha was turning a little pink, or perhaps her coloring was still a direct result of Mrs. Brombel's special potions.

"I might," Agatha said. "Although I will admit that every single time I enter a basket, I have this horrible fear it'll just sit there without a single bid."

"I'll bid on it, Miss Watson," Daniel said, stepping forward. "You just tell me which one it is, and I'll see what I can do."

Felicia bit back a grin when Zayne's eyes turned stormy. She cleared her throat. "I don't think that would be a good idea, Daniel."

"Why not?"

Felicia sent a pointed look to Agatha, who returned the look with one of confusion.

"*Grace,*" Felicia mouthed.

"Good heavens, I forgot all about that," Agatha muttered. She smiled at Daniel. "Perhaps it would be for the best if you didn't bid on my basket, but I can't exactly disclose the reasoning at the moment." She turned to Zayne. "You can bid on it though, and make certain it's a respectable bid."

Daniel looked around. "Is anyone else as confused as I am?"

"I'm not confused in the least," Felicia said before she grabbed Robert's arm and began pulling him toward the ballroom floor, looking over her shoulder. "Well, isn't someone going to bring Agatha along?"

It didn't escape her notice that even though Jeffrey and Daniel moved forward, Zayne was the first to grab hold of Agatha and lead her after them.

"I thought you said you didn't want to dance with me," Robert muttered.

"True, I did say that," Felicia admitted, "but I changed my mind."

"I have no idea who you are anymore, Felicia."

"I'm the same woman I've always been, Robert, just better garbed."

Robert swung her around once they reached the dance floor and took her hand in his. "You're not; you're different."

"And you don't like me different."

"I didn't say that," Robert countered. "I'm just not used to you being . . . happy."

Now, that was an unusual observation.

Before she had an opportunity to reply, the music began and Robert steered her around the room, complaining every so often about her apparent impression she was the one who ought to lead. By the time they left the dance floor, her good humor had been restored and she was suddenly anxious to seek out Grayson, if only to make certain he'd recovered from their little adventure and from finally admitting to everyone the truth regarding his past.

Unfortunately, he did not seem to be in attendance.

She was always aware of when he was in her vicinity—something she just then realized—because the air always seemed to be charged with little bursts of something disturbing. At the moment, the air felt perfectly normal.

"No more dancing for me," Agatha mumbled as she joined Felicia. "The itching it caused wasn't worth the pleasure, and I think another hive burst." She scratched at her arm for a moment and then glanced around, her eyes widening ever so slightly. "Felicia, do you know that gentleman over there, the one who seems to be staring at us?"

Felicia turned her head, her gaze skimming over the crowd and settling on a gentleman she thought Agatha might have been referring to, but the moment their eyes met, he spun around and disappeared through the crowd. "He must have mistaken us for someone else." She reached out and grabbed Agatha's hand. "Stop scratching. You'll only make it worse."

"But it's driving me insane."

"You need something to distract you. Tell me, have you seen Grayson?"

"Grayson is your distraction, not mine."

It seemed he was indeed.

"Have you seen him?" she repeated.

Agatha grimaced. "I don't think he's coming."

"What do you mean?"

"I mean I don't think he's coming."

Disappointment was immediate. "But . . . why?"

"I stopped by for a visit with Eliza this afternoon, and she mentioned that he's been having difficulties with Ming. Apparently her behavior has been less than acceptable, so Grayson wasn't comfortable leaving her with just the nannies."

"I thought he was supposed to bring her here and Grace and Lily were going to help keep an eye on all the children."

"Piper told me Ming ripped off some of the heads from Piper's dolls, so knowing that, I would have to believe Grayson is reluctant to foist his daughter on Eliza's children." She wiggled her brows at Felicia. "Its quite possible Ming's behavior might prompt the man into taking a wife."

"Yes, that's what I want him to do. Decide he needs a wife because of his motherless daughter."

"Piper told me she informed Grayson that he shouldn't ask you to marry him for that reason."

"Piper was talking to Grayson about marrying me?"

Agatha smiled a little smugly. "She told me I was her first choice as a potential wife for her uncle, but for some reason, your name got brought into the mix."

Agatha suddenly narrowed her eyes as she glanced over Felicia's shoulder. "Felicia, I don't mean to change the subject, considering it's a lively one, but that gentleman I was speaking about a moment ago seems to be heading our way."

Felicia turned and saw the gentleman she'd made eye contact with before he'd disappeared. He was somberly dressed, walking in a determined manner, his sights clearly settled on her, and . . . Cora Watson was on one side of the man, Gloria Beckett on the other, and bringing up the rear, her mother.

Good grief, they *had* been scheming.

She frowned when it suddenly struck her that none of the ladies looked particularly pleased, even though all of them were smiling.

"This should be good," Agatha whispered just before the mothers and the unknown gentleman came to a stop in front of them. Ruth scooted to the front of the group, sending Felicia what could only be described as a somewhat sickly smile.

"My dear, may I introduce to you Reverend Thomas Bannes? He's recently come to town after enjoying the company of Reverend Fraser and his wife."

Reverend Bannes stepped right up to Felicia, his gaze never

leaving her face. He bowed and then straightened, taking her hand in his. "My dear Miss Murdock," he began, "I've been longing to make your acquaintance ever since I had the pleasure of meeting Reverend Fraser." He tightened his grip on her hand as he leaned forward and lowered his voice. "I was told by the good reverend that you are a shining example of a truly devout and virtuous lady, and that's why I'm here. I am in the market for a wife."

17

Grayson had never dreamed that dealing with a temperamental three-year-old would be so exhausting.

He leaned his head back against the well-appointed seat of his carriage and closed his eyes, allowing the rattle of the carriage wheels against the stones to soothe his frazzled nerves.

The past day and a half had been an absolute nightmare as he and Ming had engaged in a battle of wills that Grayson wasn't exactly certain he'd won. He'd had no idea his daughter was so stubborn, or dramatic, or that she possessed the ability to raise welts on arms, legs, and even his stomach when she'd sunk her sharp little teeth into him.

More than once he'd thought about turning her over to the army of nannies he employed, but he'd known that doing so would mean he'd lost the battle and, more importantly, lost an opportunity to finally become a true father to the little girl who obviously needed a real parent figure in her life.

He raised a hand and rubbed his temple. It was a tough business, this fathering thing. He'd had no idea one small child could be so obstinate. As he'd carried her around and around his spacious home, trying to soothe her while not allowing her to bite him, he'd come to the understanding that a father's main job was to do what was best for his child—something he finally understood his father had been trying to do for him.

He'd begun talking to his father as he carted Ming from room to room, hoping the man could hear him from heaven. When Grayson was finished, he'd felt a small measure of peace, knowing that at last—even though the process was one-sided— he'd made a few amends with the father he'd been angry at for years.

His eyes flashed open when the carriage began to slow and then stopped, causing Grayson to lean forward, push back the curtain, and see they'd reached their destination.

He'd not planned to attend the Beckett ball, but when Ming had finally fallen into an exhausted sleep, one of the nannies assured him that she wouldn't wake until the next morning and had then given him some stellar advice. She'd told him point-blank that he'd done well with Ming, but that he should get out of the house and seek a bit of amusement, because . . . Ming would require his attention the following day.

It really was amazing how difficult attempting to be a real father was turning out to be, and it was quickly becoming clear that it wasn't a temporary situation—it was one he was going to have to embrace for years.

A footman took that moment to open the carriage door, and Grayson climbed out, noticing as he did so that there were no people milling around outside the mansion—clear testimony to the likelihood they were already deep into the ball, which meant he was more than fashionably late. He thanked the footman and began to walk toward the house, anticipation suddenly flowing through him.

Felicia would be there, and even though he kept reminding

himself that he wasn't good enough for her, she kept pulling at him even when she wasn't in his presence.

She hadn't turned from him when he'd disclosed his past. Because of that, he didn't seem to have any control over the fact that he thought about her constantly, thought about her sweetness, her quirkiness, her talent for trouble. All of those things kept roaming through his mind, keeping him up throughout the night, and those thoughts had compelled him to change into formal evening clothes and attend the ball.

He reached the steps to the house and was about to go up them when the hair on the back of his neck suddenly stood up. He turned and looked around, but other than a few footmen and coachmen standing around, he saw no one. Shrugging the feeling away, he climbed the short flight of steps, nodded to the butler who was standing with the door open for him, and walked into the house. There was no receiving line, nor had he expected one, given the lateness of the hour. He headed for the curved staircase, smiling when he saw Arabella and Theodore strolling down it.

"Did I miss the ball?" he asked.

Arabella smiled as she reached his side and gave him her gloved hand, which he promptly kissed. "Of course not, but the ball is a true crush, and the ballroom is stifling, which caused Theodore and I to seek out a little space."

"You can release my wife's hand, Grayson," Theodore muttered. "One would think that since she's securely married now, all of you poor unmarried gents would stop fawning over her."

Grayson let go of Arabella's hand and grinned. "It's difficult to ignore a beautiful lady, Theodore, no matter that she's firmly off the shelf."

Arabella took his arm, turned, and extended her other to Theodore. She steered them away from the staircase and into a parlor, breathing a sigh of relief as she let go of their arms, moved to a chaise, and sat down on it. "Ah, much better." She gestured Grayson to a chair next to her, while Theodore sat beside her on the chaise. She fanned her face with a hand for a moment before she turned her attention to Grayson.

"Piper told me you're considering asking Felicia to marry you."

Grayson blinked. "She did not. When?"

"I assure you, she did. We stopped by her house before heading to the ball. She also mentioned something about Ming needing a mother." She began fanning her face once again. "Take some advice from me, Grayson—don't bring that up when you propose. Felicia is a relatively no-nonsense type of lady, but she might reject you out of hand if she comes to believe you only want to marry her to provide Ming with a mother." She shuddered. "Hamilton did that with Eliza at first, and from what I understand, it did not go over well."

"I'm not planning on proposing."

Arabella narrowed her eyes. "But . . . you have to propose—tonight."

Grayson narrowed his eyes right back at her. "Why?"

"Because if you don't, Felicia is liable to end up with that Reverend Bannes, and I've already decided he's completely wrong for her."

Ice settled in his veins. "Who, pray tell, is Reverend Bannes?"

"I'm not certain, since I've never seen the gentleman before tonight, but he showed up at the ball and has been paying Felicia marked attention." Arabella blew out a breath. "She's danced with him at least twice, and I do believe he's trying his best to sweep her off her feet."

Grayson stood and strode to the door, temper replacing the ice. He was forced to a stop, however, when Theodore blocked his path. "Excuse me. I need to get by."

Theodore crossed his arms over his chest and shook his head.

"Not until you get that rage under control. The last thing Gloria will want at her ball is to have you taking out some poor reverend in the same way you evidently took out all those men at the pub." He winked. "I don't think mass carnage is what Gloria had in mind when she decided to host a ball to see Zayne on his way."

"I'm not intending to harm the reverend. I'm simply going to make it clear to him that he needs to maintain his distance from Felicia."

Theodore frowned. "You just said you weren't planning on proposing to her."

"True, but Arabella said this gentleman is all wrong for Felicia, so I feel a distinct need to help the lady. She has a very kind heart, you know. Pair that with her innocence and, why, there's no telling what kind of mischief she'll get herself into."

"He is wrong for her," Arabella said as she rose from the chaise and joined them. "I'll come with you. Between the two of us, we'll make short shrift of discouraging this man."

Theodore held his place. "Darling, you know I love you, but there's absolutely no possible way you can know—since the only contact you had with the reverend was to nod at him—that he's wrong for Felicia."

Arabella lifted her chin. "I'm remarkably intuitive."

"Be that as it may," Theodore continued with a fond smile to his wife, "both of you are forgetting one very important thing. Felicia went to extraordinary lengths to win Reverend Fraser's affections, which tells me she's hoping to form an alliance with a man of great faith."

He nodded to Grayson. "I'm not, by any means, questioning the strength of your faith, but a man of the cloth might be exactly what Felicia has always desired. Don't you think she deserves to make her own decision regarding this man?"

Grayson exchanged a glance with Arabella. "No."

"You're being difficult," Theodore muttered. "And a bit of

a contradiction as well, considering you quickly denied any interest in proposing to Felicia. It will not hurt to . . ." His voice trailed off when a hulking brute of a man slid into the room and joined them, whispering something in Theodore's ear before he slid on silent feet back out the door.

"And he would be?" Grayson prompted.

"That was Tiny." Theodore grinned but then sobered. "The police department has asked for my assistance with a situation developing in the city. Since I was unable to help them this evening, knowing Gloria would be more than miffed if I missed her ball, I've allowed my men to join forces with the police, and those men have been bringing me back regular reports."

Grayson tilted his head. "Do the police often ask for your assistance?"

"No, but since I'm the one who brought the activity at Posey's to their attention, and something does indeed seem to be happening, the police need all the help they can get."

Dread was immediate. "What's happening?"

"That's just it. We don't really know, but there's been an increased presence of Chinese around all the dens in the city, which has the police concerned." Theodore blew out a breath. "Anti-Chinese sentiment is high right now, so even a small increase in activities like the opium trade has people up in arms. They are demanding the police step in."

Grayson's mouth ran dry. "There are more Chinese surrounding the opium dens? Has an opium ship docked recently?"

"It appears that way, but I don't know how that could have happened. The authorities have been carefully regulating the docks for weeks."

"Money is how that happened," Grayson said. "I was once responsible for paying out huge sums so that our ships could gain access to docks in different countries. Believe me, it is not that difficult to disguise the arrival of a huge boat if the right amount of money passes hands." Horror suddenly coursed through him. "I have to get back to Ming."

Theodore shook his head. "No one can get to Ming, Grayson. I've sent ten additional guards to watch your house. She's completely safe. We should, however, discuss protection for you. I took the liberty of assigning a few men to trail you."

That probably explained why his hair had stood up on his neck—he *was* being watched.

"Do you really think that's necessary?"

"Until we figure out what's actually going on, yes. But it shouldn't—" Theodore stopped speaking as Ruth Murdock barged into the room, her color high and her expression decidedly agitated.

"Where have you been?" Ruth snapped as she came to a halt directly in front of Grayson and took his arm in a remarkably firm grip. "Disaster is nipping at Felicia's heels, and this is no time for you to be chitchatting with your friends."

"I was under the distinct impression you wanted me to keep my distance from your daughter."

"I've changed my mind." Ruth lifted her chin. "That is a lady's prerogative, but there's no time to discuss that at the moment. As I said before, Felicia is in dire danger of making yet another horrible mistake, so I need you to go after her. Be charming and allow her to see that her goal in life is not to become the wife of a minister—at least not the minister who is currently pursuing her."

Temper was immediate. "Reverend Bannes is pursuing her?"

"Ah, wonderful, you've already heard about the good reverend, which begs the question as to why you're not already at Felicia's side."

Theodore cleared his throat. "I told Grayson he should allow Felicia the opportunity to decide on her own whether or not she cares for Reverend Bannes's company."

"Don't be ridiculous, Theodore," Ruth snapped. "Felicia, even though she is an intelligent girl, has spent the past four years believing God intended her to be a minister's wife. Can't you see that she might come to the conclusion, given that her affection for Reverend Fraser was not returned, that God has sent her Reverend Bannes as an answer to the prayers she prayed over the years?"

"What if God really did send her Reverend Bannes?" Grayson asked slowly.

"Of course He didn't. God knows full well that Felicia would make an abysmal minister's wife. It's not that she's lacking in faith, far from it, but she needs a man who can give her the adventures her soul craves. Unfortunately, I've yet to meet a minister who's overly adventurous, and I certainly didn't get that impression from Reverend Bannes."

She drew in a breath, quickly released it, and continued. "Now then, before we go find her, I must warn you to tread carefully with anything you say, especially as pertains to this new gentleman. Reverend Fraser sent the man to town, and since Felicia held, and perhaps still holds, Reverend Fraser in high regard, make certain you don't inadvertently get her back up by saying anything of an unpleasant nature about the man."

"Do you really believe she still holds Reverend Fraser in high regard?" Grayson couldn't resist asking.

"I do, but not in a romantic way." Ruth surprised him when she smiled. "If you ask me, she never actually loved the gentleman. She loved the *idea* of loving him and embracing the role of his wife. She was completely mistaken, of course, and would not have been happy spending her life so demurely, but that's neither here nor there. We need to go find her."

For some odd reason, he had the distinct feeling he was being deftly maneuvered by a master manipulator.

He dug in his heels. "How exactly do you expect me to distract her from this reverend? And don't tell me to simply be charming, because that's a little vague."

Ruth's eyes turned calculating in a split second. "You could always bring up the subject I heard you and Piper were discussing."

He was definitely going to have a firm talk with Piper concerning what she should and should not disclose to people.

"You want me to tell Felicia that a six-year-old girl thinks I should marry her because I need a mother for Ming?"

Ruth tilted her head. "You know, a proposal would go far as a distraction."

"You think I should propose?"

"That's not really something I'm comfortable encouraging you to do, my dear. Whether or not you ask my daughter to marry you is a decision that should be made by you and you alone."

He'd obviously lost all control of the conversation. Not saying another word, he prodded Ruth forward, and a few moments later he finally found himself in the ballroom, craning his neck as he searched the crowd for Felicia.

"I'll leave you here," Ruth said with a nod. "We don't want Felicia to see us together and realize we're conspiring."

"Is that what we're calling this?"

Ruth sent him a cheeky grin and disappeared a second later.

He began to edge around the ballroom floor, nodding here and there to people he knew, frustration gnawing at him when he couldn't find Felicia. He was forced to a stop when a cluster of young ladies stepped over to him, all of them demanding his attention as he kissed one gloved hand after another. With promises to return and put his name on their dance card, he set off once again as the music ended and guests began to clear the ballroom floor.

His heart stopped beating when he finally caught sight of Felicia.

She was in the middle of the dance floor, and she looked enchanting.

Her golden hair was swept up on top of her head with a few tendrils left free to flit across her cheeks. Gems had been woven into her locks, and they sparkled under the light from the many chandeliers that graced the room, while that same light seemed to cause her skin to glow. His gaze lowered, and his heart began beating once again, beating so fast he felt, for a moment, light-headed.

She was wearing a gown of red silk, and it fit her form to perfection. He'd already come to the conclusion that she possessed some amazing curves, but seeing them in this particular gown left his mouth dry and his pulse racing.

A flash of temper stole through him once again when he noticed the bodice, or lack thereof, of her gown. Yes, there were many ladies tonight who wore similar gowns, cut in the exact way, but Felicia was slightly greater endowed than those ladies, and he felt the most unusual urge to rush to the nearest retiring room and search out a towel, much like the one Felicia had stuffed into the opera gown Arabella loaned her.

The temper suddenly turned to something that felt very much like rage when a gentleman Grayson had never seen before took Felicia's arm and began escorting her off the floor. The man leaned closer to her and whispered something in her ear, something that caused Felicia to laugh.

The world went red.

Grayson began to move, ignoring the nods people were sending him and pretending not to see the hopeful young ladies doing their best to garner his attention, some even going so far as to wave their dainty handkerchiefs in his direction.

His rage increased when he realized the gentleman seemed to be directing Felicia not to the line of gentlemen who were obviously waiting to ask her to dance but toward a door Grayson knew full well led to an outside balcony.

Increasing his pace when he saw Felicia and the gentleman disappear through the door, Grayson reached the door a moment later and paused. The sound of Felicia's laughter met his ears, and for a second, he reconsidered—until she laughed again and he realized her laughter seemed strained. He drew in a breath, reminded himself that Theodore had urged him not to cause any carnage, straightened his spine, shoved the door open, and stalked outside.

18

$\mathcal{D}$umbfounded was the only word that sprang to mind to describe how she was feeling as she stood in the company of a gentleman who seemed to be under the odd impression they shared some type of an understanding. That understanding apparently stemmed from Reverend Bannes's assumption she was somewhat desperate to marry a gentleman in his chosen profession.

The idea was completely ludicrous and seemed to have come about due to a conversation Reverend Bannes had with Reverend Fraser sometime in the recent past.

Felicia vowed right then and there that she was going to have a stern talk with Reverend Fraser as soon as the man returned from his wedding trip, and that talk was going to be anything but pleasant, given the extreme discomfort Felicia was currently experiencing.

To think she'd once believed Reverend Fraser had understood her.

She heard a grunt escape through her lips, the noise causing

Reverend Bannes to pause in his speech and gaze rather curiously back at her.

She forced a laugh, which returned him to his monologue—something to do with the mode of dress a minister's wife was expected to embrace.

Felicia narrowed her eyes. Surely the man wasn't chastising her over her choice of gowns.

". . . lovely, to be sure, my dear, but a more modest style might be in order for future occasions."

He *was* chastising her.

This gave credence to the idea she'd been pondering for quite some time—the one where she just might have misunderstood God's intentions for her all along. She'd been so certain her path in life was to marry a man of the cloth, but now that idea seemed foolish in the extreme. Simply because a man was called to do God's work didn't mean he was perfect husband material for her.

Now that she'd had plenty of time to think about it, even Reverend Fraser, a kind man if she'd ever met one, wouldn't have been a viable choice. She'd known him for four years, and yet the man had obviously not known her at all. He'd apparently sent Reverend Bannes to New York under the delusion that Felicia would be only too happy to fall at Reverend Bannes's feet and thank him for the attention he so benevolently bestowed upon her.

Gentlemen—it was quickly becoming abundantly clear—were pesky creatures, and she was quite certain she was just about ready to wash her hands of all of them and go out and buy a whole horde of cats. Maybe *they'd* understand her.

An image of Grayson flashed to mind. Now, there was a gentleman who did seem to understand her. He knew she couldn't drive very well, certainly couldn't sing; and she knew perfectly well that if he ever discovered she was a horrendous cook, it wouldn't bother him in the least. She couldn't say the same for Reverend Bannes. For some reason, she had the feeling he would expect his wife to be proficient in the kitchen.

"I can't cook."

Reverend Bannes stopped talking midword and blinked at her. "I'm sorry?"

Felicia grinned. "As I would be as well if you were ever forced to eat anything I prepared. Do you know I've been forbidden access to our kitchen? You would not believe the to-do made over my catching it on fire."

A muffled cough that sounded very much like laughter spun Felicia around. Her heart stopped for just a moment when she saw Grayson stepping out of the shadows. He was more than handsome in his evening attire, and her heart began beating a rapid tattoo when he settled his gaze on her and strode forward, determination in every step. The look in his eyes was something new, something intense, and something only for her. The dismal mood that had settled over her from the moment she'd discovered he might not be in attendance lifted.

"Grayson, this is a lovely surprise."

Grayson stopped in front of her, took her hand in his, and brought it to his lips. A spark traveled through her fingers and spread up her arm from his touch, even though his lips had touched only her glove. She couldn't seem to break eye contact with him, and he couldn't seem to remove his lips from her fingers. For how long they stood like that, she couldn't say, but a loud clearing of a throat brought her abruptly back to awareness.

Grayson sent her a wink and lowered her hand, but he kept hold of her fingers as he gave Reverend Bannes a nod. "Good evening."

Reverend Bannes cleared his throat again. "You still have Miss Murdock's hand."

"So I do," Grayson said cheerfully as he tightened his grip. "I'm Lord Sefton."

Oh . . . dear. Grayson had apparently taken issue with Reverend Bannes, because he only pulled out his title when he wanted to intimidate. She considered intervening, but the memory of Reverend Bannes criticizing her choice of attire sprang to mind, and she kept her lips pressed firmly together.

Reverend Bannes smiled a smile that didn't quite reach his eyes. "Ah, an illustrious member of the aristocracy here to take in the sights, I presume?" He didn't allow Grayson an opportunity to respond. "I am Reverend Thomas Bannes, an acquaintance of Reverend Fraser." His smile grew wider. "Reverend Fraser encouraged me to travel to New York when he learned I was in the market for a wife. My dear wife, Susan, departed this world for the hereafter a year ago, leaving me with four motherless children." He turned to Felicia. "Reverend Fraser assured me you would be delighted to receive my attentions."

Felicia felt an urge to stick her finger in her ear and jiggle it, because surely there must be something wrong with her hearing. The man couldn't have just blithely announced that he was in the market for a wife because he had four motherless children on his hands.

She tilted her head and considered Reverend Bannes for a long moment, realizing he was serious. In fact, he was staring back at her with expectation stamped all over his face, as if he'd just extended her a special treat and was waiting for her to acknowledge that.

It took every ounce of self-control she possessed not to roll her eyes. Honestly, what type of a treat would it be for her to accept this gentleman's attention, knowing full well he was only pursuing her in order to obtain a mother for his *four* children? Add in the troubling notion that he'd admitted he'd heard she was devout—which seemingly made her more acceptable for the role he intended—and he was lucky she was only considering rolling her eyes.

Irritation began to snake over her, but before she could open her mouth to put Reverend Bannes firmly in his place, Grayson tightened his grip on her hand and took one step forward.

"I really have no idea why Reverend Fraser would encourage you to pursue someone else's fiancée."

It was rare for Felicia to find herself without words, but no words were available to her. She could only stand in mute amazement as Reverend Bannes's smile disappeared—and then he did the same a moment later.

Even after he'd gone, she still couldn't speak. The ramifications of what Grayson had just done were swirling through her mind even as lovely warmth swept over her.

"I have no idea why I said that," Grayson muttered.

The lovely warmth disappeared.

"You didn't mean it?"

Grayson blinked. "Ah . . . well . . . you see . . ." He tugged on his tie as if it had suddenly become too tight. "That is to say . . . I have been pondering the idea of marriage lately, but I hadn't come to any firm conclusions as of yet."

Felicia arched a brow.

Grayson swallowed. "Piper and I had a lovely conversation regarding that very subject recently, and your name did come up."

"You sought marital advice from a six-year-old girl?"

"Piper is intuitive for her age."

"Intuitive or not, she's still a child, and I'm at a loss as to why you were even participating in that conversation in the first place."

Grayson began rubbing the top of her hand with his thumb, and Felicia yanked it away. She'd forgotten he'd been holding her hand, and with the direction their conversation was heading, she certainly didn't need to become distracted. She took a deliberate step back, earning a wounded look from him that she blithely ignored.

Grayson released a sigh. "It was not my intent to offend you."

"What was your intent?"

"As to that, I'm not certain, but I didn't care for that Reverend Bannes at all, and when he proclaimed he was here to offer you his attention, I fear I might have spoken a bit rashly."

"You do realize he's going to bring up the fact that we're supposedly engaged to someone at the ball, don't you?"

Grayson winced. "I didn't consider that."

She didn't appreciate the wince. "You should have. Honestly, Grayson, if word spreads about an engagement and then everyone learns it's nonexistent, I'll become the object of pity once again. I don't enjoy pity—loathe it, in fact. I hate when everyone takes to patting my hand as if I'm on my sickbed and speaking to me in hushed tones."

Grayson tilted his head. "I wouldn't be opposed to marrying you."

Felicia raised a hand to her heart. "And doesn't that just make me feel all aflutter."

"Are you being sarcastic?"

Her response to that was one extremely unladylike snort.

"You *are* being sarcastic."

"Why in the world would you believe I need to descend into sarcasm? I've been having such a pleasant time this evening. First, I've been forced to spend time with Reverend Bannes, who, it turns out, has traveled here to offer me a lovely proposal—one that would have me assuming the role of mother to his four children. Then you announce to him that we're engaged, but it turns out you didn't really mean it, so apparently you are now reconsidering and wouldn't be opposed to giving me your esteemed name."

"At least I don't want you for the sole reason of becoming a mother to Ming," Grayson said with a distinct trace of sulkiness in his voice.

Felicia blinked. She hadn't realized he was prone to that particular emotion. For some reason, odd as it seemed, she found it rather endearing. She shook herself. Now was not the time to dwell on that type of nonsense. She cleared her throat. "You probably decided not to point out what an excellent mother I'd be to Ming only because Piper advised you against it."

Grayson's face turned a shade darker, causing Felicia's mouth to drop open. "She *did* warn you against bringing that up, didn't she?"

"Ah, well . . ."

"Is everything all right, Miss Murdock?"

Felicia turned and discovered Mr. Blackheart lurking beside the stone wall that encompassed the balcony. She motioned him forward. "Mr. Blackheart, I need your assistance, if you please."

Mr. Blackheart was by her side in less than a second, causing Felicia to blink. For such a large gentleman, he was remarkably light on his feet.

"Did you need me to dispose of Mr. Sumner?" Mr. Blackheart asked in a soft voice that one might use when inquiring about the weather.

Felicia swallowed the laugh that threatened to escape and settled for shaking her head. "That won't be necessary. What I need from you is a man's opinion, and you're a man, so you'll do nicely."

Mr. Blackheart turned the scowl he'd been sending Grayson on her. "I'm not paid to offer opinions, Miss Murdock."

"I understand, Mr. Blackheart, but as you're paid to look after my welfare, and my welfare is unquestionably at risk at the moment, I'm really going to have to insist."

Mr. Blackheart crossed his arms over his chest and let out a grunt.

Felicia smiled. "Mr. Sumner believes I have no reason to be put out with him because he's announced to Reverend Bannes that we're engaged when it turns out he didn't actually mean it. Now he has decided he wouldn't be opposed to marrying me since there will be repercussions from his rash statement, and I was just wondering whether you think I'm being silly or if I have just cause to be annoyed."

Mr. Blackheart shot a glance to Grayson and then turned on his heel and strode away as quickly as he could without a single word, disappearing over the balcony wall.

Men were certainly strange creatures. She lifted her head and found Grayson grinning, the sight causing her temper to flare once again.

"It's not amusing."

Grayson's grin widened. "I do believe you terrify that poor man. He just jumped over the balcony, and we're two stories up."

"Good heavens, you're right." Felicia rushed over to the edge, peered down, and felt her lips curl when the sight of Mr. Blackheart casually strolling over to stand beneath a gas lamppost met her gaze. She'd expected to find his poor, mangled body lying on the cobblestones. Instead he sent her a tip of his hat, crossed his arms over his chest, and began to turn his head this way and that, evidently returning to what he was paid to do, search for trouble.

She straightened and turned. "He's fine, but just to be clear, I'm hardly terrifying. It not my fault Mr. Blackheart has issues with the simple act of conversing."

Grayson blew out a breath. "I wasn't insulting you, Felicia. I find your formidable nature delightful, but you must know that many gentlemen aren't comfortable associating with an opinionated lady." He smiled. "You don't terrify me in the least, and for that reason alone, I really believe you should consider marrying me, especially since I'm sure you're right that word about our engagement will spread quickly."

Felicia opened her mouth and discovered that, once again, she was completely at a loss for words. Disappointment cascaded over her, and she found she was no longer willing to ignore the reason behind it. She'd allowed Grayson—unwisely, it now seemed—to burrow into her heart over the past few weeks. In fact, if she were honest with herself, the thought of marriage to him had flickered through her mind more than once. She'd tried to push her feelings aside, especially after he'd disclosed the nastiness of his past, but she'd come to realize that his past did not define the man he was today.

He wasn't a comfortable gentleman by any stretch of the imagination. He was impetuous, surly, and downright grumpy at times, but he was also chivalrous and kind and seemed to make a habit of coming to her defense.

If only he'd declared himself to be a bit in love with her, she would have been the happiest woman alive, because somehow, even knowing his past, she'd fallen a touch in love with him.

That was the reason behind her disappointment.

She wanted him to love her, but it was becoming perfectly clear he did not.

Oh, he cared for her—she realized that—but . . . it wasn't enough.

A knot formed in her stomach, caused when another uncomfortable truth sprang to mind.

She'd never truly loved Reverend Fraser, because her heart had never felt this heavy even when that gentleman had done the unthinkable and married someone else.

What she felt for Grayson was completely different. It was unruly, messy, and frustrating. Her eyes welled with tears. Even though she wanted more than anything to accept his offer, she knew she was going to have to refuse.

She couldn't marry the man simply because he felt obligated to right the situation he'd created.

She drew in a deep breath and slowly released it, turning

her head ever so slightly to blink away the tears without him detecting them.

She didn't want his pity.

She blinked again when she noticed a slight shifting in the shadows on the far side of the balcony. She turned to Grayson, took a step closer to him, and lowered her voice. "Someone's watching us."

"What?"

"Over there. Go see."

Grayson ignored her request, taking her arm instead and pulling her toward the door. "You need to get inside."

She shook out of his hold.

"Get inside," Grayson said.

"Mr. Sumner, wait up. It's just me—Sam."

Grayson dropped his hold on her and spun around, as did Felicia. To her surprise, she discovered a ragged-looking boy standing on the balcony, shifting on his feet and smiling at Grayson.

"You know this boy?" she asked, moving forward until she was right in front of the lad.

Grayson joined her. "Felicia, this is Sam. Sam, this is Miss Murdock." He nodded to Felicia. "He's the young man who helped me get my horse after that debacle in the pub." He ruffled Sam's hair. "I've been waiting for Eliza to tell me you've gone to see her. I thought we had an understanding."

Sam scuffed his shoe against the stone floor. "My sisters didn't want to go to the orphanage."

Felicia frowned. "You live on the streets?"

Sam nodded.

She rounded on Grayson. "You knew this and didn't do anything?"

"I did, and before you begin giving me another lecture, I've tried to locate him numerous times, taking quite a few rides on my horse through the slums, but Sam's a tricky little guy, and I never met with any success."

Grayson would have been entirely more unlovable if he'd simply turned his back on the boy instead of trying to find him.

Sam tugged on the skirt of her gown, drawing her attention. "You shouldn't be mad at Mr. Sumner, Miss Murdock. He gave me money. It was my choice to stay on the streets, mostly because of my sisters. For now, we're fine."

"Why don't your sisters want to go to an orphanage?" Grayson asked.

"They've heard too many stories." Sam shrugged. "Even though I told them Mrs. Beckett's orphanage is different, I think they're afraid we'll get separated. But that's not why I'm here. Something strange is going on with the opium dens."

"You've been snooping around the opium dens?"

"No one notices me, Mr. Sumner, so I hear things. It wasn't hard for me to snoop, and you did help me out with that money. I owed you, and I knew you were somehow involved with those Chinese, since you had me scoot around to avoid them on the streets that day."

"You owe me nothing, Sam. You did me a huge favor, and I don't like the idea of you mingling with those men. You have no idea what they're capable of, and I would hate to see you hurt. I can only hope you haven't drawn their attention."

"No, they haven't seen me," Sam said. "I'm very good at going undetected." He looked at Felicia. "Except for tonight, that is."

Felicia grinned. "I have three brothers, Sam. Like you, I'm very good at going undetected when I spy, so that's probably why I saw you. But in all honesty, I only saw your shadow."

"Mr. Sumner hasn't seen me at all since I've been following him."

"You've been following me?"

Sam nodded. "Because you gave me all that money, I didn't

have to scrounge for food, so I had some time. I figured I'd keep an eye on you. I thought you might be the type of fellow to get into trouble."

"Which I'm perfectly capable of handling on my own, but I do thank you for your thoughtfulness." Grayson tilted his head. "Were you watching me when I arrived here tonight?"

"I followed your carriage. I was hoping to catch you at your house, but there was an awful lot of screaming coming out of it all day, so I just bided my time. I must have fallen asleep, because the next thing I knew, your carriage was trundling past me. A nice bloke offered me a ride on the back of his horse and dropped me off right as you got out of your carriage."

Felicia bent down. "But how in the world did you get on the balcony? It's two stories above ground."

"Oh, that was easy. There are vines on the side of the house, and I used them to help me climb." He smiled. "I was trying to figure out how to sneak into the ball, or at least get a message to Mr. Sumner, but then, well, both of you came out here and . . . I didn't want to interrupt."

"How much did you overhear?" Felicia asked.

"Um, not much," Sam said as he scuffed his toe against the stones once again.

Felicia began to tap her toe against the same stones Sam was scuffing.

Sam stilled and blew out a huff. "I don't want you to be offended, Miss Murdock, but if I was you, I'd take him up on his offer. You're not getting any younger, and you might not get another chance."

The night just kept getting better and better. Grayson had turned away from her, and his shoulders were shaking suspiciously, but before she could come up with a suitable response to Sam's statement without hurting the child's feelings, the door burst open and her mother, followed by Gloria and Cora, rushed out.

"My dears, I've just heard the exciting news," Ruth exclaimed as she came to a stop in front of Felicia and beamed. "I had high hopes this would happen, but I never imagined it would occur so quickly." She turned to Grayson and swatted him on the arm. "You gave me no indication at all that you were truly considering a proposal."

"Ahh . . . I . . . "

Felicia lifted her chin. "He didn't really propose."

Gloria shook her head. "Oh no, not again."

"It's Eliza and Hamilton all over," Cora added.

"Or Arabella and Theodore," Gloria added. "We mustn't forget that disastrous proposal." She looked to Grayson. "What, pray tell, did you do?"

"Ahh . . ."

Sam stepped forward and coughed, attracting everyone's attention. "That reverend fellow insulted Miss Murdock, and Mr. Sumner didn't care for that, so he suddenly announced they were engaged, which got rid of the reverend, but then . . . Miss Murdock got mad at Mr. Sumner because she didn't think he really meant it, and I can see her point, seeing as how he was a bit dodgy about the whole thing, and so, I'm not sure they're getting married."

Ruth tilted her head. "Who are you?"

"This is Sam, Mother," Felicia said. "He's a friend of Grayson's."

"And is what he said true?" Ruth pressed.

Felicia shrugged. "More or less."

Ruth looked from Felicia to Grayson, back to Felicia again. "I cannot believe how the two of you turn every simple little matter into a fiasco." She turned to Grayson. "If you were uncertain how to go about a proposal, you should have just said so when we spoke earlier."

Felicia moved closer to Grayson, ignoring the wariness now

residing in his eyes. "Did you, besides speaking with Piper, speak to my mother regarding marriage?"

"Well, not exactly, I mean, it was a rather vague conversation."

"Vague in regard to what?"

Ruth blew out a breath. "Darling, I was just concerned that perhaps you might—just might—form an unrealistic attachment to Reverend Bannes. He is a man of the cloth, after all. It seemed to me that you'd made a decision you were meant to marry one of them, and I'm not certain you've abandoned that decision quite yet."

Hurt and anger warred inside her. She took a deep breath and was pleased when the tears she longed to shed did not appear. "I know everyone believes I've been a bit of an idiot regarding my belief that God had a specific plan for me, but I understand now what His true intentions were. It's just taken me a while to understand. I'm not meant to specifically marry a minister—I'm meant to marry a man who can love and accept me for who I am, even with my many faults."

She squared her shoulders and forced herself to meet Grayson's gaze. "Since you don't seem to possess that emotion toward me, we have nothing further to say to each other." She sent a nod to her mother. "And you need to have more faith in me instead of thinking I would jump at the chance to marry a complete stranger simply because he's a man committed to spreading God's word."

Feeling a single tear leak out of her eye, Felicia spun on her heel and with her head held high set her sights on the ballroom, determined to keep what little dignity she had remaining. She heard Grayson call to her but didn't pause as she entered the house, marched through the throngs of guests and down the stairs, and stalked through the front door, not surprised in the least to find Mr. Blackheart waiting for her with the carriage.

She paused for a just a moment. "How will my mother and brothers get home?"

"No need to worry about that, Miss Murdock. I'll send the coachman back after we get you settled."

She swallowed past the lump that had formed in her throat. "Thank you," she managed to get out as Mr. Blackheart helped her into the carriage.

He waited until she settled down against the seat, and then he leaned forward, surprising her when he gave her arm a gentle pat. "You're a special lady, Miss Murdock—annoying, but special. Never forget that, and never forget that you deserve love."

With that, Mr. Blackheart closed the door and said something to the coachman. Felicia felt the carriage sway, leaving her to believe Mr. Blackheart had once again resumed his position of guard. The carriage rumbled into motion a moment later, and as she watched the Beckett house disappear from view, she felt tears begin to fall. Not bothering to wipe them away, she allowed herself the luxury of crying all the way home, wondering why, if she was so special, Grayson couldn't love her.

19

Grayson was rapidly coming to the conclusion that his life was unraveling right before his eyes. Felicia was no longing speaking to him, Ming's behavior had not improved—if anything, it had gotten worse—and . . . he'd somehow managed to obtain three additional children, all of whom were counting on him to find them a permanent home, one where they could live together. But until that time, *he* was responsible for their welfare.

Grayson pulled his attention away from the carriage window and glanced at Sam, then Beatrice, and then Harriet, all of whom were wearing new clothing and sporting remarkably clean faces in preparation for the Fourth of July picnic.

The very idea that he was now responsible for them was a little daunting, given his abysmal performance thus far as Ming's father.

Ming wasn't exactly happy with this new circumstance. In fact, she'd spent a lot of her time during the past week tormenting Beatrice and Harriet. When she'd taken to trying to divest the two little girls of any new clothing Grayson bought them, he'd saddled up his horse, rode to B. Altman's, and placed a large order for matching dresses for all three girls. That decision had create a small amount of peace in his household and explained why all three girls were currently dressed in identical pink dresses, white shoes with bows on them, and matching pink ribbons in their hair.

To top matters off, matchmaking mothers and their eligible daughters had descended on his house in droves, apparently believing he was distraught over Felicia turning down his proposal.

She'd been right about rumors starting regarding that, and in order to spare her the pity she'd been loath to garner, he'd let it be known that she was the one who'd rejected his suit.

"Do you think Miss Murdock will be at the celebration?"

Grayson looked to the left and smiled at Sam, who was looking dapper in his pristine white shirt, trousers, and a straw hat Sam had proclaimed made him feel like a gentleman. "I'm certain she will be, Sam, but I'm also certain she'll do her best to avoid me."

"Like she did when you and I went to try to speak to her the day after the ball?"

"*Tried* being the operative word," he muttered.

Sam grinned. "It sure was funny when, after Miss Murdock refused to see you, we went to find her and she dove out that window to get away from you. She must've really not wanted to talk to you, especially since she was on the third floor of her house at the time."

"She about gave me a heart attack."

"Good thing that tree was right outside the window, although . . ." Sam paused and then shuddered. "I don't think that Mr. Blackheart was too happy he had to scale up the tree and rescue Miss Murdock when she got stuck."

No, Mr. Blackheart had definitely not been happy. He'd told

Grayson in no uncertain terms that he was, from that moment forward, to leave Felicia alone, and if he didn't, there were going to be severe consequences.

Felicia, to his annoyance, had been standing by Mr. Blackheart's side when the man had issued that statement, her arms slightly scratched from her encounter with the tree and her expression decidedly stubborn. Instead of even bothering to give him the courtesy of any type of response, she'd stuck her nose in the air, thanked Mr. Blackheart for rescuing her, and marched back into the house without another word.

He'd contemplated going after her, but Mr. Blackheart had pulled out his pistol, and even though Grayson was fairly sure, having the advantage of the skills he'd learned in China, he'd win in a hand-to-hand fight with the man, he was no match for a bullet. Plus, he would hardly have been setting a good example for Sam if he'd allowed himself to get shot because he couldn't abide a straightforward request.

"I bet if you told Miss Murdock you love her and long to marry her, she'd start talking to you."

Grayson frowned. "How old are you again?"

"I'm eleven, Beatrice is nine, and Harriet is six. Ming's three, if you've forgotten."

"I know how old Ming is."

"Just checking, Mr. Sumner." Sam smiled. "So what do you think about my idea?"

"I'm not certain I'm quite ready to proclaim myself in love with Felicia."

"You don't love her?"

"I'm not sure."

Sam tilted his head. "Do you feel all mushy inside when you're around her?"

"I normally just feel irritated, but . . . sometimes there might be a slight feeling of mushiness."

"Do you think she's pretty?"

"I think she's beautiful."

"Does she make you laugh?"

"She does."

Sam crossed his arms over his chest. "Then you love her, but don't wait too long to tell her. I heard that Reverend Bannes is still in town, and I think he's only remaining here so he can try to convince Miss Murdock to marry him."

"Where in the world did you hear that?"

"I have my sources."

Grayson arched a brow.

Sam blew out a breath. "I've spent a lot of my time down in the kitchen. A person can learn a lot down there. Servants are the best sources when it comes to what's happening in the city."

"Perhaps when you're older, we should consider setting you up with Theodore Wilder. I have a feeling you'd make a fine investigator."

"I don't think you and I will still know each other by then, Mr. Sumner. It was kind of you to take me and my sisters into your home and all, but you and I agreed that it wasn't forever, just until your sister can find us a real home."

A thread of something uncomfortable settled over him. After Felicia had left the ball, he'd noticed Sam trying to make his way back to the edge of the balcony and realized the boy was about to disappear again. He couldn't abide the thought of Sam and his sisters remaining on the street and called him back, insisting that the boy return home with him after they picked up his sisters. But Sam, apparently realizing Grayson wasn't exactly father material, had struck a deal—one where he and his sisters would stay with Grayson only until other arrangements could be made, as long as those arrangements didn't consist of any orphanages.

Grayson had met with Eliza the day after the ball and sought out her advice as to how he should proceed. She'd offered to begin the search for a family who'd be willing to take in three children but had told him that it would be difficult. Grayson knew it wouldn't be fair to ask her to take the children, especially since she'd just opened up an orphanage on the outskirts of the city. If the children from that orphanage learned she'd invited other orphans to live with her, feelings would definitely get hurt.

Grayson summoned a smile when he realized Sam was watching him oddly. "How about we think of something for you and your sisters to call me besides Mr. Sumner?"

Sam frowned. "I wouldn't feel right calling you Grayson, sir. My parents expected us to mind our manners."

"They did," Beatrice said, shaking her head up and down, which sent her red curls bouncing.

Harriet didn't speak a word, but she also gave a nod, just one, but it was a small nod and didn't make her brown curls bounce at all.

His heart gave an unexpected lurch. These children had suffered so much loss, and yet they were still concerned about their manners. He summoned up a smile. "I think you should call me *Uncle Grayson*."

"But you're not our uncle," Beatrice said slowly. "We don't have any uncles 'cause we're orphans."

"True, but I think *Uncle Grayson* has a nice ring to it, and I would consider it a great honor if you three would agree to call me that."

It was clear in that moment that the three children were truly siblings. They spoke not a word but seemed to communicate with their eyes. Beatrice gave another nod, Harriet bit her lip, and Sam turned back to Grayson. "We think that would be nice, Uncle Grayson."

"Me too," Ming suddenly said.

"I'm your father, Ming, not your uncle."

"Nope."

Not particularly caring to arrive in Central Park with Ming screaming, Grayson decided against arguing that ridiculous point. She was only three, after all, and hopefully, she'd soon forget about calling him Uncle Grayson.

The carriage began to slow, and then it stopped, causing anticipation to immediately flow through him.

Felicia would be in attendance, and he was determined to speak with her. Because the park was such a public place, and because quite a few members of society would be at the celebration, given that they'd come back to the city for the ball, he doubted Felicia would make a scene and refuse to talk to him.

A footman opened the door, and he got out first, followed by Sam, who helped Beatrice out and then Harriet, then stepped aside so Grayson could get Ming.

"Want Sam."

"Honestly, Ming, you're being exceedingly difficult, and . . ."

"I'll just get her, Uncle Grayson," Sam said. "And just so you know, I don't think a three-year-old knows what *exceedingly* means. In fact, I don't know what it means."

Hmm . . . maybe that had been part of the problem. Maybe Ming hadn't been able to understand a lot of the things he'd said to her.

"Thank you, Sam. That's some excellent advice."

"You're welcome." Sam got Ming out of the carriage, set her on the ground and took her hand, then reached out and snagged Harriet's hand. He nodded to Beatrice. "Are you all right not having a hand to hold?"

"She may hold mine."

Grayson lifted his head and found Agatha, accompanied by Zayne, standing a few feet away. Agatha walked over to Beatrice and smiled. "You must be Sam's sister, and I'm guessing you're Beatrice."

Beatrice's eyes were huge. "I am Beatrice."

"I'm Miss Agatha Watson, but you may call me Agatha. And you"—she looked at Harriet—"are Harriet."

Harriet nodded, her eyes huge but her expression solemn.

"She's a little shy, Miss Watson."

Agatha looked at Sam. "You're Sam. I've heard a lot about you from Felicia."

Grayson's ears perked up. "You've spoken with Felicia?"

"Of course. She's not put out with *me*."

"What has she said?"

Agatha gave a sniff. "I'm not divulging secrets, Grayson. You'll have to ask her what she's been saying."

"She's avoiding me."

"Of course she is, and I can't say that I blame her. You made an utter mess of things the night of the ball."

Zayne stepped forward and grinned. "That's why we hurried up to meet you when we saw you get out of the carriage. Agatha and I are going to help you set matters to rights." His grin widened. "We're well equipped to offer you some steadfast advice on how to go about winning Felicia back."

Oddly enough, he found himself interested in hearing what Agatha and Zayne had to say, even though they were completely *ill equipped* to give out relationship advice.

It was a clear mark of how desperate he'd become.

"If the two of you can figure out how to get her to talk to me, I'd be most appreciative."

Agatha shifted a basket Grayson just then noticed she was holding from one hand to another. Then she turned to Zayne and thrust it at him. "Here, make yourself useful. It's getting heavy." She rubbed her hands together. "Now, where were we?"

"Felicia . . . talking to me . . . your advice."

"Ah, yes, exactly right. Well, we'll have to arrange it so that the two of you can have some time alone, but . . . that might be difficult since you now have so many children to look after."

Grayson gestured toward a phaeton just pulling up that was driven by one of his coachmen and filled with three of his nannies. They appeared to be a little squished.

"Three nannies?" Zayne asked somewhat weakly. "Isn't that a bit much?"

"Ming's tricky," Grayson admitted. "And not only do I have an abundance of nannies, I have a good many guards as well. But they'll be more difficult to pick out, considering they're paid to be stealthy."

"You're still in danger?" Agatha asked.

"Perhaps, but I don't really care to discuss that today, especially not in front of . . ." He glanced to the children, all of whom were watching the interaction closely—except for Ming, who was squatting down, poking at what looked to be an anthill. He moved over to her, scooped her up into his arms, and to his surprise, instead of screaming, she sent him a beautiful smile.

He couldn't help but wonder if he'd ever understand anyone under the age of five.

"I'm surprised you had your nannies driven here in your phaeton, knowing Felicia will be here," Agatha said, stepping forward to take Beatrice's hand, the little girl looking completely delighted by the action. "I wouldn't put it past her to agree to talk to you, but only if you'll let her drive your phaeton again."

That thought had crossed his mind, and quite honestly, he'd decided he would brave another ride with Felicia at the reins if that was what it took to get her to speak with him.

"She's not that bad of a driver," he muttered.

"She is, and you know it, but hopefully we can come up with something else that will get her talking to you again."

Agatha looked at Sam and his sisters and then frowned. "Just don't make a point of bringing up that you've taken three more children into your home. Felicia knows about your generous act, of course, but if you bring it into the conversation, she might think it was done to impress her, and that won't earn you any points."

"I didn't bring Sam and his sisters into my home to impress Felicia."

"I know that, but Felicia's in a sensitive frame of mind right now, and you did blunder rather badly when you asked her to marry you, if one can even consider what you did a proposal. You'll need to tread lightly with her." With that, Agatha began walking toward an area bedecked with flags and ribbons where a large crowd had begun to assemble.

Grayson looked over his shoulder and nodded to the nannies, who began walking behind them. He'd told them he wasn't planning for them to take over the care of all the children today, wanting to try his best to spend as much of his time as possible with them, but he wasn't delusional. He knew perfectly well he had limits, thus the reasoning behind bringing in professionals in case he found himself in over his head.

Zayne fell into step beside him as Sam, holding Harriet's hand, walked a few feet in front of them, chatting happily to his little sister and pointing out things of interest.

"It was a good thing you did for them," Zayne said softly, nodding his head toward the children.

"I keep getting this unusual urge to keep them myself, but I know they need a proper family, and I can't provide that."

"You could if you married Felicia."

"Shh . . . Don't say that out loud. Honestly, Zayne, if Felicia hears even a snippet of something that suggests I'm only interested in her so I'll be able to keep Sam and his sisters, well, she really will never speak to me again."

"Hurry up," Agatha called over her shoulder.

"It would be easier to hurry if this basket of yours wasn't quite so heavy," Zayne called back.

Agatha stopped walking, and she and Beatrice waited for them to catch up. "I wanted to pack an extraordinary lunch this year. That way I'll be certain to get bids."

"You know I promised you I would bid on it," Zayne muttered.

"True, you did, but since the proceeds for this basket auction go completely to the church, I thought I should make my lunch as appealing as possible so that it drives up the bids."

Grayson frowned. "A basket auction? What is that exactly?"

"Oh, I do beg your pardon, Grayson," Agatha said. "Even with that accent of yours, I sometimes forget you're a foreigner. It's a tradition, mostly in small towns, that on the Fourth of July, ladies prepare a picnic lunch, and then gentlemen bid on the baskets, and the gentleman with the highest bid gets to eat the lunch and spend that lunch with the lady who prepared the basket."

She smiled. "Felicia organized the first auction a few years ago for those of us who stay in town over the Fourth of July. Some families were finding it more difficult to spend time at their summer homes, and she remembered how fun it had been when she went to the auctions in Newport as a child."

Grayson felt a thread of irritation run through him. "She stayed in the city because of Reverend Fraser, didn't she?"

"I do believe that was the case, but Felicia started a wonderful tradition here, and I'm so thankful she did." Agatha sent Zayne a rather smug smile. "I'm interested to learn how much money you'll have to turn over in order to secure the winning bid."

"You never said I had to secure the winning bid," Zayne said slowly. "You only said I had to bid so that your basket wouldn't be sitting there forlorn and unnoticed."

Agatha stuck her nose in the air. "Fine, don't make the winning bid. I mean, you are leaving in the next day or so, and we'll probably never see each other again, but apparently you're not going to miss my friendship."

"Fine, I'll win the basket."

"Lovely," Agatha said before she turned to Grayson. "I don't know why I didn't think of this before, but all you have to do to get Felicia to speak to you is make the highest bid on her basket."

Zayne shook his head. "I don't think that's a good idea."

Grayson ignored him. "Felicia couldn't avoid me through an entire meal."

"Exactly, which is why I hope you brought a large sum of money with you," Agatha said with a grin. "I've seen Felicia today, and she's looking absolutely darling in a gorgeous gown of purple that brings out the color of her eyes. I'm afraid she's attracted quite a bit of attention from the gentlemen who arrived early for the festivities. You'll need to be diligent with your bidding in order to win the day."

"Piper, Ben." Ming squealed and began to squirm in his arms.

He watched Piper and Ben walking toward them in the company of Eliza and Hamilton and had no choice but to set Ming down, afraid he would otherwise drop her or suffer another one of her bites. "Behave yourself," he said before he let go of her, and she flew on tiny legs over to Piper and gave her an enthusiastic hug before she did the same with Ben.

Perhaps she would actually behave herself. Maybe his refusal to allow her to spend time with her cousins this past week had finally gotten through to her, which might, hopefully, cause a change in her behavior.

Agatha tugged Beatrice over to Piper and Ben and introduced them to one another, then gestured for Sam and Harriet to join them. Piper looked absolutely delighted to have new friends, and with barely a nod to him, she took Ming by one hand, Harriet by the other, and with Sam, Ben, and Beatrice taking up positions beside her, she called over her shoulder that they were off to find some treats, and away they went.

Grayson took a step forward. "I should go with them."

Eliza put a hand on his arm. "They're fine, Gray. Children like to be by themselves sometimes. Besides"—she gestured with her head—"Gloria and Cora have already joined them, and you know those ladies love nothing more than having children to spoil. You really shouldn't ruin their fun, and your nannies are also keeping an eye on them from a distance."

Grayson turned his head, and sure enough, Ming's nannies were standing a few feet away from where the children were chatting with Gloria and Cora, who'd somehow managed to get cookies into everyone's hands and appeared thrilled they had so many little faces turned their way. He looked to the right and found, much to his relief, some somber-looking gentlemen watching the children, their somberness giving testimony that the guards hired to protect the children were taking their assignment seriously. He turned back to Eliza.

"Any luck finding a family for Sam and his sisters?"

"Not yet. There aren't many families who are willing to open their homes to three children, but we'll find someone." She smiled. "Are you finding it's a little difficult to care for four children?"

He returned the smile. "Maybe, but I have to say, Sam, Beatrice, and Harriet are wonderful children and haven't caused any problems—whereas Ming . . ."

Whatever he was going to say next slipped out of his mind as a laugh he knew only too well floated to him on the breeze. He took a step forward, and then another, coming to a stop when he caught sight of Felicia and felt his temper kick in.

As Agatha had mentioned, she was dressed in a delightful gown of purple, her hair attractively arranged with some type of barely there hat attached to her crown. He took no issue with the way she was dressed, but he did take issue with the fact that she was surrounded by gentlemen trying to win her favor. His lips thinned into a straight line when one bold gentleman picked up her gloved hand and pressed a far too intimate kiss against her knuckles.

"Don't do anything rash," he heard Eliza mutter right as he began moving again.

He pretended he hadn't heard that bit of nonsense, set his sights on Felicia once again, and decided that a rash act was exactly what was needed.

20

Felicia forced out yet another laugh, the odd thought coming to her that it was slightly pathetic that she wasn't enjoying herself. Here she was, surrounded by delightful and eligible gentlemen, all of whom were vying for her attention, but . . . she wasn't having much, if any, fun.

Not one of the gentlemen gathered around her seemed capable of making her pulse race even the slightest bit, and it was entirely Grayson's fault.

He'd ruined her, probably for life, in the matter of racing pulses. Since he hadn't tried to contact her again after her unfortunate decision to climb out her window, she was fairly certain he'd come to the conclusion she was a crazy lady and was through with her forever. That meant her pulse was destined to simply plod through her veins instead of gallop for the rest of her days.

". . . and the sanctuary is almost as lovely as the one here in New York," Reverend Bannes said, causing Felicia to blink out of her thoughts as she tried to concentrate on the conversation at hand.

Reverend Bannes was turning out to be a somewhat pleasant gentleman, when he wasn't pushing the idea of marriage on her, or his belief of what a perfect wife should be, or how she could obtain such perfection. He'd toned down his wooing efforts, much to her relief, but she knew he hadn't given up just yet. She had the sinking feeling he was determined to win her picnic lunch.

Felicia shuddered at the thought of having to watch him eat what she'd prepared. She'd only attempted a sandwich with a salad, but unfortunately, the bread had turned slightly soggy, and the salad . . . How could she have known making boiled eggs would prove to be so tricky?

"Miss Murdock, are you paying attention?"

She certainly wasn't going to admit that her attention had not been on whatever it was he was saying. She summoned up a smile. "I'm sure the sanctuary at your church is lovely."

"I was inquiring as to when you'd like to visit."

"Ah . . ."

The rest of her response—whatever it would have been, since she really had no idea what to say to that inquiry—was deemed unnecessary when the sea of gentlemen surrounding her parted and an uneasy silence settled over the group.

"Forgive me for interrupting, but I need to speak with Felicia."

Her gaze immediately found Grayson, right as her pulse began to flutter. He was staring at her all too intently, and from what she could tell, there was a distinct hint of surliness in his tone.

He was never more attractive to her than when he was surly.

She shook herself slightly over that ridiculous idea, remembered she was still supposed to be put out with the gentleman—even though she readily admitted, at least to herself, that she'd missed him dreadfully—and lifted her chin. She opened her mouth to respond but was interrupted by Reverend Bannes, who seemed to have a vast number of words at his disposal.

"Now, see here, Lord Sefton. This is not well done of you. It is common knowledge that Miss Murdock has refused your suit, so hear me well—I won't stand idly by and allow you to badger the lady."

Grayson arched one aristocratic brow. "Felicia thrives on badgering."

It was suddenly perfectly clear that it was about to turn into a very interesting day.

"Demure young ladies such as Miss Murdock do not enjoy badgering, let alone thrive on it," Reverend Bannes returned.

"Miss Murdock, although she's been able to put on a good show of it the past few years, is not demure in the least."

For some odd reason, Grayson's words, which might have been seen as an insult to most ladies, caused her heart to sing, to sing until he opened his mouth again and a distinct expression of grumpiness stole over his face.

"My patience is waning rapidly, Felicia. So either you can agree to come along peacefully and speak with me, or I will resort to flinging you over my shoulder and carting you away in order to say my piece."

One corner of her mouth curled up. Grayson, it seemed, was in an unusual mood, but he apparently had forgotten he was standing in the midst of numerous gentlemen, all of whom were now muttering rather fiercely. She felt the other corner of her mouth begin to curl, but it stopped midcurl when all the mutters abruptly ceased, evidently because Grayson was sending the men one of his all too dangerous glares.

She couldn't help but be slightly impressed by his determination—even though it was somewhat annoying to learn that her bevy of admirers, who'd moments ago been only too keen to seek out her company, didn't seem as keen to defend her from the seemingly insane gentleman who'd wandered into their midst.

Grayson took that moment to crack his knuckles. She couldn't help it—she grinned.

"You've lost your mind, Mr. Sumner. While I would adore nothing more than to speak with you, especially since you've asked in such a pleasant yet demanding manner, I see my mother signaling over there, and I do believe the bidding on the baskets is about to begin."

To her surprise, he smiled, but it was a somewhat frightening smile, especially when he stopped cracking his knuckles and rubbed his hands together. "Wonderful, let the bidding begin."

Before Felicia could so much as blink, Grayson strode forward, took her arm, and ignoring the halfhearted protests of the men she'd been speaking with, towed her away from them. He strode through the crowd and brought her to a halt right in front of the makeshift stage that had been created for the day's festivities.

Ruth stood on that stage, her eyes gleaming with excitement. Felicia was suddenly a little wary, knowing her mother had never run the auction before. She had stepped in for Reverend Fraser, who was still away on his wedding trip.

"Happy Fourth of July," Ruth called. "It's a lovely day for our celebration and a lovely day to bring in much-needed funds for the church." She narrowed her eyes as she scanned the crowd. "I expect the bids to be generous." She smiled as laughter filled the air, turned, and strolled casually down the row of baskets, plucking up a delightful-looking red basket decorated with red, white, and blue ribbons, holding it high for everyone to see.

Felicia wondered why she hadn't realized her mother would start with her basket. Considering the food resting on the inside was probably not edible, she was thankful she'd taken extra time to make certain the outside of the basket looked presentable.

"This delightful basket has been created by my dear daughter, Miss Felicia Murdock," Ruth called as she held the basket even higher. "I must tell you, she is a fine cook. I'm certain she's made a delicious feast for any gentleman who wins this basket."

She really needed to have a chat with her mother regarding her frequent exaggeration of her talents.

"I bid five dollars."

Felicia swung around and barely had time to look at the man who'd placed the bid before another man yelled a higher bid, and to her amazement, a fierce bidding war erupted around her.

It was disconcerting to be the object of such attention, but . . . She narrowed her eyes as her gaze settled on Grayson.

Why was he just standing there? Had he changed his mind and decided he didn't want to win her basket? Had he come to the conclusion she wasn't worth the effort? Was he truly going to allow some other man to make off with her basket and win her company?

The urge to swallow her pride and tell him she'd made a mistake by refusing his offer swept out of nowhere, causing her to forget to breathe. She had made a mistake. She didn't want to lose him, and . . . she wanted another chance.

She also didn't want to eat lunch with the burly man who'd just shouted out a bid of fifty dollars.

She reached out a hand to him, but before she could make contact, he stepped forward.

"One hundred dollars."

Relief and a thrill of something she couldn't quite name coursed through her.

"Are you certain, Mr. Sumner?" Ruth called.

Grayson tilted his head. "Better make it two."

Breath came charging back, filling Felicia's lungs with air. She stepped toward him. "That might be a little too generous. The last bid before yours was only fifty dollars."

Grayson, much to her surprise, let out what sounded remarkably like a snort. "I'd pay double that, triple even, to win your basket."

Right then and there, Felicia's knees began to wobble.

"You know I can't cook."

"I'm not a particularly picky eater."

"Sold," Ruth shouted, "to Mr. Sumner for two hundred dollars."

Nerves suddenly made themselves known, most likely brought on by Grayson's gazing at her oddly, with what seemed almost like tenderness in his eyes. She cleared her throat and struggled to come up with something to say. "Ah, well, you've just made my mother's day. She's been nagging at me all week to talk to you."

"She's not still put out with me?"

Felicia smiled. "Hardly. She's been reserving her ire for me, mostly because I wouldn't talk to you."

"We have much that's left unresolved between us. Perhaps we can get some matters solved while we eat your picnic lunch."

"I'm not certain it's advisable to eat the lunch I made. I wasn't being modest when I admitted I couldn't cook."

Grayson stepped closer to her, causing her knees to go all wobbly once again. "We don't have to eat, Felicia. There are so many—"

His words were interrupted when Reverend Bannes appeared right behind them, his face red and his brow perspiring. "Lord Sefton, or Mr. Sumner, or whatever you're calling yourself today, I fear I must insist on speaking frankly to you, although I do hope you'll refrain from hitting me after I'm done."

Grayson frowned. "My good man, I don't normally attack people, especially men of the cloth."

Reverend Bannes wiped a hand over his perspiring brow and simply looked at Grayson for a long moment.

Grayson turned to her. "Why does he think I'll hit him?"

"Because you were sending him and all the rest of the men who were around me one of your dangerous glares."

"I was doing no such thing."

She patted his arm before she turned to Reverend Bannes. "He won't hit you, Reverend Bannes, so please continue."

Reverend Bannes eyed Grayson a bit warily for a moment and then nodded. "Well, I've come to the conclusion that you, Miss Murdock, are distressed regarding Lord Sefton winning your basket, so I and some other gentlemen thought we'd pool our money together to beat Lord Sefton's winning bid. That way, *we* could eat lunch with you, even if your basket doesn't have enough food in it."

"I'm perfectly capable of exceeding any amount you and those other gentlemen can scrape together," Grayson said, his eyes going all too dangerous once again.

She punched his arm this time instead of patting it. "Be quiet."

She turned back to Reverend Bannes. Even though he was a rather blustering sort, he was a dear man at heart, but . . . he wasn't meant for her, nor were any of the other men she'd been speaking with.

"Reverend Bannes, forgive me, but I do believe you've been suffering from a few delusions in regard to me. While I appreciate that you were willing to face Mr. Sumner and his temper by approaching us, it isn't fair to allow you to continue believing you and I would make a good match."

"But . . . from what Reverend Fraser told me, you'd make the perfect minister's wife. He said you're a lady of exceptional faith."

"Which I am, but I'm not demure, which is what you claimed you were looking for in a wife. Quite honestly, I'd drive you insane if you spent much time in my company. I'm afraid you're going to have to look elsewhere."

"But you're going to have to eat lunch with him now," Reverend Bannes said slowly.

Felicia smiled. "So I am."

"You don't seem distressed about that."

Her smile widened. "I'm not distressed in the least."

Before she could say another word, and with barely a nod to Reverend Bannes, Grayson took her arm and pulled her through the crowd, not stopping until they reached a spot well away from the people still bidding on the baskets. She couldn't help but notice that after he let go of her arm, he took hold of her hand.

"Why aren't you distressed?" he demanded.

Here it was, the opportunity she'd been dreaming about, the opportunity to tell him the truth. "I, ah, well . . ." She lifted her chin and met his gaze. "I wanted to have lunch with you."

Grayson's eyes darkened and he leaned forward, lowering his head. All the breath left her in a split second when she realized he was going to do the unthinkable and kiss her right in the middle of Central Park.

"Uncle Grayson."

Grayson stilled, released a breath, the air from it fanning her face, and then he pulled back and turned. Felicia turned as well and discovered Piper marching up to them, a mutinous-looking Ming by her side, while three nannies trailed behind them, all looking somewhat resigned.

Piper tugged Ming over to them and stopped. "Ming is being difficult. She keeps trying to bite everyone, and when her nannies tried to help us, she threw herself on the ground and began screaming for you. So here she is."

Piper let go of Ming's hand, sent her a disappointed look, spun on her little heel, and marched off, one of Ming's nannies falling into step beside her.

"Would you care for us to try again?" one of the two nannies left asked, stepping forward.

"I'll take her from here, Clare. Why don't you and Mary return to keep an eye on Sam and his sisters." He sent Felicia a resigned smile. "On second thought, why don't you bring them to join us? Miss Murdock and I were just about to eat lunch."

Clare frowned. "Begging your pardon, sir, but Sam, Beatrice, and Harriet are having a wonderful time with Piper and Ben. I'm sure they wouldn't mind eating lunch with you, but since they haven't had much fun in their lives, do you think it might be possible to allow them to eat with their new friends? We'll watch over them—not that they need much of that since Mrs. Beckett and Mrs. Watson haven't let them out of their sight—and we'll bring them to you after they're done eating."

"That'll be fine, Clare," Grayson said. "And thank you for the suggestion. Miss Murdock and I will take over with Ming, and do make certain you and the other nannies get some lunch as well."

Clare nodded and then walked away with Mary, leaving Ming staring angrily after them. Felicia moved over to the little girl and crouched down. "Shall we go and find a lovely spot for a picnic?"

Ming's lip jutted out. "No."

"That was my favorite word when I was a child, Ming, but we're going to have a picnic, and you're going to enjoy it." Not giving Ming an opportunity to protest, she scooped her up and ruffled her hair, causing the girl to smile ever so slightly. "Now, we need to go and fetch our basket."

Grayson grinned. "No we don't, because your mother's heading our way, and it looks as if she has two baskets."

Felicia looked up, and sure enough, Ruth was strolling their way, a huge smile on her face and clutching in her hands not one but two basket handles. Grayson stepped forward and took them from her, earning himself a pat on the cheek from Ruth once she had use of her hands again.

"You're a dear boy."

"Why did you bring us two baskets, Mother?"

"You don't think I would actually allow anyone to eat what you've prepared, do you?"

Grayson laughed. "I swear I heard you make the claim just a short time ago that Felicia was a wonderful cook."

"Did I? Hmm. I don't recall." She turned but then looked over her shoulder. "Do try and find a nice shady tree to eat under. It's growing quite warm, and I wouldn't want any of you to take in too much sun."

Felicia looked around and realized that the nearest grove of trees that had available space underneath them was quite some distance away.

Her mother, it appeared, was back to her plotting ways.

She fell into step beside Grayson, and they strolled across the grass, Ming, surprisingly enough, chatting in the way three-year-olds were prone to do about everything and anything under the sun. They reached the grove of trees, but Grayson continued forward, pointing to another grove that was even farther away and would apparently lend them even more privacy.

Felicia found she didn't have a single objection to that idea.

By the time they reached the second grove, she could feel perspiration beading her forehead. She set Ming down, swiped her brow with her gloved hand, and set about helping Grayson unfold a blanket they found in her mother's basket. Once she had Ming situated on the blanket, she began pulling out food but paused when she felt Grayson's gaze on her.

That gaze had heat warming her cheeks, and not a heat caused by the warmth of the day.

"Have I told you how lovely you look today?"

Her mouth felt remarkably dry. "Um, no, I don't believe you have."

"Well, you do. Stunning, in fact."

Incapable of summoning up a response, she simply sat down beside Ming and watched as Grayson began to inspect their lunch. He handed Ming a sandwich—out of her mother's basket, of course—then handed her one, but then . . . he pulled over the basket she'd prepared, pulled out the sandwich she'd assembled, and moved to sit down right beside her.

Right then and there, Felicia knew without a shadow of a doubt that she was well and truly in love with the man.

She waited with bated breath as he took a bite, thought she heard something crunch as he chewed—which was odd because tomatoes and eggs really weren't supposed to crunch—and then almost dissolved into a puddle of mush right beside him when he swallowed and smiled, not a single trace of a grimace on his face.

"Delicious."

He was delicious, and she wanted nothing more than to have him lean forward once again and finally kiss her.

Unfortunately, he didn't move forward but simply took another bite of the dreadful sandwich she'd made, even though his eyes had gone somewhat dark.

Perhaps, since she'd been giving him the cold shoulder over the past week, he wasn't aware that she was feeling more charitable toward him.

She leaned ever so slowly in his direction but froze when Ming scooted between them and let out a giggle.

Good heavens, she'd forgotten all about Ming.

Knowing her cheeks had to be bright red, she turned back to her sandwich and struggled to come up with something to say.

"Eliza told me you're taking care of Sam and his sisters."

"Yes, well, Agatha told me not to bring that up in case you got it into your head, if I proposed again, that I was using the children as a way to soften your heart."

Her pulse leaped through her veins. "Were you considering proposing again?"

She heard the sound of carriage wheels in the distance, and the buzzing of a bee sounded right by her ear, but Felicia didn't let those distract her as she kept her attention squarely fixed on Grayson.

He set aside the sandwich and leaned forward, almost obscuring Ming from view as her giggles rang out once again, but before he could say anything, or kiss her, for that matter, the sound of the carriage wheels grew unusually loud, and he pulled back from her right before he jumped to his feet.

"Take Ming and run," he yelled as a carriage pulled up right next to them. The door flung open, and a man jumped out brandishing a pistol, and that pistol was directed right at Ming, who was already nestled in Felicia's arms.

"I do beg your pardon for interrupting what seems to be a most touching scene, but I need to speak with you, Gray, and I'm afraid I'm going to have to do so far away from here. Don't want any of those pesky guards you've been surrounding yourself with to interfere. I'm sure you understand."

Grayson's hands clenched into fists, and his stance suggested he was about to pounce. "I thought you were dead, Francisco."

The man let out a hearty laugh, the sound more menacing than amused. "I'm delighted to report that I am not." He gestured with the pistol toward Ming. "Get in the carriage, and bring Ming with you."

Was it possible this was Grayson's partner from China? How was it that he was in New York?

Francisco smiled at Felicia, the smile causing pure terror to settle over her. "I won't be needing you, darling—well, not in the carriage."

He looked up and nodded to the driver of the carriage, a driver who turned out to be a woman. Alarmingly enough, she too was holding a pistol, one that was trained on Grayson. "If any of them make an untoward move, my love, don't hesitate to shoot them. We mustn't forget that Grayson has some rather formidable skills at his disposal, which is why I feel prompted to reveal that I won't balk in the least with shooting any of you, including Ming."

Grayson's eyes turned dangerous. "In case you've forgotten, she's your daughter."

"An interesting point, and one that we'll discuss at a later time, once we're well on our way." Francisco took a step closer to Grayson. "Now then, to the business at hand. You and Ming are going to come with me, and your little lovely here is going to go on an errand for us."

"Leave Felicia out of this. She has nothing to do with anything regarding China."

"True, but I need someone to fetch those jewels you so foolishly made off with." He growled under his breath. "What could you have been thinking? Those jewels are worth a fortune. You couldn't have believed no one would realize you'd taken them with you when you left China so abruptly."

"I took them for Ming. They are her inheritance, and I was hoping everyone would think I'd been killed along with the rest of the Wu family."

"But I wasn't killed either, was I? But enough about that for now." He turned to Felicia. "Do you know where he's stashed the jewels?"

Felicia swallowed. "Ah . . . well, no. Truth be told, I've never even been in his house."

"Then we shall provide you with directions, my dear, if that's where Gray has hidden the loot."

"Francisco, let Felicia and Ming go. I'll take you to get the jewels. I don't need or want them, and there's been too much bloodshed as it is. There doesn't need to be more."

"That remains to be seen, but the jewels aren't the only thing I need. And that is why, again, this lady is going to go fetch them for us."

Felicia lifted her chin. "I can do it."

"Felicia, no, you can't."

She ignored Grayson's protest even as she moved closer to

305

him. "Just tell me where they are, and I'll go get them." She looked to Francisco. "Where do you want them delivered?"

"I'll send you a note after I feel sufficient time has been given for you to recover them."

Felicia narrowed her eyes. "Meaning . . . you're going to have someone trail after me, aren't you?"

"But of course, my dear. That way I'll be certain no one is coming to your rescue, especially that annoying Theodore Wilder, who has been all too diligent in his efforts to figure out why there's been a bit of unusual activity of late surrounding the opium dens." He smiled. "As an added incentive for you to not pick up any assistance, remember, I'm the one holding the gun, and it would be a shame if Grayson or little Ming would have to suffer from a bullet to the heart because you've done something . . . stupid." He lifted the hand not holding the pistol and waved it. "Now, hand over the child."

Her arms instinctively tightened around Ming, who had a death grip around her neck, but the strength of a small child was no match for Francisco. He wrenched Ming away and brought her to the carriage within a span of a few seconds. Someone in the carriage grabbed the child and pulled her inside. Francisco had brought reinforcements.

Grayson took a step forward but froze when Francisco turned the pistol on Felicia. "Careful, Gray. Just because it's handy to have her here to do my bidding doesn't mean she's not disposable, or rather, replaceable." He smiled yet again. "So, be a good boy and tell her where you've stashed the jewels."

"I need your word that you won't harm her after she brings them."

"Fine. For what my word's worth, you have it."

Grayson and Francisco stared at each other for a moment, and then Grayson gestured her closer. She moved on trembling legs to his side, tears stinging her eyes.

"It'll be fine," he muttered, rubbing her back.

"I wish I could believe you, but I—"

"No chitchatting," Francisco barked. "Get on with it before any of those guards come running, not that they can see right now since the carriage is blocking you from their view, but I don't want to take any chances."

Grayson sent him a glare before returning his attention to her. "I know you've never been in my house, but do you know where it is?"

"Thor and I have driven past it . . . ah . . . well . . . a few times this week."

His eyes widened ever so slightly. "We'll discuss the reasoning behind that after we get out of this latest bout of trouble, but"—he lowered his voice as he brought his lips next to her ear—"there's a safe hidden behind a horrendous painting of a rather large lady in my house. The combination is 42, 17, 34, 12."

"42, 17, 34, 12?"

"Exactly. Can you remember that?"

She'd never been good with numbers, but she didn't think mentioning that would be very reassuring to Grayson at that moment. "Perhaps I should write them down."

Before she had time to blink, Francisco shoved a piece of paper and a pencil at her. She scribbled down the numbers, showed them to Grayson, and when he nodded, drew in a breath and released it. "I'll need to find a ride, but I'll get to Grayson's house as soon as I can."

Grayson tilted his head. "Take my phaeton. It's parked by my carriage. If anyone asks, just tell them you're fetching something for Ming. No one will think anything of it, considering how proficient you are with the reins."

Hope was immediate.

Everyone knew she was an abysmal driver, and perhaps someone, anyone, would take notice and realize something was amiss. All she had to do was pray that someone was discreet and wouldn't draw undue attention from whomever Francisco was going to have follow her.

"I think that's all the time you lovebirds need," Francisco said cheerfully.

Even though there was so much Felicia felt still needed to be said, she could only watch with tears dribbling down her face as Francisco cocked the pistol and aimed it at Grayson. A second later, Grayson sent her a look filled with something indescribable and climbed into the carriage.

21

Grayson settled into the seat and gestured to the Chinese man holding Ming. "Give her to me."

The man—the same man he'd recognized in the pub— simply looked at him, his expression curiously blank.

Apparently, he'd not been imagining things. His presence in that pub had been noticed, and evidently, he too had been recognized. But did the Chinese want more from him than the jewels, and why was Francisco involved? And how had he escaped the attack against the Wu family?

Francisco flicked a hand toward the man and spoke something in rapid Chinese, whatever he said causing the Chinese man to lean across the space that separated them and thrust Ming onto Grayson's lap. Ming immediately burrowed against him, her little body trembling and not so much as a single sound escaping her lips as the carriage lurched into motion.

The poor child had seemingly been terrorized into silence.

"I imagine you have quite a few questions."

Grayson patted Ming's head and turned to Francisco. "Just a few."

"None of this would have been necessary if you'd stayed in China instead of fleeing on the first ship available following the Wu family situation."

"I hardly think the slaughter of an entire family can be called a 'situation.'"

Francisco ignored the statement. "Why didn't you just stay?"

"I was fairly certain my life, as well as Ming's, was in danger, since the entire Wu family had been killed."

"I was a member of the Wu family, yet I wasn't killed."

"How did you manage to escape?"

Francisco smiled. "I didn't need to escape, considering I helped orchestrate the raid. You being alive today was due to me and my plans, but unfortunately, you did the unthinkable by leaving China—taking Ming with you, and taking the jewels."

"You helped orchestrate the deaths of dozens of people?"

"That I did. But I also arranged for that captain to keep you late at your office, which ensured you would live." Francisco released a grunt. "Feel free to thank me at your leisure."

"You believe I should thank you, even though you're responsible for killing Lin?"

"But of course you should thank me. It was on my order that she was a specific target. I arranged her death so that you could finally be free of her."

Grayson could only sit there, stunned, as horror robbed him of speech. Francisco's admission was unthinkable and . . . evil. He swallowed past the bile that had risen in his throat and then cleared it. "Why would you have done such a thing?"

"Lin was a hag, and you deserved better. She wasn't a real wife to you, and now, well, you're well rid of her."

"I never wanted her dead."

Francisco shrugged. "Well, she is, and there's nothing I can do about that now."

"And what about Mei? Your own wife . . . the mother of your child."

"I did what needed to be done."

"Why?"

"Money, of course."

"Wu Wah Hing paid you handsomely."

"Yes, he did. There was just the pesky little problem of him wanting me dead."

"What?"

"You heard me. Wu Wah Hing had put out the word he wanted my head on a platter. I wasn't willing to part with my head, being rather fond of it, you see, so I put into motion a plan of my own."

"You murdered an entire family."

"*I* didn't murder them. *I* only gave pertinent information— such as drawings of every building, schedules, and the number of people residing in the Wu compound—to members of the Zang family. They took care of everything from there."

"You were in league with the Zang family?"

"Indeed, but I'll explain how that came to be later. We've arrived at the docks."

The carriage rumbled to a stop, and Grayson had no choice but to get out, holding Ming tightly as he climbed down. Apprehension was immediate when he saw a ship right in front of them, a ship that had numerous Chinese sailors swarming around it.

"After you," Francisco said with a wave of his pistol.

Grayson followed the woman who'd been driving the carriage across the docks. What was a lady with fair skin and red hair doing mixed up with the Chinese? He didn't have long to wonder. When they reached the boat and began walking up the plank, Francisco said, "Darling, do run and tell everyone I've returned, won't you?"

The lady glanced over her shoulder, sent Francisco a nod and a smile, and then hurried forward and soon disappeared.

"She's my wife."

"Didn't take you long to replace Mei, did it."

To his surprise, Francisco laughed. "Ah, my old friend, there are still so many things you don't understand."

Slipping on the wet surface, Grayson steadied himself and held Ming a little tighter. As he stepped onto the deck, he wondered if he was going to make it out alive, and what Felicia would do when she realized he'd given her the wrong combination to his safe.

He'd done so in order to protect her, while at the same time he'd hoped that Mr. Blackheart would be following closely, careful to remain undetected. He'd keep Felicia safe.

Now all Grayson had to figure out was how to escape Francisco and keep himself and Ming alive.

Francisco directed him into a cabin and gestured to a chair. Grayson took a seat and arranged Ming on his lap. "How did you find me?"

Walking over to a table bolted to the floor, Francisco took a moment to pick up a decanter filled with an amber liquid, poured out two glasses, moved to hand Grayson one of the glasses, and then sat down in another chair. He took a sip of his drink and smiled. "You've led me on a merry chase, Gray, not one I appreciate, by the way. Once we were finally able to sail from China, I went to England, figuring you'd return home, but discovered you'd already taken off."

He shook his head. "Your house in London is impressive, and I was somewhat taken aback when I learned you have numerous estates throughout the country. Finding out you were in America was slightly confusing. If I've learned one thing about you, my friend, it's that you thrive on the challenge of business. What more profitable business could there be than that of estates you already own?"

"Surely we have more important matters to discuss than what I've chosen to do with my estates back in England, Francisco."

Francisco settled back in his chair. "I was simply curious, that's all, but if it's a sensitive topic, by all means, what would you care to discuss instead?"

"You mentioned you wanted something besides the jewels."

Francisco took another sip of his drink, set it aside on a nearby table, and sat forward. "I want Ming, of course."

Felicia wiped the tears off her face with her sleeve and stifled the urge to run through the crowd screaming. Not wanting to be stopped by family or friends, all of whom would most likely notice something was decidedly wrong, she skirted around the crowd and made for the parked carriages and horses, her pace slowing slightly as she caught sight of Mr. Blackheart out of the corner of her eye. When it appeared he was heading directly her way, she gave a tiny shake of her head, keeping her gaze forward even as she prayed he would see the shake.

She looked around the conveyances that were lined up in a row, picking Grayson's phaeton out a moment later. Summoning up a smile, she strode over to it and moved to stand in front of the coachman, who was polishing the side of the phaeton with a cloth.

"May I help you, miss?"

She drew in a breath and quickly released it. "Mr. Sumner has given me permission to borrow this phaeton, so I'll need you to step aside."

The coachman blinked. "I'm afraid I can't allow you to simply take off with Mr. Sumner's property without him giving me his approval."

Frustration flowed freely. She lifted her chin, glanced to the right, and saw two Chinese men watching her as they leaned against a tree a few yards away. She chanced a glance in the other direction, and relief edged over her when she spotted Mr. Blackheart, already on his horse, casually speaking to a pretty lady who was twirling a parasol. If she hadn't come to know the gentleman quite well, she would have sworn he was just a man enjoying the attention of a lady, not the trained and quite dangerous guard she knew he really was.

Feeling better because she was not totally alone, she returned her attention to the coachman. "I really am going to have to insist you stand aside."

The coachman's eyes went wide. "Are you threatening me?"

Felicia blinked. "Well . . . no, er . . . yes, yes I am threatening you, because I am Mr. Sumner's fiancée, and if you don't step aside, I'll be forced to inform him about your disappointing behavior."

"I didn't hear Mr. Sumner was engaged."

"He just asked me today, in the park, right after he bid on my basket." She forced a smile. "He paid two hundred dollars for it."

"Mr. Sumner is the one who bought that basket?" the coach-man asked before he shook his head. "That must have been some lunch, but . . . I'm not certain I should allow you to take the phaeton. It's incredibly fast, and you're just a tiny little lady."

"I've driven it before, over to Mrs. Beckett's house." She lifted her chin. "Mr. Sumner was surprised by my driving abilities."

The coachman still appeared reluctant, so taking matters into her own hands, Felicia brushed past him, climbed up and into the phaeton, grabbed the reins in a less-than-practiced hand, and gave them a flick, causing the coachman to leap out of the way as the horses bolted into motion.

The speed she quickly obtained had her falling back against the seat as she thundered down street after street, calling out apologies one after another as she left mayhem in her wake. She finally took to talking to God, out loud, with her voice sounding shrill even to her own ears, asking Him to keep Grayson and Ming safe, while at the same time keeping her from running over any people.

She soon found herself barreling down Fifth Avenue and wondered how she was going to get Grayson's horses to stop, but much to her amazement, they slowed down on their own, veered to the right, and stopped directly in front of his house. A groom came running toward her, and she took his hand and on trembling legs climbed down and glanced around the street.

She didn't see Francisco's men, or Mr. Blackheart, but that wasn't too surprising. Her mad dash through the city had been quite erratic. She would have been difficult to follow.

Sending the groom a nod, she hurried up the steps to Grayson's home and found the butler already standing with the door open, watching her warily. She forced another smile, but her smile dimmed when the butler looked down his nose at her and informed her that Mr. Sumner was not at home, right before he began to shut the door.

She had to find the jewels, and she had to do so quickly. So in desperation, she stuck out her foot and bit back a yelp when the door caught it. The butler's eyes widened considerably when she pushed past him, entered the house, and began running from room to room, looking for a painting of an ugly lady.

Unfortunately, Grayson's house was filled with such paintings, and she couldn't help stomping her foot, just once, in frustration when she peered behind yet another painting of an unattractive woman and found absolutely nothing.

"I've just convinced the butler you're not a lunatic on the loose, so I don't think he's going to summon the police, but you should probably hurry with whatever it is you're doing."

Felicia jumped straight up into the air, landed back on her

feet, brought her hand to her chest, and gawked at Mr. Blackheart. "How did you get in here? Good heavens, do you think anyone saw you?"

Mr. Blackheart let out a grunt. "I didn't come in through the front door. If you'll recall, I'm good at scaling trees."

"If you climbed in through a window, how were you able to calm down the butler? Didn't he find it odd you didn't come through the front door?"

"I told him I did use the front door, although I'm not certain he believed me since he found me already at the top of the stairs. However, I convinced him I'd been sent to deal with you, and without a blink of an eye, he allowed me to continue." Mr. Blackheart's lips twitched just a touch. "I think the poor man believes you're deranged."

The world, it seemed, was turning more peculiar by the moment.

"Tell me, what are you looking for?"

Felicia blew out a frustrated breath. "A safe, one that Grayson told me was behind a picture of an unattractive lady."

"It'll be in his bedroom." Mr. Blackheart motioned her forward. "Lead the way."

Felicia straightened her spine. "I certainly don't know where that is located."

Mr. Blackheart's lips twitched once again, and then he nodded and strode forward, checking one room after another as Felicia told him all she knew about Grayson's capture.

"Here it is," Mr. Blackheart said, walking into a room decorated with masculine furniture but without a smidgen of style. He moved over to a painting of a large woman holding a bowl of fruit, swung it open, and nodded to Felicia. "What's the combination?"

Felicia pulled out the small piece of paper she'd shoved into her glove and read it off, holding her breath as Mr. Blackheart spun the dial, then spun it again in the opposite direction, then back again. He tried spinning it different ways for a full minute, then held out his hand. "Let me see those numbers."

Felicia handed him the paper and watched Mr. Blackheart read it, his lips mouthing the numbers. Then he looked up and shook his head. "He gave you the wrong combination."

"What?"

"You heard me, but I bet he did so to protect you."

Temper was swift. "I'm going to . . . Well, I don't know what I'm going to do when I see him, but . . . Now what are we going to do?"

Mr. Blackheart looked around and then, to Felicia's annoyance, smiled.

"There is nothing amusing about this, and you never smile. Why are you smiling now?"

"Because Grayson is only renting this house, and the furnishings, while nice, aren't made of the most expensive materials, which means, neither is this safe." He walked over to where a pitcher of water and a glass rested on a table, picked up the glass, and then moved back to the safe.

"You know how to crack safes?"

"I know a lot of things."

"Like what?"

"Stop talking."

The man might have smiled earlier, but it was clear he'd rapidly returned to his normal grouchy self.

Felicia fidgeted as Mr. Blackheart placed the glass to his ear and then to the safe, and began slowly turning the dial. Fear settled over her as the minutes ticked away.

Would Francisco let Grayson and Ming go if she was able to deliver the jewels, or was the man just playing a cruel joke? Did he and whomever he was working with want something beside the jewels—something she thought Francisco might have hinted at?

"Got it."

Felicia watched as Mr. Blackheart swung open the door of the safe, extracted a fairly large black case, and then turned. "We should make sure the jewels are in here." He walked over to the bed, set down the case, opened it, and drew in a sharp breath. Felicia couldn't say she blamed him. Rubies, diamonds, and what looked like a tiara encrusted with priceless gems winked back at her from the case.

"I guess I understand Francisco's incentive to cross an ocean," Mr. Blackheart muttered. "But now, how to proceed?"

"We wait for instructions, and then I take these to wherever they want."

"I've been paid to protect you, Miss Murdock, not watch you place yourself in danger."

"I won't let Grayson and Ming die."

"I'll make the delivery."

A loud cough had Felicia and Mr. Blackheart spinning around. Grayson's butler was standing in the doorway, looking more confused than ever and holding a slip of paper in his hand. "I've been instructed, by two Chinese men who spoke only limited English, to give this to the young lady who burst into the house."

Mr. Blackheart walked to the butler's side, pried the piece of paper out of his hand, and read it. "They want you to take the . . . case to the docks. Someone will meet you there."

The butler coughed again. "Should I mention that those men are waiting on the front stoop?"

Felicia's nerves began to jingle. "Well, there's nothing to do but go through with this."

"I can't allow that," Mr. Blackheart growled.

"You can follow me. I know perfectly well you'll keep me safe."

Mr. Blackheart looked at her for a long minute, then reached into his jacket, pulled out a gun, and pressed it into her hand. "Can you shoot?"

"About as well as I can drive."

"God help us all, then."

Felicia made Mr. Blackheart and the butler turn around before she lifted her skirt, looked around for a place to stash the pistol, and finally settled for shoving it underneath her garter. She wasn't certain her garter was up for the task of holding it for long, and if it did fall off, she could only hope she wouldn't shoot herself in the process.

She shoved her skirts back into place, squared her shoulders, and released a breath. "I'm ready."

Mr. Blackheart caught her eye. "I'll be behind you, although I'll have to keep out of sight." He moved closer to her and surprised her by taking her hand. "You're a lady of faith, Miss Murdock. Don't forget that, and remember, no matter that you'll be driving the phaeton alone, God will be sitting right next to you. Draw courage from that."

Felicia smiled ever so slightly and headed for the door, realizing that Mr. Blackheart was exactly right and that God, in His way, would show her what to do.

22

The minutes kept ticking away, and with each tick, Francisco seemed to become more agitated.

What would he do when he discovered Felicia was not coming back?

Surely she would have discovered she couldn't get into his safe by now, and surely someone, hopefully Theodore and Mr. Blackheart, had taken note of her making off with his phaeton, realized something was amiss, and would be protecting her from the men Francisco had sent to follow her.

"Your ladylove is dragging her feet."

"So it would seem." Grayson settled Ming more comfortably against him, relieved to discover that even amidst the mayhem they were now in, the little girl had fallen asleep. "You said you didn't track me down simply for the jewels but also for Ming. May I assume you intend to use her in some manner to take over where the Wus left off?"

"Don't be ridiculous. Ming's a baby, and she's not the heir to the Wu fortune."

Now they were finally getting somewhere. "So . . . you need me more than Ming?"

Francisco frowned. "I'm not certain I'm following you."

"Am I the heir—being the surviving husband of the eldest daughter?"

Francisco looked at him, his eyes widened, and then he laughed. "Of course you're not the heir, you idiot. Really, Grayson, did you ever understand the Chinese at all? They wouldn't tolerate a white man running one of their most lucrative businesses."

Confusion was immediate. "I'm afraid you have me at a disadvantage then, Francisco. If I'm not the heir, and Ming's not the heir, why were we not killed along with the rest?"

"You are still alive because I hoped, as did my new employers, that you would be willing to join us as we combined both families' resources and created the strongest opium network in the world. The Zang family was quite impressed with your abilities to secure trade routes. I convinced them you would be only too willing—for a substantial fee, of course—to lend those abilities to their organization. To my dismay though, you did the unthinkable and fled China, taking Ming and the jewels."

"You're not intending to kill Ming, are you?"

"Of course not. Ming's just a child, and she's the reason I've been promised a rather nice reward."

"I'm afraid I don't—"

The cabin door opened and two men entered, causing Francisco to scowl at them, his scowl turning to a look of disbelief when . . . Felicia followed the men, carrying the case filled with jewels in one hand and a pistol in the other.

Grayson felt the urge to shake her and kiss her all in the same breath.

"Hello," Felicia said with a smile as she sauntered into the room. "I've got the jewels, and a pistol, as you can see, and just so everyone understands, my mother makes the claim that I'm entirely too proficient when it comes to the matter of shooting."

The urge to kiss her overtook the urge to shake her. She was smiling in an entirely too confident manner, but her eyes were blazing, and it was apparent, at least to him, that she was furious. All he could do was hope she wouldn't start shooting, because who knew what she'd hit.

"Now then," Felicia said briskly as she dropped the case to the floor, "since you're getting the jewels—they are quite extraordinary, I might add—I think it only fair that you allow me, Grayson, and Ming to leave."

Francisco narrowed his eyes. "Grayson can leave, but not Ming."

"I'm afraid that's not acceptable."

"I'm afraid it's nonnegotiable," Francisco countered before he raised a hand that had been hanging at his side and pointed the pistol clutched in that hand directly at Grayson. "I'll shoot him. I've already told him that the only reason he was kept alive when the Wu family was killed was to have him help my new business associates secure trade routes. Since it's become abundantly clear Grayson no longer considers me a friend, has no interest in working with us, and is actually appalled that I was the one behind the Wu family's destruction, he's of no use to me anymore."

To his surprise, not only did Felicia not lower her pistol, she laughed. "You can't shoot Grayson while Ming's on his lap. You could miss and hit her, and since it's *abundantly* clear you've traveled all this way not only for the jewels, but for her as well, I think you're bluffing."

Francisco cocked the pistol, the sound loud in the room.

Before Grayson could brace himself, a scream echoed right outside the door, and then a woman rushed into the room, the sight of her causing his mouth to drop open.

"Mei," was all he could whisper.

Ming's mother spared him not a single glance as she brushed past Felicia and began speaking in rapid Chinese, shaking her finger at Francisco, which had him uncocking his gun and putting it aside. When he'd done that, Mei slowly turned and set her sights directly on her daughter. Her eyes filled with tears, and she began speaking again in Chinese, and even though Grayson didn't understand the language, he understood all too well what she wanted.

He looked down and found Ming's eyes open, her attention firmly fixed on Mei.

What was he supposed to do?

Ming surely wouldn't recognize her mother. She'd only been two when they'd fled China, but Mei *was* her mother, which meant . . .

"Hand Ming over," Francisco said.

Mei held out her arms.

"She's Ming's mother?" Felicia asked.

Grayson nodded.

"I thought she was dead."

"Just like Francisco, she's not. I'm not certain how that happened, but . . ." Grayson drew in a sharp breath. "*She's* the heir to Wu Wah Hing's empire."

Mei said something else, this time with a distinct note of pleading in her voice. Grayson was helpless against that plea. He leaned his head forward, pressed his lips against Ming's hair, and turned her on his lap so she faced him. "Ming, I want you to meet someone, someone you knew a long time ago, your mama."

Ming looked up at him and scowled. "Mama?"

"Yes."

He glanced to the door as a well-dressed Chinese man strode through it. The man came to an abrupt halt as his eyes went immediately to Ming.

"And there's your papa," Francisco said, causing silence to descend on the room.

"What? I thought you were Ming's father," Felicia said slowly.

"No, I'm not, nor was I even married to Mei—our marriages were, in fact, much the same, Gray. This is the eldest Zang son, Zang Chao. He and Mei secretly married before we arrived in China. Since I picked up Chinese rather easily, I was able to understand her when, right after she learned her father was insisting she marry me, she told me she was already married. She offered me a significant amount of money to go through with a farce of a wedding ceremony and to keep their secret."

He released a breath. "Unfortunately, Wu Wah Hing discovered the truth and believed his daughter and I had dishonored him. When I learned there was a price on my head—as well as on Mei's and Ming's—I went about destroying every other Wu."

Grayson held Ming a little tighter as a wave of revulsion swept through him. "Mei didn't mind that you ordered that her sister be killed?"

Francisco shrugged. "Mei thinks I arranged for Lin to be saved too. She believes her sister's death was an accident—just like it was an accident we lost Ming for a while. Ming was supposed to be smuggled out of the main house by a servant, but that servant was caught, and we thought Ming had been killed, until we started receiving reports about you leaving China with a small child." He nodded to Mei. "She promised me I could have the jewels you took if I helped her and her husband locate their daughter." He turned to survey all in the room. "Mission accomplished, I would have to say."

Mei began speaking again, more rapidly than before.

"She wants to hold her daughter, Grayson, and as she is the child's mother, it is her right."

"Tell her I'm concerned for Ming's future—the opium trade is a dangerous world."

Francisco rolled his eyes but turned to Mei and spoke. Whatever he said caused Mei and her husband to shake their heads and start shouting things at Francisco. He held up his hand and the shouting stopped.

"Mei says she's done with the family business, as is her husband, because that business caused the death of her beloved sister. They want me to assure you that after returning to China, they will be taking Ming to live far away from the opium world."

"Down," Ming suddenly demanded.

"I don't think that's a good idea, darling."

"Down."

Grayson's hold instinctively tightened on the little girl as she began to squirm. He glanced up and caught Felicia's eye, and she nodded ever so slightly, even though her expression was decidedly wary. He drew in a breath, slowly released it, and helped Ming scoot off his lap. His vision blurred, and he wanted to pull her back into the safety of his arms, but the minute her feet hit the ground, she twisted out of his hold and scampered across the space that separated her from her mother. She stopped directly in front of Mei and tipped back her head.

"Mama?"

Tears coursed down Mei's face as she bent down and cupped her daughter's chin in her hand.

The next second, Ming was wrapped in her mother's embrace, with her father's arms around both of them, all of them crying—crying in a way that couldn't help but warm Grayson's heart, even though it ached at the same time.

Felicia let out a sniff, wiped her eyes with the hand that wasn't holding the pistol, and nodded to him. "I think it might be best for everyone if we were to get on our way."

Grayson simply stood there for a moment as everything he'd learned in the past couple hours whirled around his mind.

Quite a few things he'd believed regarding his past had

changed, most importantly, the belief he'd been carrying around that he'd been responsible for the murder of his Chinese family.

"Grayson, are you all right?"

He turned to Felicia and opened his mouth but shut it as his gaze drifted down and he saw that the hand she was using to hold the pistol had begun to shake. Striding to her side, he took the pistol and smiled. "I'll be fine." He nodded to Francisco. "Was there anything else you needed to say before we take our leave?"

"Do you really think we're free to go?" Felicia asked before Francisco could respond.

"Yes," Mr. Blackheart said as he burst into the room, "Miss Murdock, you're definitely free to go." Theodore, Zayne, and Hamilton followed right behind, all of them armed, and all of them looking rather lethal.

Grayson smiled. "Gentlemen, you have no idea how glad I am to see you."

Theodore returned the smile. "I'm sure you are, and just so you know, the police are here as well. They're waiting on the docks for my signal to board."

"They have no reason to board this ship," Francisco snapped. "We've done nothing wrong, and Grayson I were just finishing up a business deal."

"Kidnapping is a serious offense, and . . ." Theodore gestured to the case. "Mr. Blackheart told me you forced Felicia to bring that case filled with jewels in order to keep Grayson and Ming alive, so you're looking at attempted theft as well."

Grayson shook his head. "The jewels are Mei's to do with as she wishes."

"Who is Mei?" Zayne asked, looking confused.

"Ming's mother," Grayson said with a nod toward Mei, who was clutching Ming tightly against her as her husband stood in front of them, obviously trying to protect them.

"I thought Ming's mother was dead," Theodore said.

"Yes, well, so did I, but clearly she is not."

Francisco rubbed his hands together as he walked over to the case of jewels, bent over, and picked it up. He released a hearty laugh. "Since everything is wrapping up so nicely, and since it should now be clear that I'm not a jewel thief, I'll just take my prize out and leave all of you to conclude your business."

"Wait."

Grayson, along with everyone else, turned to stare at Mei, who handed Ming to her husband before she stepped forward.

Francisco was standing stock-still, his face turning deathly white as he clutched the case of jewels against his chest. "You speak English?"

Mei smiled a smile that was less than amused. "Enough to understand."

Sweat began to immediately dribble down Francisco's cheek. "Understand what?"

Mei moved up beside him and tilted her chin. "You kill Lin."

"It was an accident."

Mei shook her head. "No. For that, you pay."

"You promised me a reward if I got Ming back for you."

Mei's smile turned downright frightening. "You not die. That be your reward. But you pay for my sister's death."

She shouted something in Chinese that turned Francisco white as a sheet, and before anyone had a chance to move, two Chinese men—one of them the man with the scar Grayson had recognized in the pub—entered the room. Theodore and Mr. Blackheart shifted and repositioned their guns but made no other move. The Chinese men took Francisco by the arms and, without a single word, pulled him through the doorway, his protests drifting back into the room.

Grayson cleared his throat. "What will you do with him?"

Mei stepped closer to him and shrugged. "Why you care?"

Grayson looked at Mei for a long moment. "I would not want him to die."

"I said he will not, but . . . not your concern. We deal with Francisco. No more about him." She smiled a genuine smile. "Thank you for helping my Ming." She turned and gestured to her husband, speaking rapidly in Chinese. Chao stepped forward and, to Grayson's surprise, held Ming out to him.

Grayson took the little girl and drew her close.

"We leave. You say goodbye." Mei looked to Mr. Blackheart and Theodore, and then to Hamilton and Zayne. "You go too." She waved toward the door, and everyone—including Felicia, who sent Grayson a reassuring smile—walked out of the room, leaving him with Ming in his arms. He moved to a chair and sat down, tilting Ming's chin up so he could look her in the eye. He forced a smile.

"I have to go now, darling, but you have your mama and papa back."

Ming frowned. "You come."

Grayson blinked when he felt tears sting his eyes. He drew in a breath and slowly released it. "I'm afraid I can't. You belong with your mama, and she loves you very much. She crossed an entire ocean to find you, as did your papa."

Ming's little brow wrinkled, but then she smiled and patted his cheek. "Okay."

And that was it. He set her down, she ran to the door, and then Mei was there, scooping her up. He didn't see them leave because his eyes were now filled with tears, but then Felicia was back by his side, taking his hand into hers and squeezing it tightly.

"She'll be fine, Grayson. She's where she belongs now."

"I know, but it's difficult to let her go."

"Yes, it is, but it's the right thing to do."

"You two, come on, now," Mr. Blackheart said, poking his head into the room. "We're getting the distinct impression the crew is readying this ship to leave, so if you don't want to end up in China, may I suggest we make our way to the dock?"

Grayson got to his feet, kept Felicia's hand tucked into his, and followed Mr. Blackheart through the ship, down the plank, and finally to the dock. He looked around, noticed far too many policemen to count, and grinned. "So Theodore wasn't exaggerating when he said the police were here."

Mr. Blackheart returned the grin. "He takes this type of matter very seriously and began setting things into motion right after he saw Felicia drive off in your phaeton—something, I might add, that took years off my life as I was forced to watch her careen through the streets." Mr. Blackheart shuddered. "It took everything I had to keep up with her and yet stay out of sight."

Grayson frowned. "When did you meet up with Theodore, Hamilton, and Zayne?"

"Here at the docks. Sam told Theodore, right after Felicia was seen driving away from the park, that they should go to the docks. He's a bright boy, that Sam, but stubborn too. He was not pleased when Theodore wouldn't let him come here but instead made him promise to look after his sisters."

Felicia smiled. "That was a wise choice on Theodore's part. Sam would never refuse to look after his sisters." Her smile suddenly disappeared. "I think they're pulling up anchor."

Grayson turned and watched as the anchor was lifted and the ship began moving. He realized he'd never see Ming again, but instead of feeling the grief he'd been expecting, he found himself happy for the child, knowing she wouldn't face the prejudices she would have if she'd remained with him.

His eyes welled with tears when Ming suddenly appeared at the railing, held fast in her mother's arms as she waved cheerfully at him. His hand, seemingly on its own accord, rose and waved back, waved until the boat moved so far away that he couldn't make Ming out any longer. He turned to face Felicia and found a river of tears trailing down her beautiful face.

"She'll be all right," he said.

Felicia took a deep breath and nodded. "She's not the one I'm worried about."

Grayson took a deep breath of his own and slowly released it. "I'm fine, really. Strange as it may seem, I feel better than I have in years. I know you'll find this odd, coming from me, but I get this feeling that God might have had His hand in this business today."

"I'm sure He did, but what do you mean?"

"Everything got wrapped up so nice and tidy. I found out the truth regarding my past, Ming found her parents again, Francisco will not get rewarded for the evil he has done, and . . ."

He looked up and found Theodore, Mr. Blackheart, Zayne, and Hamilton watching them. He narrowed his eyes, which caused all the gentlemen to grin back at him, but they dutifully turned around and disappeared down the dock.

"Where was I?"

"You were saying 'and . . .'"

"Ah, quite right, well, and . . . since everything is coming together so nicely, it might be exactly the right moment for me to tell you that, since I'm no longer a murderer, well, I would be delighted if you would agree to marry me."

"You want me to marry you because you're not a murderer?"

"Well, I mean, I love you—"

Before he could get another word out, he felt a sharp shove against his chest, and the next second, cold water washed over him as he tumbled off the dock. He splashed to the surface, pushed his sopping wet hair out of his face, and scowled up at Felicia, who was peering at him from the edge of the planks.

"Are you out of your mind?" he sputtered.

"I do beg your pardon, Grayson," Felicia called down to him.

"I might have acted a touch hastily. Did you, perhaps, actually make the claim that you love me before you hit the water?"

She really was incredibly exasperating. He dipped under the water for a brief second, kicked his feet, resurfaced, and then, after he spit water out of his mouth, managed a nod.

A brilliant smile blossomed over Felicia's face. "But, that's marvelous because I love you too and would be honored to become your wife. Although, you really do need to work on your romantic side."

Grayson went motionless at her declaration and promptly sank. He struggled back to the surface, spit out another mouthful of horrible-tasting sea water, and blinked when he discovered Felicia bending down to offer him her hand. He took it, hefted himself to the dock, and before the infuriating woman could get a single word out of her mouth, he kissed her.

Epilogue

ONE WEEK LATER

Felicia knew she was grinning like a lunatic, but she had no control over it whatsoever. She'd been grinning on and off for no apparent reason ever since Grayson had proposed, and even though people were beginning to watch her a little oddly, she simply couldn't help herself.

"I must say, this is a lovely day to be out and about. Central Park is absolutely gorgeous at the moment, but . . ." She looked down at her gown and then lifted her head, catching Arabella's gaze. "I feel rather overdressed. Are you quite certain this rally we're attending is to be a formal event?"

Arabella evidently didn't hear her, because instead of answering Felicia's question, she turned to Ruth, who was waving a delicate fan in front of her face and standing underneath the shade of a large tree. "You must be tickled pink that Felicia and Grayson are engaged."

Ruth smiled. "Indeed, I'm beyond thrilled. Although . . ." She

333

caught Felicia's eye. "I am disappointed that you won't allow me to plan a large wedding. Why, every mother dreams of the day she gets to see her daughter exchange vows, yet all you're willing to allow me to plan is a simple service at the church with a small gathering back at the house afterward. Add to that the fact that you've yet to tell me when you'd like to hold this all too small affair, and I must admit, I'm not having much fun."

Felicia wrinkled her nose. It was somewhat odd, but for a woman who was supposed to be downright disappointed, her mother's eyes seemed to be sparkling quite a bit. She blew out a breath, wondering what plotting was currently going on in her mother's diabolical mind. "I don't want a large wedding, Mother. After that debacle with Reverend Fraser and having wasted so many years trying to be someone I'm not, now that I've finally found the gentleman who loves me for who I am, well, I don't see the need for a lot of fuss. I just want to marry the man—simple as that."

"That's rather sweet . . . and nauseating at the same time," Agatha said, slipping up to grab Felicia's hand. "I am happy for you, my darling, but I do wish you weren't going to be moving so far away."

"Grayson wants to resume his role as earl and finally take over his estates back in England."

"Noble of the man," Ruth said with a nod. "And he did tell me and your father that we'd be welcome to visit any time." She grinned. "Since the man has six homes, I'm fairly certain there'll be room enough for everyone to visit, including you, Agatha."

Arabella stepped closer to her. "I've just realized something— you're going to be a countess."

"Don't remind me. That thought makes me a little queasy."

Ruth shook her head. "Nonsense, you'll make a fine countess, and have you told everyone you and Grayson have decided to adopt Sam and his sisters?"

"Well, no. There hasn't been much time, what with everything going on, but after the rally today, I'm sure I'll be able to have a chance to catch up with everyone." Felicia looked around. "And speaking of the rally, shouldn't we keep moving? I wouldn't want to miss it."

Arabella opened her reticule, pulled out a watch, looked at it for a moment, dropped it back into her reticule, and nodded. "I suppose it is almost time, which means we should get moving."

Agatha gave Felicia's hand a tug, and the ladies began walking, chatting about this and that as they strolled along.

"I thought Eliza was joining us today," Felicia said as she peered into the distance, unable to detect even a hint of a crowd just yet. "And forgive me, but wouldn't it have been easier if we'd had the carriage deposit us a little closer to the rally?"

"Eliza's probably already waiting for us," Arabella said, "and it was such a marvelous day that I thought everyone would enjoy a nice long walk."

Felicia noticed that everyone was acting more and more peculiar the farther they walked. "I'm all for long walks, Arabella, but since this is a formal affair and we're dressed in silks, this hardly seems the appropriate time."

Arabella shot an unreadable glance to her, then turned her head forward again. "Ah, well, you see, the walk is actually a way to allow Agatha time to gather her emotions before she has to once and for all bid Zayne goodbye. He is leaving tomorrow, if you recall, and this time he says he means it."

"I can't believe you just said that," Agatha exclaimed before she let out a good snort. "I'm fine with Zayne leaving, as I've said over and over again."

"Of course you're fine, now that you've walked off all those pesky lingering emotions," Arabella muttered before she nodded her head ever so slightly in Felicia's direction.

Felicia narrowed her eyes and was considering demanding an explanation immediately, but before she could get a single demand out of her mouth, Agatha suddenly came to an abrupt halt, tugging Felicia to a halt in the process. She then grabbed onto Felicia's arms and tried to turn her around, while Arabella suddenly began waving her hands to the side, as if she were trying to swat away a bee or . . . distract someone.

Felicia dug in her heels and swiveled her head. "I think that's Eliza up ahead. Eliza, wait up," she called.

Eliza turned rather slowly, looked down, thrust a bouquet of flowers she was holding behind her back, and sent them what appeared to be a halfhearted wave.

Everyone was behaving quite oddly. Felicia drew in a breath and opened her mouth to insist someone start talking, but snapped it shut when a familiar voice spoke directly behind her.

"Ah, Miss Murdock, you're here."

She turned and found Reverend Fraser smiling back at her. "Reverend Fraser, this is a surprise. I thought you were still on your wedding trip."

Reverend Fraser's smile widened. "Mrs. Fraser and I got back just last night, and I'm thankful we did. I wouldn't have wanted to miss this special occasion for the world." He lowered his voice. "Before I say another word though, please allow me to apologize most profusely for sending Reverend Bannes to New York. I had no idea you'd settled your affections on Mr. Sumner, or I would never have attempted to meddle in your life." A rather sheepish expression crossed his face. "It would appear I did you a grave disservice, Miss Murdock, seeing as how I failed to realize you thought of me as something other than your minister."

Felicia waved the remark away and grinned. "You mustn't give it another thought, Reverend Fraser. I fear I was simply suffering from a bad case of delusions for quite a few years. You were meant to be with your lovely Julia, just as I'm meant to be with my Grayson. But tell me, you said something about a special occasion. Are you and Mrs. Fraser planning on attending the rally as well?"

"Rally? No, I'm here for the . . . Good heavens, do you not know?"

Ruth came marching up beside them, took Reverend Fraser's arm, and pulled him away, something about "a surprise" drifting back to Felicia on the breeze.

She looked at Arabella. "What surprise?"

"It really would be nice if just one of my ideas would go according to plan."

Felicia swiveled on her heel and found Grayson standing a few feet away from her. For some reason, the man had thrown what looked like a large burlap sack over his clothing. "Why are you wearing that?"

"You know the bride isn't supposed to see the groom's outfit before a wedding," he muttered, "but I saw that mayhem was about to descend, so I had no choice but to intervene."

All the breath left Felicia's body in a split second. "Wedding?"

"It was supposed to be a surprise, but obviously that's gone the way of the wind now."

"You're not supposed to see the *bride*," Felicia heard herself say, having no idea why those particular words came out of her mouth. Her pulse was galloping through her veins as pure happiness settled over her. Something odd was indeed going on, and that something seemed to be a wedding—hers.

Grayson had apparently taken it upon himself to give her a romantic adventure, one that seemingly had been planned with the help of her family and friends.

In that moment she realized once again that he was the perfect gentleman for her—a gentleman who understood she had a talent for trouble, but a gentleman who would save her from that trouble every time.

He understood her as no one else ever had or ever would.

Before she could say another word, Grayson whipped the sack off himself and threw it over her head. "These pesky traditions. How's a man supposed to keep them straight?"

She snorted through the burlap. "You've already seen me."

"Yes, well, I'll pretend I haven't."

"Honestly, Grayson, why are you trying to smother poor Felicia?" a voice she recognized as Eliza's asked. "If you must know, tradition states you're not supposed to see the bride before the wedding, but we'll have to settle for you not seeing her in her bridal dress."

"But I did see her dress. It's quite lovely," Grayson said.

"She's not wearing the gown she currently has on. Her mother only suggested she wear that gown so that she wouldn't feel out of place traveling here with Agatha and Arabella, who insisted on dressing properly for the wedding. I've brought her a real gown."

"Which I won't be able to wear if I lose consciousness from having this hot sack over my head," Felicia called.

"Oh dear, I do beg your pardon," Eliza said, and a second later the sack was pulled from her, but it wasn't Eliza who stood before her—it was Grayson.

"Better?" he asked.

"Much."

"There's no time for smoldering looks just yet," Eliza said firmly, stepping between them. "We need to get Felicia ready."

"I need to speak with her first."

"You'll have your entire life to speak with her, Grayson."

Felicia grinned when Grayson arched one aristocratic brow at his sister, which had Eliza arching her own aristocratic brow in return, right before she threw up her hands and stepped to the side. "Fine, but make it snappy."

Grayson looked around, seeming as if he wanted to ask all

of their friends and family members who were currently in their vicinity to leave, but then smiled at them instead right before he took her hand in his and brought it to his lips.

Her pulse hitched up another notch.

"Before we exchange our vows, I wanted to tell you some things." He smiled and drew her closer, pressing a kiss on her forehead before he leaned back. "I love you, and I want nothing more than to spend the rest of my life with you."

"I love you too."

"I wasn't done."

He really was somewhat of an impatient gentleman at times, which made her love him all the more.

"I know you've always wanted a husband who was a man of faith, and I do think I'm on the right path. I've made my peace with God and asked Him for His forgiveness. Because my very soul seems to be lighter, I believe He's accepted my plea and granted me my request."

Felicia's eyes brimmed with tears, and she gave a loud sniff.

Grayson dug into his pocket, produced a handkerchief, and pressed it into her hand.

"You will make the perfect countess because you're such a compassionate woman, and we will have countless tenants who will welcome you and who you'll be able to fuss over and . . ."

Felicia reached up and placed her fingers over his lips, effectively bringing his speech to an end. "I'm going to marry you no matter what you say."

Grayson grinned. "Are you insinuating that you'd like to get this wedding underway?"

"Yes, please."

Grayson turned and motioned Ruth forward. It was apparent her mother had been weeping throughout Grayson's speech, but she took Felicia's arm, let out one hiccup, straightened her spine, and nodded to Eliza, Arabella, and Agatha. Her friends escorted her a short distance away to where a tent had been set up. Piper, Beatrice, and Harriet were standing in front of the tent, all dressed in identical purple dresses, matching bows, and clutching what appeared to be bouquets of violets.

"We're your flower girls," Piper proclaimed. She nodded to Sam, who was standing off to the side. "He's going to be Uncle Grayson's best man, and Ben's going to be the ring bearer."

Piper steered Felicia into the tent, and before she knew it, with the help of her mother and friends, she was dressed in a stunning gown of white trimmed with delicate lace, a sheer veil hiding her face from view.

Ruth let out a sniff. "You look exquisite, and I must tell you, it was exceedingly difficult for me not to let you in on the secret. I knew you wouldn't mind not being in on the planning of the wedding, but . . ." She suddenly dissolved into tears but waved Felicia's offer of an embrace away. "No, my tears will stain the silk." She drew in a shuddering breath. "I'm just so happy for you, my dear. You've found your prince charming."

"I'm not certain Grayson's a prince charming, Mother, but whatever he is, he's mine." She turned and smiled when her father ducked into the tent. "I was wondering if you were going to be here."

"Your mother sent me a telegram, and it was a close call." He grinned. "It would have been nice to have been given a little warning that you'd fallen head over heels in love, and with a foreigner, no less, but Ruth says you're deliriously happy, so let's go get you married."

Her father gave her his arm, and she walked with him out of the tent and back into the beautiful summer day. Butterflies flitted in front of her as anticipation began to flow through her.

She watched as Jeffrey, Daniel, and Robert escorted Ruth to her seat. Then she glanced around, unable to help but smile when she realized that somehow Grayson had turned this corner of Central Park into a beautiful outside church, replete with pews and a choir.

She would miss her church's choir.

A grin teased her lips as the thought came to her that the members of the choir would probably not miss her overly much.

The sound of a harp filled the air, and she took a deep breath as she waited for Piper, Beatrice, and Harriet to walk ever so slowly down the white runner spread over the grass. They reached the end and took their places, and she shifted her attention to Grayson.

He really was an extraordinarily handsome gentleman.

Her feet set to motion, and she quickened her stride, causing her father to laugh even as he increased his pace. "I don't think he's going anywhere, darling."

Felicia glanced at her father. "I think you might be right, but no need to take any chances."

They reached the end of the aisle in no time at all. Her father turned her to face him, lifted her veil, pressed a kiss against her cheek, and then passed her over to Grayson and took a seat next to her mother.

Grayson leaned closer to her. "You're beautiful," he whispered, right before he kissed her.

The world melted away until Reverend Fraser coughed, loudly. "May I suggest the two of you hold off with that until after the vows are spoken?"

Grayson pulled back, straightened, and grinned. "Just don't make it a long ceremony, Reverend."

Every vow spoken sang to Felicia's soul, and when Grayson placed a large gold band surrounded with diamonds on her finger, she barely spared it a glance, which had him turning a bit sulky.

"Don't you like your ring?" he whispered, his lips only an inch away from hers. "I picked it out myself."

"I'm sure it's lovely," she whispered back, "but right now, I find I'm more interested in your kiss than your ring."

Grayson laughed and proceeded to oblige her. As his lips pressed against hers, she realized that God had indeed known what was best for her. He'd given her not what she'd believed she wanted but what He'd known she needed—a gentleman who would love her, flaws and all, forever.

ACKNOWLEDGMENTS

I am incredibly fortunate to be surrounded by so many people who offer me their encouragement and support as I journey through the publishing world. All of you have my deepest appreciation.

To my editors, Raela Schoenherr and Karen Schurrer, thank you for all of your suggestions and for pushing me to produce a better story. Your advice and expertise are invaluable to me.

To John Hamilton and Paul Higdon, thank you for a spectacular cover. This one literally stole my breath away.

To Steve Oates, Noelle Buss, Debra Larsen, Anna Henke, Brittany Higdon, Stacey Theesfield, Chris Dykstra, Jennifer Parker, and Elisa Tally, thank you for everything you do to get my books published and promoted.

To John and Paulette Tangelder, my in-laws extraordinaire, thank you for your unconditional love and support. It means the world to me.

To Gail Broyles, a wonderful librarian and friend, thank you for being so enthusiastic about my work.

To the friends of my heart, the girls I grew up with and the girls responsible for shaping the woman I am today—Barbara Porter Petrozzi, Lachell Favede McFadden, Paula Waddell Henwood, Kim Terhlan Yates, Lynne Porterfield Lim, Rita Wood, and the late Amy Sessi Harris—thank you for all the laughter and adventures we've shared. Love you, ladies!

To Al and Dom, my guys, thank you for amusing me on a daily basis.

To the readers, thank you for enjoying my words.

And to God, thank You for . . . everything.

DISCUSSION QUESTIONS

1. Felicia goes to extraordinary lengths to make herself attractive to Reverend Fraser. Have you ever changed your appearance or personality in order to impress someone? What resulted from your changing?

2. Grayson has made a vow to never marry again because of his past. Do you believe that was noble of him or just misguided?

3. Felicia came to the conclusion that God sent Reverend Fraser to her because of a prayer she'd prayed, only to come to the realization that she'd been greatly mistaken. Have you ever thought God sent you something you'd asked for but then learned differently? What was your reaction to that realization?

4. Felicia and Eliza tell Grayson that all he needs to do to have God forgive him for his past is to ask, but Grayson doesn't accept that right away. Why do some people find it difficult to accept the idea of God's grace? Has there ever been something you've had trouble accepting or offering forgiveness for?

5. Felicia feels that she's been helping the needy for all the wrong reasons, but do you really think that was true? Have you ever been in a situation where you were doing the right thing for the wrong reasons?

6. Why was it so important for Grayson to tell Felicia the truth about her singing?

7. Ruth Murdock has the tendency to exaggerate her daughter's abilities. Why does she do this? Do you think this is a good habit? Why or why not?

8. Did Francisco deserve to be left at the mercy of Mei and Chao? What would you have done in the same situation?

9. Many people assume that those who possess great wealth are content with their lot in life, yet Grayson certainly wasn't. Why do you think some people aren't satisfied with their circumstances, no matter their monetary standing? Have you ever experienced this?

10. Well before the beginning of this story, Grayson finally realized that his participation in the opium trade had ruined people's lives. Will he always carry around some guilt over his past actions, and how can he experience relief from it? Is there anything in your past that you still feel guilty about?

11. Felicia believes at the end of the story that God sent her not what she'd asked for, but what she'd needed. Has this ever happened to you? How did you react?

Jen Turano, critically acclaimed author of *A Change of Fortune* and *A Most Peculiar Circumstance*, is a graduate of the University of Akron with a degree in Clothing and Textiles. She is a member of ACFW and makes her home outside of Denver, Colorado, with her husband and teenage son. Visit her website at www.jenturano.com.

More Lively Historical Romance From Jen Turano

To learn more about Jen and her books, visit jenturano.com.

Arabella Beckett is in the business of helping other women, but she's not in the habit of accepting help herself. She certainly doesn't want assistance from the narrow-minded knight in shining armor her brother sent to fetch her home. But private investigator Theodore Wilder is just as stubborn as she is. Has this feisty suffragette finally met her match?

A Most Peculiar Circumstance

Lady Eliza Sumner has lost everything—her father, her fiancé, her faith, and now her fortune. Masquerading as Miss Eliza Sumner, governess-at-large, she's on a mission to find the man who ran off with her inheritance and reclaim what's rightfully hers. It will take a riot of complications for Eliza to realize that God may have had a better plan in mind all along…

A Change of Fortune